These High, Green Hills

The Original Mitford Classic

JAN KARON

These High, Green Hills

RIVEROAK®
Good News in Fiction

COOK COMMUNICATIONS MINISTRIES
Colorado Springs, Colorado • Paris, Ontario
KINGSWAY COMMUNICATIONS LTD
Eastbourne, England

RiverOak® is an imprint of
Cook Communications Ministries, Colorado Springs, CO 80918
Cook Communications, Paris, Ontario
Kingsway Communications, Eastbourne, England

THESE HIGH, GREEN HILLS
©1996, 2005 by Jan Karon
Originally published in 1996 by Lion Publishing.
Previous ISBN: 0-7459-3741-1

This story is a work of fiction. All characters and events are the product
of the author's imagination. Any resemblance to any person, living or
dead, is coincidental.

Cover Design: Jeffrey P. Barnes
Cover Illustrator: Ron Adair

Printed in the United States of America

1 2 3 4 5 6 7 8 9 10 Printing/Year 09 08 07 06 05

Excerpt on page 101 taken from *Life Together* by Dietrich Bonhoeffer.
English translation © 1954 by Helen S. Doberstein. Used by permission
of HarperCollins Publishers, Inc.

Library of Congress Cataloging-in-Publication Data

Karon, Jan, 1937-
    These high, green hills / Jan Karon.
        p. cm.
    Originally published: Colorado Springs, CO : Lion Pub., 1996. (The
Mitford years)
    ISBN 1-58919-064-5
    1. Mitford (N.C. : Imaginary place)--Fiction. 2. Church membership
--Fiction. 3. North Carolina--fiction. 4. Episcopalians--Fiction.
5. Clergy--Fiction.   I. Title. II. Series: Karon, Jan, 1937-   . Mitford
years.
PS3561.A678T48 2005
813'.54--dc22

                                                    2005019509

For my precious grandmother,
Fannie Belle Bush Cloer,
Mama, Redwing, The Storyteller.
1893–1993

With sincere thanks to:

Miss Read (Dora Saint); Rev. Rocky Ward; Marrion Ward; Dr. Greg Adams; Dr. "Bunky" Davant; Dr. Greg Hawthorne; Flyin' George Ronan; Jim Atkinson; Dr. John C. Wolf, Jr.; Billy Wilson; Dr. Buck Henson; Dr. Cara Roten-Henson; David Watts; Tony di Santi; Dr. Ken McKinney; Fr. James Harris; Ruth Bell Graham; Earl and Nancy Trexler; Sonny Klutz; Richard J. Foster; Dr. William Standish Reed; Jim Barber; Diane Grymes; Steve Sudderth; Bear Green; Bob Moody; Fr. Chuck Blanck; Fr. Rick Lawler; Fr. Russell Johnson; Raney MacArthur-Ratchford; Maribelle Freeland; Julie Q. Hayes, R.N. BSN, Blowing Rock Hospital; Pam Collette, R.N. BSN, Clinical Nurse Mgr., Donna Joyner, Assistant Clinical Nurse Mgr., and Pamela Thomas, R.N. BSN, of the Burn Center, North Carolina Baptist Hospitals, Inc., Winston-Salem; Dana Watkins, R.N. BSN, Sanger Clinic, Charlotte; Rev. James Stuart; Fr. Kale King; Dr. Ross Rhoads; Doug Galke; Shirlee Gaines Edwards; Bertie Beam; Nancy Olsen of Quail Ridge Books; Shirley Sprinkle of The Muses; my friends at Gideon Ridge Inn; Liz Darhansoff, my gifted and indefatigable agent, and Carolyn Carlson, my visionary Viking Penguin editor and friend; Jerry Burns, the small-town newspaperman with the big heart; and the vanishing breed of old-time Gospel preachers (especially the late Vance Havner and the still-present Arndt Greer), who brought conviction to their calling and color to the language.

Last but never least, thanks to the wonderful booksellers who have enthusiastically spread the word, and to the many readers who have cheered me on, given my books to family and friends, and come to feel comfortably at home in Mitford.

Contents

INTRODUCTION 11

ONE: Through the Hedge 17

TWO: Bread of Angels 34

THREE: Gathered In 54

FOUR: Passing the Torch 73

FIVE: A Close Call 89

SIX: Love Came Down 109

SEVEN: Flying High 128

EIGHT: Serious About Fun 151

NINE: Locked Gates 172

TEN: The Cave 192

ELEVEN: Darkness into Light 208

TWELVE: Lace 227

THIRTEEN: Homecoming 244

FOURTEEN: The One for the Job 264

FIFTEEN: And Many More 281

SIXTEEN: Loving Back 298

SEVENTEEN: Sing On! 316

EIGHTEEN: Every Trembling Heart 335

NINETEEN: Starting Over 354

TWENTY: Send Me 373

TWENTY-ONE: These High, Green Hills 394

READERS' GUIDE 413

Introduction

Mitford and Father Tim have been good to Jan Karon. She is now among that small group of celebrated authors who can demand substantial fees for public appearances and speeches. Although she turns down more of these opportunities than she accepts, she does enjoy the occasional foray to visit her readers. And what does she do with the fees? The money goes to the Mitford Children's Foundation. All of it.

Facts like these help explain the burgeoning popularity of Karon's fiction. Readers sense that she's not in it for the fame or the fortune. She says she wants to give her readers two things: "consolation and laughter." In this third novel of the Mitford series, she does just that, again inviting her readers to a temporary residence in Mitford, a place not quite "with it" in contemporary cultural terms and all the more eye-catching for being out of step.

In addition to her masterful handling of the romance of Cynthia and Father Tim, Karon takes us this time from the humor of Tim's trying to learn to use a computer to the ugliness of child abuse. This book has joyful conversions juxtaposed against a death so wrenching that it "broke her heart," she says, as she forced herself to tell the story that unfolded in her dreams. But the range here never obscures the central intention "to write about a life of faith." We come back to Mitford, not merely to pass time, but to revisit the life of a good man, "a foot-washer," Karon labels him. Father Tim simply wants to be a pastor and despite everything—his inhibitions, his perfectionism, and his sense of inadequacy—he manages to minister in humility and compassion. He teaches us something about forgiveness, about living well instead of just living. He returns to the word "pastor" some of the dignity it has lost in our contemporary newspaper reports.

In Karon's fictional southern town, God is in the everyday, and remarkable conversion is enmeshed in the fabric of the place. By simply writing the books that she "wanted to read," Karon has tapped into a thirst for optimism, a longing for the heroism of ordinary life. "Where Christ is, cheerfulness will keep breaking in," Dorothy Sayers says, and such a revolutionary notion pulses at the center of this Mitford place. We've had plenty of novels to remind us of phoniness and desolation. Karon believes we need something else. We need to know that "cheerfulness is okay," she says, adding, "Some people just don't know what cheerfulness is until you give them a demonstration."

So here it is—a novel that reassures and affirms. Once again there's plenty of baked ham and livermush, but there are also the complicated lives of Dooley and Lace—lost children whose tragedies move this narrative. There's Sadie's decline toward death and Father Tim's thoughts of retirement. There's a frightening day in a cave, a scary airplane excursion, and a stern reminder to Tim that the "future belongs to God." And finally, there's Karon's steady insistence that "day is as real as night."

Dale Brown
Professor of English
Calvin College
Grand Rapids, Michigan
March 5, 2005

These High, Green Hills

The Lord's Chapel

The Rectory

The Local

MITF

— Lilac Road —

— Wisteria Lane —

— Main Street —

— Old Church

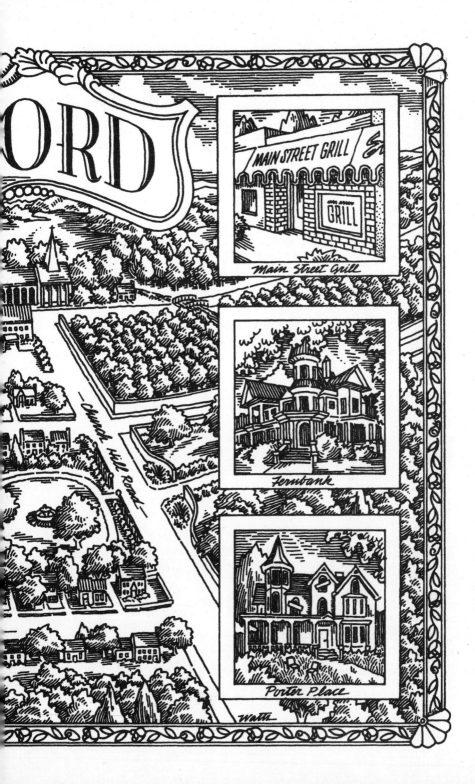

ORD

Main Street Grill

Fernbank

Porter Place

Church Hill Road

Watts

ONE

Through the Hedge

He stood at the kitchen window and watched her coming through the hedge.

What was she lugging this time? It appeared to be a bowl and pitcher. Or was it a stack of books topped by a vase?

The rector took off his glasses, fogged them, and wiped them with his handkerchief. It was a bowl and pitcher, all right. How the little yellow house next door had contained all the stuff they'd recently muscled into the rectory was beyond him.

"For your dresser," she said, as he held the door open.

"Aha!"

The last thing he wanted was a bowl and pitcher on his dresser. The top of his dresser was his touchstone, his home base, his rock in a sea of change. That was where his car keys resided, his loose coins, his several crosses, his cuff links, his wallet, his checkbook, his school ring, and a small jar of buttons with a needle and thread.

It was also where he kept the mirror in which he occasionally examined the top of his head. Was his hair still thinning, or, by some mysterious and hoped-for reversal, growing in again?

"Cynthia," he said, going upstairs in the wake of his blond and shapely wife, "about that bowl and pitcher ..."

"The color is wonderful. Look at the blues. It will relieve all your burgundy and brown!"

He did not want his burgundy and brown relieved.

✳

He saw it coming.

Ever since their marriage on September seventh, she had plotted to lug that blasted armoire over for the rectory guest room.

The lugging over was one thing; it was the lugging back that he dreaded. They had, for example, lugged over an oriental rug that was stored in her basement. "Ten by twelve!" she announced, declaring it perfect for the bare floor of the rectory dining room.

After wrestling the table and chairs into the hall, they had unrolled the rug and unrolled the rug—to kingdom come. It might have gone up the walls on all four sides and met at the chandelier over the table.

"This is a rug for a school gym!" he said, wiping the pouring sweat from his brow.

She seemed dumbfounded that it didn't fit, and there they had gone, like pack mules, carting it through the hedge again.

The decision to keep and use both houses had been brilliant, of course. The light in the rectory would never equal that of her studio next door, where she was already set up with books and paints and drawing board. This meant his study could remain unchanged—his books could occupy the same shelves, and his vast store of sermon notebooks in the built-in cabinets could hold their place.

Marrying for the first time at the age of sixtysomething was change enough. It was a blessed luxury to live with so few rearrangements in the scheme of things, and life flowing on as usual. The only real change was the welcome sharing of bed and board.

Over breakfast one morning, he dared to discuss his interest in getting the furniture settled.

"Why can't we keep things as they were … in their existing state? It seemed to work.…"

"Yes, well, I like that our houses are separate, but I also want them to be the same—sort of an organic whole."

"No organic whole will come of dragging that armoire back and forth through the hedge. It looks like a herd of elephants has passed through there already."

"Oh, Timothy! Stop being stuffy! Your place needs fluffing up, and mine needs a bit more reserve. For example, your Chippendale chairs would give a certain sobriety to my dining table."

"Your dining table is the size of something in our nursery school. My chairs would look gigantic."

She said exactly what he thought she would say. "We could try it and see."

"Cynthia, trust me on this. My chairs will not look right with your table, and neither will that hand-painted magazine rack do anything for my armchair."

"Well, what was the use of getting married, then?"

"I beg your pardon?"

"I mean, if no one is going to change on either side, if we're both just going to be our regular, lifetime selves, what's the use?"

"I think I see what you're getting at. Will nothing do, then, but to cart those chairs to your house? And what about my own table? It will be bereft of chairs. I hardly see the point." He felt like jumping through the window and going at a dead run toward the state line.

"One thing at a time," she said happily. "It's all going to work out perfectly."

deAr stuart,

thanx for your note re: diocesan mtg, and thank martha for the invitation to put my feet under yr table afterward. however, I must leave for home at once, following the mtg—hope you'll understand.

while i'm at it, let me ask you:

why are women always moving things around? at Sunday School, jena iivey just had the youth group move the kindergarten bookcAses to a facing wall.

on the homefront, my househelp has moved a ladderback chair from my bedroom into the hall, never once considering that i hung my trousers over it for 14 years, and put my shoes on the seat so they could be found in an emergency.

last but certainly not least, if C could lift me in my armchair and put it by the window while i'm dozing, she would do it.

without a doubt, you have weightier things to consider, but tell me, how does one deal with this?

i hasten to add that ii've never been happier in my life. to tell the truth, i am confounded that such happiness—in such measure—even exists.

He signed the note, typed on his Royal manual, thankful that Stuart Cullen was not merely his bishop, but his closest personal friend since the halcyon days of seminary.

Fr Timothy Kavanagh,
The Chapel of Our Lord and Savior
Old Church Lane, Mitford, N.C.

Dear Timothy:

In truth, it is disconcerting when one's househelp, SS supervisor, and wife do this sort of thing all at once.

My advice is: do not fight it. It will wear off.

In His peace,
Stuart

P.S. Martha would add a note, but she is busy moving my chest of drawers to the far side of our bedroom. As I am dealing with an urgent matter with the House of Bishops, I could not be browbeaten to help, and so she has maneuvered it, at last, onto an old bedspread, and I can hear her hauling the whole thing across the floor above me. This particular behavior had lain dormant in her for nearly seven years, and has suddenly broken forth again.

Perhaps it is something in the water.

✳

He could see, early on, that beds were a problem that needed working out.

They had spent their wedding night in his bed at the rectory, where they had rolled down their respective sides and crashed together in the middle.

"What is this *trough* doing in your bed?" she asked.

"It's where I sleep," he said, feeling sheepish.

They had been squeezed together like sardines the livelong night, which he had profoundly enjoyed, but she had not. "Do you think this is what's meant by 'the two shall be one flesh'?" she murmured, her cheek smashed against his.

The following night, he trooped through the hedge with his pajamas and toothpaste in a grocery bag from The Local.

Her bed was a super-king-size, and the largest piece of furniture in her minuscule house.

He found it similar in breadth to the state of Texas, or possibly the province of Saskatchewan. Was that a herd of buffalo racing toward him in the distance, or a team of sled dogs? "Cynthia!" he shouted across the vast expanse, and waited for the echo.

They had ordered a new mattress for the rectory immediately after returning from their honeymoon in Stuart Cullen's summer house. There, on the rocky coast of Maine, they had spent time listening to the cry of the loons, holding hands, walking along the shore, and talking until the small hours of the morning. The sun turned her fair skin a pale toast color that he found fascinating and remarkable; and he watched three freckles emerge on the bridge of her nose, like stars coming out. Whatever simple thing they did together, they knew they were happier than ever before in their lives.

One evening, soon after the new mattress and springs were installed at the rectory, he found her sitting up in bed as he came out of the shower.

"I've had a wonderful idea, Timothy! A fireplace! Right over there where the dresser is."

"What would I do with my dresser?"

She looked at him as if he had toddled in from the church nursery. "Put it in the alcove, of course."

"Then I couldn't see out the window."

"But how much time do you spend staring out the alcove window?"

"When you were parading about with Andrew Gregory, a great deal of time." His face burned to admit it, but yes, he'd been jealous of the handsome antique dealer who had squired her around for several months.

She smiled, leaning her head to one side in that way he could barely resist. "A fireplace would be so romantic."

"Ummm."

"Why must I be the romantic in the family while you hold up the conservative, let's-don't-make-any-changes end?"

He sat down beside her. "How quickly you forget. When we were going steady, you said I was wildly romantic."

She laughed and kissed him on the cheek. "And I was right, of course. I'm sorry, old dearest."

He regretted being anyone's *old* dearest.

"Old dearest, yourself," he said grumpily. "I am, after all, only six years your senior."

"By the calendar," she said imperiously, referring, he supposed, to something decrepit in his overall attitude about life.

In any case, the fireplace issue did not come up again.

❋

In truth, he had no words for his happiness. It grew deeper every day, like the digging of a well, and astounded him by its warmth and power. He seemed to lose control of his very face, which, according to the regulars at the Main Street Grill, displayed a foolish and perpetual grin.

"I love you ... terribly," he said, struggling to express it.

"I love you terribly, also. It's scary. What if it should end?"

"Cynthia, good grief ..."

"I know I shouldn't talk of endings when this is a blessed beginning."

"Don't then," he said, meaning it.

❋

That Barnabas had so willingly given up the foot of his master's bed to sleep on a rug in the hall was a gesture he would never forget. Not only did his dog enjoy eighteenth-century poets and submit to his weekly bath without rancor, his dog was a gentleman.

❋

The decisions were made, and both parties were in amicable accord.

They would sleep at the rectory primarily, and on occasion at the little yellow house. Though she would work there, as always, they would treat it much as a second home, using it for refreshment and private retreat.

He promised to have his sermon well under control each Saturday afternoon, with time to relax with her on Saturday evening, and he would continue to make breakfast on Sunday morning.

He showed her where his will was, and promised to have it rewritten. She confessed she didn't have a will, and promised to have one drawn up.

If they should ever, God forbid, have a misunderstanding, neither would dash off to the other house to sulk.

He would continue to have the cheerful and enterprising Puny Guthrie, née Bradshaw, clean the rectory three days a week, and Cynthia would use her services on a fourth day, next door.

They would go on with their separate checking accounts, make some mutual investments, counsel with the other about gift offerings, and never spend more than a certain fixed sum without the other's prior agreement.

He suggested fifty dollars as the fixed sum.

"One hundred!" she countered.

He was glad he had opened the bidding low. "One hundred, then, and I keep that old jacket you earmarked for the Bane and Blessing sale."

"Done!"

They laughed.

They shook hands.

They felt relieved.

Getting a marriage off on the right foot was no small matter.

✳

"I reckon you're gone with th' wind," said Percy Mosely, who rang up his lunch tab at the Main Street Grill.

"How's that?" asked the rector.

"Married an' all, you'll not be comin' in regular, I take it." The proprietor of the Grill felt hurt and betrayed, he could tell.

"You've got that wrong, my friend."

"I do?" said Percy, brightening.

"I'll be coming in as regular as any man could. My wife has a working life of her own, being a well-known children's book writer and illustrator. She will not be trotting out hot vittles for my lunch every day—not by a long shot."

Percy looked suspicious. "What about breakfast?"

"That," said the rector, pocketing the change, "is another matter entirely."

Percy frowned. He liked his regulars to be married to his place of business.

✳

He looked up from his chair in the study. Curlers, again.

"I have to wear curlers," she said, as if reading his mind. "I'm going to Lowell tomorrow."

"Lowell? Whatever for?"

"A school thing. They want me to read *Violet Goes to France* to their French class, and then do a program in the auditorium."

"Must you?"

"Must I what? Read *Violet Goes to France*? That's what they asked me to read."

"No, must you go to Lowell?"

"Well, yes."

He didn't want to say anything so idiotic, but he would miss her, as if she were being dropped off the end of the earth.

A long silence ensued as she curled up on the sofa and opened a magazine. He tried to read, but couldn't concentrate.

He hadn't once thought of her traveling with her work. Uneasy, he tried to let the news sink in. Lowell. Somebody there had been shot on the street in broad daylight.

And another thing—Lowell was a full hundred miles away. Did she have good brakes? Plenty of gas? When had she changed her oil?

"How's your oil?" he asked soberly.

She laughed as if he'd said something hilariously funny. Then she left the sofa and came to him and kissed him on the forehead. He was instantly zapped by the scent of wisteria, and went weak in the knees.

She looked him in the eye. "I love it when you talk like that. My oil is fine, how's yours?"

"Cynthia, Cynthia," he said, pulling her onto his lap.

✳

"Guess what?" said Emma, who was taping a photo of her new grandchild on the wall next to her desk.

This was his secretary's favorite game, and one he frankly despised. "What?"

"*Guess!*"

"Let's see. You're going to quit working for the Episcopalians and go to work for the Baptists." He wished.

"I wish," she said, rolling her eyes. "Try again."

"Blast, Emma, I hate this game."

"It's good for you, it exercises the brain."

"Esther Bolick's orange marmalade cake recipe is coming out in the *New York Times* food section."

"See? You don't even try. You're just talking to hear your head roar. One more guess."

"Give me a clue."

"It has to do with somebody being mad."

"The vestry. It must have something to do with the vestry."

"Wrong. Do you want me to tell you?"

"I beg you."

"Marge Wheeler left her best basket in the kitchen after the bishop's brunch last June, and Flora Lou Wilcox put it in the Bane and Blessing sale. Somebody walked off with it for a hundred dollars! Can you believe a hundred dollars for a basket with a loose handle? Marge is mad as a wet hen, she threatened to sue. But Flora Lou said she doesn't have a leg to stand on, since you're always running notices in the pew bulletin to pick up stuff left in th' kitchen."

"Ummm. Keep me posted."

"It's been four months since the brunch, so I can see Flora Lou's point that Marge should have picked it up and carted it home. Anyway, how could Flora Lou know it was handmade by Navajo Indians in 1920?" Emma sighed. "Of course, I can see Marge's point, too, can't you?"

He could, but he knew better than to intervene unless asked. His job, after all, was Sales and Service.

He rifled through the mail. A note from his cousin, Walter, and wife, Katherine, who had done the Ireland jaunt with him last year.

Dear Timothy,

Since Ireland is now old stomping grounds, why don't you and Cynthia plan to go with us next summer? Thought we'd plant the seed, so it can sprout over the winter.

We shall never forget how handsome you looked on the other side of the pulpit, standing with your beautiful bride. We love her as much as we love you, which is pecks and bushels, as ever, Katherine

PS, Pls advise if canna and lily bulbs should be separated in the fall, I'm trying to find a hobby that has nothing to do with a pasta machine

Yrs, Walter

He rummaged toward the bottom of the mail stack.

Aha!

A note from Dooley Barlowe, in that fancy prep school for which his eldest parishioner, Miss Sadie Baxter, was shelling out serious bucks.

Hey. I don't like it here. That brain in a jar that we saw is from a medical school. I still don't know whose brain it is. When are you coming back? Bring Barnbus and granpaw and Cynthia. I culd probly use a twenty. Dooley

There! Not one 'ain't,' and complete sentences throughout. Hallelujah!

Who could have imagined that this boy, once barely able to speak the King's English, would end up in a prestigious school in Virginia?

He gazed at the note, shaking his head.

Scarcely more than two years ago, Dooley Barlowe had arrived at the church office, dirty, ragged, and barefoot, looking for a place to "take a dump." His grandfather had been too ill to care for the boy, who was abandoned by a runaway father and alcoholic mother, and Dooley had ended up at the rectory. By grace alone, he and Dooley had managed to live through those perilous times.

"I've been wondering," said Emma, peering at him over her glasses. "Is Cynthia goin' to pitch in and help around the church?"

"She's free to do as much or as little as she pleases."

"I've always thought a preacher's wife should pitch in." She set her mouth in that way he deplored. "If you ask me, which you didn't, the parish will expect it."

Yes, indeed, if he could get the Baptists to take Emma Newland off his hands, he would be a happy man.

*

"Miss Sadie," he said when she answered the phone at Fernbank, "I've had a note from Dooley. He says he doesn't like it in that fancy school."

"He can like it or lump it," she said pleasantly.

"When you're dishing out twenty thousand a year, you sure can be tough, Miss Sadie."

"If I couldn't be tough, Father, I wouldn't have twenty thousand to dish out."

"You'll be glad to know the headmaster says he's doing all right. A little slow on the uptake, but holding his own with those rich kids. In fact, they're not all rich. Several are there on scholarship, with no more assets than our Dooley."

"Good! You mark my words, he'll be better for it. And don't you go soft on me, Father, and let him talk you into bailing him out in the middle of the night."

"You can count on it," he said.

"Louella and I have nearly recovered from all the doings in June...."

"June was a whopper, all right."

"We're no spring chickens, you know."

"You could have fooled me."

"I'll be ninety my next birthday, but Louella doesn't tell her age. Anyway, we're going to have you and Cynthia up for supper. What did we say we'd have, Louella?"

He heard Louella's mezzo voice boom from a corner of the big kitchen, "Fried chicken, mashed potatoes, gravy, an' cole slaw!"

"Man!" he exclaimed, quoting Dooley.

The announcement rolled on. "Hot biscuits, cooked apples, deviled eggs, bread and butter pickles ..."

Good Lord! The flare-up from his diabetes would have him in the emergency room before the rest of them pushed back from the table.

"And what did we say for dessert?" Miss Sadie warbled into the distance.

"Homemade coconut cake!"

Ah, well, that was a full coma right there. Hardly any of his parishioners could remember he had this blasted disease. The information seemed to go in one ear and out the other.

"Ask Louella if she'll marry me," he said.

"Louella, the father wants to know if you'll marry him."

"Tell 'im he got a short mem'ry, he done married Miss Cynthia."

He laughed, contented with the sweetness of this old friendship. "Just name the time," he said. "We'll be there."

*

Autumn drew on in the mountains.

Here, it set red maples on fire; there, it turned oaks russet and yellow. Fat persimmons became the color of melted gold, waiting for frost to turn their bitter flesh to honey. Sassafras, dogwoods, poplars, redbud—all were torched by autumn's brazen fire, displaying their colorful tapestry along every ridge and hogback, in every cove and gorge.

The line of maples that marched by First Baptist to Winnie Ivey's cottage on Little Mitford Creek was fully ablaze by the eleventh of October.

"The best ever!" said several villagers, who ran with their cameras to document the show.

The local newspaper editor, J.C. Hogan, shot an extravagant total of six rolls of film. For the first time since the nation's bicentennial, readers saw a four-color photograph on the front page of the *Mitford Muse.*

Everywhere, the pace was quickened by the dazzling light that now slanted from the direction of Gabriel Mountain, and the sounds of football practice in the schoolyard.

Avis Packard put a banner over the green awning of The Local: *Fresh Valley Hams Now, Collards Coming.*

Dora Pugh laid on a new window at the hardware store featuring leaf rakes, bicycle pumps, live rabbits, and iron skillets. "What's th' theme of your window?" someone asked. "Life," replied Dora.

The library introduced its fall reading program and invited the author of the *Violet* books to talk about where she got her ideas. "I have no idea where I get my ideas," she told Avette Harris, the librarian. "They just come." "Well, then," said Avette, "do you have any ideas for another topic?"

The village churches agreed to have this year's All-Church Thanksgiving Feast with the Episcopalians, and to get their youth choirs together for a Christmas performance at First Presbyterian.

At Lord's Chapel, the arrangements on the altar became gourds and pumpkins, accented by branches of the fiery red maple. At this time of year, the rector himself liked doing the floral offerings. He admitted it was a favorite season, and his preaching, someone remarked, grew as electrified as the sharp, clean air.

"Take them," he said one Sunday morning, lifting the cup and the Host toward the people, "in remembrance that Christ died for you, and feed on him in your hearts by faith, with thanksgiving."

Giving his own wife the Host was an act that might never cease to move and amaze him. More than sixty years a bachelor, and now this—seeing her face looking up expectantly, and feeling the warmth of her hand as he placed the bread in her palm. "The body of our Lord Jesus Christ, which was given for you, Cynthia."

He couldn't help but see the patch of colored light that fell on her hair through the stained-glass window by the rail, as if she were being appointed to something divine. Surely there could be no divinity in having to live the rest of her life with him, with his set-in-concrete ways and infernal diabetes.

They walked home together after church, hand in hand, his sermon notebook tucked under his arm. He felt as free as a schoolboy, as light as air. How could he ever have earned God's love, and hers into the bargain?

The point was, he couldn't. It was all grace, and grace alone.

✳

He was sitting in his armchair by the fireplace, reading the newspaper. Barnabas ambled in from the kitchen and sprawled at his feet.

Cynthia, barefoot and in her favorite robe, sat on the sofa and scribbled in a notebook. One of his antiquated towels was wrapped around her damp hair. He still couldn't get over the sight of her on his sofa, looking as comfortable as if she lived here—which, he was often amazed to realize, she did.

"Wasn't it wonderful?" she asked.

"Wasn't what wonderful?"

"Our wedding."

"It was!" She brought the subject up fairly often, and he realized he'd run out of anything new to say about it.

"I love thinking about it," she said, plumping up a needlepoint pillow and putting it behind her head. "A tuxedo and a tab collar are a terrific combination."

"No kidding?" He would remember that.

"I think you should dress that way again at the first possible opportunity."

He laughed. "It doesn't take much for you."

"That's true, dearest, except in the area of my new husband. There, it took quite a lot."

He felt that ridiculous, uncontrollable grin spreading across his face.

"It was a wonderful idea to ask Dooley to sing. He was absolutely masterful. And thank goodness for Ray Cunningham's video camera. I love the frames of you and Stuart in his bishop's regalia, standing in the churchyard … and the part where Miss Sadie and Preacher Greer are laughing together."

"Another case of two hearts beating as one."

"Would you like to see it again? I'll make popcorn."

"Maybe in a day or two." Hadn't they watched it only last week?

"It was very sweet and charming, the way you insisted on baking a ham for our reception."

"I always bake a ham for wedding receptions at Lord's Chapel," he said. "I'm stuck in that mode."

"Tell me something …?"

"Anything!" Would he really tell her anything?

"How did you unstick your mode long enough to propose to me? What happened?"

"I realized … that is, I …" He paused thoughtfully and rubbed his chin. "To tell the truth, I couldn't help myself."

"Ummm," she said, smiling at him across the room. "You know I love that you knelt on one knee."

"Actually, I was prepared to go down on both knees. As soon as I dropped to one, however, you saw what was coming, and seemed so happy about it, I didn't bother to advance to the full kneel."

She laughed uproariously, and held her arms out to him. "Please come over here, dearest. You're so far away over there!"

The evening news was just coming on when the phone rang. It was his doctor and friend, Hoppy Harper, calling from the hospital.

"How fast can you get here?"

"Well …"

"I'll explain later. Just get here."

He was out the door in thirty seconds.

TWO

Bread of Angels

"Dr. Harper's in the operating room, Father, he can't come out. He said put you in his office."

Nurse Kennedy opened a door and firmly pushed him inside.

"He said for you to pray and pray hard, and don't stop 'til he comes in here. Pray for Angie Burton, she's seven. Dr. Harper says it's a ruptured appendix, septic shock. We're all praying—except Dr. Wilson."

Nurse Kennedy, who generally looked cheerful, looked strained as she closed the door.

In Hoppy's cluttered office, only a lamp burned.

Angie Burton. That would be Sophia Burton's youngest. He thought of Sophia, who was well known for taking her two girls to First Baptist every Sunday morning, rain or shine, and for teaching them the Twenty-third Psalm as soon as they could talk. Working in the canning plant in Wesley, she kept bravely on in the wake of a husband who had totaled their car, tried to burn down their house, and disappeared into Tennessee only yards ahead of the law.

He phoned home and asked Cynthia to pray, then fell to his knees by Hoppy's desk.

"God of all comfort, our only help in time of need, be present in your goodness with Angie...."

✳

It was nearly midnight when Hoppy opened the door. "I owe you an apology," he said. "I could have asked you to pray at home, but all I could think of was having you here—on the premises."

The rector had seen that look on his friend's face before. It was utter exhaustion. "How did it go?"

There was a long pause. Hoppy looked up and shook his head. "We did everything we could."

He sank wearily into the chair at his desk. "Ever since we prayed for Olivia's transplant and I saw the miracles that happened, I've been praying for my patients. One day, I asked Kennedy if she would pray. Then she told Baker, and soon we discovered that the whole operating room was praying.

"I never talked to you about it, I kept thinking I would.... Anyway, we've seen some turnarounds. No miracles, maybe, but turnarounds. We felt something powerful was going on here, something we wanted to explore."

Hoppy took off his glasses and rubbed his eyes. "The bottom line is, we prayed, you prayed, and Angie Burton didn't make it."

What could he say, after all?

✳

Angie Burton's death was something the village could hardly bear.

Winnie Ivey was grief-stricken—Angie and her sister, Liza, often visited the Sweet Stuff Bakery after school. To them, she was Granny Ivey, who hung their school drawings on the wall in the Sweet Stuff kitchen.

The editor of the *Mitford Muse*, who scarcely ever spoke to or acknowledged a child, was moved to sudden tears over breakfast at the Grill and excused himself from the booth.

Coot Hendrick went to Sophia's house with a pie his elderly mother had baked, but, not knowing what to say, ran before anyone answered the door.

The members of First Baptist mourned the loss. So many of them had been involved in Angie's life; had held her as a baby, taught her in Sunday School, and made certain that she and Liza regularly got a box of decent clothes. In recent years, some had quietly paid the drugstore bill when the girls were sick with flu.

After the funeral, the rector went with his wife to the rented house behind Lew Boyd's Exxon station, still known to most villagers as the Esso.

He didn't say much, but sat on the sofa and held Sophia's hand, against a background murmur of neighbors bringing food into the kitchen.

Next to him, Cynthia cradled Liza on her lap, caressing the damp cheek that lay against her shoulder.

When Liza began to sob, Cynthia began to weep quietly with her. Then, somehow, they were all weeping and clinging to each other, huddled together on the sofa.

It was at once a terrible and a wondrous thing. He didn't care that he suddenly had no control, that he had lost it, that his grief was freely pouring forth, apart from his will.

They held each other until the wave of their sorrow passed and he was able to pray. They all knew that he had no answers, though they had hoped he might.

Afterward, he and Cynthia walked down the path to their car.

"Blast," he said, clenching his jaw.

She looked at him, at the way this death had moved and stricken him. In the car, she took his hand and drew it to her cheek. "Thank you for being a loving priest."

He didn't feel loving. He felt helpless and poured out.

❋

"Upside down and backwards," the new Baptist preacher had assured him yesterday.

The usually cheerful preacher looked as if he'd swallowed a dose of castor oil. "Plan to spend the first six months in misery and confusion, and the next six months merely in confusion."

For someone who could barely heat coffee in a microwave, the thought of what lay ahead was mind-boggling. Yet, for all the gloom and doom he had heard on the subject, he knew his vestry was right—it had to be done. Death, taxes, and computer systems. This was the law of the land, and no getting around it.

"Emma, I don't know how to tell you this. But the vestry wants us to go on computer."

She looked at him over her glasses. "What? What did you say?"

"I said the vestry wants us to go on computer. The bishop thinks it will bring some consistency to the affairs of the diocese. And chances are, it will do as much for the affairs of Lord's Chapel. You'll think so, too, once we get the hang of it."

"No way, José!"

She rose from her chair, doing that thing with her mouth that made her look like Genghis Khan with earrings.

"No one hates it more than I do," he said. "But it's going to happen."

"I work here fourteen years, day in and day out, and this is the thanks I get? I labor over these books like a slave, watching every penny, checking every total, and how many mistakes have I made?"

"Well," he said, "there was that pledge report five years ago ..."

"Big deal! As if a measly fourteen thousand dollars was something to get upset about."

"... and the incident with Sam McGee ..."

"Sam McGee! That skinflint! Anybody can say they put a thousand dollars in the plate and the check was lost by the church secretary! I hope you're not telling me a *computer* could have found that stupid check he probably never wrote in the first place!"

"Ah, well ..."

"So!" she said, inhaling deeply. "Go and find some young thing with her skirt up to here, and pay her out th' kazoo. Does the vestry take into consideration the kind of money they'll be shellin' out for her, while the money they save on *me* goes to Sunday School literature and soup kitchens? Ha! Never entered their minds, is my guess!"

He had expected Mount Vesuvius—and he was getting it.

✳

They were in bed at the rectory, propped against the huge pillows she had carted from her house in leaf bags. He had to admit it was a comfort, all that goose down squashing around back there. He could hardly get past the first page of his book without nodding off.

"Timothy, do I snore?"

He liked the way her questions sometimes bolted in from the blue, contained within no particular context that he could see. Good practice for a clergyman.

He removed his glasses and looked at his wife. "Snore? My dear, I don't know how to tell you this, but you positively rattle the windows. I think it could be overcome, however, if you would sleep with your mouth closed ... which might also eliminate the drooling problem."

"Timothy!"

"See how it feels? You told me I mutter in my sleep and grind my teeth. So, tit for tat."

"*Please* tell me you're kidding. I don't really snore, do I?"

"To tell the truth, no. You never snore. Maybe a whiffle now and again, but nothing serious."

"And no drooling?"

"Not that I've witnessed."

She looked smug. "You really do mutter in your sleep, you know."

"Worse has been said."

He never failed to wonder how all this had come about. If he had known that being together was so consoling, he would have capitulated sooner. Why had he been so terrified of marriage, of intimacy, of loving?

He had read again this morning about the wilderness trek of the Israelites and the way God miraculously provided their needs. Manna every day, and all they had to do was gather it.

"Men ate the bread of angels," was how the psalmist described it.

That appeared, somehow, to illustrate his marriage. Every day, with what seemed to be no effort at all on his part, he received God's extraordinary provision of contentment—there it was, waiting for him at every dawn; all he had to do was gather it in.

"… bread of angels," he mused under his breath.

"See! You mutter even when you're not sleeping!"

"I hardly ever knew what I was doing 'til you and Dooley Barlowe came along and started telling me."

She leaned against him in her striped pajamas and yawned happily.

"You're so comforting, Timothy. I never dreamed I would find anyone like you—sometimes, I hardly know where I end and you begin."

It was true for him, as well, but he said nothing.

"I think our love fits into the miracle category," she said.

"Right up there with the Red Sea incident, in my opinion."

"Do you think the people who love you are happy about us? Isn't some of the parish feeling a bit ... betrayed?"

"Never. They're glad to have someone look after me, so they don't have to. Of course, they never had to, but bachelor priests are thought to require extra attention."

He put his arm around her shoulder and pulled her close.

She kissed his chin. "Dearest?"

"Ummm?"

"Shall we bring the armoire over this Saturday?"

Out of the blue, again! He had to be quick. "This Saturday, I'm taking you for a little ... recreation."

"I love recreation! What are we going to do?"

In all his life, he had never been able to figure out what to do for recreation. As a bachelor, he was forever dumbfounded by the way people planned ahead for this very thing. "What are you doing this weekend?" someone might ask, and the respondent would roll off a daunting list of activities—a ball game, a movie, dinner out, a play, hiking, a picnic, and God knows what else. If he were asked such a question, he always wound up scratching his head, speechless. He never knew what he might do until he did it.

"It'll be a surprise," he announced.

"Good! I love surprises!"

"Cynthia, Cynthia. What don't you love?"

"Exhaust fumes, movies made for TV, and cakes baked from mix."

"I'm all for a woman who knows what she likes—and doesn't like." He cleared his throat. "As for me, I like this."

"This what?"

"This ... living with you."

"Then why did you fight me tooth and nail for longer than it took to build the Brooklyn Bridge?"

"No vision," he admitted. "No imagination. No—"

"No earthly idea of heaven!"

"You said it."

"Well, then …"

He leaned over and kissed her mouth, lingering.

"Oh, my goodness," she murmured at last. "Who would ever have thought …?"

❋

"Barnabas!" he called, coming in the kitchen door.

It was time for recreation, and he'd better hop to it. Otherwise, he'd have to leg it to the hardware to rent a back brace for the lugging over.

Barnabas raced from the study, skidded through the kitchen on a rag rug, and leaped up to give his master a lavish bath around the left ear.

"If we confess our sins," the rector quoted hastily from First John, "he is faithful and just to forgive us our sins, and to cleanse us from all unrighteousness!"

Barnabas retreated on his hind legs, lay down, sighed, and gazed up at his master.

His was the only dog in creation who was unfailingly disciplined by the hearing of God's Word. Now, if all of humankind would respond in the same vein …

"I'm ready!" she said, appearing from the study. She was dressed in blue jeans and a sweatshirt, tennis shoes and a parka, looking like a girl.

"Ready for what?" he inquired, grinning.

"What you said.…"

He was as excited as a boy, and no help for it.

"Here we go," he announced, offering his arm.

❋

Barnabas lay in the high grass, his tongue hanging out from the long climb uphill.

They had walked around Mitford Lake twice, their cheeks red with the sting in the air, eaten lunch from a paper bag, sat on a log and laughed, and then headed up Old Church Lane to rest on the stone wall overlooking what he called the Land of Counterpane.

In the valley, with its church steeples and croplands, tiny houses and gleaming river, they saw the retreat of autumn. Only the barest hint of color remained in the trees.

"I have a great idea," he said.

"Shoot!"

"Why don't we do something like this every week? Both of us can get bogged down with work, and maybe this would be a way around it. Even for a few hours, let's plan to get away." He was learning something new, he could just feel it. Who said you can't teach an old dog new tricks?

"Lovely!"

He pressed on with mounting enthusiasm. "Even in the dead of winter!"

"Wonderful! I couldn't agree more."

There. Since all the stuff about checking accounts, where to sleep, and how much to spend without the other's consent, this was their first important pact.

"Shake," she said.

They sat on the wall until a stinging wind blew in from the north, then walked briskly down Old Church Lane and through Baxter Park.

"Look," he said, "there's our bench."

"Where we were sitting when the rain came ... where you said you felt like thin soup, and invited me to go with you to see the bishop."

He was impressed with his wife's memory, as he didn't recall saying anything about thin soup.

"By the way," he wondered, "who's supposed to cook dinner this evening?"

"I can't remember," she said, wrinkling her brow.

✳

Percy shuffled to the back booth and poured coffee for the rector, who had come in for an early lunch. "How d' you like it?"

"Same as ever. Black."

"That ain't what I'm talkin' about."

"So what are you talking about?"

"How do you like bein' married?"

"I like it."

This was the first time since he'd returned from the honeymoon that any of the crowd at the Grill had really questioned his new circumstances. He had strolled in one day during Percy's beef-stew special, looking tanned and thinner, fresh from Maine, and not one word had Percy Mosely, Mule Skinner, or J.C. Hogan said about it.

All he could figure was, they were ticked off at knowing somebody for nearly fifteen years who suddenly upped and married. It required a certain change of mind, which, as Emerson had pointed out, was a blasted inconvenience.

"If I had it t' do over, I wonder if I'd do it," said Percy.

"You know you would. Where else would you get those terrific grandkids?"

"Oh, yeah," said the Grill owner, brightening.

"I'd do it over in a heartbeat," said Mule, sliding into the booth. "Fancy's better lookin' today than she was when I married her."

J.C. slid in on the other side. "I wouldn't touch it with a ten-foot pole. You couldn't get me to do it for a million dang dollars."

"Before or after taxes?" Mule wanted to know.

J.C. mopped his face with what appeared to be a section of

paper towel. "Once was one time too many. I'd rather be shot by a firin' squad."

"Is that caf or decaf?" Mule asked Percy. "Fancy's got me on decaf, I been stumblin' around for two days tryin' to get awake. Hit me with a little shooter of both."

J.C. held his cup out to Percy. "I tried decaf for a week, and it was all I could do to get th' paper printed. We whittled that sucker down to four pages, I couldn't paste up an ad without droppin' to the floor to take a nap." He blew on the steaming coffee. "Nossir, I wouldn't be married for all the tea in China, women want to run your business—they put you on fiber, take you off bacon, put you on margarine, take you off caffeine."

"You're mighty talkative today," said Mule.

"I was up half the night with the fire department. Omer Cunningham's old hay barn caught fire and the sparks jumped over and started on the shed where he stores that antique airplane. The fire engine came, and it was fish or cut bait 'til three in the mornin'."

"I thought I might go into newspaper work," said Mule, "but I got over it."

"If that airplane had caught, you might've found a landin' gear on your front porch."

"Had gas in it, did he?"

"You know Omer, he's always ready to fly. All he needs is a cornfield that hasn't been plowed. He said he's moving it to a hangar at the airstrip."

Mule stirred cream into his coffee. "Somebody told me Mack Stroupe's going to run in the next mayor's race."

"Mack's for change," said J.C. "Development, progress, and change—that's his platform."

"I like the platform we've got," said the rector. "'*Mitford takes care of its own*'!" he recited in unison with Mule.

Everybody in Mitford knew Mayor Esther Cunningham's platform, including the students at Mitford School, who had painted it on a nylon banner that was annually carried in the Independence Day parade up Main Street.

"You know how he built on to his hot-dog stand when he thought Percy was goin' out of business? He's goin' to use that side of th' building for his campaign headquarters."

"Right," said J.C. "And I'm the pope. You couldn't get this town to vote for anybody but Esther Cunningham if you paid 'em cash money. They'll carry her out of office in a coffin."

"He'll never run," said the rector, "so we might as well forget it. Mack's no genius, but he's not stupid, either."

Mule leaned out of the booth, searching for Velma. "Are we goin' to order, or did I come in here for my health?"

"You definitely didn't come in here for your health," said J.C.

Percy's wife, Velma, magically appeared with her order pad. "Order th' special."

"What is it?" asked the rector.

"Ground beef patty with a side of Hi-waiian pineapple."

"How's th' pineapple cut up?" Mule inquired. "I like slices, not chunks."

Velma frowned. "It's chunks."

"I'll have a grilled cheese, then. No, wait." Mule drummed the tabletop with his fingers. "Give me a bowl of soup and a hot dog all the way. Fancy's got me off cheese."

"I'll take a double cheeseburger all the way, plenty of mustard and mayonnaise, and large fries." J.C. gave his order louder than usual, to make it clear he was a free man.

"You don't have to bust my eardrums," said Velma.

Mule sighed. "On second thought, hold th' onions on my hot dog, they give me indigestion."

Velma eyed the rector, who was inspired by the sting he felt in the late October air. "Beef stew!" he announced.

"Cup or bowl?"

"Bowl."

"Roll or crackers?"

"Crackers."

"Change my order and bring me th' beef stew," said Mule. "I always like what he orders. But no crackers for me, I'll take the roll. And skip th' butter."

"I never heard of a *cup* of beef stew," said J.C.

"Crackers are for sick people," said Mule.

"Lord!" Velma ripped the order off her pad and delivered it to Percy.

Mule turned to the rector. "One thing I've been wondering ..."

"What's that?"

"How do your dog and her cat get along?"

"Violet lives in the house next door, and Barnabas keeps to himself at the rectory."

Actually, Cynthia fed Violet her evening meal at five, then popped through the hedge to the rectory, after which Violet curled up on Cynthia's love seat and slept until her mistress returned to work the following morning and opened one of those canned items whose odor could knock a man winding at fifty paces.

"A cat with a house," said J.C. "That's some deal."

"So her cat and your dog don't cross?"

"Not if we can help it."

"One time you told me Barnabas slept on your bed."

"Now he sleeps in the hall."

There was a reflective silence.

"Anybody been up on the hill?" asked the rector.

He had just come from the site of Hope House, the five-million-dollar nursing home that Sadie Baxter had given as a memorial gift to Lord's Chapel. By the look of things, it would be a year before it was up and running with staff.

"I shot two rolls up there Wednesday. Doin' a feature page next week."

"That's going to be some deal," said Mule. "I wouldn't mind movin' in there myself. I hear there's goin' to be a fountain in the lobby."

"And an aviary in the dining room," the rector announced proudly.

Mule scratched his head. "Did I hear it'll have its own church?"

"A chapel. A small chapel. Local millwork, a rose window. First-rate."

Velma carried two lunch plates on her left arm, and a third in her right hand.

Mule looked on with approval. "That's a trick I always thought highly of."

"Beef stew with crackers. Beef stew with roll, no butter. Double cheeseburger all the way, with large fries." Velma set the plates down in no particular order and stalked off.

The men dropped their heads as the rector asked a blessing.

"Amen," said Mule, rubbing his hands together.

"How's your boy?" asked J.C., who was busy pouring salt on his burger and fries.

"Great. Couldn't be better. He'll be home for Thanksgiving."

"He's not gettin' the big head in that fancy school, is he?"

"Nope. Dooley Barlowe might get a lot of things, but the big head won't be one of them."

"Did you read my story on Rodney hirin' a woman?" J.C. was not a pretty sight when he talked with his mouth full.

"You don't mean it."

"I bloomin' well do mean it. She starts the middle of November. A woman in a police uniform.... I can't see it."

"Why not? It's the law, no pun intended."

"Would you want a woman preachin' in your pulpit?" asked J.C., spilling coffee on his tie.

"Depends on the woman."

"I can't see a woman carrying a pistol."

"How come you don't like women?" asked Mule. "I like women."

"I told you. They're in the overhauling business."

"Maybe you could use a little overhaulin'."

"I *been* overhauled, buddyroe. Dropped fifty pounds, quit cigarettes, gave up red meat, and quit readin' trashy books. Oh, yeah. I even got shots for smelly feet. Was that good enough? No way. She was outta there the year the Dallas Cowboys defeated the Denver Broncos twenty-seven to ten."

"Big year," said Mule. "The Yankees won the World Series."

"Not to mention the *Chicago Daily News* went belly-up."

None of this information gave the rector a clue as to what year they were talking about, and he had no intention of asking.

"So," said Mule, "did the shot work, or have you still got smelly feet?"

Lunch at the Grill, thought Father Tim, was what kept life real. He had to confess, however, that he could hardly wait to get back to the office and finish the C. S. Lewis essay entitled "Thought, Imagination, Language."

＊

Cynthia gave him a hug as he came in the back door. "We've been invited to Miss Rose's and Uncle Billy's for banana pudding this evening."

"Oh, no! Please, no!"

"Dearest, don't be stuffy."

"Stuffy? Miss Rose has been hospitalized with ptomaine poisoning twice—and nearly sent a Presbyterian parishioner to her reward. You're the only person in town who'd put your feet under her table."

"So, pray for protection and let's go," she said, looking eager.

It didn't take much to delight Cynthia Kavanagh. No, indeed, it hardly took anything at all. What's more, she loved flying in the face of mortal danger.

"Besides, they've invited us for banana pudding practically since the day I moved here, so we can't disappoint them."

"Of course not."

"Next Wednesday," she said, "Miss Sadie and Louella are having us up for supper."

"Right."

"Fried chicken and mashed potatoes."

"We'll be there."

"And homemade coconut cake!"

"I've made a reservation in the emergency room," he declared, sitting down at the kitchen table.

"Don't worry, I'll watch you every minute. You mustn't have the gravy or the cake, and only the tiniest portion of potatoes, they'll be loaded with butter and cream."

He was glad J.C. Hogan wasn't around to hear this.

"Then," she said, adjusting her half-glasses to read from a list, "Ron and Wilma invited us for Friday evening."

"Ummm."

"Hal and Marge want us for dinner at the farm, the first Sunday of November."

"Aha."

"And the mayor has asked us for a family barbecue the following Sunday. What do you think?"

"Book it."

She looked faintly worn. "So much social activity! I thought you led a quiet life."

"I did," he said, "until I got married."

"Oh."

"Everybody wants a look at you."

"But they've seen me for ages!"

"Not in your new circumstances."

She sighed. "And then there's Thanksgiving!"

"And the All-Church Feast, which we must attend, and Dooley and Russell Jacks and Betty Craig for turkey here the day after, and … You look all in, what's up?"

She sighed again. "I've started a new book, and it has a crushing deadline."

All or nothing at all. That's what he liked about this new life.

✳

They walked to the Porter place—cum—town museum, holding hands. A Canadian cold front had moved in, inspiring them to wrap like mummies.

"I went to see Miss Pattie this morning," she announced, her breath sending puffs of steam into the frigid air.

"You did?"

"I gave Evie two hours off."

"God knows when Evie's had two hours off. You're a saint."

"I'm no such thing. We played Scrabble."

"Scrabble? With Miss Pattie?" Evie Adams's mother hadn't been in her right mind for a decade, causing Evie to call the church office with some frequency, in tears of frustration.

"She spelled one word—'go'—and declared herself the winner. Then we had an imaginary lunch and she showed me her imaginary doll."

"Knowing you, you can describe that doll in detail."

She laughed. "Dimples. Blue eyes—one won't shut. It had lost its socks and shoes, and I think its toes were once chewed by a puppy. I told Evie I'd come again."

He stopped and put his arms around her. "I've always wanted a deacon. You're hired." He kissed her on both cheeks and then on the mouth.

"Dearest ... everyone will talk."

"It's time I gave them something to talk about," he said, meaning it.

※

"I'll be et for a tater if it ain't th' preacher! Rose, come and look, he's got 'is missus with 'im."

They stood at the back door of the museum that led to the apartment the town had remodeled for Miss Rose and Uncle Billy Watson.

The old man's schizophrenic wife of nearly fifty years peered around the door. The rector thought she looked fiercer than ever.

"What do they want?" she demanded, staring directly at the shivering couple on the steps.

Uncle Billy appeared bewildered.

"You invited us for banana pudding!" said Cynthia. "Yesterday, when I saw you on the street."

"I did?" Miss Rose put her hands on her hips and gave them a withering look. "Well, I don't have *any* banana pudding!"

"Oh, law," said Uncle Billy, "did you go an' forget you invited th' preacher and 'is missus?"

"I certainly did not forget. It's too close to Thanksgiving to make banana pudding. I would never have had such an idea."

Uncle Billy looked anguished. "You 'uns come on in, anyway, and set where it's warm. I've got somethin' for you, Preacher, hit's nearly burnt a hole in m' pocket."

"That's all right, Uncle Billy, we'll come another time." Talk about a lifesaving turn of events.

"Nossir, I need t' give you this. It's somethin' that belongs to th' Lord, don't you know."

They trooped in as Miss Rose eyed them with suspicion.

The rector observed that she was still dressing out of her long-dead brother's military wardrobe. Under a worn housecoat whose belt dragged the floor, she was wearing Army pants and a World War II field jacket. He was almost comforted by the sight of her unlaced saddle oxfords, which were her all-time favorite footwear.

"I cain't set down, cain't lay down, an' cain't hardly stand up," said Uncle Billy, who was leaning on a cane. "Ol' arthur's got me, don't you know."

They hovered timidly by the kitchen table while Miss Rose stood at the stove and gave them a thorough looking-over.

"Preacher, could you step in here a minute?" Uncle Billy opened the door to the unheated part of the house, admitting a blast of arctic air, and led the way. As the door closed behind them, the rector looked back at his wife, who was trying to appear brave.

"I put it over yonder," said Uncle Billy, turning on a light in a room stacked with old newspapers. "I've kep' it hid from Rose— she wouldn't take t' me doin' this, don't you know."

He felt thoroughly refrigerated by the time the old man located the stack of yellowed papers and withdrew an envelope. With a trembling hand, he gave it to the rector.

"It's m' tithe," he said, his voice breaking. "Th' Lord give me that money for my pen an' ink drawin's that Miss Cynthia sold, and I'm givin' his part back."

The rector was so moved, he could barely speak. "May the Lord bless you, Bill!"

"Oh, an' he does. Ever' day, don't you know."

✳

"I'm glad we went," he said, buttoning his pajama top.

"Me, too. Even if Miss Rose does scare me half to death!"

She put her hands on her hips and said fiercely, "I don't have any banana pudding!"

"Thanks be to God!" he shouted, as they collapsed on the bed with laughter.

THREE

Gathered In

Y

"You lookin' at th' las' supper," said Louella.

As Fernbank's dining room was closed off for winter, they were sitting at the kitchen table.

"Louella's having her knee operation on Thursday," Miss Sadie reminded her guests. "She won't be able to cook like this again for a long time." His hostess, who was also his oldest, not to mention favorite, parishioner, appeared wistful.

"Who's driving you to Winston-Salem?" asked Cynthia, who had offered to do it a month earlier.

"Ed Malcolm. I don't know how Mr. Leeper heard about it, but somehow he did, and gave Ed the day off so he can drive us. Have you ever?"

"Extraordinary," said the rector. Buck Leeper, the abrasive, profane, don't-tread-on-me supervisor of the Hope House project ...

Cynthia helped herself to another deviled egg. "How long will you be there?"

"Five days, we think," said Miss Sadie.

"What will you do down there for five days? And where will you stay?"

"I'll have a cot in Louella's room!"

"She goan baby me," said Louella, looking sunny. Miss Sadie had babied Louella, who had been born at Fernbank, since they were children. In recent years, however, circumstances had begotten the reverse.

Five nights on a hospital cot? he thought. Not good.

"Louella would do the same for me."

"Amen!" pronounced Louella, passing the mashed potatoes. "Y'all eat these up. We don't have no puppy dogs t' feed 'em to."

He could tell that his wife was in seventh heaven, eating like a trencherman and happy as a child. She looked at him and smiled. "Keep your eyes off the gravy, dearest."

Lord knows, he was trying. "What will you do when you come back? Surely the stairs …"

"Louella will sleep down here in the kitchen."

"For how long?"

"The doctor said no stairs for three months."

"We ain't tol' him our stairs go almos' to th' Pearly Gates. How many we got, Miss Sadie?"

"Twenty-nine! Papa wanted thirty, but it didn't work out."

Sadie Baxter alone at night on that cavernous second floor? And what if Louella were to take a tumble on this cracked and broken linoleum? He didn't like the sound of the plan, not at all.

"When we go up at night, we go together," said Louella. "But sometime, it's more settin' down than goin' up."

"That's right. Sometimes it takes so long to get to the top, it's nearly time to start back to the bottom!"

"Me an' Miss Sadie, we sing our way up. I say, Do you remember 'To You Before the Close of Day …'? She say, Sho' I do, you start and I'll jump in. We set there and sing a verse, then we climb up another little step or two. Sometime, we go through two or three hymns jus' to lay our bones down."

"And *sometimes*," said Miss Sadie, inspired by the excitement of revelation, "we don't come *downstairs* at all."

"Miss Sadie, she keep candy in her vanity, an' I keeps Spam and loaf bread in my bureau. We watch th' soaps and th' news."

"We play checkers, or go ramble in the attic. I love to ramble in the attic. It keeps me young to remember old times."

"Many a day," said Louella, "we read th' Bible out loud, or Miss Sadie jus' sleep 'til dark."

"Louella, you don't need to tell that!"

"It's th' gospel truth."

Miss Sadie looked suddenly tired. "This old house ..." she murmured. "I don't know...."

You can learn a lot over a platter of fried chicken, he thought. Why had Miss Sadie never told him any of this? She always made everything seem bright and shining. They had no business rattling around in this clapboard coliseum alone. But what could be done? Hope House wouldn't be finished and staffed for another year. Maybe good help was the solution, someone to come in at night.

Or ... well, now. That was a thought. Why hadn't it occurred to him before? The fine old house on Lilac Road, bequeathed to Olivia Davenport by her mother ... perfect!

Only months ago, Miss Sadie had found something she never knew she had—blood kin. The beautiful Olivia was her great-niece, a surprising revelation that had thrilled both women. It was, however, a revelation they chose to keep secret, as it pointed to an illegitimate child by Miss Sadie's own mother.

Now, Olivia was married to Hoppy Harper, who had engineered her miraculous heart transplant. As they were living happily in the doctor's rambling mountain lodge, Olivia's house on Lilac Road sat quite empty. And didn't it have a brand new furnace, wall-to-wall carpet, and every imaginable convenience, all on one floor?

He wouldn't introduce the idea just now, however. He'd make his move on Monday.

The shrill ring of the phone sounded in the hallway.

"I'll get it!" said Cynthia.

He would ask Olivia if there were any plans to sell her house. If not, he'd work on breaking down Miss Sadie's resistance to the idea of leaving Fernbank. She had lived in the house her father built since she was nine years old—more than eighty years. One didn't casually walk away from such a bond.

"Miss Sadie, it's Olivia."

As Miss Sadie left the room with her cane, Louella leaned over and whispered, "Honey, this ol' house killin' me and it killin' her, don't let her fool you. 'Sides that, when I say Miss Sadie, you 'member this hymn, she say she do, but she don't. Miss Sadie doan want you to think she doan remember. And ramblin' in th' attic? She could stay up there 'til Jesus comes, kickin' up all that dust."

"I don't like the thought of you two being twenty-nine stair steps apart at night," he said.

"An' I don't like th' idea of Miss Sadie doin' th' cookin' aroun' here! Fact is, she don't cook—she sets out. She sets out mustard, she sets out baloney, she sets out light bread. Bless th' Lord, we in a pickle!"

Cynthia put on Louella's apron and announced she was washing the dishes. She handed her husband a drying towel.

Miss Sadie came back to the kitchen and closed the door. "I declare, if it's not one thing to muddle over, it's two. You'll never guess what that was all about."

"I could never guess," Cynthia admitted.

"Olivia said, 'Aunt Sadie, I want you to come and live in Mother's house, we're worried about you and Louella.'"

"Thanks be to God!" said the rector.

"Praise Jesus!" boomed Louella.

"Bingo!" exclaimed Cynthia. "And what did *you* say?"

Miss Sadie sat down and met each pair of eyes. "I said I'd have to think about it."

Cynthia spoke up at once. "I hope you'll think about the fact that it's all on one floor."

"And think about the heating system," he added, "and the insulation, and those good, tight windows, all brand-new. Warm as toast!"

"Think 'bout where it is!" crowed Louella. "One block from th' grocery! Aroun' the corner from th' post office!"

"You all don't have to preach me a sermon!"

After a respectful silence, he plunged in again. "Twenty-nine steps and nobody to sit and sing a hymn with. I wouldn't want to do it."

Miss Sadie looked at him coolly.

"I'll be sleepin' in th' kitchen, listenin' to th' roof leakin' in th' buckets," moaned Louella.

"Is the roof leaking again?" he asked. "I thought it was fixed."

"I thought it was fixed, Miss Sadie thought it was fixed. But it ain't fixed."

"It's fixed everywhere except the entrance hall!" said Miss Sadie, looking stern.

"Yas 'um," Louella muttered. "An' when it rains, it take a soup pot, a Dutch oven, an' a turkey roaster t' catch it!"

Miss Sadie thumped the floor with her cane. In all his years of knowing her, he'd never seen her do such a thing. "Shush!" she commanded. "I said I had to *think* about it. I didn't say how *long* I had to think about it. Coming down the hall, I thought about it."

Nobody said a word.

"And I have every intention of doing it!"

✳

"Save us from troubled, restless sleep," he sang softly in the darkened room, "from all ill dreams Your children keep ..."

"How lovely," she murmured, lying beside him. "What are you singing?"

"A verse from Louella's hymn, 'To You Before the Close of Day ...'"

He sang again, "... so calm our minds that fears may cease, and rested bodies wake in peace."

"Amen," she whispered, taking his hand.

✳

The crowd at St. Andrews in Canton had hammered out a description of what every parish was looking for, and sent him a copy.

> The perfect pastor preaches exactly ten minutes. He condemns sin, but never hurts anybody's feelings. He works from eight in the morning until midnight and is also the church janitor. He is twenty-nine years old and has forty years experience. He makes fifteen house calls a day and is always in the office.

Right up there with what's currently expected of Cynthia Kavanagh, he thought.

"They asked me to be president of the ECW," she said, looking pale.

"What did you say?"

"I said I have full-time work and that it wouldn't be fair to be president of anything, for I would surely have to shirk my duty."

"Well put."

"And so they invited me to head up the Altar Guild."

They had discussed this very thing, long before he proposed to her on the night of his birthday last June.

"Of course I said no, thank you. That's when they asked me to chair that awful Bane and Blessing sale, which has put at least two women flat on their backs in bed."

"True."

"When they got to a nomination for program chairman, every eye turned to me. I excused myself and went to the ladies' room. It was awful."

She sighed. "Well, dearest, I turned down six things in a row— they were all positively glaring at me. It took enormous courage."

"I'm certain of that." Where the Episcopal Church Women were concerned, he personally wouldn't have the guts to turn down six things—in a row or otherwise.

She took a deep breath. "That's when I announced that I'm reserving my energies to give a parish-wide tea in the spring."

Aha! He knew the fondness of his parish for a roaring good tea.

"I was off the hook in a flash. You should have seen the look of forgiveness in their eyes! Now, guess what."

"What?"

"Now I have to do it!" she wailed.

✳

The Hope House Board of Directors was searching for an administrator.

According to Hoppy, all was going well. As a graduate of Harvard Medical School, and the personal friend of a distinguished heart man at Mass General, his contacts had already turned up the names of several promising candidates.

It would take something like fifty people to run the two-story, forty-bed nursing home, and Miss Sadie had insisted on a full-time chaplain into the bargain. Finding the right candidate, the rector learned, was his job.

There would be RNs, LPNs, nurses' aides, business staff … the list went on and on, and most would have to be hired from outside the area. All of which would give a boost to merchants up and down Main Street and beyond.

No doubt about it, Hope House would be a shot in the arm for Mitford's economy.

"Who needs a canning factory?" asked a jubilant Mayor Cunningham at a town meeting.

✳

Puny had been looking a bit peaked, in his opinion. Somehow, she wasn't the same girl he had escorted down the aisle in June and given in marriage to the mayor's grandson.

"Do you have to scrub the floor like this?" he asked his house help on Monday. Seeing Puny on her hands and knees on his kitchen floor always distressed him. "You know I'll buy you a mop."

"You always say that. When I scrub on my hands and knees, I wisht you'd look th' other way. I don't know why it makes you s' mournful, it's the same as my granmaw did it, and my mama, too, and it's th' way I'm goin' to do it."

She seemed to scrub the worn kitchen tiles even harder. "Some gloves, then!" he said. "Rubber gloves!" He had taken to worrying about the freckle-faced, red-haired Puny Guthrie as if she were his own blood.

"Ooooh, I jis' hate it when you preach!" she said.

"Preach? If you think that's preaching, wait 'til you hear the real thing, young lady."

She looked at him and smiled, and pushed her hair from her eyes. "I kind of like it when you boss me."

"I'm not bossing you, and you know it. But you look a little … pale, somehow. Are you feeling your usual self?"

"Well," she said, sitting back on her heels, "if you're goin' to hound it out of me, th' truth is, I ain't. I'm give out, sort of. I don't know what it is."

"You want a few days off? We can push along."

"Nossir, I don't want a few days off! Me an' Joe Joe are addin'

a bathroom on our house an' puttin' on a new roof. I sure don't
need to be takin' days off, with roofin' at twenty dollars a square."

Since she walked in and took over his house two years ago,
Puny had been like a candle against the darkness—he wouldn't
take the world for her cheerfulness, her vigor, her adamant faith,
and the life she had brought to his household. Joe Joe Guthrie had
won himself a pearl beyond price.

"OK, I'll hush."

"Good!" she said, grinning up at him.

✳

He woke in the middle of the night, searching for the glass of
water on the nightstand. He took a swallow and lay there listening to her breathe. He was confounded over and over again that
she was lying beside him. He hadn't known what to expect, after
all, when it came to sleeping with someone.

Would he feel hemmed in? Invaded?

But he had never felt hemmed in or invaded, not once. He felt,
instead, a kind of awe that made him lie very still, scarcely breathing. How this could have happened, he couldn't imagine. During
the day, he could imagine it, and muse over the slow and gradual
process that had brought them to this place. But at night, it
seemed a miracle, defying reason.

Oddly, he could feel himself becoming something more, as
one might discover new rooms in a house he had lived in all his
life. Doors had opened, shutters had been cranked back to let in
new light. When he lay there and simply let the wonder of it sink
in, he was suffused with a kind of joy he'd never known before.

This joy was different from what he felt when the Holy
Spirit broke down his defenses and circumcised his heart. But
both these joys produced in him a tenderness that was nearly
unbearable.

"Thank you, Lord," he whispered.

"Hmmm?" Cynthia said, sleepily. "What did you say, dearest?"

"I said ... thank you," he croaked.

"You're welcome," she sighed, falling back to sleep.

✳

He walked to the Grill with Barnabas on his red leash, feeling the keen, pure cold of the day. Overhead, he heard the drone of a small airplane and looked up. Omer Cunningham, he supposed, who had nothing better to do than dip and soar in the wild blue yonder, while the rest of them had to fetch and carry like so many ants on a hill.

He reflected on Dooley's call last night—not once had he said "ain't," a piece of grammatical mayhem that Cynthia particularly disliked. That boy was a quick learner, he could say that for him. But there was something held-back in him, also—something cautious and wary like the old Dooley, yet more severe.

"How's Tommy?" Dooley had asked.

"Missing you, I think. Doing fairly well on his crutch. Dr. Harper is hopeful there won't be a limp." The friend who had fallen from a collapsing pile of lumber had survived a terrible wound to the head and a leg slashed to the bone.

"Can he talk right?"

"Nearly as well as the rest of us, I'd say."

Silence.

"How are you? How's your science class?"

"All right."

"And math? You're killing them, I take it."

"It's OK."

"The chorus is coming along—you're singing?"

"Uh-huh."

If only he could see his face. "We're wanting to see your face, pal. In just ten days, you'll be home."

"Yeah."

Was the "yes, sir" he'd once managed to gouge out of Dooley now gone with the wind? He felt an inexpressible love for the boy who had changed his life, who had turned it upside down and backward, and had come to be like his own son. They had toughed it out, they had made it through.

Or had they? "Are you OK?"

"Yeah."

Blast it, he was not OK, but there was nothing he could do about it on the phone. In no time at all, he and Cynthia would fetch him home from school, and everything would be fine. All Dooley Barlowe needed, after all, was a good dose of family and friends and somebody to catch up his laundry.

✷

Hoppy Harper had called the church office earlier, saying merely, "I need to bust out of here, and I need to talk. What about lunch?"

His friend was already in the front booth, looking, as Emma once remarked, "like a young Walter Pidgeon."

"Track me on this," said Hoppy. After years of exhausting himself as the only doctor in town, he had learned the economy of never mincing words.

"Hippocrates said that in the body, there's no beginning—in a described circle, no beginning can be found. He believed that if the smallest part of the body suffers, it imparts suffering to the whole frame."

The rector nodded. If the smallest part of the spirit suffers, it imparts suffering to the whole being. He'd seen this principle at work too often. "Keep going."

Velma appeared with her order pad. "What're you havin'?"

"What's the father having?" asked the doctor. "Give me the same."

"Chicken salad on whole wheat, no mayonnaise," said the

rector, "with a cup of vegetable soup." Why did people always want to order what he ordered? Did they think he had some special sign from Providence about what to order for lunch?

Hoppy leaned toward him, his brow furrowed. "So, nothing happens to any part of the envelope that affects us in an isolated area. And part of the envelope is the spirit—right in there with the lymphatic and enzymatic and neurological and circulatory factors.

"Even Socrates jumped on this. He said the cure of a lot of diseases was unknown, because physicians were ignorant of the whole. His bottom line was, the part can never be well unless the whole is well."

"I'm with you," said the rector.

"For the first few months, the staff and I prayed silently before operating, and that was good. It got us up for the job ahead in a whole new way. Now we usually ask the patient if we can pray aloud before we begin the surgical procedure.

"It works for me, it works for the staff. That alone has to be of some benefit. But it's working for the patients, too. I think it helps them go under the anesthetic as a complete entity, not merely a diseased bladder or a ruptured appendix."

"Makes complete sense."

"Besides, wouldn't God care as much about our bodies as our souls? Isn't redemption total? Doesn't it involve body, soul, mind—all?"

"Absolutely all."

"By the way, Olivia read that in certain primitive cultures, the doctor and the priest are one and the same person."

"Quite a packaging concept."

He had never before seen his friend so passionate about anything—except, perhaps, securing the miraculous heart transplant that saved the life of the woman he married last June.

Hoppy ran his hand through his disheveled hair. "As I said, there's nothing in this you can print out, nothing you can prove. Yet I know it's real, it's right, it works—even though we see through a glass darkly."

They didn't notice that Velma had set their orders on the table, until Percy dropped by to refill their cups.

"Your soup's gettin' cold," he snapped. "And your san'wiches are dryin' out."

Percy Mosely did not like his customers to be indifferent to his fare. No, indeed.

✳

The annual All-Church Feast, convening this Thanksgiving Day at Lord's Chapel, was drawing its largest crowd in years. Villagers trooped across the churchyard hooting and laughing, as if to a long-awaited family reunion.

It was one of his favorite times of the year, hands down.

People he saw only at the post office or The Local were, on this day, eager to give him the details of their gallbladder operation, inquire how he liked married life, boast of their grandchildren, and debate the virtues of pan dressing over stuffing.

This year, the Presbyterians were kicking in the turkeys, which were, by one account, "three whoppers."

Esther Bolick had made two towering orange marmalade cakes, to the vast relief of all who had heard she'd given up baking and was crocheting afghans.

"*Afghans?*" said Esther with disgust. "I don't know who started such a tale as that. I crocheted some pot holders for Christmas, but that's a far cry from *afghans.*"

Miss Rose Watson marched into the parish hall and marked her place at a table by plunking her pocketbook in a chair. She then placed a half dozen large Ziploc plastic containers on the table, which announced her intent to do doggie bags again this year.

Ray Cunningham came in with a ham that he had personally smoked with hickory chips, and the mayor, who had renounced cooking years ago, contributed a sack of Winesaps.

Every table in the Lord's Chapel storage closets had been set up, and the Presbyterians had trucked in four dozen extra chairs. The only way to walk through the room, everyone discovered, was sideways.

Cynthia Kavanagh appeared with two pumpkin chiffon pies in a carrier, Dooley Barlowe followed with a tray of yeast rolls still hot from the oven, and the rector brought up the rear with a pan of sausage dressing and a bowl of cranberry relish.

Sophia and Liza arrived with a dish of cinnamon stickies that Liza had baked on her own. Handing them off to her mother, she ran to catch Rebecca Jane Owen, who had grown three new teeth and was toddling headlong toward the back door, which was propped open with a broom handle.

Evie Adams helped her mother, Miss Pattie, up the parish hall steps, while lugging a gallon jar of green beans in the other arm.

Mule and Fancy Skinner, part of the Baptist contingent, came in with a sheet cake from the Sweet Stuff Bakery.

And Dora Pugh, of Pugh's Hardware, brought a pot of stewed apples, picked in August from her own tree. "Get a blast of that," she said, lifting the lid. The aroma of cinnamon and allspice permeated the air like so much incense from a thurible.

In the commotion, George Hollifield's grandchildren raced from table to table, plunking nuts and apples in the center of each, as Wanda Hollifield came behind with orange candles in glass holders.

In his long memory of Mitford's All-Church Feasts, the rector thought he'd never seen such bounty. He thought he'd never seen so many beaming faces, either—or was that merely the flush from the village ovens that had been cranked on 350 since daybreak?

The face he was keeping his eye on, however, was Dooley Barlowe's.

✳

Following the regimental trooping to the dessert table, someone rattled a spoon against a water glass. No one paid the slightest attention.

Somebody shouted "Quiet, please!" but the plea was lost in the din of voices.

Esther Bolick stepped to the parish hall piano, sat down, and played the opening bars of a ragtime favorite at an intense volume.

A hush settled over the assembly, except for the kitchen crew, who was lamenting a spinach casserole somebody forgot to set out.

"Hymn two-ninety!" announced the rector, as the youth group finished passing out song sheets. "And let me hear those calories *burn!*"

Esther gave a mighty intro, and everyone stood and sang lustily.

> *Come, ye thankful people, come*
> *Raise the song of harvest home*
> *All is safely gathered in*
> *Ere the winter storms begin*
> *God, our Maker, doth provide*
> *For our wants to be supplied*
> *Come to God's own temple, come*
> *Raise the song of harvest home.*

Baptists warbled with Anglicans, Presbyterians harmonized with Methodists, and the Lutherans who had trickled in from Wesley gave a hand with the high notes.

The adults soldiered on through two more hymns, followed by the Youth Choir, who fairly blew out the windows with three numbers in rapid succession. The grand finale was a solo from Dooley Barlowe, whose voice carried all the way to the back of the room and moved several of the women to tears.

"He ain't got th' big head no more'n you or me," said Dora Pugh.

It was some time before anyone could move to help clear the tables.

"Let's just lay down right here," said Mule Skinner, pointing to the floor.

"You 'uns cain't be alayin' down," said Uncle Billy. "You've got baskets to take around, don't you know."

Somebody groaned. "Tell us a joke, Uncle Billy!"

"Well, sir, this feller had a aunt who'd jis' passed on, an' his buddy said, 'Why are you acryin'? You never did like that ol' woman.' And th' feller said, 'That's right, but hit was me as kept her in th' insane asylum. Now she's left me all 'er money an' I have t' prove she was in 'er right mind.'"

Groans and laughter all around. "Hit us again, Uncle Billy!"

"Well, sir, this feller was sent off to Alaska to do 'is work, and he was gone f'r a long time, don't you know, and he got this letter from his wife, and he looked real worried an' all. His buddy said, 'What's th' matter, you got trouble at home?' An' he said, 'Oh, law, looks like we got a freak in th' family. My wife says I won't recognize little Billy when I git home, he's growed another foot.'"

Miss Rose Watson sat silent as a stone, concerned that the Ziploc bags of turkey and dressing would shift under her coat.

Good-byes were said, hugs were given out, and everyone shook the hand of the rector and his new wife, thanking them for a fine Feast. Several inspected Dooley's school blazer and commented that he'd shot up like a weed.

The contingent organized to deliver baskets waited impatiently as the packers worked to fulfill a list of sixteen recipients. These included Miss Sadie and Louella, Homeless Hobbes, and Winnie Ivey, who had shingles.

"You doin' a basket run?" Mule asked the rector.

He nodded. "Over to Miss Sadie's new digs on Lilac Road, then back here to help clean up. What about you?"

"Headed to Coot Hendrick's place. His mama's weak as pond water since th' flu."

"I thought J.C. was coming to the Feast this year."

"He probably boiled off a can of mushroom soup and ate what he didn't scorch."

"It's a miracle he's alive."

"Ain't that th' truth?" Mule agreed.

"There's nothin' wrong with J.C. that a good woman couldn't cure," said Fancy, who was dressed for today's occasion in fuchsia hot pants, spike heels, V-neck sweater, and a belt made of sea shells sprayed with gold paint.

"Don't hold your breath on that deal," said Mule.

Sophia came over and hugged the rector around the neck, as Liza clasped his waist and clung for a moment. "We love you, Father," said Sophia. He leaned down and kissed Liza on the forehead.

"Lord have mercy," said Mule, as Liza and Sophia left. "I don't know what these people will do when you retire. I hate t' think about it."

"Then don't," snapped the rector.

He saw the surprised look on his friend's face. He hadn't meant to use that tone of voice.

"Line up and collect your baskets," hollered Esther Cunningham, "and hotfoot it out of here! This is not a cold-cut dinner you're deliverin'."

The delivery squad obediently queued up at the kitchen door.

"If you could knock th' Baptists out of this deal," said Charlie Tucker, "we'd have somethin' left to go *in* these baskets. Baptists eat like they're bein' raptured before dark."

"It wasn't the *Baptists* who gobbled up the turkey," said Esther Bolick, appearing to know.

"Well, it sure wasn't the Methodists," retorted Jena Ivey, taking it personally. "We like fried chicken!"

"It was the dadgum Lutherans!" announced Mule, picking up the basket for Coot Hendrick's mother. "Outlanders from Wesley!"

Everyone howled with laughter, including the Lutherans, who had personally observed the Episcopalians eating enough turkey to sink an oil freighter.

✳

Abner Hickman came in the back door of the parish hall, returned from taking his kids home.

"Y'all want to see a *sunset*?"

A little murmur of excitement ran through the cleanup crew. Mitford was a place where showy sunsets were valued.

"Better get up to th' wall," declared Abner, "and step on it."

Esther Bolick parked her carpet sweeper in a corner. "Drop everything and let's go! Life is short."

They piled into vans and cars and screeched out of the parking lot, gunning their engines all the way to the steep crest of Old Church Lane, where they tumbled out and raced to the stone wall that overlooked the Land of Counterpane.

"Good heavens!"

"That's a big 'un, all right."

Little by little, the sharp intakes of breath and the murmurs and whooping subsided, and they stood there, lined up along the wall, gazing at the wonder of a sunset that blazed across the heavens. Where the sun was sinking, the skies ran with molten crimson that spread above the mountains like watercolor, changing to orange and pink, lavender and gold. A cool fire of platinum rimmed the profile of Gabriel Mountain and the dark, swelling ridges on either side.

He put one arm around Dooley's shoulders and the other around Cynthia's waist. The fullness of his heart was inexpressible.

All is safely gathered in ...

He knew it could not always be this way. No, nothing ever remained the same. If he had learned anything in life, he had learned that such moments were fragile beyond knowing.

Ere the winter storms begin ...

FOUR

Passing the Torch

The light from the street lamp in front of the rectory shone through the hall window, reflected into the mirror at the top of his dresser, and bounced softly onto the bedroom ceiling.

Because a mimosa tree had grown up beside the old street lamp, the light gleamed through its leaves, casting shadows overhead. He could tell when a breeze was up, as the shadow of the leaves danced above him.

"Timothy?"

"Hmmm?"

Cynthia turned over and lay facing him. "I can feel you lying there stiff as a board. Something's on your mind, I just know it. Can't you tell me?"

He didn't want to say it to himself, much less to anyone else. "It's Dooley."

"Yes."

"What's happened to him?"

"I've been wondering that, too."

"He's different. Was I so wrong to send him away to school?"

"I don't know." She sighed. "At least he isn't saying 'ain't.' But that's no consolation."

"God's truth, as much as I fought him on it, I miss hearing him say it."

Cynthia turned and lay on her back. "The wind is up," she said, looking at the ceiling.

"I sense something hard in him, something harder than before."

"He hates that school."

"I can't help but wonder if I should bail him out. Or trust the old adage that time heals all wounds. Maybe it's just a matter of time until he puts down roots where he is. He put roots down here—his very first—then I hauled him off to Virginia. Transplanting is always risky business."

"Look what happened," she said, "when I moved my white lilac in the middle of summer. How did I know it should be moved in early spring?"

"Yes. Maybe it was timing, maybe we should have waited a year to send him away."

"Have you talked to him?"

"He won't talk. He's hard as stone—face, heart, spirit."

"He needs to spend time with Tommy," she said. "He's avoiding his best friend."

He despised losing sleep over any issue. Broad daylight was the time for fretting and wrestling—if it had to be done at all. "Don't worry about anything," Paul had written to the church at Philippi, "but in everything, by prayer and supplication, make your requests known unto God. And the peace that passes all understanding will fill your hearts and minds through Christ Jesus." In the last hour, he had twice given his concerns to God and then snatched them back, only to lie here staring at the ceiling, worried.

"What were you like when you were thirteen? What was going on in your life? Maybe that will help us."

"My best friend was named Tommy, also. We did everything together. My father despised him."

"Your father. What was it, Timothy, that made him so cold? Did you ever do anything that pleased him?"

He thought about it. No. He really couldn't remember doing anything that pleased his father. His grades had been very good, but never good enough. There was the incident with the bicycle, but he didn't want to remember that. He didn't want to talk about his father. It was the middle of the night and he suddenly felt the weight lying on his chest.

"Let me rub your neck," he said, turning to her. "I know you had a long day over the drawing board."

"But, dearest—"

"There. How's that?"

"Lovely," she murmured.

The softness of her skin, the warmth of the down comforter, the leaves moving softly above them ...

He was asleep in two minutes.

✳

He drove to the country to see the ninety-year-old preacher he'd hooked up with Homeless Hobbes and the residents of Little Mitford Creek.

Every Wednesday night, in clement weather, Homeless cooked a vast pot of soup and fed any who would come to his one-room shack on the creek bank. Homeless's broader concern for their spiritual feeding had moved the rector to ask Absalom Greer to preach a summer meeting, his last call before retiring from his "little handfuls" at three mountain churches.

The old parson had willingly gone into the desperately

impoverished area, where alcohol, drugs, and violence had eaten into the Creek like cancer.

"I quit!" said Absalom Greer, opening a cold bottle of Orange Crush and passing it to the rector.

"I hate to hear it," said Father Tim.

"Every time I try to get loose of preachin', there's somebody who hates to hear it, and so I fall to doing it again, goin' like a circle saw. But this is it, my brother, as far as churches and camp meets go. The Lord paid me off, showed me the gate, and told me to trot."

The two men sat by the ancient soft-drink box in Absalom Greer's country store, twelve miles from Mitford. Among the comforts of this life, the rector once said, was sitting in Greer's Store in the late afternoon, with the winter sun slanting across heart-of-pine floors laid nearly a century ago.

"I'll do my preaching from the drink box, from here on out. There's many a lost soul comes down that road looking to quench their thirst, thinkin' they can do it with a Pepsi."

The rector nodded.

"Used to, I could give 'em a soft drink and a sermon for a nickle. Now the drink companies gouge a man for the best part of a dollar." The preacher's pale blue eyes twinkled. "Some days, it's hard to come up with a dollar's worth of preaching."

"Amen!"

The rector gazed with affection on the man who, more than sixty years ago, tried to win the hand of Sadie Baxter, and lost— the self-educated man who, to the horror and delight of his parishioners, had supplied the pulpit at Lord's Chapel while Father Tim hustled off to Ireland last year. What was more extraordinary was that Absalom Greer had packed them in—after the initial shock wore off.

"Tell me about your stint on the Creek. Homeless said wonderful things happened."

"My brother, they were a rough bunch—a handful and a half! I was preaching on sin, and they didn't like it a bit—same as the fancy churches, where the very mention of sin empties the pews.

"But a man has to start somewhere, and that's where the Lord told me to start—with sin and repentance.

"Folks like to think sin is what everybody else is doing, but the mighty book of Romans lays it out plain and simple—'For all have sinned and come short of the glory of God.'

"I didn't go on about drinking and fornicating, or backbiting and stealing. Nossir, I jumped right to the heart of the matter and preached the taproot of sin, which is found in the middle of the word, itself—*I*! I want this, I want that, and I want it right now. I want to run things, I want to call the shots, I want to be in charge....

"When we turn from our sin, and have the blessed forgiveness of the Almighty, then we can ask him to run things, and let him be in charge. But boys howdy, folks don't want to hear that, either.

"Nossir, they like to keep control, even if their little boat's pitchin' around in the storm and takin' on water and about to be swamped."

Preacher Greer took a long swallow of his cold drink.

"I got to chasing rabbits there for a minute. You asked how it went.

"Wellsir, you know how you stick a seed in the ground and you squat down and look where you planted it, and you get up and walk around a little bit, waiting for something to happen, and the rain falls and the sun shines, and you water that seed some more ... and still nothing pokes up. So after a while, you're tempted to go off and lay down under a tree, and plumb quit on that seed.

"Week after week, I was preaching the living redemption of our Savior, and I look out and see dead faces and stony hearts. A rough life had killed back their feelin's like a hard freeze on a peach crop.

"Some nights I'd go home and cry like a baby for the way they were hangin' on to their hurt.

"But I plowed on. One evenin', we preached the Word where it tells us the wages of sin is death, but the gift of God is eternal life through Jesus Christ.

"We told how Christ died for us out of love, which is mighty hard to understand, saved or unsaved.

"Then, we preached that noble verse from Revelation that makes me shiver to hear it—'Behold, I stand at the door and knock! If any man hears my voice and opens the door, I'll come in to him, and will sup with him, and he with me.'

"I said the Lord Jesus will knock and keep knocking 'til you let him come in and make you a new creature. He'll never break down the door. Nossir, the Lord is a gentleman. He waits to be *invited*."

The bell jingled, and a customer walked in. "Brother Greer, I need a box of oatmeal!"

"Comin' up," said Absalom, leaving his guest.

The rector noted the slowness of the old man's gait as he walked toward the shelves. He hadn't seen that last year and felt troubled by it. Deep down, he expected the people he loved to live forever, no matter how many funerals he had performed during his years as a priest.

Absalom rejoined the rector and sat again.

"My brother, I was in deep prayer as I preached, that the Holy Ghost would knock through the crust on every heart along that creek—but I have to tell you, my own heart was sinking, for it looked like the vineyard wasn't givin' off a single grape."

"I hear you."

"That's the way it was goin' when I noticed a young girl sitting on a limb of that big tree by the water.

"Usually, a good many young 'uns would sit up there for the preaching, but somebody had put a board across some rocks that evenin', and all the young 'uns but her was sitting on the board. I pay a good bit of attention to young 'uns, having been one myself, but I'd never spotted Lacey Turner before.

"You talk about listening! Her eyes like to bored a hole in me. If a preacher had a congregation to sit up and take notice like that, he'd be a happy man. It seemed like every word the Holy Ghost put in my mouth was something she craved to hear. I got the feeling my words were like arrows, shooting straight at that long-legged, barefooted girl, but still missing the souls on the ground.

"Wellsir, that young 'un slid off that limb and landed on her feet right in front of me, blam!

"Strikin' the ground like that kicked the dust up around her feet. I looked at that dust and looked at that girl, and I knew the Lord was about to do a work.

"She said, 'I'm sorry for th' bad I've done, and I want to git saved.' It was as matter-of-fact a thing as you'd ever want to hear.

"Well, the young 'uns on the board, they started in laughing, but that girl, she stood there like a rock, you should have seen her face! She was meaning business.

"I said, 'What would you be repenting of?' And she said, 'Bein' generally mean and hatin' ever'body.'"

"My brother, that's as strong an answer as you're likely to get from anybody, anywhere.

"I said, 'Do you want to be forgiven of meanness and hatred?' and she squared back her shoulders and said, 'That's what I jumped down here for.'

"I said, 'Well, jump in here and say a prayer with me and turn your heart over to Jesus.' And we both went down on our knees right there by the water, saying those words that's changed the lives of so many lost and hurting souls.

"'Lord Jesus,' she prayed in behind me, 'I know I'm a sinner. I believe you died for my sins. Right now, I turn from my sins and receive you as my personal Lord and Savior. Amen.'

"Wellsir, I looked up and half the crowd had moved over to that big tree and was going down on their knees, one by one, and oh, law, the Holy Ghost got to working like you never saw, softening hearts and convicting souls 'til it nearly snatched the hair off my head.

"We stayed kneeling right there, and I led first one and then another in that little prayer, and before you know it, brand-new people were getting up off their knees and leaping for joy!

"Oh, you know the lightness that comes with having your sins forgiven! It's a lightness that fills you from one end to the other and runs through your soul like healing balm."

The rector could feel the smile stretching across his face.

"My brother, I scrambled down the bank to that creek, and that little handful swarmed down over rocks and roots, some crying, some whooping for joy, and we baptized in the name of the Father and the Son and the Holy Ghost 'til I was sopping wet from head to toe."

The old preacher was silent, then he smiled. "I've never seen anything to top it."

"Nor I," said the rector.

Absalom got up and set his empty bottle in a crate.

"You can baptize anywhere you've got water," he said, "but to my way of thinking, you can't beat a creek. It's the way ol' John did it—out in the open, plain and simple.

"Only one thing nags me," he told the rector. "Who's goin' to disciple those children of God?

"What's goin' to become of Lacey Turner, as pert and smart a young 'un as you'll ever see, with a daddy that's beat her all her life, and a mama sick to death with a blood ailment?

"I can't keep goin' back in there. My arthritis won't hardly let me get down the bank from the main road." The old man shook his head. "It grieves me, brother, it grieves me."

The knot in the rector's throat was sizable. "I don't know right now what we can do," he said, "but we'll do something. You can count on it."

They walked out to the porch and looked across the pasture and up to the hills. The sun was disappearing behind a ridge.

"How's Sadie?" asked Absalom.

"Never better, I think. She has a heart like yours."

"Well ..." said the old preacher, gazing at the hills. They stood on the porch for a moment, silent.

Absalom Greer had passed a torch, and Father Tim had taken it. The only problem was, he had no idea what to do with it.

✳

He was fixing dinner as Dooley stood at the kitchen door, staring into the yard. Cynthia looked up from setting the table and walked over and put her hand on his shoulder. He shrugged it off.

"What is it, Dools?"

"Nothin'."

"Why won't you talk to us, be with your family for the two days you've got left of your school break?"

Dooley turned around and they saw that his face was white with anger. "You're not my family. I don't have a family."

He stalked from the kitchen, slamming the door behind him.

✳

On Saturday, Cynthia popped through the hedge for an early call from her editor, so he hotfooted it to the Grill, with Barnabas on the red leash. Advent was coming up, and still no snow, or promise of snow. Perhaps they would have a white Christmas—but, God forbid, not a blizzard like the one that paralyzed them last winter.

He took his cup off the hook at the counter and poured his

own coffee. "Poached," he said to Percy, who was flipping bacon on the grill. Percy frowned. He had never liked doing poached, which he considered too time-consuming.

In the rear booth, Mule was reading the paper, printed on the *Muse* presses overhead. "How'd we get th' pleasure of your company this morning?"

"I lost the pleasure of my wife's company," said the rector.

"I know th' feelin'. Fancy was up doin' highlights and a perm at six-thirty." He folded the *Muse* and laid it on the table. "You see J.C.'s story?"

"'Getting to Know Your MPD,' I think he called it."

"He drove around in a squad car for a couple of days, gathering material."

"Very readable," said the rector. "Well done. Anybody seen the new police officer?"

"You mean th' woman?"

"Right."

"Fills out 'er uniform pretty good. She was in here before you, picked up a coffee with cream and sugar. Forty, if she's a day. Name's Adele Lynwood."

"Where's J.C.?" wondered Father Tim.

"Gettin' barbered. I saw him leggin' it up th' steps to Joe Ivey an hour ago. Speakin' of which, you're lookin' a little lank around th' collar."

"Always drumming up business for Fancy. If she did as much for your real estate interests, you'd be rolling in dough."

"I call it like I see it, and you could use a trim."

"Man!" said J.C., sliding into the booth. "He shaved me for boot camp."

"That's Joe's deal," said Mule. "Take it all off at one whack. Fancy's of the new school. She believes in trimmin' a little at a time. More natural."

"And more money," said J.C., wiping his face with a paper napkin. "Six bucks here, six bucks there. Joe gives you fifteen dollars' worth for five."

"And sends you out needin' a hat to keep your head warm," said Mule.

Given the surprised, newly hatched look of J.C. Hogan, the rector thought he might dodge Joe Ivey this time and step over to Fancy's himself.

"Good story," said the rector. "One of the best in some time. I didn't know the chief played minor league baseball."

"Nobody else did, except his mama and daddy, and maybe his wife."

"Journalism at its best!" announced Mule.

Percy poured a round of coffee and eyed J.C. "What'll it be?"

"Give me a bowl of Wheaties, skim milk, a cup of yogurt, and dry toast ... whole wheat."

There was a stunned silence. "Call nine-one-one!" said Mule.

Percy dug a finger in his ear. "Am I goin' deef?"

"And snap to it," said J.C. "I could eat a horse."

Mule blew on his coffee. "You'll have to drink a saucer of grease to let your stomach know it's you."

"Why didn't you come to the Feast?" asked the rector.

"Too much carryin' on."

"You could use a little carrying on, if you ask me."

"I didn't ask you," said J.C.

One thing he could say for his collar—it never earned him any respect at the Grill.

After breakfast, he walked out with Mule and untied Barnabas from the bench.

"I don't get it," said the realtor. "Clean tie. Haircut ..."

"Dry toast. Skim milk ..." mused the rector, shaking his head.

✳

"I just thought ... we've been wondering ... is anything going on at school that we should know about? Dooley's not himself, not at all."

"Glad you asked," said the headmaster, who promised he didn't mind being rung up on a holiday. "I thought the trip home might do him good, so I didn't say anything."

"Say anything about what?" He was afraid to know.

"About what happened. He made friends with one of the boys, one of the ... disadvantaged boys, if you will, and he talked to him about his family, about his mother and what happened to his brothers and sisters. I think it was hard for him to talk to someone about this. I think it plagues him a good deal. The bottom line is, Dooley spilled his guts to the boy, and the boy betrayed him. He told it around school."

Dear God. So that was what had chilled Dooley to the bone and hardened his heart all over again.

"While we're at it," said the headmaster, "Dooley was caught smoking on the grounds. This put his name on a roster that's posted in the hall for all to see. He's also skipped chapel a couple of times. Not a good start. He mustn't think that's a way to make a name for himself around here. I've spent a bit of time with him, Father, he's got strong potential. But there may be equally strong liabilities."

"What can I do?"

"Well, for one thing, you can increase his allowance, if it seems appropriate. Even with the few students from lower economic backgrounds, this is a school for the privileged, and there's no getting around it. He sees the boys buy expensive school sweatshirts or take off on weekend field trips to Washington, and his allowance doesn't stretch that far. Perhaps the generous woman who's sending him here would—"

"What kind of money are we talking about?"

"A hundred and fifty dollars a month. I think that's fair."

"Consider it done," he said.

After the phone conversation, he stared out his office window. He had to hand it to Dooley Barlowe. The boy had never once complained about his allowance, and only once had he asked for money.

He took his checkbook out of his jacket and sighed. Then he called home. Dooley answered.

"I'm taking you to Wesley for a cheeseburger," he said.

"I don't want a cheeseburger."

"I'll pick you up in ten minutes. Flat."

Shelling out a hundred and fifty bucks a month did not put him in the mood to mince words.

Sitting in the fast-food restaurant, he laid the check on the table and went over the program.

"Get caught smoking again, and you're back to what you've been getting. Got it?"

No answer.

"Got it?"

"Yeah."

"No yeah."

"Yes, sir."

"Another thing. Skip chapel again and you blow off seventy-five bucks a month. Period."

Dooley looked at him.

"I've talked with Dr. Fleming and I know what happened. Hear me on this. Your friends *will* betray you. Not all your friends, but some of your friends. That's life. Let it teach you this: *You* mustn't betray *your* friends. Ever."

"I could kick his guts out."

"You could. But for what?"

Dooley stared out the window.

"You can make it or break it in that school. You can stick in there and obey the rules and suck it up and learn something, or you can come crawling home for the world to know you couldn't hack it up there with the big guys.

"Listen, pal, life is tough. School's no picnic. But you'll be home again at Christmas. That's not far away. Take it a little at a time. A little at a time. You're going to be OK up there. I promise."

Dooley wadded his burger wrapper into a ball and lobbed it into a trash can.

"You said the other day you don't have a family. That hurt. It made us feel rotten. I want you to know that. The truth is, you do have a family, because we love you and care for you and we're sticking with you, no matter what. That's family."

Dooley dropped his gaze. "I didn't mean it," he said.

"I know you didn't. Go call Tommy and ask if he wants us to bring him a cheeseburger, and does he want waffle fries or seasoned."

It was only there for a moment, but he saw it—Dooley Barlowe couldn't fool him. It was an instant of happiness in the boy's eyes, something like hope or relief.

※

He'd pop a load of Dooley's laundry in the machine, then swing by Winnie Ivey's for a sack of donuts to take on the trip back to school tomorrow. A bitterly cold wind was gusting through the village.

"I wish I could go with you to take Dooley," Cynthia said. "I hate to see him leave."

"Ummm."

"Did you hear me?" she asked, peering at him.

"What's that?"

"Sometimes you're a thousand miles away."

He grinned. "The rest of me is a stick-in-the-mud, but my mind has always liked to wander. Living alone so many years didn't help matters any."

"A likely story."

"I'll try to do better, I promise. What are you up to today?" His wife, he knew, was always up to something.

"I'm mending two of Dooley's shirts and then working on an illustration of bluebirds in a nest."

"Your new book is about bluebirds?" Things had been so frantic, they hadn't found a chance to discuss her book.

"I think so," she said, "but I'm not sure, yet. I feel it should *open* with bluebirds, but I don't know if it's *about* bluebirds."

Sounded like the way he wrote his sermons.

"I've always wondered what it's like to be a bird—soaring around in the clouds, sleeping in trees. I think children would want to know that. All we see from the ground is that lovely, winged freedom. But they must have perils and scrambles like the rest of us, don't you think?" She peered at him over her glasses.

"I'm inclined to think so, yes."

"I can hardly wait 'til spring to go out with my sketchbook," she said, getting that abstracted look in her eyes.

"Ummm."

"I hope you'll come with me! You can exegete Jeremiah while I draw birds."

"I'd rather draw a bird any day than exegete Jeremiah!" he said with feeling.

"By the way, dearest, what's blooming around the rectory in May?"

"Let's see. A fine grove of white mountain trillium, a border of primroses which are pretty showy ... and there's lily of the valley, of course, a side yard full."

"Perfect!"

As he kissed her good-bye, he was struck again by the endlessly compelling blue of her eyes. Would he one day take them for granted, or would they always draw him in like this?

❋

He was unplugging the coffeepot on Monday morning when he heard Puny let herself in the front door.

She came down the hall at a trot and disappeared into the downstairs bathroom, where she remained for some time. When she came out, he was leaving for the hospital.

He couldn't help seeing that she was an odd green color— something in the mint family, to be precise.

"Good heavens, Puny, what is it?"

She sighed. "Remember I said Joe Joe and me won't be in any hurry to have babies?"

"Yes. I remember that."

"Well, *we* forgot to remember," she said, looking ghastly.

FIVE

A Close Call

It might have been a nest of copperheads, for the cold dread he felt when seeing the boxes left by UPS on Emma's desk.

"Get it off my desk," she said, her shoulders rigid.

"Where would we put it? The shower stall is filled with everything from 1928 prayer books to the office Christmas wreath."

"Set it on the visitor's bench."

"But we usually have visitors." Why couldn't the people it came from have kept the blasted thing 'til they were ready to install it?

She turned and eyed his desk, a cue that he ignored.

"Put it on the floor, then," she said with disgust. "In front of your bookcase."

"Then we can't open the front door all the way."

"You ought to see the nice preacher's office at First Baptist," she said, glaring around their nine-by-ten-foot confinement. "Enough room for a bowling alley!"

He saw it coming—the Baptist preacher's office would grow into a stadium, a coliseum, the Parthenon.

"Emma," he said, "why don't you take the day off?"

He was sure someone would be around tomorrow to plug it in.

Or whatever.

✳

But nobody came on the morrow.

Reluctantly, he read what was printed on the boxes: 420 drive megabytes. Eight megabytes of RAM. PCI architecture. He might have been reading Serbian. If you couldn't make sense of the box, he reasoned, what sense could you make of its contents?

"Put it in your car," said Emma. "You could put it in mine, but Harold's storing hay in the backseat."

"*Hay?*"

"It's wrapped up with old blankets to keep from makin' a mess, you can't tell it's hay. He wanted to keep it dry and didn't have any room left in that little barn he built."

"Aha."

"Just stick it in your trunk, if it'll fit."

He had to hand it to her—Emma Newland could come up with a really good idea once in a while.

"Don't worry," he told her as he hauled the largest box out the door, "somebody said a child could operate it."

He knew he was repeating a barefaced lie, told by someone who foolishly believed clergy to be ignorant of reality and bereft of common sense.

✳

"Hello, Rodney!"

He hadn't had a call from the Mitford police chief in quite a while, not since they'd done all that business together before his trip to Ireland.

During the dognapping of Barnabas that had led to the drug bust, and the drama of the jewel thief who had lived in the church attic and turned himself in during a Sunday service, he'd seen Rodney Underwood nearly every day for a couple of months.

"Father, I need to talk to you about somethin'. We could meet at the Grill—or how about me comin' by your office?" Rodney sounded worried.

"Why don't I come by your office? I haven't been there in a while. Got anybody I can visit, while I'm at it?"

"Not a soul. I released a DUI this mornin'. We've done cleaned th' cell and mopped th' floor." Rodney was the only police chief he'd ever heard of who kept house like a barracks sergeant and provided back issues of *Southern Living* for inmates.

At the station, Rodney met him at the door. "Looks like marriage is treatin' you right."

"It is, thank you."

"How's Dooley? I been meanin' to ask."

"Fine. Doing great."

"Not gettin' the big head, is he?"

If there was anything the village didn't want Dooley to get, it was the big head. "Let that be the least of your concerns."

Rodney took him into his office and closed the door. "It's Miss Sadie," he said, hitching up his gun belt.

He distinctly felt his heart skip a beat. "What happened?"

Rodney sat on the corner of his desk and invited the rector to take a chair. "She's done run that Plymouth up on the sidewalk one time too many.

"You know I've closed my eyes and looked the other way ever since I stepped into this job—but only where Miss Sadie's concerned. She's th' only one I'd look th' other way for."

The rector nodded. If there was ever an honest man, it was Rodney Underwood.

"Drivin' up on th' sidewalk ain't goin' to hack it from here out. This mornin', she hauled up in front of The Local so close you'd bust out the store window if you opened the passenger door. I mean, we got new people movin' in here, it's not just homefolks anymore. These are modern times. Why, there's somebody from Los Angelees, California, livin' on Grassy Creek Road."

"I'll be darned."

"The way I figure it, that car rolled off the line when Eisenhower was in office. If it hit a Toyota, it'd send it all the way to Wesley—air express. Another thing. She hugs th' yellow line like it was laid out for her to personally run on. People scatter like chickens when they see her comin' in that Sherman tank."

The police chief looked closely at the rector, to be sure he was getting the point. Clearly, he wasn't. "What I'm sayin' is, she's got to do better or we got to get her off th' street."

"Aha." He didn't want to hear this, no indeed, he liked things to go along smoothly, business as usual. Sadie Baxter had been driving up on the sidewalk for years. What was the big deal?

"My men have spoke to her twice, but it ain't sinkin' in. Next time, we're givin' her a citation. And if she don't do better then, I'm turnin' her in to th' MVB for reevaluation."

"Can *you* discuss it with her?" asked the rector, knowing the answer already.

"That's what I'd like you to do, Father."

"I hate to meddle," he said, knowing full well that he would have to do it, anyway. Actually, someone once told him that meddling was his job. Godly meddling, they'd called it, though it hardly ever felt godly to him.

"I don't call it meddlin' when you might be savin' somebody's life, not to mention hers. How she even sees over the dashboard is more than I can figure, low as she is."

"Ah, well," he said weakly. He had rather be horsewhipped than tell Sadie Baxter she'd have to park at the curb like everybody else and stick to her own lane. He had seen the stern way she rapped the floor with her cane before Louella's operation. To tell the truth, he might be a little afraid of Sadie Baxter.

Maybe Cynthia would do this uncomfortable deed, and let him out of it altogether.

✳

He had shaved and showered, and was about to walk into the bedroom when he realized his wife would be there.

He shook his head as if to return some sense to it. His *wife*. He more than relished the company of his wife; there were times he could hardly wait to see her. But when would his heart stop this foolish pounding on nearly every encounter? When would the comfort of merely being two old shoes kick in?

She was sitting up in bed in something blue, with Barnabas on the floor beside her. "I gave Evie a little break today."

"You're wonderful."

"Never! What do you think Miss Pattie and I did?"

"I can't even begin—"

"We danced."

"No!"

"Yes."

"The rumba? The fox-trot?"

"Free-form."

"You had … music?"

"She turned on the radio. It was something about calling the wind Mariah."

"Aha."

"When Evie came home and saw her little mother dancing, she cried."

"Evie always cries."

He loved the open expectancy that so often lit her face. He sat on the bed next to her. "It all sounds amusing, but I know it isn't, really. You're brave and good to let Miss Pattie express something of her spirit."

"I'm not good, dearest, and I'm certainly not brave. I really don't like going over there at all. It's hard. But when I think how hard it is for Evie ..."

He took her hand, grateful.

"There's something terribly winsome and sweet about Miss Pattie," Cynthia said. "She looks rather like the Pillsbury Dough Boy in a dress, don't you think?"

"Exactly!" He wouldn't talk to her about Miss Sadie tonight.

"I thought I might take her to ride one day. Rodney Underwood used to take her to ride in his squad car, but he's too busy now. Do you think a Mazda would do just as well?"

Yes, indeed, he thought, angels were very real. Miss Pattie and Evie Adams had been given one of their own, in the flesh. As had he.

✳

"Ah, Father!" It was Hope Justice, appearing out of the fog as the rector jogged his final lap up Main Street.

He stopped, panting. He always liked seeing her face. And since she worked the night shift and slept most of the day, he didn't see it often.

"I wanted to thank you and the missus for what you did for our Benjamin and all. It was mighty big of you in every way. We just appreciate it, Father." He saw tears welling up in Hope's brown eyes.

"Why, think nothing of it!"

"It helped more than you know," said Hope, pulling out a handkerchief.

Jogging away in the damp December cold, he couldn't help but wonder what he had done for Hope Justice. He didn't want to seem dense, but the last time he could remember doing anything was years ago, when her husband was laid off from the glove factory.

✳

Puny Bradshaw Guthrie was getting back to her old self. In fact, he'd never seen her look better.

"Stop starin' at my belly!" she said, giggling. "I can jis' feel you starin' down there to see what's what. I prob'ly won't even show for another month or two!"

He felt that uncontrollable grin spreading across his face. His Puny, with the red hair and freckles and the soul of a saint.... "And what does your mother-in-law, the mayor, think?"

"She's excited as anything. This'll be her eighth great-gran."

"And twenty-five grans, I believe?"

"Twenty-six, countin' her youngest girl's little boy that popped out last week."

"I got you something and don't sass me for doing it." He went to the pantry and took out the mop.

"It's a squeegee with a flexible handle, and look here, you don't ever have to bend over again, just work this lever...."

She eyed the demonstration with suspicion.

"And another thing," he said. "I want you to eat a good lunch and stop pecking around here like a bird."

She laughed and saluted him. "Yes, sir!"

He sighed. "I don't know what I'll do without you when—"

"You don't have to do without me! I'll bring it to work with me!"

"You ... you will?"

"I sure will! And I won't mind a bit if you play with it!"

"You won't?"

"That little train you set up at Christmas, you could run that an' all. That would be entertainin'."

There was a thought, he mused, scratching his head.

✳

Out of sight, out of mind.

He had forgotten the three boxes shifting around in his car trunk, until the computer company called to say they'd be heading up the mountain "real soon."

While he had them on the line, he said, maybe they could tell him what to expect. No problem, said the caller. They would come and install the computer, the monitor, the printer, and the bookkeeping system, and give a two-hour introduction. Then they'd come back every week or so for a couple of hours until the church office could handle it on their own.

How long, he wondered, would it take for his office to ... handle it? About a year, no problem, piece of cake, said the caller. Father Tim felt his stomach wrench. As for scheduling, they'd install it the week after Christmas, if that was all right with him.

All right? He couldn't thank them enough for their inexcusable, unprofessional delay in getting the blasted job done.

When she heard the news, it seemed to him that Emma was her old self again. Not that this was any improvement.

"Lord!" she said. "What I wouldn't give for a chocolate Little Debbie, to celebrate!"

Emma had given up Little Debbies for Lent three years ago, a sacrifice he deeply appreciated. Being in the same room with a Little Debbie of any variety was more temptation than he could handle.

Emma eyed him. "She's watching your diet, I suppose?"

"Somebody has to."

There was a prickly silence.

"I hear the ECW wanted her to be president."

"They did."

"I hear she wouldn't be program chairman, either."

"You heard right."

"My, my," said Emma, twisting her mouth in that way he so thoroughly disliked.

✳

He stopped by Mitford Blossoms only a hair before closing time and bought three roses of good breeding, along with several stems of freesia. Jena Ivey wrapped the bouquet in crackling green florist paper and tied it with satin ribbon—an extra business expense she willingly assumed for the fine presentation it made.

"Special occasion, Father?" Jena liked to know what was up with her customers, and would look a man straight in the eye until she got the answer.

He said it all together, as one word, "Marriedthreemonths."

On the back stoop of the rectory, he straightened his collar, held the bouquet behind his back, and marched into the kitchen.

"Cynthia!"

Barnabas came bounding down the stairs, sailed toward him, airborne, and gave his face a fine licking before he could summon a scripture. "You got me that time," he said, wiping up the damage with his coat sleeve. The excited barking of his good dog filled the rectory like the bass of the Lord's Chapel organ filled the nave.

It was a wonderful thing, to be greeted as if you were the very pope, but where was the woman who had moved in with him and shared his bed and left hilarious notes in his sock drawer?

"Cynthia!"

Maybe she was late coming home from work, from the little yellow house next door.

He ran some water in a vase and put the roses and freesia in it. The barest whiff of scent came to him.

He stood in the middle of the kitchen floor, holding the vase, and listened for her footsteps on the back stoop. Barnabas sat at his feet, staring up at him.

"Come, then, old fellow, we'll go for a walk." Barnabas danced on his hind legs, barking.

Cynthia would be home by the time they got back from the monument, and he'd take her to dinner in Wesley. Why not? He had done it once before, and she seemed to enjoy it immensely. He set the roses in the center of the kitchen table, wrote a hasty note on the back of the electric bill, and propped it by the vase.

> Gone to the monument. Back in a trice. Taking you to dinner.
> Love, Timothy

He loved the soft shine of the street lamps in their first hour of winter dark. And now, Christmas lights added to the glow. Up and down Main Street the tiny lights burned, looping around every street lamp with its necklace of fresh balsam and holly.

If he never left Mitford at all, it would suit him. He had been happier here than in any parish of his career. To tell the truth, there wasn't even a close second, except, perhaps, for the little mission of fifty souls where he had served at the age of twenty-seven. They had taken him under their wing and loved him, but refused to protect him from sorrow and hardship. Indeed, there had been plenty of both, and that little Arkansas handful had made a man and a priest of him, all at once.

He looked up to see clouds racing across the moon, as Barnabas lifted his leg on a fire hydrant.

A line came to him, written by a fellow named Burns, who put out the newspaper in a neighboring village.

> *Big cities never sleep, but little towns do.*

At barely six o'clock, Mitford was already tuckered out and tucked in, poking up the fires that sent wafts of scented smoke on the December wind. He drew the muffler close around his neck.

"Father!"

It was Bill Sprouse, the new preacher at First Baptist,

bounding along behind something that looked like a tumbleweed on a leash. Barnabas growled.

"Good evening, Reverend!" He was glad to see the jolly face of the man who was working wonders at First Baptist and was liked by the entire community. Last summer, he and Bill and two other Mitford clergymen had pushed peanuts down Main Street with their noses to raise funds for the town museum. If nothing else had come of that miserable experience, it had bonded the local clergy for all time.

"That's Sparky," said Bill Sprouse, with evident pride.

The two dogs sniffed each other.

"What breed?"

"Beats me. We think it was a rag mop that mated with a feather duster. He was left on our doorstep in a cracker box twelve years ago. Rachel and I are foolish about the little so-and-so."

"I know the feeling."

"How's the computer coming? Learned your way around a menu yet?"

"A menu?"

Bill Sprouse laughed. "Do you have Windows? CD-ROM?"

He didn't even pretend to know what Bill was talking about. "It hasn't been installed yet. Right after Christmas, they say. My secretary has threatened to quit."

"I lost two secretaries in the start-up at my old church. To get a computer system going in a church office takes youth, stamina, and the faith of an early martyr." Bill Sprouse grinned knowingly.

"Aha."

"I guess I'd liken it to having all your wisdom teeth pulled, with no gas to knock you out." The two dogs continued in a circle, sniffing. "No, wait, that's too mild. It's more like ..."

The rector stepped back, ready to turn and run.

"... having a frontal lobotomy. Yes! That's it!"

"Bill, good seeing you. My best to Rachel. So long, Sparky."

As he hurried toward the monument, did he hear Bill Sprouse guffawing, or was it the wind? He bitterly resented the thought of wrecking the peace of his workplace—not to mention the infernal aggravation of reworking the budget to accommodate the cost of the system.

He saw the squad car coming, but noted that the passenger in the front seat didn't see him. J.C. was too busy laughing. J.C. laughing? He turned his head to get another look, but the car disappeared around the corner.

He quickened his steps toward home.

Cynthia would be waiting.

✳

But Cynthia wasn't waiting.

He shouted through the rectory, finding it empty as a tomb. Then he dialed the house next door. No answer.

Still in his coat and muffler, he popped through the hedge, noting with dread that the only light shining against the darkness was the one over the back stoop.

"Cynthia!"

He walked into the dark kitchen, turning on a light, and raced to her small studio. He was alarmed at what he might ...

But she was not there, which gave him an ironic mixture of dread and relief.

"Cynthia!" He turned on the hall light and bounded up the stairs and into her bedroom. What was that on the bed ...

Good Lord!

But it was only a pile of clothes she had stacked there for the Bane and Blessing sale.

He went in the bathroom and drew back the shower curtain.

Would she have driven to The Local for groceries? But they

shopped only yesterday. Had she gone out to the FedEx drop on the highway to Wesley? But why wouldn't she have told him or left a note? She had never before caused him to wonder at her whereabouts.

He looked at his watch. Six-thirty. She was always home by five-fifteen, sometimes earlier. He must not panic, no indeed. His wife was a grown woman, fully capable of taking care of herself and having plenty of common sense into the bargain.

He found he was pacing the bedroom floor.

Should he call Rodney Underwood? That was a dark thought. Rodney would have his force swarming over the town and fanning out into the woods, not to mention taking fingerprints in both houses and talking over a radio crackling with static. He hated even thinking of it.

Violet! He realized there was no Violet trooping along at his heels, trying to scratch him on the ankle.

He could just feel it—Violet was definitely not in the house, or she would have made herself present at once.

He went back to the kitchen and looked under the shelves in the pantry. The cat carrier was gone.

The serenity of the little house was maddening—it revealed absolutely nothing. Everything was the same, yet everything was disturbingly different.

He went to the sink and leaned against it and prayed.

"Look here, Father, this is serious business. Protect Cynthia wherever she is, bring an end to the fear I'm feeling, and give me wisdom. Show me precisely what to do, through Christ our Lord, Amen." Direct and specific. Plain and simple. Any tendency he had to pray like a Philistine fled before such confused anxiety as this.

✳

Her car was, of course, gone from the garage.

He sat on the study sofa at the rectory, where he had often sat to figure things out. But he could not figure this. It was past seven o'clock and his wife was two hours late arriving home on a cold, dark, and windy night in December.

He would call his cousin, Walter, in New Jersey. But what would he say? Katherine would get on the phone and insist he call the police at once.

Well, then, he would call Marge Owen, his friend ever since coming to Mitford, and the wife of the finest senior warden he'd ever had. She would know what to do.

But he couldn't make the call. He went out to the back stoop of the rectory and waited for Cynthia's car lights to come down the driveway on the other side of the hedge.

The wind was blustering, now, lashing the trees in Baxter Park.

He couldn't bear the torment any longer, and he wouldn't consider the consequences. At eight o'clock, he went to his kitchen phone and called Rodney Underwood at home.

"Hello, Rodney?" His voice sounded like the croaking of a frog. "Tim Kavanagh here."

Did he hear something outside? "Excuse me a moment ..."

He raced to the stoop and saw her car, parked in the driveway next door with its lights on. "Hello, dearest!" she called through the hedge.

He sprinted back to the phone.

"Rodney! About that talk we had yesterday. Just wanted you to know I'm working on it, consider it done. Good-bye!"

✳

He couldn't hold her close enough.

"Timothy, you're smashing *by doze*," she said, coming up for air.

"Cynthia ..."

"I know you were frantic, and I don't blame you. I should have told you again this morning, but you see, even *I* forgot! I didn't remember my one o'clock at Trent School until nine-thirty, and it's a four-hour drive! I flew down the highway. I'm telling you, if they had nailed me for speeding, I would be on bread and water in solitary confinement in some little town that's not even on the map!

"I screeched to the door practically on the dot of one, and you should have seen the children, Timothy! They brought flowers, they'd made posters, one little girl brought apple jelly from her grandmother's tree and wrote a poem for the lady author. Nearly everyone had drawn pictures of Violet. I can't wait for you to see them, some are better than mine!

"If I hadn't shown up, it would have been terrible, they had looked forward to it so much. We sat on the floor and read and talked and had a wonderful time for two whole hours, and Violet was her best-behaved in years.

"And then I had to start home and I was famished because I'd gone without lunch, and when I stopped for a hamburger, I took a wrong turn and drove an hour in the opposite direction.

"It was horrible, horrid, I can't tell you. I wanted to stop and call you, but I thought it would be best to spend time driving, because I *told* you I'd be late. Finally, I did stop and call—it was six-thirty—but there was no answer."

"I was combing your house and trying to keep myself calm," he said.

"I'm so sorry, darling, but I did tell you I was going. I did! I was very specific. We were sitting at the kitchen table when I told you just the other morning ... but Timothy, you must not have been listening."

So that was the penalty for not listening—mortal terror.

Actually, he seemed to recall that she'd mentioned Trent

School, but beyond that, he drew a blank. "Must you do this again, these school visits?"

"Yes." There was a note of finality in her voice, and he didn't press the issue.

But even if she *had* told him, she owed him one, he could say that. Tomorrow, he would ask her to talk to Sadie Baxter.

✻

"No way," said Cynthia.

"Please."

"You're the priest, Timothy, I'm merely the deacon. This is a job for the top dog."

You owe me, he wanted to say, but didn't. "I can't do it," he said flatly.

"You're scared."

"You're right."

"So who can we get to do it?"

"If I had an answer to that, I wouldn't be here practically begging on my knees."

"You're cute when you're desperate."

"You're so good at this sort of thing ..."

"At what? Asking people to change their ways, give up familiar habits?"

"Habits maintained at the possible expense of human life?"

Cynthia frowned. He had her there, he could tell.

"Oh, poop," she said. "I'll do it."

He sat down, immeasurably relieved.

"But you owe me," she said, narrowing her blue eyes in that way he'd come to know as meaning business.

✻

It happened on the fourteenth day of Advent, the date marked on the calendar to take his Buick to Lew Boyd for a tune-up and muffler. Nor was it a day to be walking around without a car. He might have stopped by the house and borrowed Cynthia's, but no, he had pressed toward the office from the service station, his head bent into the first falling snow of the season.

Ron Malcolm slowed down, pulled to the curb, and lowered his window. "Father! Good morning. Been wanting to ask when our computer system's going in."

"After Christmas!" he snapped.

Ron blanched. "Want a ride?"

No, he did not want a ride. If he had wanted a ride, he would *have* a ride.

He looked into the face of one of the most loyal parishioners on earth, suddenly feeling like two cents with a hole in it. "Sorry, my friend. The very mention of that computer system is like gall in a wound. I need to grow up, get with it."

"I understand. We hooked one up in my construction company right before I retired. Actually, that's why I retired."

"That bad, huh?"

"Something like getting gored by a bull, in slow motion."

The snow was melting on his hatless head. "Got time for a cup of coffee at the Grill?" He went around the car and opened the door, and slid in with his Hope House building committee chairman.

"Speaking of retiring," said Ron, as he pulled away from the curb, "I guess that's something you're thinking about."

"It certainly isn't. I never think about it." The unbidden coldness came into his voice again. If he couldn't control his peevish tongue, who could?

They drove in silence until Ron found a parking place across the street from the Grill.

"Thinking about it isn't so bad ..." said Ron, turning off the ignition, "once you get the habit of doing it."

"Maybe." Why should his retirement be anyone's concern? If

Lord's Chapel wanted him to leave, that was one thing. But retiring was his own blasted business.

Hadn't Churchill begun writing *A History of the English-Speaking Peoples* while in his eighties? Hadn't Eamon de Valera served as Ireland's president when he was ninety-one? It was a litany he often recited to himself. And George Abbott, the Broadway legend—Good Lord, the man never even married until he was ninety-six! What was all the blather about retirement? He despised the very word.

"Coffee straight up," said Ron to Percy, "and make his a double."

＊

Just before noon, the phone rang. Emma handed him the receiver with patent distaste. It was the computer company.

"Father, we've had some schedule changes. Would it be all right if we come at two o'clock today and get you up and running?"

He was sick of the whole affair. "Perfect!" he said, without consulting his secretary. "Come ahead!"

Emma winced when he told her. "No use to fret," he declared. "We might as well get it behind us and enjoy the Christmas season."

"And you might as well bring the dern thing in and have it ready when they get here."

There was only one problem. The dern thing was in the trunk of his car.

He dialed Lew Boyd, but the line was busy. He was still getting a busy signal when Emma unwrapped her sandwich at the noon hour.

"Why don't you take my car and run up there?" she asked. "It's still got hay in it, but at least you could go and tell Lew to bring those boxes over here in his truck."

Emma was a clear thinker, all right.

The wall clock said twelve-thirty when he arrived at the station, where Lew and Bailey Coffey were playing checkers with the phone off the hook.

"I've got to get something out of the trunk of my car," he told Lew. "It's three boxes, and I'd appreciate it if you could run them down to my office in your truck before two o'clock. I'd take them in that big Olds out there, but it's, ah, full of hay."

Lew looked sheepish. "I hate to tell you, but I just sent Coot t' Wesley to pick up your muffler—in your Buick. Th' rear end's been lockin' up in my truck, and I can't drive it 'til it's fixed. Sendin' Coot in your car was th' only way to get your part in here today."

"Aha. What time will Coot be back?"

"I'd give 'im a half hour if I was you," said Bailey Coffey. "He hain't been gone more'n ten minutes. Take a load off your feet."

"Don't mind if I do," said the rector, perching on a vinyl-covered dinette chair and peering at the checkerboard.

※

Beyond the unwashed windows of the service station, the flakes spiraled down as in a snow globe.

He had given Coot thirty minutes, then forty-five. "Stopped off for a burrito, is my guess," said Lew.

It was nearly two o'clock when the phone rang. Lew Boyd turned white as a sheet.

"You're lyin'! You ain't lyin'…. Call Bud and get 'im to tow it in."

Lew stared at the rector, who was checking the wall clock with mounting aggravation. "It's your Buick," said Lew, looking stricken.

"What about it?"

"Somebody rear-ended Coot after he pulled out of the parts place. Plowed right into 'im."

"Good grief!"

"I don't know how t' tell you this, but them boxes in the trunk of your car ..."

He stood rooted to the spot.

"... they're tore up pretty bad. He looked in there, said he couldn't tell from jig what it was in 'em, but said whatever it was is history."

"Hallelujah!" He was shocked at what flew out of his mouth.

"What's that?" said Lew.

"I said thank you!" He grabbed Lew's hand and shook it. "Thank you, thank you!"

"I'm awful sorry, I cain't tell you how—"

"No problem. Quite all right. Good. Fine. Excellent!" Knowing some insurance companies, it could take weeks on end, even months, to put things straight. His neck was out of the noose. Good-bye and good riddance!

The two men watched the rector roar out of the station in the lavender Oldsmobile.

Bailey Coffey shook his head. "Seem like he wanted to hug your neck for gettin' his car tore up."

"Th' man is a saint," said Lew, meaning it.

Six

Love Came Down

He was without a car again, but so what?

Hadn't he once given up his car for Lent and, liking the idea, gone without it for eight years? He could always use Cynthia's car, or, if push came to shove, haul his motor scooter out of mothballs.

After all, their winter weather was nearly like spring. They'd been given a couple of snow flurries and a few bitter winds, but beyond that, temperatures had been unseasonably mild.

He would think all of Mitford would leap for joy about this weather. But no.

"You talk about a flea problem this summer!" Dora Pugh grumbled to him at the hardware. "With no cold weather to kill 'em off, they'll be swarmin' over your dog like ants over jam. An' wait'll you see th' Japanese beetles. Your roses'll look like Swiss cheese."

The Collar Button man was complaining that he couldn't sell his winter topcoats and practically had to give them away, the Irish Woolen Shop was stuck with a load of boiled-wool sweaters from the British Isles, and Percy Mosely railed that his ice-cream business had cranked up again, which tended to overwork his wintertime "skeletal crew."

Those who slogged through last year's blizzard, saying they never wanted to see snow again, grumbled about not having any. And Bud Bradley made it known that without rotten weather to send people crashing into ditches, his tow truck business was suffering.

On the bright side, Father Tim called Dooley and learned the school had just gotten a fine snowfall.

"Went sledding, did you?"

"Yep. Me'n Harvey Upton crashed."

"Into a tree?" That's what he'd always crashed into when he went sledding.

"Into one another."

"Anybody hurt?"

"Ol' Harvey busted his hands when he run in the back of me."

"You OK?"

"He sent me windin', but I rolled down th' hill."

"How's your computer stuff coming along?"

"I been on th' Internet."

"You what?"

"You wouldn't understand."

"Truer words were never spoken, thanks be to God. What did you learn on the, ah ..."

"Internet."

"Right."

"Learned about Labrador retrievers. When I get out of this school, I want one."

"Fine. You got it."

"They eat th' furniture and rugs an' all."

"Ummm."

"But they get over it."

"How long does it take them to get over it?"

"'Bout three years."

"Aha. Well, listen, son, we miss you."

Silence.

"Christmas break will be here soon. We're coming to get you, save up your laundry. You'll see your granpaw, he's been asking about you, and you'll see Tommy. He can spend the night anytime you like."

Silence.

"Shoot straight with me, buddy. Are you OK?"

Dooley hesitated, but only for a moment. "Yeah."

He heard the ache in the boy's voice. It was something no one else would hear, he supposed, but he had gotten to know Dooley Barlowe, gotten to love....

Dooley was in his prayers throughout the day, and as he prayed with Cynthia in the evening, which gave him the confidence to watch and wait.

He decided not to consult with the headmaster again until after the Christmas holy days.

❋

"It's done," said Cynthia, looking gloomy.

"It is?"

"But I didn't do it."

"You didn't?"

"Miss Sadie did the thing herself."

"Aha."

"When Miss Sadie tried to raise one of Olivia's silk shades, it flew up and wrapped itself around the roller, so Miss Sadie climbed on the divan, as she calls it, and tried to pull the shade down and lost her balance."

A broken hip! Ninety years old ... months in a wheelchair, or worse, in bed....

"She fell off the sofa," said Cynthia, "and broke her wrist."

"Thanks be to God!"

"Timothy! How could you?"

"I mean I'm thankful that it was only her wrist that was broken. Think what could have happened."

"I know. She was very brave about it ... wanted to set it herself to save a doctor bill. But Louella called Hoppy and they sent the ambulance, which made Miss Sadie furious because it cost a fortune. Of course, it went through town blasting the siren, which she really didn't like, and now her arm is in a sling."

"I'm having what's called mixed emotions."

"Me, too. Now Louella and Miss Sadie are both down for the count. But Olivia will visit every day and I'll check on them faithfully, plus The Local delivers, and there's a mail slot in their front door, so ..."

"So, all's well that ends well," he said.

"For now," she replied, looking concerned.

✻

J.C. Hogan must be hitting the skim milk pretty hard, he thought, as he saw the editor hiking along the other side of the street, toting his briefcase in one hand and hitching up his pants with the other.

✻

They were hurtling toward Christmas, which left little time for lunch at the Grill.

There were multiple meetings with the choir director, the Hope House building committee, the vestry, the new Evangelism Committee, and the Sunday School supervisor, not to mention his involvement in the mayor's projects to repair and paint Sophia Burton's house, and a Lord's Chapel Christmas party at Children's Hospital.

He also felt led to attend an overnight with the youth group, during which they made tree ornaments, wolfed pizza, and listened to loud music until he went home at 2:00 a.m., wildly energized by teenage adrenaline.

Woven into the fabric of this seasonal tapestry were his daily hospital visits and a desperate jog up Old Church Lane four afternoons a week.

Seizing the moment on Wednesday, he dashed from the office to the Grill and slid into the rear booth on the stroke of noon, literally panting.

"We thought you'd died and gone to heaven," declared Mule.

"I'm working on it."

"Still haven't had your neck cleaned up."

"My neck has been in the noose," he said testily. "Where's J.C.?"

"Probably blown away by a strong wind. Have you seen him? He's droppin' off to a stick."

"Yeah," said Percy, pouring coffee, "if he don't watch it, he'll walk out of his britches right on Main Street."

"That," said the realtor, "would be a sight for sore eyes. What'll it be?"

"Soup du jour!" said Father Tim. "A bowl and a roll."

"You'll like the soup," Percy announced. "It's got fresh broccoli in it."

"I don't like broccoli," said the rector.

"I don't have time t' argue about it. Have th' soup," said Percy.

"Fine," he sighed, too exhausted to care.

Mule leaned toward his lunch companion. "So, what do

you think is goin' on with J.C.?"

"Beats me. I guess we finally talked some sense into his hard head before he fell out with a stroke."

"I don't think it's got anything to do with health. Do you think he's interviewin' for a job and wants to look sharp?"

"What kind of job would he interview for? The Wesley paper is against his politics."

J.C. slammed his briefcase onto the bench and slid into the booth. "Been hangin' around the hospital for three dern hours."

Mule eyed him suspiciously. "You're not gettin' shots for smelly feet, are you?"

"I got a dadgum physical to the tune of two hundred bucks," snapped the *Muse* editor.

"It didn't improve your disposition any," said Mule.

"Turns out I've lowered my cholesterol, brought my blood pressure down, and passed the treadmill test—"

"That's worth two hundred right there," said the rector.

"You did all that with yogurt?" asked Mule.

"Lookit," said J.C., grabbing the waistband of his pants and pulling it away from his stomach a full two inches.

After lunch, the rector stood and talked with the realtor in front of the Grill.

Mule furrowed his brow. "Did you notice his shoes were shined?"

"Did you notice he was carrying a handkerchief instead of a paper towel?"

They eyed each other.

"And the handkerchief was clean."

They went their separate ways, deep in thought.

＊

"Puce," said Cynthia, staring at the walls of the rectory dining room.

"I beg your pardon?"

"Puce. Your dining room color. I just figured it out."

"Spell it," he said.

"P-u-c-e. I loathe puce. Besides, who wants a brown dining room?"

Nobody, if her wrinkled nose was any indication.

"Dearest, I've been thinking. We've set the date of the parish-wide tea for May fifteenth. It should be a happy time, definitely not a time for brown—especially not ancient brown. This paper must have been on these walls since Lord's Chapel was a mission church!"

"The turn of the century, then."

"Look at this stuff!" She waved her hand at the walls he'd never fully seen, somehow, until now. They were brown, all right. With a tint of muddy purple.

"I agree."

"Agree with what?"

"That you can have it repapered."

"That's not what I had in mind, exactly."

"Aha."

"Close your eyes and imagine this. We steam off the paper. Put on a coat of primer. Paint over that with a wonderfully soft, rich pumpkin. And then use a creamy bisque color to rag it."

"What it?"

"Rag it. Go over it with a rag and make it look like the walls of an old Italian villa. What do you think?"

"But it's not an old Italian villa."

"Timothy."

"Well," he said, "it isn't."

"Lord's Chapel has a Norman tower, and the church isn't in England. Not only that, but your gardens are full of French and German roses and this—must I remind you?—is Mitford!"

No two ways about it, his wife was a quick thinker.

"Go for it!" he said, with feeling.

✴

Placing the phone on the hook, he sank into a chair at the kitchen table as Cynthia walked in from next door.

"Timothy! What is it?"

"You won't believe this."

"Tell me!"

"Dooley isn't coming home for Christmas."

"But why? What's wrong? Is he—"

"He's going to Europe."

"*Europe?*"

"To sing. In the school chorus. They're leaving next week. They'll be gone fourteen days."

She sat down, too.

"A boy has pneumonia, and Dr. Fleming said the choirmaster pulled Dooley off the bench, as it were. All expenses paid. It's part of a grant."

"Why, I'm … it's … I'm speechless. It's too wonderful for words!"

"I was just going to bring the electric train down from the attic," he said, looking dazed and forlorn.

She reached over and took his hand. "Don't worry, dearest. We'll get it down, anyway. I love electric trains."

✴

A hastily scrawled note from Dooley:

> Here's ten dollars to get a present for Tommy. Merry Christmas.
> P.S. If I could I would buy you a world globe with a light in it.

A world globe with a light in it! Merely the present he'd wanted all his life. Amazing that the boy recalled something he'd mentioned only once, a very long time ago.

✴

He had found a few precious moments to make notes in his sermon notebook, while a fire blazed on the hearth, the Christmas tree lights glimmered, and Cynthia made dinner.

It was a type of grace, this small hour he'd been given during the haste and hurry of Advent. He gazed away from the notebook, giving thanks for small things.

"We look for visions of heaven," Oswald Chambers had written, "and we never dream that all the time God is in the commonplace things and people around us."

He went to his bookshelf and took down a volume. He was thankful merely for the time to go to his bookshelf and look with leisure for a reference.

He thumbed the pages. Dietrich Bonhoeffer had talked of the small things, too, saying in *Life Together*:

> We prevent God from giving us the great spiritual gifts He has in store for us, because we do not give thanks for daily gifts.
>
> We think we dare not be satisfied with the small measure of spiritual knowledge, experience, and love that has been given to us, and that we must constantly be looking forward eagerly for the highest good. Then we deplore the fact that we lack the deep certainty, the strong faith, and the rich experience that God has given to others, and we consider this lament to be pious....
>
> Only he who gives thanks for little things receives the big things.

Cynthia came in quietly and set a cup of tea before him. He kissed her hand, inexpressibly grateful, and she went back to the kitchen.

When we view the little things with thanksgiving, he thought, even they become big things.

✳

Where his hair was concerned, it was fish or cut bait. Some of the youth group mentioned it, asking when he was getting an earring.

He'd been to Fancy Skinner only twice. On both occasions, his longtime barber, Joe Ivey, was either down with the flu or in Tennessee with relatives. Whatever Fancy had done, he'd liked it, noting both times that he looked suddenly thinner—a look he could currently use, if the tightness of his collar was any indication.

Joe Ivey, however, was in town and healthy as a horse, and he couldn't figure out how to give his business to Joe's competition without being found out.

"When are you gettin' your neck cleaned up?" asked Emma. She considered it her business to remind him about haircuts, shoe shines, and a variety of other personal services.

"Ah ..."

"Christmas is on top of us and you look like a wise man who's been travelin' from afar." She peered at him over her glasses. "They traveled two years, you know."

Whatever that was supposed to mean.

"I'm surprised Cynthia hasn't made you get a haircut."

In his secretary's view, his wife was doing nothing for the church, much less ministering to the needs of her husband.

"Anyway," she said, "if I were you, I'd try Fancy Skinner. Joe Ivey makes you look like a chipmunk."

Permission! Is that what he'd been waiting for like a schoolboy? He was out the door in a flash.

✳

"Lord!" said Fancy, who had worked him in between her eleven-thirty trim and twelve o'clock perm. "Look at this mess, it's cut in three different lengths. I hate to say it, but I hear Joe Ivey gets in th' brandy, and if your hair's any proof, his liver's not long for this world.

"How's your wife? I'm glad you married her, she's cute as anything and really young. How much younger is she than you, anyway? Lord, I know I shouldn't ask that, but ten years is my guess.

"So, what are you givin' Cynthia for Christmas? Mule's givin' me a fur coat, I have always wanted a fur coat, I said, 'Honey, if you buy me a fur coat at a yard sale, do not come home, you can sleep at your office 'til kingdom come.' I know it's not right to wear fur, think of the animals and how they feel about it, but it gets so dern *cold* up here in th' winter. Of course, it's not been cold *this* winter, they say th' fleas will be killer this summer.

"D'you want some gum, have some gum, it's sugarless.

"Speakin' of sugar, I hear you're diabetic, how does that affect you? I hear it makes some people's legs swell or is it their feet? Lord, your scalp is tight as a drum, as usual—you ought to be more relaxed now that you're married, but of course, some people get more uptight when they tie th' knot. I bet married people come bawlin' to you all th' time, I don't know how you have a minute to yourself, bein' clergy.

"My great uncle is clergy, they handle snakes at his church. Mule says for God's sake, Fancy, don't tell that your uncle handles snakes, so don't say I mentioned it. Have you ever seen anybody handle snakes, it's in th' Bible about handlin' snakes, but if you have to do that to prove you love th' Lord, I'm goin' to hell in a handbasket.

"Oops, I like to poked a hole in you with that fingernail, it's acrylic.

"How's Dooley, I hope he don't get th' big head in that fancy school. I've never been to Virginia, I hear seven presidents were born in that state, I think we had one president from our state, maybe two, but I can't remember who it was, maybe Hoover, do you think he had anything to do with th' vacuum cleaner, I've always wondered that. Speakin' of school, they asked me to come to Mitford School and talk about bein' a hairdresser for Occupation Day, I think I'll do a make-over, wouldn't that be somethin'? I'd like to make over th' principal, that is the meanest school principal in the world! I'd dye her hair blue in a heartbeat, then swing her around in this chair and say, 'Look at that, Miss Hayes, honey, don't you just love it, it's *you!*'

"See there? Aren't you some kind of handsome with all that glop cut from over your ears? You looked like you were wearing earmuffs. Oooh, yes! Cute! I'll just swivel you around so you can look at the back, your wife'll eat you with a spoon...."

He paid Fancy and reeled out of her shop, his ears ringing. By dodging the Skinners' driveway and taking the footpath, he was able to avoid the next customer, who merely glimpsed his back as he fled the premises.

﹡

Not only was he at a loss about what to give Cynthia, he couldn't figure out what to buy Tommy with Dooley's ten bucks.

It came to him while he was walking home from Fancy's. Just go by the bank and exchange it for ten silver dollars. A great idea! His new haircut clearly helped him think better. He felt as if he'd just hatched out of an egg for the lightness of spirit that overcame him.

And what the heck would he get Dooley? He'd better knuckle down and come up with something pronto. Maybe a parka. But he already had one, and besides, Dooley Barlowe did not consider clothing items to be gifts.

Tommy's mother welcomed him with a hug.

"We're so glad to see you, Father. Tommy is doing better each day. He'll be back in school after Christmas, Dr. Harper said."

"Wonderful news!"

"Come down the hall and see him. He's reading a new book. It's been awful hard to keep up with his schooling. I can't help him a bit with his math, and his daddy says he never even heard of diagramming a sentence."

"What a grand tree!" he said, stopping to look at the bedecked Fraser fir that stood in the corner. A veritable sea of gifts lay under its branches.

"See those three big packages by the sofa? They're from Mr. Leeper! He's been wonderful, Father. Thank you for asking him to look in on Tommy."

"Oh, but I didn't have a thing to do with it. It was all Mr. Leeper's idea."

"I've heard he's not a very nice person, but I disagree, don't you?"

He looked at the gifts, given by a man who was also healing—not from a terrible accident, but from other, far deeper, wounds. He would go and see Buck Leeper over Christmas and sit with him in the room where the drunken Hope House supervisor had hurled and smashed a bottle and a chair around his head, venting a black rage that lasted for hours. He would never forget that night, and his inability to get up and walk out on the pain that was forged by a brutal father, years of alcoholism, and Buck's part in the death of his younger brother.

He smiled at Tommy's soft-spoken mother. Seeing the three large presents under the tree was somehow a gift to him, as well.

✳

A collect call from France? He couldn't imagine who ...

Yes, of course, he would accept the charges, if only out of curiosity.

"*Bonejure, messure!*" said a strange voice through a crackling phone line.

"Ah ... *bonjour.* Who's calling, please?"

Dooley Barlowe laughed like a hyena.

"*Dooley?*"

"*Oui, messure! Come on talley voo.*"

"Unbelievable! I'm thrilled you called."

"They made us do it. Everybody had to call home."

Home! If Dooley Barlowe had used that word before, Father Tim hadn't heard it. "Merry Christmas, pal! Where are you?"

"Paris, France. We been lookin' at statues and paintin's and I don't know what all, and we're singin' tonight in a big church, a cathedral. Man, it's huge."

"You know all those songs?"

"I'm learnin' quick as I can. Ol' Mr. Pruitt, he'll knock you in the head if you don't get it right."

Good old Mr. Pruitt. "I've never talked to anybody in Paris, France, before. How's the tour going?"

"Great. We're singin' in Austria or somewhere tomorrow night. I'm about wore out."

"We miss you, buddy."

Expensive silence.

"We put the train under the tree."

"I bet ol' Cynthia likes that train."

"How did you know?"

"She likes everything."

"I'll get a present off to you when you're back at school."

"That's OK. You give me a lot of money an' all."

He felt a mild lump in his throat. "Will you send Miss Sadie and Louella a card, like I asked? You wouldn't be in Paris, France, if it weren't for Miss Sadie."

"I already done—did it. It had th' Eiffel Tower on it. Did

you take Tommy his present?"

"Ten silver dollars!"

"Cool."

Thank goodness he'd done that right. He wished Cynthia was here to say hello. It would do her good to hear Dooley's unconcealed excitement.

"Tell ol' Cynthia I said hey. And ol' Barnabas. Well, I got to go. 'Bye."

"Dooley? Dooley!"

But Dooley was gone.

✳

With the jam-packed schedule of the holy days, he'd never been able to settle on a good plan for opening gifts.

To do it on Christmas Eve meant doing it in broad daylight before the five o'clock and midnight masses. That didn't seem quite the ticket.

To do it after arriving home at one-thirty in the morning never had much appeal.

To do it on Christmas morning meant stumbling around in the dark at 5:00 a.m., mindlessly racing through the gift opening, then sprinting to church for two services.

To do it on Christmas day, after the high moments of His birth, seemed paltry, somehow.

Consequently, he had done it differently every year, by the seat of his pants, with a mild semblance of tradition kicking in only when Dooley Barlowe came under his roof.

Now he had a wife who would tell him how to do it.

✳

When his flock thronged into the midnight service, there was wonder on every face at the newly hung greens and the softly flickering candles on each windowsill. To the simple beauty of the historic church was added fresh, green hope, the lush scent of flowers in winter, and candle flame that cast its flickering shadows over the congregation like a shawl.

> *Holy, holy, holy ...*
> *Joyful, joyful, we adore Thee ...*

The choir packed their creaking stall, and leaving the exertion of the eternal crush behind, their voices carried from behind closed doors onto the soft December air.

Lord's Chapel could not, on that night, contain the joy.

"Listen!" murmured the elderly widow who lived next door to the church. "It sounds like angels!" In the hushed and sleep-drugged village, voices stole upon the midnight air, blessing the Lord of Hosts and praising his holy name.

To every weary and overworked soul came some new energy that flowed through the nave like a current.

> *Unto us a child is born, unto us a Savior is given ...*
> *Alleluia! Alleluia!*
> *Come let us adore Him ...*

New life to replace the old, the old one that so often disappoints us and lures us into forgetting the Birth, sending us into despair.

It was no surprise that with the joy came tears for those whose hearts felt a crust falling away....

*

Cynthia had gone through it with him like a trouper. Up and out to nearly every service, making his breakfast, preparing the early dinners he had no appetite for, praying for his stamina, rubbing his shoulders....

"I can't let you do this," he said, loving the feel of her hands on his tense muscles.

"But why not?"

He had no answer. Why not, indeed? "I'll do something for you."

"You're always doing something for me."

"I am?" Why did she think that? His wife had a certain innocence.

"Timothy, dearest, you have an innocence that amazes me."

He allowed the resistance to go out of his body.

"That's better. Sometimes you make it hard to do anything for you, because you've been so ... self-sufficient."

"Ummm," he said, his face smashed into the pillow.

She had suggested they open their gifts on Christmas evening in front of the fire, dressed in their favorite robes. Thank heaven her gift had arrived—and already wrapped, into the bargain. He'd had it delivered to Dora Pugh at the hardware, in case he couldn't be found at his office to sign for it.

It was all too easy, he thought. Just call toll-free and talk to someone solicitous and give them a credit card number. It seemed a man should suffer a bit over what to give his beloved. Next year, he would do better.

❋

"Are you crying?" he asked, as she stared into the small box.

"Definitely!" she said, the tears coursing down her cheeks.

"It's to go with your wedding band. I hope ... I do hope ... you don't think it ..." Gaudy, he wanted to say, or tacky. The emeralds glimmered in the firelight.

She threw her arms around his neck, weeping. Nothing discreet about Cynthia Kavanagh's tears—they were honest and forthright. He patted her fondly on the back. He wished she wouldn't do this ... yet, there was something touching about so much carrying on.

"I love emeralds!" she pronounced, pulling away from him to wipe her tears on the hem of her robe. "I'm so glad you didn't give me sapphires to *go with my eyes*...."

Like her former husband, who had been cruelly unfaithful, he thought.

"It's beautiful, and I'm so proud of it. Thank you, my darling. Is all this a lovely dream?"

He kissed her.

"Well, is it?"

"I think we'll get used to it, somehow."

"You mean we'll become old shoes, and all that?"

"Very likely. They say it happens."

"I can't imagine it happening. I think you're the most delicious, attractive, fascinating man in the world."

"Cynthia, Cynthia …" he said, touching her face. "I'm only a country parson, foolishly in love with his wife. Nothing more."

"Shall I go fetch what I have for you?"

"Wait," he said, holding her close to him. "Wait."

✳

She had turned the Christmas music on and gone off to the garage. He heard it creaking across the kitchen linoleum, then over the hardwood floor and onto the rug of the study.

"Don't open your eyes yet," she insisted.

Whatever it was, she had rolled it next to the crackling fire, then he heard something that sounded like a cord being plugged into the socket at his desk.

"Now," she said, almost shyly.

He saw it, but could hardly believe what he was seeing. It was a magnificent world globe, lit from within and bathed in the glow of the firelight.

He got up slowly and went to it and gazed at it, and was speechless.

"Dooley told me you've always wanted one," she said, slipping her arm around his waist.

He spread his hands over the parchment seas and conti-
nents, as if some inner warmth were coming from inside.
There was the seductive blue of the Gulf of Bothnia, and, as he
twirled the globe, the vastness of Arabia, and the emerald
masses of the Angola and Argentine Basins.

"I love you, my dearest husband."

"And I love you," he said, resting his cheek against the top
of her head. Grace, and grace alone.

The music was only a flute, and a clear, simple voice
singing what Christina Rossetti had written.

✳

> *Love came down at Christmas*
> *Love all lovely, love divine*
> *Love was born at Christmas*
> *Star and angels gave the sign.*
> *Love shall be our token*
> *Love be yours and love be mine ...*
> *Love was born at Christmas ...*
> *Love incarnate, love divine ...*

SEVEN

Flying High

Lady Spring's Grand Surprise
—*by* Mitford Muse *reporter, Hessie Mayhew*

Lady Spring has surprised us yet again.

Arriving in our lofty Citadel prematurely this year, she caught us looking to the mending of our winter mittens. As early as mid-April, the first bloom of the lilac peeked out, whilst in years past, not one of us had caught its virtuous scent until May. Last April at this time, you may recall, we were shivering in our coats as white icing lay upon the bosom of our Village as upon a wedding cake.

In any case, Lady Spring has left her calling card in our expectant Garden—this little Niche where, upon the margin of a rushing streamlet, the woods violet first revealed its innocent face on yesterday morn.

Those with an eye for fashion will wonder what fanciful attire our Lady is wearing this year. I have as yet glimpsed her only briefly, and cannot be certain of every detail, but she appears to have arrayed herself in lacy ferns from her maiden

Breast to her unshod feet, and crowned her fickle head with trumpet vines and moss.

At any moment, she will make her couch upon the banks of Miss Sadie Baxter's hillside orchard, so that every rude Cottage and stately pile might have a view of Heaven come down to earth.

Gentle Reader, may fragrant breezes fan thy brow this Spring, and whether you meet our Lady upon the wild summit or in the sylvan glade, please remember:

DO NOT PLANT UNTIL MAY 15.

He dropped the newspaper beside his wing chair, laughing.

Hessie Mayhew had been reading Wordsworth, again, while combing the village environs with looking-glass and flower press.

Rude cottages and stately piles, wild summits and sylvan glades! Only in the *Mitford Muse,* he thought, unashamedly proud of a newspaper whose most alarming headline in recent months had been "Man Convicted of Wreckless Driving."

Though Hessie had given him a good laugh, he realized he hadn't been much amused lately.

The rectory dining room and kitchen were upside down and backward, and the plunder from the two rooms had been scattered throughout the parlor and along the hallway, not to mention dumped on either side of the steps all the way to the landing.

On Easter Monday, his dining chairs and china dresser had been hauled to the foyer, along with a stack of pots, pans, dishes, and nine boxes of oatmeal. As he hadn't cooked oatmeal in two or three years, he had no idea where it came from, and was afraid to ask.

He saw his wife on occasion, but hardly recognized her,

smeared as she was with pumpkin-colored paint, and her hair tied back with a rag.

"Cynthia?" he said, peering into the dining room. He might have stuck his head inside a cantaloupe, for all the brazen new color on his walls.

She looked down from the top rung of a ladder. "H'lo, dearest. What do you think?"

He honestly didn't know what he thought.

What he wondered was how much longer they'd be dodging around paint buckets and ladders, not to mention that he'd stepped in a skillet last night as he went up to bed. His study was the only place on the ground floor that hadn't been invaded by the haste to transform the rectory into an old Italian villa before May fifteenth.

The kitchen, which certainly hadn't been painted in his fourteen-year tenure, was becoming the color of "clotted Devon cream," according to Cynthia. She was also doing something with a hammer and sponge that made the walls look positively ancient.

If anything, shouldn't they be trying to make the place look more up-to-date?

As worthless as guilt was known to be, he couldn't help feeling it, seeing his wife work herself to exhaustion for a parish tea that would last only two hours.

"Yes," said their friend Marge Owen, "but they'll talk about it for two years!"

He tried once to help her, but he'd never held a paintbrush in his life.

"You bake," she finally said, exasperated, "and I'll paint. For starters, I need ten dozen lemon squares—they freeze beautifully. When you're through with those, I need ten dozen raspberry tarts and fourteen dozen cookies, assorted ..."

She rattled off a baking list that sounded like the quarterly output of Pepperidge Farm.

Why couldn't they just do vegetable sandwiches and straw-berries dipped in chocolate ... or something?

"We're also doing those, but not until the last minute," she said, peering down at him from a ladder. She was always on a lad-der. Except, of course, for the times she popped through the hedge to work on her book, which had an ominous deadline.

"I can't even *think* about the deadline," she wailed. "I can't even *think* about it!"

At night, she rolled over and expired, while he stared at danc-ing shadows on the ceiling and listened to Barnabas snore in the hall.

✳

"We're thrilled," said Esther Bolick. "I can't remember when something this big has happened and I didn't have to bake a cake for it!"

"You're not hurt that we didn't ask you to bake?"

"Hurt? I should say not!"

He could tell, however, that Esther wouldn't have minded doing a two-layer orange marmalade.

He was relieved to see that Emma was softening toward the coming event. But she made it clear to him that Cynthia should at least get involved in Sunday School and chair the parish brunches.

The ECW called to offer help in serving and pouring, and promised to line up four or five husbands to keep the tea traffic untangled on the street in front of the rectory.

Hessie Mayhew stopped by, wanting an interview, just as Father Tim trekked home to pick up his sermon notebook.

"Talk to my wife," he said, "it's all her doing." He hoped that Hessie would not read any Coleridge before she wrote the story.

Clutching her notepad, Hessie grilled Cynthia, who was painting dentil molding from the top rung of a ladder. "What are you serving? How many people? What time of day? Any special colors? Do you have a theme?"

He ran from the room.

Going out the back door five minutes later, he heard Cynthia announce that the event would be called the "First Annual Primrose Tea."

Hessie gave a squeal of delight, which was definitely a good sign.

✳

He had talked to local clergy over the winter, but wasn't encouraged.

Bottom line, Creek people were not known to welcome meddling preachers, and especially not meddling town preachers.

When he reminded them that Absalom Greer had gone in there every week for an entire summer, they reminded him that not only was Greer elderly, which generally translates to non-threatening, but he was a native—always an advantage.

"From what I've heard," said Bill Sprouse, "I wouldn't mess around in there. I hear they'd as soon shoot you as look at you, and there's no question that drugs and alcohol are serious problems."

"Isn't something being done through social services?"

"When it comes to the Creek, I don't think much gets done one way or the other."

"Tell me what else you've heard."

"The usual intermarrying, as you might guess. Used to be a nest of bootleggers in there, and before that the Creek was where they made corn whiskey. A lot of poverty. Houses where you can see through the walls, kerosene stoves in winter, a fair amount of families get burned out."

"Where do they go when that happens?"

"They don't usually come into Mitford or Wesley. They stay with their own. Of course, once in a while you'll see some of the older kids hanging around town, but not often. The Creek buys its groceries and gets doctored over the county line, in Ipswich—that's where they get their schooling, too, if they get any. I think the county line runs along the creek bank for several miles."

"Go in there with me," he said. That was radical, but was anything worthwhile ever accomplished without radical action? Preaching the gospel was radical, forming the church had been radical. Heaven knows, marrying Cynthia—at his age—had been radical.

"Brother, I've got all the sick and hurting I can say grace over. I don't have to go to the Creek to find suffering. My organist is dying of a brain tumor, and one of my finest deacons is too depressed to get out of bed in the mornings." The usually jovial preacher looked solemn.

"Yes, well …"

"Not to mention that Rachel's old mother just passed and me and Sparky are on our own while she's in Springfield cleaning out the home place."

"My condolences to Rachel."

"I keep on a tight string with what the Lord's laid at my own back door," said Bill.

Yes, but if they didn't do something, who would?

"Tell you what," said Bill, looking jovial again, "I'll commit to pray about it."

Father Tim felt strangely restless and annoyed. Certainly he had prayed about it and would continue to pray about it, but he was moved to act, as well. Somehow, he could see the girl who had jumped out of the tree; he could see her as plainly as if she'd landed at his own feet.

※

"Big doin's comin' up at your place," said J.C. "A real front-pager." He slid into the rear booth, protecting a bandaged hand.

"Why don't you run your story *after* the fact?" queried the rector. "You know, one of those good-time-was-had-by-all deals."

"We're running a story before *and* after," said the editor, looking as if he owned the world.

"Aha."

Mule stirred cream into his coffee. "Your wife's tea party is sure rackin' up business for Fancy. She's booked solid through the morning of the fifteenth for perms and color, not to mention acrylic nails."

He had never thought that a rectory tea might boost the local economy. "What happened to your hand?" he asked the editor.

"Jabbed a knife in it."

"How come?"

"Tryin' to punch another hole in my belt. The knife slipped and I punched a hole in myself."

"That's a mighty neat-looking bandage. Did you do that?"

"Not exactly," said J.C.

"You better get some nourishment. You look like you've been sent for and couldn't go," Mule told him.

"Ten more pounds and I'm home free."

"You'll need a whole new set of clothes. That'll hit you up for a bundle."

J.C. mopped his face with his handkerchief. "I'll shop yard sales like some people I know, and dress myself with pocket change."

"Who's shakin' the sheets to find you of a mornin'?" Velma asked the editor as she poured coffee.

J.C. grinned hugely. "That's for me to know and you to find out. And by the way, I'll take the check for this booth."

"My hearin' just went bad," said Mule. "What'd you say?"

"I said I'm pickin' up the check."

"Why?" asked the rector.

"It's spring!" said J.C., still grinning.

*

"Miss Sadie's sleepin'," Louella whispered, answering his knock on the door. "Come in an' drink a glass of tea. I ain't put th' sugar in yet."

Louella led him into the kitchen on tiptoe and closed the door. "Now!" she said. "You can talk yo' head off and Miss Sadie can't hear nothin'!"

"How's your knee doing?"

"Stiff, honey, but perkin'."

"Are you cooking?"

"One time a day. I said Miss Sadie, pick yo' time, she said lunch! So, I cooks lunch, then we put them dishes in th' dishwasher and set back and listen to it go. It's a treat an' a half to have a dishwasher!"

"I wouldn't know," he said. "I've never had one."

"Father, you ought t' get more modern, now you're a married man."

"Right. How's Miss Sadie's wrist?"

"Oh, law. Law, law, law!" Louella shook her head. "Gittin' better."

"That's not good?"

"Soon's that little bone git strong, Miss Sadie goan be drivin' that car hard as she can go! You see this pore ol' gray head? Thass not ol' age, honey, thass Miss Sadie's drivin'."

"Ummm."

"When she break her wrist, I said, 'Thank you, Jesus, now we both goan live longer!' I hate to cross over Jordan meetin' head-on with a truck. I'd 'preciate crossin' in my sleep with a smile on my face!"

"She'll be ninety in June. Won't she have to take another test?"

"She don't have t' test again 'til she hit ninety-two. And Miss Sadie, she test good. She test real good."

They sat in silence for a moment, sipping their tea.

"I don't know what to do," he said, meaning it. "But I'll do something."

Why was he always offering to do something he had no earthly idea how to do? Was his ego so twisted that he had to seize control over outcomes? No, it was almost worse than that. He was driven to console people, to bind them up, to protect them from the worst—an ambition that often got in the way of the Holy Spirit's ministrations.

"This boy," the old bishop of Mississippi had said to Tim's mother, "will make the sort of priest God can use around his house. Timothy will pay attention to his flock in the small particulars, and most of all ... he'll love them."

He didn't know if it was so loving to protect people. Perhaps really loving meant not protecting them.

He certainly hadn't protected Dooley Barlowe. Sending him off to school with those fancy rich kids was like throwing red meat to wolves. But hadn't the boy turned up in Paris, France, singing in a cathedral?

✳

"I never thought I'd live to see the day ..." said Cynthia, lying prostrate in bed.

"Which day?"

"The day I'd be in bed at eight-thirty."

"You've become a true Mitfordian. The mountain air has finally gotten the best of your big-city habits."

"Did I clean my face? I forgot. Could you look? I hope I did, because I can't get up, I'm sore all over."

"I've been meaning to ask ... why are you giving one colossal, backbreaking tea when you might, say, give a couple of medium-size teas?"

"Medium-size does not hack it in today's world, dearest. Medium, tedium. The idea is to kill yourself once a year and keep them talking, and then I don't have to be president or chairman of anything, and everybody still speaks to me and respects my husband."

"Aha."

"Do you really like the dining room?"

"I really do. Very much. It's wonderful. But I was wondering ..."

"Ummm ..."

"... what happened to the drapes."

"I unhooked them from the rod and Puny wore a mask and caught them in a laundry basket and took them to the Dumpster. We would have burned them in the backyard, but there's a law."

"That bad, huh?"

"Historic."

He looked at the ceiling. No wind or breezes tonight. "Sorry I messed up that batch of lemon squares."

She yawned hugely. "It's OK. Puny and I are baking all day tomorrow. I know I could have accepted help or called on the ECW, but those women already work like slaves, and I want to give everyone a lovely break. I want them to feel honored and special.

"I don't mind all this work, really I don't. It's my own fault that I decided to redecorate, but it had to be done, you know, it was like a cave down there. Next year will be a breeze. Oh. Can you help me with the vegetable sandwiches Wednesday morning, and melt the chocolate and dip the strawberries?"

"My pleasure," he said, meaning it.

"I need your moral support more than you imagine. To tell the truth, it will mean everything. It's the first time out for the rector's new wife, you know."

He took her hand. "Mark my words, it's going to be the grandest event since the unveiling of the statue at the town museum."

"Just one more day to go," she said, "and then boom, a hundred and twenty women all talking at once! I have a feeling Uncle Billy will come with Miss Rose, don't you?"

"I'd be surprised if he doesn't."

"I hope he does. It will add an air of intrigue."

Uncle Billy? Intrigue?

"Do you really like the kitchen, Timothy?"

"Greatly. I think it's … interesting … that you knocked the plaster off the wall in forty-seven places."

"It's that wonderful ruined look. Are you laughing?"

"I am not."

"I see your stomach jiggling."

"The kitchen might go over a few heads on Wednesday."

"When we leave, I'll replaster," she said.

There was a long silence.

She looked at him. "We never talk about when you—we—might … leave."

"That's because I don't have the faintest idea," he snapped.

Why had he snapped at her? Because Stuart Cullen was always pushing him to consider his retirement—what he was going to do and when he was going to do it. He wouldn't know until he did it, and that should be enough for anybody.

The phone by the bed gave a sharp blast.

"Father? Richard Fleming."

"Yes?" he said cautiously.

"I'm very embarrassed about something. Do you have a moment?"

"I do." He sat straight up.

"Nearly four weeks ago, we sent a hand-addressed mailing to all parents, an invitation to a special choral concert here at the school. I walked over to the office tonight and saw that yours has just come back. Where it has languished for so long, I can't say, but it was marked Return to Sender."

"Aha."

"We'd made the regrettable mistake of addressing it to Milford, a slip of the pen, as it were, though you're in our computer correctly.

"What I'm getting around to is, this concert is the most ambitious thing we've done all year. Very important. I wondered why you hadn't responded, and Dooley was very concerned that we had no reply from you.

"I must tell you this means a great deal to him. The parents are turning out in enthusiastic numbers, and, well, I'm dreadfully sorry about the mix-up...."

"Quite all right," said the rector. "I'm sure we can make arrangements. Whatever it takes, I'll be there. You have my word."

"Excellent! A great relief!"

"When is it ... exactly?"

"Wednesday morning—the day after tomorrow—at eleven o'clock. It's followed by a luncheon at one. We had a conflict at the weekend and were forced to schedule a weekday, but the parents have been very accommodating. Well, then, this is lovely. Shall I jot you down for two Kavanaghs?"

He looked at his wife, feeling stricken. He had given Richard Fleming his word.

"No," he said hoarsely. "Just one."

*

To be there at eleven, he would have to leave Mitford no later than six, maybe six-fifteen, after melting the chocolate and dipping a hundred and fifty strawberries. Puny had agreed to come early and do the vegetable sandwiches.

Cynthia had been gravely disappointed, but tried hard not to show it. His wife, however, had the complete inability to hide her feelings. They were right out there for all to see, as accurate as a top-of-the-line wall barometer.

"Of course you must go," she said. "Dooley would be heart-broken if you didn't. I'll pack him a box of treats, and you don't have to do the strawberries, it's too much—"

"It's no such thing. I'll do them and that's that."

She sighed. "Puny will be here all day, and Hessie Mayhew is collecting primroses from every garden and insists on helping clean up, and Marge Owen wants to help, too, so—"

"So I'll be back around six-thirty, and anything that's left to clean up, I'll do it."

"I love you madly," she said, looking brave.

He finished setting out squares of chocolate and a double boiler for the morning. Then he turned and drew her to him and took her face in his hands. "In truth," he said, "it's the other way around."

✳

He was thirty miles out of Mitford when, without warning, his engine quit.

He managed to steer his car onto the shoulder of the road, where it sat at the edge of a ditch. He tried the ignition several times, to the sound of nothing but a click. The engine, the battery, whatever, was as dead as a doornail.

"Blast!"

Agitated, he got out of the car and looked up and down the road. He had thoroughly enjoyed the eight years he traveled by foot. Not once had he been forced to put up with the aggravation and expense of car trouble.

He saw a house situated at the end of a pasture. In the other direction, some kind of low building set back from the road, with a sign out front.

He walked toward it quickly, feeling the cold sting of the clear spring morning. Seven-fifteen. He had three and a half hours or so to drive the network of time-saving back roads that led to Dooley's school.

The sign had rusted, but was still readable.

Beaumont Aviation
Charters and Instruction
Have a nice day

If he could get to a phone and call Lew Boyd, Lew could call and ask Cynthia to follow Lew's tow truck. He could use her car, though he'd definitely be late.

He didn't see anybody when he opened the door. "Hello!" he shouted.

Silence.

"Hello! Anybody here?"

He spied a phone on a table. Knowing Lew's number by heart, he dialed it. Busy.

Dadgum it, if Lew Boyd was sitting around playing checkers this time of morning ...

He glanced out the window and saw somebody tinkering with a little plane on the grass landing strip.

He dialed Lew again. Still busy.

One problem. If Lew called Cynthia, what could she do, after all? And what a rotten thing it would be to have her drive a half hour from home on a morning when every moment was vital to her.

He'd stick it out for Lew, however.

Still busy.

Lord, show me where to step here. We've got a boy who's

looking for a familiar face in the crowd. We can't let him down.

He paced the floor. If Mule Skinner drove out to loan him his car, how would Mule get home? He certainly couldn't ask the man to drive all the way to Dooley's school and back, as if he had nothing better to do.

Ron Malcolm! He didn't know how Ron could help, but Ron had a solution for everything. Wilma's voice on the machine said, "We're out of town. If you're Tommy, Rachel, or Nell, please call us in Boca Raton at—"

He hung up, took a dollar from his billfold, and laid it next to the phone.

"Mornin'," said a man coming in the door. He wiped his hands on a rag.

"Good morning. I just made a phone call to Mitford. I left a dollar on the table."

"Can I help you?"

"I wish you could. My car broke down. I think the engine quit."

"Could be a timing belt," said the man, still wiping. "Maybe your ignition switch."

"Could you take a look at it?"

"I'm not much good around automobiles. Coffee?"

Outside, he heard a car screech onto the gravel and park near the door.

"No, thanks. I've got to be at my boy's school in Virginia at eleven o'clock, come hell or high water."

Omer Cunningham strode in, wearing a leather flying jacket and a grin. "Hey, Preacher, I thought I seen your car out there. You here to charter or take lessons?"

"Omer!" He felt like a man in a foreign country who sees a face from home. "My car broke down and I've got to get to Virginia, Dooley's singing in a concert, and Lew Boyd won't

answer the blasted phone, and ... can you drive me into town? I
could pick up my wife's car." This would put him at the school a
little past noon. He felt sick with regret.

"Where you goin' in Virginia?"

"White Chapel, and running late."

"I'll fly you," said Omer.

"Oh, I don't think—"

"When you got to be there?"

"Eleven o'clock."

"It's goin' on eight. You'll never make it runnin' home t'
Mitford."

He felt the blood drain from his face. *Lord, if this is an
answer to prayer, I don't believe I can take you up on it.*

"I've flew in and out of White Chapel many's th' time. We
could borrow a pickup at the airstrip and whip you over to that
fancy school in ten minutes. I know where it's at."

"You could?"

"I'll take you in m' little rag-wing tail dragger!" Omer's face lit
up like a Christmas tree.

"Your ... what?"

"Rag-wing tail dragger. She's a honey, a little J-3 Cub. Fabric
stretched over a few tubes of steel, wheel under th' tail. You don't
see 'em much anymore."

Fabric stretched over a few tubes ... ?

"Better built than anything out there today. Get your plunder,
and let's go. You'll be there ten-thirty sharp, with time to spare."

"Is, ah, your pilot's license current?"

"Omer's license is always current," said the man, grinning.

Father Tim hobbled to his car, his knees nearly giving out.
When he reached for his jacket, he saw that his hand was visibly
shaking.

He couldn't do this.

His aversion to flying had kept him stuck to Mitford like moss on a log for fourteen years—except for that witless sojourn to New York, which his heart had forced him to make, and the long-ago jaunt to write the paper on C. S. Lewis. As for the trip across the pond to Ireland, that had been his bishop's idea. He had flown six interminable hours with his jaw set like a stone.

Lord, if this is your answer, then you've got to help me do this thing. I know how you feel about fear, and I agree. But I'm scared stiff and you know it, and I'm needing a generous hand-out of grace.

The little yellow plane looked like a toy sitting on the green airstrip. While merely walking to it was a problem, climbing into the thing was worse. His knees were Silly Putty, his breathing labored, his palms drenched.

Omer settled in and pulled on a cap. "I don't reckon you'd want t' fly with th' doors off?"

"I don't … reckon so."

"Yessir," said Omer, displaying a mouthful of teeth the size of piano keys, "flyin' my little tail dragger is th' most fun you can have with y'r clothes on."

✳

"Hang tight!" yelled Omer.

He felt as if he were lashed to a jackhammer as they tore along the grass strip for what seemed an eternity.

At last the little plane nosed up, up, up into the blue. His stomach crawled under his lung cage. Perspiration dampened his forehead like summer fog. The racking vibration in the cockpit bounced his glasses on his nose.

Flying with Omer Cunningham, he suspected, was aviation's equivalent of eating Rose Watson's cooking. Wasn't he the guy who, years ago, flew so low over a pasture that he soured the milk in a farmer's cows? The farmer had sued—and won.

Omer leaned toward him and shouted at the top of his lungs, "Beautiful day for flyin', ain't it?"

He ran his tongue around the inside of his teeth, to make sure he wasn't losing any. "Yes, indeed!" he yelled back.

He regretted even the few strawberries he'd eaten for breakfast. *Lord, please don't let me make a mess of this man's airplane.*

Clearly, he was gaining a whole new perspective on St. Paul's admonition to pray without ceasing.

✳

"Dooley, this is Mr. Omer Cunningham, my pilot."

"Your *pilot*?"

"He flew me up here."

"You *flew*?"

He held his thumb and forefinger about three inches apart. "In a little yellow plane about this big."

"Man!"

He shook Dooley's hand. "You were great, son. Words fail me. It was a thrilling experience."

"Real good," said Omer, with feeling.

While Omer smoked a cigarette by the pickup truck, he and Dooley walked to the school green and sat under a tree.

"I'm glad you could come. I wish ol' Cynthia could've come."

He handed over the samples from the First Annual Primrose Tea. "She sent you a box of stuff that will melt in your mouth."

"I want t' open it now."

"Go to it."

Dooley opened the box, popped an entire lemon square into his mouth, and reached for a cookie.

"Chew before you swallow is my advice."

He looked at the place where Dooley's cowlick used to spout up like a geyser, and wondered how it had mysteriously vanished. He looked at his tennis shoes, which were size eleven, and the long legs, which had grown longer just since Thanksgiving.

It seemed only yesterday that he'd been chosen as the one to take the boy in, and already Dooley was gone—growing up, finding his own way. Why did time seem so short, so fleeting?

"How're you doing, buddy?"

"All right."

"Really and truly?"

"Yep."

"No kidding?"

"Yep."

"You going to make it up here?"

"Yes, sir."

"You're sticking with it?"

"Yep."

"That concert was as fine as anything I've heard anywhere. A lot of hard work in that."

"Yes, sir."

He put his arm around the boy. "I love you, pal."

"Looky here," said Omer, walking over to the tree. "Don't you want me t' take th' boy up for a little spin?"

"Well…"

"Man!" said Dooley, jumping to his feet.

Walking to the office to get the headmaster's permission, he reflected that there was a full lunch, two lemon squares, and three cookies in that boy. He was thrilled there was only one passenger seat in the little plane, which meant he'd be forced to stick it out on the ground during this particular joyride.

✳

When they dropped Dooley back at school, he hugged him, and got a good, hard hug in return.

That was worth the trip right there, he thought, choking up.

"*Boneswar, Messure!*" Dooley yelled after him.

✳

They vibrated toward Mitford, having altered their return course so Omer could give his passenger an aerial view of the rectory.

"Where's the Creek?" he shouted. "Do we fly over the Creek?"

"If you want to, we do!" Omer shouted back. The rector thought he could count thirty-two piano keys in his pilot's grin. "But it ain't scenic."

"I'm not looking for scenic!"

Omer veered to the right and dipped, only slightly ahead of the rector's stomach.

"Over yonder, see that power station?"

"I see it!"

"Th' Creek's on th' other side. Comin' up!"

After roaring over the power station and a patch of woods, he saw a ribbon of water gleaming in the sunlight. Then he saw the open sore on the breast of the creek bank—ramshackle, unpainted houses, tin-roofed sheds, houses that had burned and stood in their rubble, rusted trailers and vehicles abandoned in the weeds or sitting on blocks. A few hens pecked at the ground, which appeared to be hard, baked clay.

Dogs ran out and barked at the sky. A few people stood, shading their eyes, looking up. Near the woods, piles of abandoned stoves, refrigerators, tires, and other debris flowed down the bank to the water's edge.

"It ain't Dollywood!" shouted Omer, as they roared over the treetops and gained altitude.

✳

"I'm buzzin' Lew's place first!"

Man alive, he thought, seeing the station sign come closer.

EXXON. Coot Hendrick stood at the gas pumps, gawking and waving.

"OK! Here comes your house!"

The trees were so close, he might have stripped the leaves off a maple.

"Isn't this against the law?" he yelled.

"I cain't hear you!" shouted Omer.

"I don't see the rectory!"

"Yank up y'r floor mat and I'll spot 'er for you!"

He peeled back the mat, revealing a sizable hole, as Omer careened to the left and dipped.

He recognized the monument, then the school and First Baptist—and, by George, there was the Grill! Somebody stepped out to the sidewalk and looked up, but Omer roared on before he could tell who it was.

"There you go!" hollered his pilot.

Just below, tucked beside the little yellow house with the tile roof, was the place where a hundred and twenty women had devoured as many lemon squares this very day. He could see the pink and white trilliums blooming in the backyard. He could number the slates on his roof.

If he looked through that hole another minute, he would deposit his calling card all over Wisteria Lane. He slapped the mat back in place.

"What else you want t' see?" hollered Omer, nosing them straight up. Omer was getting a second wind.

"That'll do it!" he shouted. "Just take me to my car!"

Please!

※

He drove to Mitford with Omer.

"What do I owe you?" he asked Mayor Cunningham's brother-in-law.

"Oh, about three or four hundred! But seein' as I owe *you* for th' pleasure of doin' it, you can give me fifty."

"Fifty? Surely—"

"I ain't licensed to charge commercial. I can only charge gas, and that's fifty on th' button. Besides, you're clergy."

He peeled off two twenties and a ten. Here he was, a small-town priest flying around in a chartered plane, shelling out bucks like an oil field executive.

His legs were still wobbly, but he managed to give Omer Cunningham an invigorating slap on the back, as Omer put the money in his pocket and grinned hugely.

"That was a ride I won't forget," said the rector, meaning it.

✳

Cynthia was in bed, her face mashed into the pillow.

"I never thought I'd see the day."

"H'lo, dearest," she murmured. "What day?"

"The day my wife would hit the hay while it's still daylight." It was, in fact, only a little after seven o'clock.

She moaned.

"That bad, huh?"

"They had a wonderful time. I'm a heroine, Timothy. Your good name is untarnished. But I can't move."

"The house looks wonderful. I can't tell anybody's been here. How did the food hold out?"

"You'd think they hadn't eaten in days. There's nothing left but a couple of hazelnuts, which rolled under the primroses."

"Off the hook for another year, are you?"

She moaned again.

"Speak," he said, sitting on the bed and rubbing her back.

"They thought the tea was so fabulous, they asked me to do the bishop's brunch in June."

"No rest for the wicked, and th' righteous don't need

none," he quoted Uncle Billy.

"You'll be glad to know I flatly refused."

"Well done!"

"Now it's your turn. Tell me everything about our Dools." She rolled over and looked at him. "Why, Timothy! You're beaming like a light tower! An eight-hour drive and up before dawn, and you look positively … wonderful!"

"Dooley's the one who was wonderful. The whole choral presentation was outstanding. You would have been proud. He missed you."

She took his hand. "I miss him every day. Is he going to make it?"

"He's going to make it," he said.

"I knew he would."

"Well … we both have lots to tell."

She leaned up and kissed him. "I want to hear everything. There's supper in the oven."

"Thanks, maybe later."

"Then take your shower, why don't you? I'll be here waiting, and we can have our prayers."

She was there waiting, all right, but dead asleep doing it.

He snuggled up to her back, conforming to her soft contours. "Spoons" is what this marital position was called in their part of the South.

He lay there, comforted by his bed and his room and his house and his wife, and thanked God silently.

He didn't realize it until after he prayed, but blast if he hadn't had a good time today in that little yellow tail dragger.

EIGHT

Serious About Fun

J.C. had been to the dentist and was sucking tea through a straw. "That crazy Omer Cunningham was flyin' so low yesterday, he could have picked my pocket."

"No kidding?" said the rector.

Mule whistled. "I wouldn't go up in that plane for a million bucks before taxes. What is it but a bed sheet wrapped around a bale of chicken wire?"

J.C. sucked his tea to the bottom of the glass. "I've personally never met the fool who'd fly with Omer Cunningham."

"What're you grinnin' about?" Mule asked the rector.

"Grinning?" he said. "I didn't know I was grinning."

❋

He was in Wesley buying a new shaving kit, when he happened to glance out the shop window into the mall. He saw J.C. walking with a police officer. When they stopped for a moment, the rector threw up his hand and waved, but J.C. didn't see him. It appeared that J.C. glanced around to see if anybody was looking, then he hugged the police officer and the officer hugged him back.

He fogged his glasses and wiped them with his handkerchief and looked again. The two parted and went in opposite directions.

Aha. That was no police officer J.C. had hugged. It was a woman.

He pressed his nose to the shop window.

Actually, it was a woman police officer.

✳

After Omer Cunningham told Lew Boyd at the Esso on North Main, word spread to the end of South Main with the speed of a brush fire.

The rector noticed that people dropped what they were doing and nodded respectfully when he walked by. The postmaster pitched in a nickel when he ran out of change for a stamp. Uncle Billy gave him a strawberry-flavored sucker as a token of admiration. The following Sunday, his congregation proffered their rapt and undivided attention throughout the sermon.

Four hours in an airplane had given him more credibility than thirty-six years in the pulpit.

✳

He wasn't seeing much of his wife.

What with working on her book, visiting schools, turning the rectory into a villa, and giving a tea for a hundred and twenty women, which, at the last minute, had numbered a hundred and thirty-one, she hardly had time to roll her hair, much less sit and talk at the breakfast table.

At the office, he uncovered his Royal manual, bent on giving a hundred percent to his sermon, which was largely inspired by a saintly challenge. "Preach the gospel at all times," St. Francis had said. "If necessary, use words."

"Guess what?" asked his secretary.

"What?" he snapped.

"Oooh. Touchy."

"Try again."

"It's something we just got. Three guesses."

Defend us, deliver us ...

"Come on!" Emma said. "Be a sport, for Pete's sake."

"Would it be asking too much for you to give me a clue?"

"It's brown."

"Ah. That's helpful. A new suit for Harold."

"You know he hates to wear a suit."

"Runoff from the Clark River."

"Please."

"I give up."

"You always give up. OK, it's a dog."

He had never seen Emma Newland beam. Smile, maybe. Laugh, certainly. But not beam.

"You? Harold? A *dog*?"

"A brown poodle named Snickers."

"A poodle! What does Harold think of that?"

"He thinks all dogs should live outside. He was raised in the country, you know, and that's how country people think."

"So, where's Snickers going to live?" he inquired.

"Inside!" she said, looking determined.

✳

He walked up to Fernbank after he left the office, to check on Miss Sadie's house. He could sense the worry when he talked with her on the phone. Had that dead tree crashed onto the porch during a recent storm? And what about the old washhouse—could rain have come in where the handmade bricks had fallen out of the chimney, and ruined the pine table that belonged to her mother?

"I'll go," he said.

"Oh, Father, I promise I wasn't asking you to run up there. I was just thinking out loud."

"Glad to do it," he said, meaning it.

He veered off Church Hill Road along a path through the ferns on the steeply pitched bank. The path, which led from the road to the orchard, had been worn by locals over the past few years, owing to Miss Sadie's invitation to the town. "Come and get them!" she said annually, unable to have the apples picked.

He was halfway up the bank and had stopped to rest by a huge oak when he saw movement ahead, among the ferns. It looked like a young boy, who was facing away from him and digging.

He watched intently. The boy was digging ferns with their root balls, and putting them into a sack, looking constantly to the left and right, but not behind. Clearly, he thought he was well-protected from behind by the tree.

Certain people, he recalled, often dug ferns and rhododendron on someone else's property and sold them to nurseries who looked the other way. He knew, too, about the flourishing traffic in galax leaves, and local moss, which was peeled off the ground or pulled from logs in large, unbroken sheets and sold to florists.

The ways and means of making a living in these mountains had never been easy, he knew that, but let an incident like this go by, and Fernbank could be stripped of the very resource that inspired its name.

As he started to move away from the tree, he saw the boy take off his hat. Long hair spilled down and fell over his shoulders. Actually, it appeared to be a girl, a girl wearing boy's clothes, or even a man's clothes, given the way they hung on her. She had sashed the oversized shirt with vines.

"Hello," he called.

She whirled around, letting the mattock drop. He saw the fear in her eyes, then the anger.

"I ain't done nothin'," she said harshly, standing her

ground as he walked toward her. He saw that she noted his clerical collar.

The point was to speak kindly, he thought. She might have been a wild rabbit for the look in her eyes and the fierce way she glared at him. He knew a thing or two about rabbits, having raised them as a boy. They didn't like sudden moves.

"These ferns are pretty special."

"I don't care nothin' about 'em."

She backed away from him and put her foot on the mattock handle.

He stopped about a yard from her and glanced toward the sack.

"I'll knock you in th' head if you lay hands on my sack. I don't care if you are a preacher."

"Miss Sadie Baxter's ferns are a town treasure." He spoke as if he had all the time in the world. If he had a stick, he would have whittled it with his pocket knife. "These banks have been covered with the wild cinnamon fern for many years—there's not another stand like it anywhere, I hear."

"Don't mean nothin' t' me," she said, edging toward the sack.

"Ferns grow in families, like most other kinds of plants. Actually, there are four different fern families ... and look at this. See how the leaves curl at the tip of the stem and curve around? That's called a fiddlehead."

She was going to grab the mattock and sack and run for it, he could tell by the language of her movements.

"I'd personally appreciate it if you'd replant everything you just dug," he said kindly. "In fact, I'll help you do it. And I won't say anything to anybody about it, unless I see you here again."

She reached down and grabbed the mattock and dived toward the sack. Quick as lightning, she threw it over her shoulder and was away, racing down the bank like a hare.

He saw that she was barefoot and that she'd left her hat lying at his feet.

Had he done or said the right thing? He didn't know. He had never liked the pressure to do and say the right thing because he was a preacher. He was also a human being, blast it, and he stumbled along like the rest of humankind.

He squinted his eyes and watched her disappear over the curve of the green bank.

She had not looked back.

※

What they needed, he thought, was an adventure, some recreation. Hadn't they agreed on that very thing not long after their honeymoon? He had boldly declared they'd do something interesting every weekend, even in the dead of winter. In fact, they'd shaken hands on it.

But what were they doing? Why, working, of course. And falling into bed like two logs, with scarcely a fare-thee-well.

Once again, he'd let the puzzling mystery of recreation hold him back. What was fun, after all? And how did one go about having it?

He'd been so fired up the day they shook hands; the possibilities had seemed endless. Now, all he could think of was going out to dinner in Wesley. But they'd done that twice. Besides, anybody could go out to dinner. What was needed here was something fresh and new, something unexpected, to captivate the imagination of his highly imaginative wife.

Then again, if she was so highly imaginative, why not ask her to think of something?

He would not. It was his own bounden duty to come up with a solution.

He walked around his rosebushes. He pulled a wild burdock out of the daylilies. He sat on the stone bench and stared at a tree. Maybe he should ask somebody for an idea. But who?

Not Emma Newland, who thought fun was watching TV game shows and nagging Harold to eat his vegetables.

Not Mule Skinner, who thought fun was clipping cents-off coupons and going to yard sales.

Not Ron and Wilma Malcolm, who thought fun was packing their car to the roof and driving nonstop to Boca Raton, where the temperatures would roast a pork loin.

Come to think of it, he didn't know anybody who was good at having fun, except, of course, Omer Cunningham, who clearly knew how to have a good time—and all for the price of a few gallons of gas.

Oh, well. He would think about it. He would make some notes. He might go to the library. In the meantime, he knew he couldn't count on reading Wordsworth aloud forever. Somehow, that had been just dandy while they were going steady, but now it didn't go over so well. Cynthia's gaze wandered around the room, she fidgeted, she got up and made notes that had absolutely nothing to do with Wordsworth.

Even Barnabas, once so attracted to the romantic poets, went to sleep before the end of an opening stanza.

There was nothing for it but to come up with a whole new ball game in the area of recreation.

✳

He stopped by the rectory for his checkbook, in transit to the Children's Hospital in Wesley.

Puny Guthrie looked exceedingly plump, not to mention smug and self-satisfied. Everything about her had gained a certain largesse—her hair seemed redder and curlier, her freckles bigger, her eyes greener.

"Guess what?" she said, turning from the sink where she was peeling potatoes.

"I promise I can't guess," he said.

"Remember you said you'd play with it, an' all, when I brought it to work with me?"

"Now, Puny ..."

"Well, th' only thing is—it's not an it."

"It's not?"

"It's *twins!*"

"No!"

"Yes!" she exclaimed, looking joyful.

He thumped down into a chair at the kitchen table.

She rubbed her stomach, giggling. "You'll have two t' play with! Don't that beat all?"

"You can say that again," he replied, loosening his collar.

✳

"Dearest," she said, before popping through the hedge to her drawing board, "why don't you come with me to Hastings School tomorrow? You never take a real day off, and besides, it would be *fun!*"

Fun? "Sure!" he said without hesitation.

Emma could cover for him. They also had an office answering machine, didn't they? Besides, it was true—he hardly ever took a real day off.

"I'll be reading *Violet Visits the Queen*. Oh—I just thought of something!—you could read the part of the palace guard!"

He looked dazed.

"Just say yes!" she implored. "Remember the first time you took me to visit Miss Pattie, and let me see into *your* work? This way, you can see into mine. That will be the most fun of all!"

To hear her tell it, this sojourn would be loaded with the very thing he'd been trying so hard to get a bead on.

✳

"I'll tell you how the sun rose ..." she said, zooming down the road in her Mazda.

"Tell me!" he said.

"A ribbon at a time—

The Steeples swam in Amethyst—

The news, like Squirrels, ran—

The Hills untied their Bonnets—

The Bobolinks—begun—

Then I said softly to myself—

That must have been the Sun!"

"Mark Twain!" he said recklessly, leaving all care behind.

"Timothy, you're not trying! Guess again."

Women wanted you to guess something every time you turned around. "Christina Rossetti?"

"No, but you're close. One more guess. Listen—steeples, amethyst, bobolinks. Who writes like that?"

"Hessie Mayhew!"

She laughed uproariously. It didn't take much for his agreeable wife. Give her an inch of amusement and she'd convert it to a mile's worth.

"Emily Dickinson, for Pete's sake. Now it's your turn."

"Can't we play cow poker?" he wondered, gazing out the window for a pasture.

"I can't be mooning into ditches counting cows while I'm driving. No, you have to do a poem or something. And not Wordsworth."

"Blast! A man can't take a day off …"

She whipped around a truck. "Something from the eighteenth century would be nice."

After yowling from Mitford to Holding, Violet had finally curled up and gone to sleep in her carrier. Now, at least, he could think straight.

"Ye fearful saints, fresh courage take

The clouds ye so much dread

Are big with mercy, and shall break
In blessings on your head.
His purposes will ripen fast
Unfolding every hour
The bud may have a bitter taste
But sweet will be the flower."

"Are you sure that's not Wordsworth?" she asked, slowing down for an intersection.

"Positive," he said. "One of his friends, however."

"Cowper, then."

"Yes, from the hymn that opens with 'God moves in a mysterious way, His wonders to perform.' Most people think that line is from Scripture."

"'The bud may have a bitter taste, but sweet will be the flower.'" She laughed, looking happy. "That's our courtship and marriage he was writing about!"

It was grand to be on the road with a comfortable companion.

✳

"And this is Miss Coppersmith's husband, Mr. Coppersmith."

The students applauded.

"And they're both going to read about one of your favorite friends."

"Violet!" shouted the class in unison.

"Let's sit on the floor with the children," Cynthia whispered.

He looked at the half-circle of bright faces, hoping his knees didn't creak like a garden gate when he sat down. Could he get up? He would cross that bridge when he came to it.

"Miss Coppersmith is very, very famous. She has won a medal for one of her books. I know Mr. Coppersmith must be very proud."

"Actually," said Cynthia, "my husband's name is not Coppersmith. It's Kavanagh."

"Oh," said the teacher. "How modern!"

"Actually, we both have the same name. Coppersmith is my writing name. OK, everybody! This is Father Kavanagh. And this is Violet!" They sat down in front of the children, with Violet's carrier. The kids scrambled close and peered inside.

"I never seen a cat that's in books," somebody said.

"Does she live in there?"

"What does she do all day?"

"Where are her kittens?"

Violet blinked imperiously from her carrier.

"I have a cat!" announced a girl. "Its name is Perry Winkle!"

"I have two dogs!" said a boy, raising his hand and flapping it. "One throws up if he eats spaghetti."

"My mom knows somebody who has a pig!" offered another. "They let it live in the house. Yuck! A pig in the house! I wonder where it goes to the bathroom."

The pupils guffawed.

"Children!" said the teacher.

"A pig in the house is no big deal," said Cynthia. "When I was your age, I had an alligator that lived in my bathtub."

"Wow!"

"Neat!"

"How did you take a bath?" More hysterical laughter.

"I didn't," said Cynthia. "I didn't take a bath for a whole month. Maybe two whole months!"

"Cool," someone murmured in heartfelt awe.

"Neat-o!"

"I took showers at my friend's house!" said Cynthia.

Groans, moans.

"How can your husband be married to you if he's your father?" inquired the boy whose dog couldn't tolerate spaghetti.

"Well, you see, he's a priest. And we call a priest 'Father.'

Now, settle down, and I don't mean maybe, because we're going to read a story. Anybody who doesn't listen, or who talks or whispers, gets to come up here and read my part—in *French*."

He thought they'd never get to the section with the palace guard, but when they did, he hoped he wouldn't mess up.

"The palace guard," Cynthia read at last, "looked down upon Violet and said ..."

He gave the line a wicked snarl. "*Aha, my fine feline, thought you'd pull the wool over my eyes, did you?*"

"Violet was very frightened," continued Cynthia. "She didn't know what to do. As the palace guard's big hand moved to catch her by the neck, she darted between his legs.

"She ran down the long corridor as fast as she could go.

"She looked behind her and saw the big, black boots of the guard. Then, other people were running behind her and shouting, 'Stop that cat!'

"As she ran, Violet's heart beat very fast. She could hardly get her breath. Boots and slippers and mops and brooms followed in hot pursuit."

He jumped on his line in the nick of time. "*We must stop that cat! The Queen hates cats!*"

"Violet rounded the corner at a very great speed, and skidded into a large room. It was bright and beautiful. The sun shone in on a polished marble floor. And there, sitting on a throne, was ... the Queen."

He heard a gasp or two. Large eyes fixed on Cynthia.

"Violet tried to stop, but the marble floor wouldn't let her. She slid right up to the hem of the Queen's royal gown. And then ... she *bowed*.

"That's when she felt the fearsome hand on the scruff of her neck.

"Suddenly, she was lifted up, up, up—and then down, down, down as the palace guard bowed, also.

"What is *that*?" the Queen demanded.

"*Your Majesty*, that *is a cat!*"

"I'm supposed to hate cats!" said the Queen.

"*Yes, Your Majesty.*"

"But *why* am I supposed to hate cats?" asked the Queen.

"*Because your father, the King, hated cats, Your Majesty.*"

"Hmmm," said the Queen. "It looks soft. Let me hold it."

"*But Your Majesty, I couldn't—*"

"Of course you could, because I am the *Queen!*"

At that high moment, Cynthia looked up to see Violet suddenly bolt from her carrier and, leaping over laps and darting past grasping hands, race through the open classroom door to the shrieks of the entire assembly.

"Oh, no!" cried Cynthia, unbelieving.

The catch on Violet's decrepit carrier had jiggled loose again.

Cynthia sprinted toward the door.

"Stop that cat!" she shouted.

Half the classroom emptied before the rector could get up.

He sat down again quickly, however, as both legs had gone completely to sleep.

✳

"You were a wonderful palace guard," she said, smiling over at him. "So fierce!"

He zoomed around an RV with a sign that read *Dollywood Or Bust*. "It was a new and different experience, all right."

"I thought it was great fun!"

"Which part? When we read the story together, or when Violet leaped through the window and was caught in midair by the assistant principal?"

"All of it!" she said, laughing.

"I've always heard that truth is stranger than fiction." He looked at Violet, who was sleeping in Cynthia's lap, the very picture of innocence.

His wife furrowed her brow. "Maybe it *is* time for a new carrier," she said.

✳

The summer people were slowly making their annual comeback to Mitford. Attendance was building every Sunday, and the Wednesday Eucharist was definitely up in numbers.

Four buildings on Main Street installed new green awnings, including The Local, which inscribed theirs with white lettering: *Fresh Meats and Produce Since 1957, Avis Packard, Grocer.*

Dora Pugh gave a sidewalk sale and moved forty-five flats of pansies in a record two hours and nine minutes. The candy tuft did not do as well. Lank Pitts drove a pickup load of rotted manure into town and parked it in front of Dora's hardware, where he sold it by the pound in garbage bags.

"Most people give that away," grumbled a customer, who nonetheless purchased two sacks full. "I pay f'r th' feed that goes in m' horses," said Lank. "Seems fair t' charge f'r what comes out."

Evie Adams, whose family home faced Main Street, received a check from an uncle and replaced the rusted porch glider, a longtime village eyesore, with two green rocking chairs. New window screens also went up, but only on the front of the house. Uncle Billy looped a hanging basket of geraniums over a nail beside his back door, where they'd be easy to bring in, in case of frost.

In all, the days were longer, the air warmer, and the Lord's Chapel youth group more restless.

"You've promised two or three times," said Larry Johnson, the group leader.

"Could I help it I had the flu the first time you went camping, and the next time you asked, I got married?"

"You better do it this time," said Larry, "or I don't know what dark revenge the kids might come up with. They really want you to go. Besides, it will be fun."

Suddenly, everybody knew how to have fun. Why bother to come up with ideas of his own?

"Oh, and they want you to bring Cynthia," said Larry.

Cynthia camping? He didn't know about that. However, a girl who'd kept an alligator in her bathtub might possibly be up for it.

✳

"How would you like to go camping weekend after next?"

"Camping?" He might have asked her how she'd like to go bungee jumping.

"With the youth group. They like you, said you'd be a blast to go camping with."

"A blast?"

"That's what they said."

"How do you go camping? What do you do?"

"You take a bedroll and a tent and a frying pan, and saunter forth," he said.

"Have you ever done it?"

"Hundreds of times!" As good as that sounded, he couldn't tell a lie. "Five or six, anyway. I've been promising the kids I'd do it, and the jig is up."

"Snakes," she said. "I hate snakes."

"Snakes hate you even more. Watch your step and you'll be fine."

"What about bugs?"

"Cynthia, Cynthia …"

"And how do you … I mean … what do you do about … ?"

"The woods."

"Oh."

"Take sketch pads and pencils—you could see a deer or wild turkeys, even beavers. It's just your dish of tea. I'll teach you to throw a line in the water, and who knows, we could catch dinner for the whole crowd, and be heroes."

"Do you have a tent?"

"Sort of," he said.

"Sort of?"

He could tell she smelled a rat. "A few poles and a blanket."

"I don't think so."

"Come on," he said, kissing her. "We'll have a blast."

She looked at him, leaning her head to one side in that way he couldn't resist. He realized he didn't want to go without her.

"Sleeping under the stars, singing around the campfire, roasting marshmallows …" He searched her face for some sign of interest. Blank.

"Walking in the woods, listening to the creek rush boldly over the rocks …" He was giving it everything he had.

"Searching yourself for ticks …" she put in.

"Didn't you say you wanted to study different kinds of moss, draw birds, go out into nature? That's where you find nature—*in the woods!*"

"Yes, but … camping?"

"Cynthia, it'll be *fun!*" he said, desperate for a merchandising tactic.

She looked at him soberly, then grinned. "OK. But just this once."

※

"You remember that dictionary I found in th' Dumpster?" Uncle Billy asked him when they met on the street.

"I do."

"I cain't hardly enjoy readin' it n' more."

"Is that right?"

"Yessir, it's one thing here and another thing there—they're always changin' th' subject, don't you know."

The rector rolled his eyes and chuckled.

"That's m' new joke, but it's not m' main joke. I'm workin' out m' main joke for spring. By th' almanac, spring comes official on June twenty-one."

"Well, then, you've got a little time," he said. "Let me treat you to a cheeseburger."

Uncle Billy grinned, his gold tooth gleaming. "I'd be beholden to you, Preacher. An' I wouldn't mind a bit if you'd tip in some fries."

He put his arm around the old man's shoulders as they walked toward the Grill. He'd be et for a tater if he didn't love Bill Watson like blood kin.

※

He sat in the living room on Lilac Road, where Miss Sadie had come to look perfectly at home.

He wanted to get the thing accomplished. He was actually losing sleep over it. What if she really did hurt someone, or herself, or both? The last time he was told to deliver a warning to another party, he didn't deliver it—and Dooley's best friend was nearly killed.

"Have you looked into getting a chaplain yet?" asked Miss Sadie.

"No, ma'am, I haven't." He suddenly felt about nine years old.

"Well ..." she said, sounding a trifle stern. She'd had to keep after him with a stick to find a school for Dooley.

"But I'll get to it. We've months to go yet."

"What have you got on your mind, Father? When you have something on your mind, it shows."

Dive in, and pray there's water in the pool. "Miss Sadie, I know your wrist is healing."

"Look there!" She jiggled her hand as a demonstration.

"Planning to drive soon?"

"I certainly am! I've nearly turned to a fossil sitting around here, and it's made me grumpy as all get-out. You know I've never been grumpy."

"No, indeed."

"It's not my nature."

"I agree completely."

"But there's a first time for everything," she declared.

"Miss Sadie, Rodney Underwood is going to give you a citation the next time you drive up on the sidewalk."

She looked at him. "Did he tell you that?"

"He did."

"Did he send you to tell me that?"

"Yes ma'am." Seven years old.

"Well, you tell Chief Underwood that he can march over here himself and do his business like a man. Sending my priest to do his dirty work is something I don't cotton to, and I don't mean maybe."

"He said his men had spoken to you before...."

"Yes, indeed, they did, and I took no notice of it. He certainly likes to send people around to do his job! Is he so overworked he can't take care of important matters himself? You and I pay his salary, Father, need I remind you?"

Sadie Baxter was in a huff, and grumpy wasn't the word for it. He wanted to sprint to the door and head for the city limits. She had fussed at him before, but he'd never been around when she unloaded both barrels.

He saw Louella peering through the doorway.

"As if you didn't have enough on your hands, Father, with the sick and hurting all around us. You know what I'd like to do?" Miss Sadie looked fierce.

"No, what?"

"I'd like to yank a knot in Chief Underwood's tail!" she said, meaning it.

He thought he'd never seen her look so young and spunky. Maybe being grumpy had done her good. In any case, he was quitting while he was ahead.

He stood up. "The construction at Hope House is moving along at a pace, everything looks terrific, and I'd like to take you up there any day you want to go. Oh. I nearly forgot." He pulled the paper sack from his jacket pocket and handed it to her.

"Donut holes!" he said. They were her hands-down favorite.

She looked at the bag and then at him. "Were these supposed to soften me up?"

"They were," he said. Why beat around the bush?

She threw her head back and laughed merrily. There was the Sadie Baxter he knew, thanks be to God.

Taking the bag, she said, "You tell Chief Underwood to pay me a call in person and stop sending his henchmen to tell me what it's his job to say."

"I will."

Miss Sadie rose from the chair, taking her cane. "And tell him to call first, so I'll be dressed."

"I'll do that."

She laughed again. "I declare, it's kind of fun to be grumpy. People jump when I speak. I never noticed people doing that before."

He put his arm around her as they walked to the door. "Cynthia and I will come and take you for a spin, drive you up to Fernbank. Maybe you've got a little cabin fever."

"I'd like that. And Father?"

"Yes?"

"You know we love you. But you're not suited to meddling."

✳

"Hessie's story on your Primrose Tea was a whopper," said J.C.

"A prizewinner," said the rector. "Cynthia had a copy laminated."

"If I paid that woman by the word, I'd be in deep manure."

Mule slid in beside the rector, wearing a chartreuse jacket. "I just did a closing that will set me up for a month of Sundays."

"Maybe now you can dump your polyester in a landfill and get you a new wardrobe," said the editor, finishing his house salad.

"Congratulations!" put in the rector.

"I just dropped a bundle at the Presbyterian parking lot sale. Two suits, a brand-new sweater, and a runnin' suit."

"You don't run," J.C. said.

"So, I'll protect my investment and start," Mule replied. "What's that smell?"

The rector didn't mention that he'd smelled something peculiar ever since J.C. sat down. So far, it had killed off all cooking odors from the grill, driven his sinuses haywire, and made the inside of his mouth feel funny.

"What smell?" asked the editor.

"Somethin' foul. Man! Stinks like cat musk." Mule sniffed the air like a beagle. "No offense," he told J.C., "but it's comin' from your direction."

"It's your upper lip," snapped the editor, grabbing his briefcase. "I'll just leave you boys to figure it out. I got to get over to th' mayor's office. *Hasta la vista.*"

J.C. left a heavy blast of scent in his wake. The two men looked at each other.

"Cologne," said the rector.

Understanding slowly dawned on Mule's face. He broke into one of his cackling laughs. "So that's it! Well, I'll be dadgum. Ol' J.C., he's ... he's ..."

"Getting overhauled," said the rector.

NINE

Locked Gates

If spring had blown in like a zephyr, its mood soon changed.

Gentle rains became wind-lashed torrents, washing seeds from furrows and carving deep gullies in driveways and lawns. Power blinked off and surged on again, those with computers kept them unplugged, and TVs went down before the lightning like so many ducks in a shooting gallery.

Sudden, startling downpours of hail unleashed themselves on the village, leaving holes the size of dimes in the burgeoning hosta, and flattening whole groves of trillium and Solomon's seal. Seedlings keeled over in the mud, and Winnie Ivey's hens and chicks scattered for high ground.

Mitford was driven indoors for three days running, to watch the mildew make its annual invasion of basements, bathrooms, and closets.

It was Tuesday morning before the village awoke to a dazzling sunrise, clear skies, and balmy temperatures. The foul weather, however, lingered on in his secretary.

"If I ever read another word about Hessie Mayhew's Lady Spring, I'll *puke*," Emma said.

"Did Harold get his potatoes in?"

"Got 'em in, watched 'em slide off the side of the mountain. Along with his peas, beans, squash, and onions."

"A regular blue plate special."

"I haven't heard you talk about a garden this year. Too busy, I suppose." Emma gave him one of her unmistakable looks-with-a-message.

"Not at all. We're filling out a couple of beds with purple foxglove, lupine, cosmos … let's see, delphinium, Canterbury bells, a dozen astilbe …"

"Humph. Astilbe. Too feathery for me. I'll take a good, hardy marigold any day."

"To each his own," he said mildly.

"That was some shindig at your place."

He had wondered when she would at last bring up the social event that was still the talk of the town. "So I hear."

"Cynthia did a good job."

"Thank you. I hear that, too."

"A little too much sugar in the lemon squares."

"I see it failed to sweeten your disposition."

"Ha ha. What do you think about your kitchen walls being banged up with a hammer?"

"The best thing to happen to the rectory since Father Hanes installed a fireplace in the study."

"I didn't think you'd go much for that deal."

"I hope you know the ruined look is the very thing to give mundane surfaces a mellow, weathered appeal. Take your old villas in Italy, for example, where the plaster is put on thickly, without superficial concern for perfection, where the surfaces ripple and change like … like life itself …"

She peered at him over her glasses.

"… where buildings shift and settle with the passage of years, where a century is but a fleeting moment in time ..."

"I get it!" she said, wanting him to stop at once.

"... where decades of smoking olive oil and burning wood wash the walls with a palette of color as subtle as the nuances of old stone or ancient marble—where, indeed, the very movement of light and shadow are captured in the golden glow of the walls, grown as redolent with history as trade routes worn by ancient Romans...." He had no idea what he was saying, but he was enjoying it immensely.

She stared at him with her mouth slightly agape.

That ought to fix her.

✳

When Cynthia wasn't bending over the drawing board with her elaborate wooden box of watercolors, she was laying a flagstone walkway through the hedge. This time, he couldn't claim ineptitude. It was down in the dirt with his wife, or else.

She was wearing one of Dooley's baseball caps, a T-shirt, blue jeans, and out-at-the-seams tennis shoes. Given how youthful she was looking and what he was thinking, he could be jailed for a violation of the Mann Act.

"I'm packing for your camping trip," she said, huffing a heavy flagstone into the hollow he'd just dug with a shovel and edger. He would have huffed it in himself, but she preferred her way of placing the stones.

"So it's my camping trip, is it?"

"Well, yes, I would never in a hundred years do this on my own."

"What are you packing?"

"Colored pencils, Snickers bars, and a change of socks and underwear."

"That ought to do it," he said, trying not to laugh.

"What are you packing?"

"They're bringing the food, so we're traveling light. Tent, flashlight, emergency candles, matches, bottled water, a Swiss army knife, an iron skillet, a coffeepot, coffee, fire starter ... ah, let's see ... inflatable pillows, ground cover, lantern, sleeping bags, bandages, toilet paper, dried fruit and nuts ... what else? A canteen, fishing poles, bait, talcum powder, mosquito repellent, Band-Aids, sunscreen, and, oh, yes ... a bucket to put the fish in. Ah, I just remembered—an egg turner to flip the fish in the skillet. And cornmeal, of course. Can't fry fish without cornmeal."

"We'll need a U-Haul," she said, muscling the stone around until it pleased her.

"We're going to pack it in to the campsite."

"You do have someone meeting us there with *a team of mules*?"

"You're looking at the team," he said, pleased with himself.

"Do we really need all that for one night?"

"They've asked us to stay two nights."

"Timothy!"

He rolled his eyes and shrugged.

"Oh, well," she said, wiping her forehead with the back of her garden glove. "Dig this one a little bigger. See that stone? It needs to go in next, I think. What do you think?" She sat back on her heels.

"Perfect."

"It will be lovely not to get mud on our shoes when we pop through the hedge."

"I'll say."

"Timothy, dearest, do you like being married?"

"Married to you, or married in general?"

"In general," she said, watching intently as he dug the hollow.

"I do. Very ..." he searched for the right word, "consoling."

"Lovely! Now, do you like being married to me?" He looked down upon her sapphire gaze under the bill of the baseball cap and squatted beside her.

"Words fail," he said, meaning it. The scent of wisteria floated out from her like scent from a bush in an old garden.

"I want to be your best friend," she said.

"You are my best friend."

"You can speak your heart to your best friend," she said.

"What is it you want me to say?"

"I want us to talk about our future. It really doesn't matter if you don't know what you want to do, or when. It would be lovely just to talk, to have it out in the open. I can't bear that closed place in you. It's like coming up to a gate that's been locked, and the key thrown away."

"Perhaps we all contain gates that have been locked."

"Perhaps," she said.

He wanted to stand up again and turn away from her and go on with their work. Wasn't that what they'd come out here to do? But he sat down in the grass and looked at her across the half-finished walkway. He was grateful for the shade because he felt warm, and suddenly peevish.

Katherine had taken it upon herself to counsel him before he got married, whether he needed it or not. "First and foremost," she had said in her salty way, "communicate! If Cynthia wants to talk, Teds, you'd better hop to it. Communicating is everything, painful as it may be. Trust me on this."

So far, so good. But he wanted to draw the line somewhere. He wanted to draw it right here and right now—but he sat and faced her, making the effort.

"I don't want to talk about it," he said, finally.

"I know." She sat, too, and took off her work gloves.

There was a long silence, filled with the chatter and song of birds. A junco dipped through the air and vanished into the hedge. They heard a neighbor's phone ring.

A nap, he thought. A nap would be the very thing. Why this Puritan work ethic pumping through them like so much adrenaline? Hadn't they come and gone through the hedge with perfect ease for the last two years? So what if they got their shoes muddy once in a blasted blue moon?

"You're angry," she said.

Yes, he was. And he didn't like it. "What good can it do, talking of something I don't know anything about? We came out here to work, why not work?"

"Lord," she prayed aloud, "will you please help us through this?"

His heart was hard toward her, something he hadn't experienced since they married, and wanted never to experience. It felt like the time she had mentioned marriage—only mentioned it. His heart had turned to stone, and remained stone for weeks on end.

"There's your gate," she said. "I'm right up against it, and it's still locked."

More birdsong. A car passing on Wisteria Lane.

"You'll have to do the talking," he said, "because I don't know what to say. I don't have a clue."

She looked at her hands, a little furrow between her brows. He thought she was weighing whether it was worth it to try and figure out their future.

"All that really matters about our future," she said, "is that we're together. I mean that with all my heart. I feel so puzzled about why you shut down like this—why does this wave of coldness seep out from you when there's any mention of your retirement? Oh, rats, Timothy, why does it have to be complicated? All I want to know is ...

"... are you going to preach 'til you keel over? Will we someday have our own home? Have you thought where we might live?"

"I mean," she said, waving her arm toward the new flower bed, "should we be planting all these *perennials*?"

He stared at the row of astilbe. "I don't know. Why do I have to know?"

"Ummm," she said, looking at him. "This is going nowhere."

"So let's get back to work." He got to his feet and picked up the shovel.

What had happened? They had been working together as one flesh and one spirit, laying one flagstone walkway to link two houses. And then it had all come apart.

They were silent as they placed the remaining stones.

He felt oddly embarrassed at his hardheaded behavior, behavior that even he didn't truly understand.

✴

They were an hour out of Mitford, headed north to the campsite, when a drumming rain began. It transformed the overloaded van into an odorous cocoon on wheels. A radio report guaranteed the downpour would last through the morning and well into the afternoon.

Turning around and going back was loudly argued among eight teenagers.

Bo Derbin, who had a surging, but nonetheless repressed, attraction to Lila Shuford, would have none of turning back. He imagined himself swinging on a vine across a broad creek or tributary, to rescue her from a human savage raised by wolves.

Avoiding eye contact with his wife, the rector voted to press on. Larry declared he had no intention of doing otherwise.

They pressed on.

✴

Eight teenagers with lower lips they might have tripped over was not a pretty sight.

"Oh, pipe down!" yelled Larry, clipping along at the front of the line as they hiked into the woods in a persistent drizzle. Though known for not taking any flack from the youth group, he was nonetheless their hands-down favorite leader, not to mention an Eagle Scout, an Orvis fly-casting school graduate, and onetime wrestler of a grizzly bear.

"When we get there," shouted Larry, "the sun will be shining, the fish will be biting—"

"And the ground will be sopping!" he heard Cynthia mutter.

Sopping was right. The ground at the campsite was like okra that had been boiled and mashed.

He had never seen his wife look so pathetic, though she didn't utter a word of complaint. The kids, on the other hand, howled and grumbled. They wanted Nintendos, they wanted TV, they wanted a bathroom with a lock on the door.

But they hadn't come two miles from civilization and forty miles from Mitford to coddle themselves.

"Strip bark!" commanded Larry Johnson, who was humiliated to find he'd forgotten the Coleman stove.

"Strip ... *bark*?" said Cynthia.

In the rector's opinion, that was where the whole thing began to slide downhill.

✳

He knelt by the sleeping bag, which, like a bicycle, was built for two.

He had endured some discomfort with the salesperson when he bought the thing in Holding, but spreading it on the ground in front of God and everybody had been worse.

The kids had snickered, Larry Johnson had cocked his eyebrow like some two-bit actor, and Cynthia had been bashful as a girl. The heck with it, he thought, unzipping his side at a little after ten o'clock on Friday night.

So what if he had forgotten the tent poles and they had no

earthly cover from whatever the weather might bring? So what if they were lying out in the open like so much carrion for wolves, bears, or worse, wild boar?

He glanced around the campsite, making certain no one watched as he slithered in beside his slumbering wife. Clearly, no one cared. Larry Johnson was playing a final tune on his guitar, which, thanks to the dense humidity that followed the rain, sounded precisely like rubber bands stretched over a cigar box.

Cynthia had almost completely enveloped herself in the bag, leaving only her nose in view. The thought of sleeping on the ground with but a thin cover under them and nothing above them had stunned her—no two ways about it. It had put a positive curl in her lip that he didn't believe he'd ever seen before.

In the end, however, the fresh air worked wonders. After crawling into the bag a little before eight-thirty, she had gone out like a light.

He drew her close, feeling how much she meant to him, and how like his own body her sleeping form seemed to be. One flesh! There were miracles in that phrase, in that unfathomable concept. He realized he sometimes felt attached to her like a Siamese twin, joined at the heart or the groin, the shoulder or the spleen.

How had he lived so long without this vital connection in his life? Where had he been all these years? How had he gotten by before he was married?

He couldn't reckon how it had been before. It was as if he'd always lain with her in this sleeping bag built for two, spooning like a farmhand, inhaling her warmth. What power it must have taken to draw him out of himself, he thought with wonder, out of his endless surmise, out of his inward-seeing self, into such a union as this.

"How lucky you are!" people continually said to him. But, no. There was never any time he thought of it as luck. Luck! What was that, after all, but so much random good fortune? It was grace, and grace alone that brought Cynthia's body close to his, made them this single mystical flesh that, once laced together like brandy in coffee, could not be riven apart—even by the world and its unending pressures.

He closed his eyes and thanked God for the crucible of peace and laughter and love that lay beside him, snoring with the galvanized precision of a chain saw.

❋

"Lila Shuford!" yelled Larry Johnson, beating on a skillet with an egg turner. A pitiful fire crackled in a ring of rocks.

"Here!"

"Lee Lookabill!" More beating.

"Here!"

Murky sunshine. Birdsong.

"Luke Burnett!"

He sat up in the sleeping bag and looked at his watch. Five after six. He hadn't slept this late since his honeymoon. Cynthia rolled over and peered at him as if he were a Canadian moose who had stumbled into camp.

"Cynthia Kavanagh!"

"Ugh!" muttered Cynthia, sitting up in a T-shirt from The Local, which was printed with a huge yellow squash. "Here, for Pete's sake!"

He reached for the camera in his duffel bag, but not before she slammed his wrist with a karate chop.

"Do it and die," she said, meaning it.

"Rats. I was going to put it on the parish hall bulletin board. Enlarged."

She grinned, surprising him entirely. "Actually, that wasn't so bad," she said, stretching. "Except I feel bruised all over. Were we sleeping on a *rock*?"

"You *slept* like a rock, I know that."

"I remember when you crawled in here with me, but I played like I was asleep. I was furious. But I'm over it."

"You knew nothing when I got in here with you. You were snoring with the might of a top-of-the-line fellerbuncher."

"What in heaven's name is that?"

"You don't want to know," he said, slithering out of the bag.

"Clarence Austin!"

Birdsong.

"Clarence! Rise and shine!"

"Clarence ain't here," said Lee Lookabill.

"Where is he?"

"I ain't seen 'im."

"Take Henry Morgan and find him," said Larry. "Bo Derbin!"

Muted laughter from the three girls who had slept under a quilt tied to four poles.

"Bo! Snap to!"

"Bo's not here," said Lila Shuford.

"Where is he?"

"He slipped off, we saw him. He went with Clarence. They've been gone a really long time."

"Prob'ly takin' a leak," said Lee Lookabill, trying to be helpful.

"Move it," Larry told the search party, "and while you're at it, strip more bark. We've got grub to cook." The rector thought Larry looked like he'd just wrestled with yet another grizzly.

"Gross to the max," muttered Cynthia, remembering last night's chicken à la king, which had come packaged in industrial-strength brown plastic.

"You're losing your vocabulary out here in the woods. Didn't you like your peach bar?"

"I hated it. I was too hungry to wait while it soaked in water, so I ate it dry. It's still reconstituting in my stomach."

"And the peanut butter. I thought you loved peanut butter."

"Can you imagine having to *knead* your peanut butter in the package before opening it? And what was that they gave you to spread it on, a flagstone for the path through our hedge? I'm so starved, I could eat a helping of moss. What's in that package you had left?"

He picked it up and squinted at it. "Sugar, salt, chewing gum, matches, and toilet tissue."

"Yum," she said, slithering out into the chill morning air. "Let's save that for afternoon tea."

✳

Lee Lookabill lost his glasses while stripping bark, and Henry Morgan returned with a report.

"We cain't find Bo 'n Clarence, and Lee's done lost 'is glasses and cain't hardly see to walk back. I thought I stepped on 'em, somethin' crunched, but it was a stick."

"Fine!" snapped Larry. "Luke, go back with Henry and help Lee find his glasses. Tim, Cynthia, look for Bo and Clarence. They can't be far. Tell 'em I said they're in deep manure. And remember—step *on* a log, not over it."

Larry squatted over the smoking fire with a skillet, trying to dignify a cement-colored block of hash browns, as the rector and his wife vanished into a thicket.

Cynthia pulled on blue jeans and a denim shirt. He got into jeans, also, and hiking boots, leaving on the turtleneck he'd slept in, and adding a corduroy shirt. The air was damp and cool from yesterday's rain, and the skies again appeared overcast.

"I'll take my day pack. We might see something worth drawing." She pulled her blond hair back and whipped a rubber band around it.

"I don't think this is a drawing trip."

"You never know," she said brightly. "Besides, I think it has two candy bars in it."

"Ummm. No substitute for Percy's poached eggs with a side of grits."

"Dearest," she said, looking at him sternly, "we didn't come on this trip to coddle ourselves."

Give his wife a little time and a good night's rest, and she could bounce back with the best of them, he thought with pride.

✻

"Bo!" he called as they stepped into a clearing in the woods. "Clarence! Give us a shout!"

"You want me to whistle?" asked Cynthia.

"Whistle?"

"Like this," she said, piercing the air with a note so high and shrill, it might have dropped the Chicago Bulls in their tracks.

"Good Lord!" he said, holding his ears. "Where did you learn to do that?"

"When I was eleven. I was in a girls' club and we all learned to do something boys did. Phyllis Pringle learned to shoot marbles, Alice Jacobs took up the slingshot, and I learned to whistle."

"Aha."

"Want me to do it again?"

"Well …"

She did it again.

"You're strong stuff, Kavanagh," he said with admiration.

They heard the answering whistle reverberate in the woods.

"Listen!" she exclaimed.

"Sounds like it came from over there."

They sprinted into the clearing and were nearly across when they saw Bo and Clarence emerge from the woods.

"Man!" shouted Bo. "You won't believe this!"

"It better be good," said the rector, meaning it.

Clarence pointed toward the trees. "There's a big cave in there!"

"Huge!" announced Bo. "And scary, too. Clarence was too chicken to go in, but I did, and you won't believe it!"

"You can believe Larry Johnson will strip your hide for leaving camp like this."

"Let's go see it," said Cynthia.

"No way," said the rector, herding the boys toward the clearing.

"Oh, please, Timothy! Where is it, Bo? Is it far?"

"It's just right in there. I was coming out when I heard you whistle. Clarence can't whistle—it was me who whistled back."

"I can too whistle!" said Clarence.

"It's right through there," said Bo, "behind that big rock. Just go in behind that rock and you'll see this *hole* in the side of the hill, kind of covered up with bushes and stuff."

"Did you see any bats?" asked Cynthia.

"Nope. Just heard water dripping, and saw all those weird things sticking up."

"Stalactites," said the rector. "Or is it stalagmites?"

"Timothy, dearest, just five minutes? The boys can go back and we'll follow right behind. I've never seen a cave. Five minutes, I promise!" She looked imploring.

"Well ..." he said.

"Wonderful!"

"Straight across the clearing, hit the trail to the left, and be quick about it," the rector told the boys.

Clarence looked disconsolate. "Larry's prob'ly goin' to whip our head."

"*C'est la vie.* Get moving."

"We're right behind you!" called Cynthia as the boys sprinted away.

Father Tim cupped his hands to his mouth. "And stay together!" he shouted.

It was a word of caution he'd soon have to reckon with himself.

✳

"Uh-oh," said Cynthia, staring at the nearly hidden opening in the side of the hill.

"What do you mean?"

"That hole! I can't go through that hole like some rabbit into a burrow."

"But you love rabbits."

"Rabbits, yes, but not burrows."

He had once seen her crawl on her hands and knees into Miss Rose Watson's minuscule play hole in the attic of the old Porter place, entirely without a qualm.

"So let's head back," he said. "I'm famished."

"Well … but I've never seen a cave. Let's at least have a look."

She climbed the short ascent to the hole, swept aside the weeds and brush, and peered in. "It drops straight down and then flattens out. I can't really see anything."

Personally, he didn't want to see anything. He had no interest in disappearing into a hole in the ground that was hardly bigger around than he was.

His stomach growled. "Remember what happened to Alice in Wonderland.…"

"Ummm," she said, sticking her head in the opening. "Ummm."

Which was it, anyway? Did stalactites go up or down? Tite. Tight. Tight to the ceiling! That's what his seventh-grade teacher, Mrs. Jarvis, had said when they studied Mississippi caves, and then actually took a bus trip to a local cave. Stalactites hang down, mites stick up! Anita Jarvis. Now, there was a force to reckon with.…

"The tites hang down!" he said aloud, looking up as Cynthia's head disappeared into the hole.

He scrambled after her. "Cynthia!"

"Slide in feet first, Timothy. That's the way to do it!"

He did it.

He might have been dropping into a tomb, for all he knew. What if there should be a landslide, a mudslide, any sort of shift in the terrain? The hole would be blocked until kingdom come. He felt his heart pound and his breath constrict.

He slid along the muddy entrance shaft on his backside and landed on his feet behind his wife. Enough light streamed into the mouth of the cave to illuminate part of the large chamber in which they stood. It resembled a subway tunnel, long and rather narrow, and he was able to breathe easily again, sensing the space that opened up around them.

Odd, how the air was different. He could tell it at once. He felt the moisture in it, and smelled the earth. Like his grandmother's basement, except better.

"Are you OK?" he asked, noting the absence of an expected echo.

"Wonderful! This is too good for words! A glorious opportunity! I've got a flashlight in here somewhere." She fished in her day pack. "There!"

The beam from the flashlight snaked up the wall. "Good heavens! Look, dearest! It's a whole rank of organ pipes!"

"Limestone. Limestone does this." The vast wall might have been formed of poured marble, richly tinted with rose and blue, and glistening with an omnipresent sheen of moisture. He had never before observed what God was up to in the unseen places. A fine chill ran along his right leg.

The beam of light inched up the wall, shining palely on formations that appeared to be folds of draperies with fringed cornices, overhanging an outcropping of limestone as smooth as alabaster.

"Heavens!" gasped Cynthia. He slipped his forefinger into the band of her jeans as they inched along the chamber wall, looking up.

"Look!" she said. "There's just enough light to see how the ceiling of this thing soars—it's like a cathedral.

"Can you believe we're under the crust of the earth, possibly where no one has ever been before, except Indians? And who knows how old this cave is? It could be millions of years old, maybe billions...."

"Hold the light close to your face for a minute," he said.

"You're interested in seeing another ancient formation, I presume?"

"Your breath is vaporizing on the air."

She turned around and shone the light toward him. "And so is yours! But it doesn't feel cold in here."

"Not cold. But different."

Cynthia strode forth again, at a gallop.

"Hey! Are you going to a fire, Mrs. Kavanagh? Slow down."

"But we only have five minutes.... Yuck! Mud. These shoes will be history. I never have the right shoes for anything. When I was in New York last year in the blizzard, I only had *pumps*—"

"What's that?" They stopped, and he turned and listened. It sounded like water dripping. Here. There. At random. Everywhere. Water falling on water. Plink. Plink. Plinkplink.

"Obviously, there's water in here," he said. "Watch your step. Maybe we shouldn't be going in so far."

"Just two more minutes," she said, shining the light on the wall that curved ahead of them. "There! See that? Doesn't it look just like the rib cage of a dinosaur?"

"Spoken like the woman who once spotted Andrew Jackson in a cumulus cloud."

She placed her hand on the limestone wall that rippled with smooth, undulating forms. "Feel it, Timothy. It's so strange to the touch. Slick. Wet. But friendly, somehow, don't you think?"

"Ummm." Larry Johnson would have that slab of potatoes browning to a fare-thee-well. A little green onion in the mix wouldn't be bad, either, not to mention a sprinkle of the Romano cheese he'd carried along in a sandwich bag. It didn't take Ecclesiastes to know there was a time to seek nourishment and a time to explore caves.

"Time to go," he said firmly.

"There at the end of the passage, dearest. See? It looks like a huge urn, doesn't it, sitting in that vault? How extraordinary, all these wonders that remind us of things on top of the earth—and yet, surely all this came long before cathedrals and urns."

"Listen, people are depending on us. We've run off exactly like Bo and Clarence did, and Larry will not like this one bit. You talk about getting our head whipped ..." He took her arm.

"What are you doing?"

"We're turning around and going back the way we came."

She sighed. "You're right, of course." They turned and began walking. "I was going to sketch something while you held the light, but I suppose there's not time."

"Darn right. How's the battery in that thing? It looks weak."

"It's just that this place is so huge and so dark, it absorbs the light."

"Let's hope so."

"I guess I'm ready to get out of here, too. I'm starved, not to mention freezing. Are you freezing? Suddenly, it's ... like a grave in here."

"Kindly rephrase that."

They walked in silence, shining the light along the walls on either side. He had no memory of the little cave in Mississippi looking anything like this; in fact, he remembered being pretty bored with that field trip. The most vivid memory of it was the picture someone took of him with Anita Jarvis, who was nearly as wide as the bus. He had tried to flee the camera, but she grabbed him by the ear and yanked him back, while everyone laughed their heads off. He had wanted to tear the resulting snapshot in a hundred pieces, but was so entranced with having a picture of himself, even with Anita Jarvis, that he couldn't do it.

"I've got an idea," she said. "Why don't we stop and turn the light off? I'd love to see how dark it really is in here."

"Cynthia, Cynthia ..."

"It will only take a minute. Then we'll go, I promise."

"Well ..."

Bright, unidentifiable images swam before his eyes, then gradually faded, leaving a velvet and permeating darkness.

He thought he heard her teeth chattering. "Maybe I should turn the light back on."

"Wait," he said, touching her arm. "Our eyes are just starting to get adjusted." They stood together in silence. "I think this place is totally devoid of light," he said at last. "We're in complete and utter darkness. Amazing."

"Scary."

"Don't be scared. I've got you." He put his arm around her shoulders, noting that the musical sounds of water-on-water seemed louder than before.

"I'm glad you're here," she whispered.

"I'll always be here."

"You will? Do you mean that?"

"Of course I mean that. I took a vow on it, for one thing."

Some fragment of a poem came swimming to him, something, he thought, by Wendell Berry: "... and find that the dark, too, blooms and sings." What was it about this darkness, the particular, nearly tangible density of it, and the odd sense that he was somehow blending into it?

"Why can't we see light from the mouth of the cave?" Cynthia asked.

"I don't know. We were standing in the light only a minute ago."

"We can't have walked completely away from the light that was coming through the hole." She switched on the flashlight, which glimmered on columns of roseate limestone.

"This isn't the way we came," she said. "We haven't seen these before."

"We must have missed a turn." He puzzled for a moment, rubbing his forehead and feeling disoriented. "You were hauling along there pretty good."

"You get in front and haul, then," she said testily.

"OK, let's retrace our steps and watch where we're going." But they had just retraced their steps....

In less time than it might have taken to recite the Comfortable Words, they'd been thrown off kilter. He felt for a moment as if his mind had walked out on him.

They had begun to move in the opposite direction when the light faded, glimmered weakly, and failed.

"No," she said, as the darkness overtook them. "Please, no."

TEN

The Cave

"Pray, Timothy!"

"I am praying. Keep moving. We're bound to come back to the light from the entrance."

"Are you sure?"

"Positive."

"It's so terribly dark. Don't you have some matches in your shirt pocket? I thought campers always took matches."

"No matches."

"Don't lose me, Timothy."

"I won't lose you. Hang on to my belt; we're doing fine. The wall is leading us."

"The flashlight battery ... I haven't used that flashlight since I moved next door and the electricity went off. I'm a terrible partner."

"Careful. Slippery here. Feels like ..."

"Water," she said. "We're stepping in water. It's soaking through my tennis shoes."

He stopped. They hadn't come through water before. His heart pumped like an oil derrick. It wasn't the darkness, exactly, that was disconcerting. It wasn't the sense of being hemmed in by walls of limestone on either side. No, the worst of it was the sudden sense of being turned around, of having no idea at all which way was north, east, south, or west. It was as if the beaters of a mixing machine had been lowered into his brain and turned on high.

"I'm terrified," she said, clinging to his back. Whatever he did, he must not let her sense his own fear.

Something like light flickered at the periphery of his vision.

"Light!" he said. "I saw light."

"Where? Thank God!"

He blinked. Then blinked again. But it wasn't light at all. He realized his nervous system was generating neural impulses that resulted in the strange, luminous flickers.

"Wrong," he said. "Something's going on with our vision. It's still adjusting."

"Poop!" she said with feeling.

The sound of dripping water was random, but constant, and now he realized it was dripping nearby.

Were they standing in a puddle they had stepped through before without noticing, or something they had walked around and missed entirely? "Wait here," he said. "I'm going to see if this stuff gets deeper."

"Don't leave me!"

"I'll be only inches away. Let me check it out."

"I'll come with you." She dug both hands under his belt and hung on.

The water definitely got deeper as they stepped forward. Then the wall on either side ended, and his hands were suddenly groping thin air. He sensed they might be entering a large chamber at the end of the passage.

"We're turning back," he said evenly.

"We keep turning back—and turning around! I'm so confused."

"Hang on." Dear God, what was a complete turn when you could see nothing? Had he been misjudging their turns? Had he been making half turns that sent them off along some other route? Why hadn't they crashed into something?

They turned slowly, as one, and began walking. He kept his hands out, feeling for the wall that had been within reach only moments ago.

There! He felt the sweat pour from his body, followed by a stinging chill as it met the cool air of the cave.

"Keep your left hand in my belt and put your right hand on the wall, and don't take it off, even for a moment. We'll come back to the light, I promise. There's no way we can't." His voice was about to gear down into the croaking mode, and he mustn't let her hear that. In him, croaking was a sure sign of depression, anger, or fear, and she knew it.

They hadn't been in here long enough for Larry Johnson to be worried. Knowing Larry, he probably thought the newlyweds were off doing a little hand holding, and he'd give them plenty of time to enjoy it.

"I'm thirsty," she said. "Stop and let me take the day pack off. I think I've got a bottle of water."

They stood with their backs to the damp wall, and she found the bottle and shook it. "There's not much left. The flashlight … the water. I can't do anything right."

"So, what did I come off with? Nothing. You get extra points."

She unscrewed the cap and reached for his hand and gave him the bottle.

"No," he said. "You first."

"I think you should be first. You're the leader."

"Drink," he said. She took the bottle and drank, and passed it back to him. There wasn't much left, but he drained the bottle and felt revived.

"Why don't I scream for help?"

"Not yet. We can find our way out." Who would hear them if they yelled their heads off?

"I forgot you're one of those men who won't stop at a service station and ask directions."

"There are no service stations anymore," he said unreasonably. "Just places to buy hot dogs and T-shirts and pump your own."

"We should be screaming our heads off. Someone will be looking for us, Timothy. They'll hear us."

He stuffed the empty bottle into her pack. "Save your breath. We've only been in here ten minutes." Had it been ten minutes? Twenty? An hour? He couldn't see his watch. He had never bought a watch with an illuminated dial, thinking it an unnecessary expense. After all, who needed to know what time it was in the dark, except when one was in bed? For that, there was the illuminated face of the clock on his nightstand.

"I hate this," she said, whispering. "It's horrid. We're sopping wet all over."

His unspoken prayers had been scrambled, frantic. He needed to stop, take a deep breath, and state it plainly. He put his arms around her and she instantly recognized the meaning of his touch and bowed her head against his.

"Father, your children have stumbled into a bit of trouble here, and we're confused. You know the way out. Please show it to us. In Jesus' name."

"Amen!" she said, squeezing his arm.

"That's the ticket."

He wanted to stand there for a moment, collect his thoughts, get a real sense of the place. Maybe that would help, maybe that would give them some idea of what to do next. They had raced into this place, after all, like two heedless children, then panicked and gotten wildly confused.

Stop. Slow down. That was definitely the answer.

He drew a deep breath. "Actually, this is the way a lot of people live their lives."

"What do you mean?"

"Never knowing, in the dark, constantly guessing. It's the guessing that's the worst."

"Always working, dearest."

"Sermons are everywhere," he said.

"Speaking of guessing—you've been guessing, haven't you, about the way to get back to the entrance?"

Why lie? "Yes."

She was silent for a time. "We can't possibly be far. It seemed so simple when we came in, just a long room with that vault thing and the urn."

"Right," he said. "We can't be more than a few yards from the entrance. If it were a snake, it would bite us."

"Did we turn right or left at that vault thing?"

"Right. We went around the corner, and there were the dinosaur ribs...."

"The dinosaur ribs came before the vault."

He made a conscious effort not to sigh, and put his arm around her shoulders. "Let's chill to the next episode, dude."

"What kind of talk is that?"

"That's Dooley's new foreign language, in addition to French. Let's take a couple of deep breaths and go from there."

"I feel as if every crawling thing ever created is lurking in here."

"Anything lurking in here is blind—if that's any comfort."

"Blind?"

"All creatures who live in caves are blind."

"That makes sense, I suppose. I mean, what good would it do them to see?"

"I learned that in the seventh grade when we went on a bus trip to a local cave. I wanted to hold Justine Ivory's hand while we were standing by the blind trout pool, but I didn't have the guts."

"In the seventh grade, you wanted to hold hands?"

"Didn't you?"

"Absolutely not. I fell in love with Russell Lowell in the fifth grade, got my heart broken, and didn't even think of boys again until high school."

"Different strokes ..."

He visualized Larry running this way right now, with the entire pack at his heels. Hadn't Bo said the cave was scary? And big? And the opening half-covered by brush? That wouldn't sound good to Larry Johnson, who was pretty savvy about things of the woods.

On the other hand, what if the boys couldn't find their way back to the cave?

"Oh, Lord, Timothy! Gross! Vile! Get it off me!"

"What?" he said, his heart thundering.

"Something fell on my head, oh, please, oh, no, it's running down my neck, oh, get it off ... !"

"Water," he said stoically, feeling a large drop crash onto his own head and roll down his back.

"Are you sure? Run your hand down my back."

It had hit with such force, it must have come from a great distance. "Water," he said again, smoothing her damp shirt.

"Timothy, we've got to get out of here. We can't just stand around talking about the seventh grade!"

"Did you say you have candy bars in your day pack?"

"Snickers. Two." She turned her back to him and he reached

into the pack and felt around among the colored pencils and the sketchbook and the dead flashlight and socks, and found them rolled up in her underwear.

He didn't know why it swam to the surface at just that moment, but he remembered Miss Sadie's story of falling in the well, of the darkness and her terrible fear, and the long night when no one seemed destined to find her because of the rain. The rain had destroyed the scent for the bloodhounds. What if it were raining out there again, erasing their scent?

But he was making mountains out of molehills. Good Lord, they'd been fumbling around in here for only ten or fifteen minutes, and already he was calling in the bloodhounds.

His adrenaline had stopped pumping, and he felt exhausted, as if he wanted nothing more than to lie down and sleep. He ate two bites of the candy, wondering at its astonishing sweetness, its texture and form, the intricate crackle of the paper, and the way the smell of chocolate intensified in the darkness.

"Please don't eat the whole thing." She had seen him in a diabetic coma once, which had been once too often.

He put the rest of the bar in her day pack, realizing he felt completely befuddled. He didn't want to press on until the sugar hit his bloodstream.

"I'm going to start walking," she said impatiently.

"Which way?"

"To my right. That's the way we were going when we stopped to reflect on our early love interests."

"We were going to your left. I was ahead of you, remember?"

"I thought I was ahead of you. No, wait. That was before."

"Trust me. We go this way. Grab my belt and hold on."

"I think it's time to scream. In fact, I think we should scream now and walk ten paces and scream again, and so on until someone comes or we see the light."

"Have at it," he said tersely.

She swallowed the last bite of her Snickers, then bellowed out a sound that would have shattered the crystal in their own cabinets, forty miles distant.

"How was that?" she wanted to know.

"You definitely get the job of screaming, if further screaming is required."

"Every ten paces," she said, feeling encouraged. "You pray and I'll scream."

"A fair division of labor." He was feeling the numbing cold, now, and the dampness of his clothes. Didn't the French keep wine in caves because of a mean temperature in the fifties? This felt like thirty degrees and dropping.

"Five, six, seven ..." said Cynthia.

His foot met thin air. He pitched wildly to the left, banging his head on a sharp object, and fell sprawling.

※

Was it blood, or mud, or the moisture that covered everything in this blasted place?

Blood. Definitely. He felt the sharp sting as he rubbed his fingers over the gash.

"Are you all right?" He heard the fear in her voice.

"I'm OK. Just a knock on the head." He was struggling to find the breath that had failed him.

"Let me help."

"Don't move!"

Her voice seemed to come from somewhere above him. He reached up, feeling nothing but air, then touched a flat rock. He inched his hand along the edge, and found the tip of her shoe. "You're standing on some kind of ledge. Back up a little, and take it easy."

"Timothy ..."

"Don't panic. I'm fine. I'm telling you, we've got to be right at the entrance. We'll be out of here in no time. Stay calm."

"Let me give you a hand."

"Back up and stay put."

He grabbed the ledge and hauled himself up. He had fallen only a couple of feet, thanks be to God.

Lord, you know I'm completely in the dark, in more ways than one. I don't have a clue where we are or what to do. I know you're there, I know you'll answer, give me some supernatural understanding here....

He stood up and leaned against the wall, and reached for her, and found her sleeve and took her hand. He had lost all sense of time. *A thousand years in Thy sight are but as yesterday when it is past, and as a watch in the night....* Was he being introduced to something like God's own sense of time?

"I'm going to scream again."

"Don't," he said, meaning it.

"Why not, Timothy? People will be looking for us. We'll never get out of here."

"Turn around."

"Turn around? Again? We're so turned around now we can't think straight. We've turned around and turned around, 'til we're fairly churned to butter!"

"Clearly, this is not the way. It vanishes into thin air."

He stepped around Cynthia, and she tucked her hands into his belt.

The sugar was beginning to work. He felt suddenly victorious as he moved along the wall, his wife attached to his belt like a boxcar to an engine.

He walked more quickly now, his hands never leaving the wet surfaces on either side. There. That felt better. His adrenaline was definitely up and pumping.

"We're out of here!" he whooped. He reached up and brushed away the blood that was running into his left eye. A handkerchief. In his pocket. He took it out, still walking, and patted it to his forehead.

When he put it in his pocket and reached for the wall on his left, he groped air.

"Why did you stop?" she said.

"The wall just ran out on the left. Maybe that's another passage. Maybe that's the way we came before I crashed. Hold on, we're backing up."

He took two steps backward and found the wall on the left, and examined it with his hand. Did it end abruptly or did it curve around?

It curved around. A fairly gentle curve. If they had come through this passage to where they were standing now, they might easily have continued around the curve to their right, which had pitched him off the ledge.

What if he left her here and explored the passage? Perhaps just around the turn, he would see light from the entrance. Or what if they both explored that passage? But they could be stumbling along passages until kingdom come. Who would have thought that an innocent-looking hole in the side of a hill might lead to such unutterable complexity?

Mush. His mind was mush.

"We need to stop again," he said.

"Why stop again? You said we were going out of here."

"We are. But we need to stop and think, right here where these two passages converge. We've got to think."

They sat with their backs to the wall, and he put his arm around her to warm her, and pulled her to him. He felt the cool slime of mud under them, but he didn't care.

In his life, he had never confronted anything like this. He had never been to war, he had never been in peril, he had never even gone to the woods and lived on berries like Father Roland once boasted of doing. No, he had lived a sheltered life, a life of the soul, of the mind, and what had it gained him in the real circumstances of day-to-day living?

He had spent nearly forty years telling other people how to live in the light, and here he was, lost in a complex maze in the bowels of the earth, in total, devastating darkness.

For no reason he could have explained, he thought of his father calling him into the house that summer night, the night the chain had broken and he had walked his bicycle home from Tommy's house.

"Timothy." The kitchen light was behind his father, throwing him into silhouette at the screen door. He had looked up and been frightened instantly. The silhouette of his father was somehow larger than life, immense.

"Yes, sir?"

"Come in and tell me why."

Come in and tell me why. He would never forget that remark. What did it mean? He knew it had something to do with why he could never do anything right. He had stood there, unable to go in, frozen.

His father had opened the screen door and held it, and he walked inside.

He saw the look on his mother's face. "Don't hurt him, Matthew."

"You're crying," Cynthia whispered, wiping the tears from his cheek. He hadn't known he was weeping until she touched his face. It was as if he stood nearby, watching two people sitting on the floor of the cave, holding each other.

"Dearest …" Cynthia whispered, stroking his arm.

The self who stood was humiliated that the priest had broken down and broken apart. The priest who would do this under pressure was a priest who could not get it right.

"I can't get it right," he managed to say, as if repeating some unwritten liturgy.

Unwritten liturgy. All these years, he had spoken the written liturgy, while underneath …

"Almighty God, to you all hearts are open, all desires known, and from you no secrets are hid.…"

I can't get it right.

"Holy and gracious Father, in your infinite love you made us for yourself.…"

I can't get it right.

"It's all my fault," she said. "I was the one who insisted we come in here. I led us on a merry chase and brought that no-good flashlight.… You mustn't blame yourself."

He didn't want to weep like this, but there was nothing he could do about it; he felt as if he'd broken open like a geode.

"I'm sorry," she said. "Please forgive me."

"He couldn't tolerate anything that wasn't perfect."

"Who, dearest? What … ?"

"That's why he was enraged when something broke. It had to be fixed at once—or thrown away. There was a terrible pressure to keep things from breaking, to keep them like new. Mr. Burton's tractor broke down along the road from our house.… Mr. Burton pushed it off the road and left it in the field for days. My father never passed that tractor without lambasting the owner's incompetence."

"Ah," she said, quietly.

"I can't retire," he told her. Why had he said that? … like a geode.

"Tell me why."

"The way things are, they're running smoothly, most of the

bases are covered. I'm trying to get it right, Cynthia. I can't stop now."

"But you have got it right, Timothy."

He didn't want to be placated and mollycoddled. He drew away from her, and she sat in silence.

He was hurting her, he could feel it, but here in this total, mind-numbing darkness, he could not summon what it might take to care. Out there in the light, out there where his ministry was, he could always summon what it took to care.

"Listen to me, dearest, and listen well." He had heard knives in her voice once before, when he'd drawn away from her prior to their marriage. It was knives he heard again, but they were sheathed, and he leaned his head against the cold wall and closed his eyes.

"I lived with Elliott for seventeen years, always trying to get it right. When I tried to kill myself and it didn't work, I remember thinking, I can't even get this right. Elliott was never there for me, not once—he was out making babies with other women, trying in his *own* confused way to get it right. During those long months when I was recovering in a friend's house in the country, God spoke to my heart in a way he hadn't spoken before. No. Erase that. He made me able to listen in a way I couldn't listen before.

"He let me know that trying to get it right is a dangerous thing, Timothy, and he does not like it."

His head pounded where the blood had congealed. "What do you mean?"

"I mean that getting it absolutely right is God's job."

The cold was seeping into him. He was beginning to feel it in his very marrow. He also felt the loss of her living warmth, though she was right beside him. He drew her to him and took her hands and put them inside his shirt and held her. She was shaking.

"Must I remind you that your future belongs to God, and not

to you? Please unlock your gate, Timothy. Leave it swinging on the hinges, if you will. This thing about our future must go totally out of our hands. We cannot hold on to it for another moment."

He smiled in the darkness. "Don't preach me a sermon, Mrs. Kavanagh." The weeping had stopped, but the geode lay open. He felt a raw place in himself that seemed infantile, newly hatched.

He stood up and helped her to her feet. He was stiff in every joint, but stronger.

"I think I should take this passage and check it out. I won't go beyond the range of your voice, I promise. Maybe I can see light, maybe this is the way."

"Don't leave me, Timothy."

"I promise I won't go beyond the range ..."

"I'll come with you."

"I feel you need to stay here and be the compass. If I don't turn anything up, I'll pop right back. We're not far from the opening. We can't be. Besides, I know Larry, and he's starting to get worried, maybe even ticked off, for Pete's sake. One way or the other—"

"Timothy ..."

"Yes?"

"You have your fears, I have mine. Don't leave me." Her own geode had come apart; he heard her panic.

"But I don't know what's along that passage. Why should we both take the risk?"

"You could go pitching headfirst into God knows what, you might not ..."

"Might not what?"

"Might not come back."

"Of course I'll come back. I'll test every step I take."

"The buddy system—they say to always use the buddy system. We're stronger together, smarter. If we only had something to scatter as we go, like bread crumbs. But then, we couldn't see them...."

Why hadn't they left something at the entrance of the cave, some sign that they'd gone in, like the nearly empty water bottle or a candy wrapper? It might have said, *If you find this, we're still in here. Start the search.*

Stay calm was still the directive. They couldn't go blasting down every passageway that presented itself. Light! If only he had the tiniest flame, the barest flicker of illumination, he would fall to his knees in thanksgiving.

In Him was life; and the life was the light of men. And the light shineth in the darkness; and the darkness overcame it not....

He refused to fear this thick, palpable darkness. As far as he knew, God had not drawn the line on caves. He hadn't said, *I'll stick by you as long as you don't do some fool thing like get lost in a cave, you poor sap.* What he had said was, *I will never leave you. Period.*

"Trust God!" he blurted to his wife.

"Don't preach me a sermon, Father Kavanagh. I am trusting him, for Pete's sake. It's you I can't get a bead on. Are we going or coming?"

"Definitely going. Let's tuck along this passageway for a bit. I won't take a step I haven't tested first. I'll keep my left hand on the wall and my right hand in front of me. Hang on. And no back-seat driving, thank you."

They moved carefully around the curving limestone wall with its thrusting formations.

"'I cannot see what flowers are at my feet,'" she murmured, "'nor what soft incense hangs upon the boughs, but, in embalmed darkness, guess each sweet wherewith the seasonable month endows.' Who said that?"

"Will Rogers!"

She laughed. "One more guess."

"Joe DiMaggio?"

"Keats!"

"Aha."

"How's it going up there?"

"Ummm. Same old, same old. But no mud. Feels like we're walking on dry clay. Does that ring any bells as to our previous sojourn?"

"I can't remember," she said. "Our sojourns all run together like so much goulash."

He was feeling more closed in than he had before, when his hand suddenly struck something in front of him. It was a wall of sheer limestone with—he moved his cold hand over it as someone blind might examine a sculpture—with a swollen formation attached to its surface.

It was another of those columns, perhaps, something like a great elephant trunk. He turned slowly to the right, reading the wall with his hands. More columns.

The columned wall, he found, continued around in a U curve.

It was a moment before he told her what neither wanted to know.

ELEVEN

Darkness into Light

He felt as if the circuits had gone down in his brain.

No logic, no reason, no common sense had worked to lead them to the opening. Every turn had been a wrong turn. Every decision had been fruitless. It was maddening.

Dear God! Now what?

The darkness seemed to fall like a heavy curtain over his mind.

"If we go back the way we came," he said, forcing himself to think rationally, "we'll come to where we were sitting. We know that turning right isn't the way; that's where I fell off the ledge. So, let's retrace our steps and turn left."

She was trembling as he put his arm around her shoulders.

"We can't be far from the opening," he said. "We're going to find it, I promise. Besides, Larry won't let this go on much longer. Hang on."

She tucked her hands into his belt and they began the return trek.

He was blasted sick and tired of this everlasting fumbling around in the dark. Where in God's name was Larry, anyway?

Putting a fly in the water and showing off the cast he learned from his Orvis seminar?

His thirst was becoming hard to ignore, and he realized how seductive the dripping water sounded. He saw them down on their hands and knees, lapping at a puddle like Barnabas and Violet. But what might the water contain, what could limestone do to the human system, what algae or larvae might be lurking in it?

"I'm so thirsty," she said, as if reading his mind. "Are we almost there?"

"The wall is beginning to curve a little, I think." Would they recognize the curve, the place where they'd been sitting, or go careening around to the right until he fell off the ledge again? Good Lord, why hadn't they marked the place they'd sat, left something there as a touchstone?

"Here. I think we're here." That was the thin slime of mud they'd been sitting on, wasn't it? Something was squishing under his shoes. It might have been a light in a window, for the moment of warm familiarity it kindled in him.

"How are your feet?"

"Frozen," she said.

"We're turning left. Hang on."

"You're sure? You're positive this is the way?"

"Positive." He wasn't positive.

Except for the time they had sat by the wall … when? How long ago? Twenty minutes ago? Except for that time, they had been constantly on the move, battling their fear, struggling to make sense of this mind-altering confusion. His knees felt weak— or was it the numbing cold and dampness that was seeping into their very bones and slowing them down?

Now. They were back to a passage he could touch on either side, thanks be to God!

"Soon," he said, hearing the despair in his voice, "we'll be at the opening. We just took a couple of wrong turns."

"Right."

He heard the echoing despair in her own voice.

＊

He didn't try to imagine how much time had passed.

He leaned against the day pack, using it as insulation between his back and the damp cold of the wall, and held her tightly between his legs.

They had groped along an endless passage strewn with boulders and low shelves of limestone, which banged up their knees and twice sent him sprawling. At a pool of water, they stopped and made the decision to go no farther.

"I think we should wait it out," he said, edging back from the pool. "We need to stop moving, and let them find us." How much deeper had they gone in, struggling to find their way out?

She didn't speak.

Exhausted, they sat away from the water, under a ledge, and prayed silently.

He felt as if they had become part of the cave. The damp cold had made such a thorough invasion of their bodies that their nervous systems had slowed to a crawl. It wasn't cold enough to freeze them to death, he reasoned, but it was blasted cold and dark and still enough to numb every limb, not to mention the mind.

Leaning with her back against his chest, she rubbed his legs and ankles, and he rubbed her arms and shoulders for warmth.

His throat was as parched as if they'd wandered the desert. Couldn't he scoop up the water in one hand, and with the other examine it for living things? He did not want to gulp down an eel or a worm or whatever else might live in these waters, and though his wife had remained substantially calm until now, straining a wriggling organism through her teeth would not improve matters.

What was going on out there in the world, anyway, where people were free to move around and look at trees and hear the call of other human voices? The kids couldn't find the cave, he was convinced of it. Furthermore, it was almost certainly raining, and no trace of their scent remained on the ground.

Drops of moisture hit the pools, plinkplinkplink. He felt a sudden shortness of breath and a racking, intense thirst.

He sat up and pulled the bag to his side and reached in and found the bottle. He also found the two soft bundles she had tucked next to her pencil case. Socks!

"Put these on," he said, handing her a pair.

It was difficult to draw his feet from his shoes, as most of the feeling had gone. The good news was, his socks were still dry, thanks to the investment he'd made in the boots. Her socks, however, were sopping. "Put on both pairs," he said.

"No, dearest. You—"

"Please mind your priest."

She pulled his feet into her lap and massaged them briskly, and put his socks on again. Then she rubbed her own feet and pulled on the dry socks. "Heaven," she murmured.

"I'm going to get water," he said.

"But—"

"How bad can it be?"

She thought a moment. "Maybe we could scoop some into our hand and feel if there's anything in it."

"Whatever."

"Don't leave me!"

"It's just over there, for Pete's sake."

"Just over there? Where is just over there? We thought the opening was just over there."

"Cynthia …"

"I'm coming with you."

"Hitch on, then."

They crawled the short distance to the pool, feeling their way, the smell of damp earth in their nostrils.

"It smells clean," he said. "That's one thing I can say for this place. And the air … no sneezing, no sinus drainage."

"No exhaust fumes, no pollen!" she said, catching the spirit.

He splashed his hand into the edge of the pool. Then, pushing up his muddy sleeve, he slid his hand into the water and tested the depth. It dropped off steeply. Thank God they hadn't bungled their way into it.

"Do you feel anything moving?"

He didn't. He scooped water into his cupped hands and recklessly drank it. Good Lord! Sweet. Sweet as sugar! It went down his throat in a great, healing stream. He scooped some more and drank.

"It's OK, you can drink it! Move up to the edge, but be careful. This pool could be pretty deep."

He splashed water into his mouth with the palm of his hand. Then he bent his head to the pool and drank freely, feeling the mentholated coolness of the water against his face, and the drops from above splatter on his back.

"Oh," she said, simply, weeping with relief as she drank.

It was as if God had touched them, instilling a new, raw hope.

They crawled back to the dry pack, and he fetched the bottle to the pool and filled it and put the cap on, and returned to where she sat under the ledge.

"Why don't I start screaming?"

"Give you a little refreshment and you're off again," he said.

"I mean it, Timothy. It would be such a help to whoever is looking for us."

"Well …"

He held his ears, and she screamed.

"Well done!"

"I'm going back to the screaming program. I don't care what you say."

"So be it," he said. "Let's get warm."

She crawled into the embrace of his legs and arms, and pulled her own legs under her chin.

"Thank God Sophia and Liza are looking in on Barnabas," he mused. "He's probably dragging them around the town monument as we speak."

"And Liza's loving it!"

"I like the way you smell," he said, burying his face in her hair. Even in this dark, damp place that reeked only of earth, he inhaled the faintest scent of wisteria.

"Tell me something."

"What?" she asked.

"Why are you especially afraid of being left?"

There was a long silence. He listened to the musical drip, dripping of the water, calling upon every discipline to avoid the sheer panic that lay beneath the surface of his outward calm. They should be finding their way out of here, executing some rationale that he couldn't seem to get a fix on. But no, stumbling around hadn't worked, he had to fight the fear with everything in him and stay exactly where they were until help came.

"Because I was always being left by someone. My mother and father … and then Elliott."

"Tell me about it."

"Well, you see …" She hesitated, then went on. "I remember when I was in fourth grade and Mother and Daddy were to pick me up from school. Except … they never came."

"Never?"

"I waited out front until all the buses had left, and Miss Phillips stayed with me. Then everyone left, and we went back inside and stood by the windows in my classroom and watched for them to drive up."

She trembled slightly.

"They ... never did come. Miss Phillips called our house over and over, but there was no answer, so she took me home with her."

He kissed her hair.

"Miss Phillips kept calling, but there was no answer, and I remember she made grilled cheese sandwiches and hot cocoa, and finally I did my homework and we went to bed. I slept on her sofa and her cat curled up beside me—his name was Alexander, as in Alexander the Great. We got up the next morning and I put my clothes back on and we went to school, and I was afraid people would know that I hadn't been home, that Mother and Daddy ... At recess, Miss Phillips said Mother called to say they'd been ..."

He waited.

"... detained."

The water dripped all around them, and he was glad for the ledge that kept them dry.

"I don't know why I remember that particular thing."

"I'll never leave you," he said, holding her.

"Not even to explore a passage?"

"Not even for that," he said.

✳

She had fallen asleep in his arms, and he sat with his eyes open, staring ahead, not wanting to miss the light when it came.

The feeling of panic had wondrously left him, and in its place had come an odd and surprising peace. Somehow, he wasn't afraid of this place anymore. He could wait.

A line from Roethke surfaced in his mind: *In a dark time, the eye begins to see.*

It was as if he were drifting through space, and every care he had was reduced to nothing. What were his cares, anyway? They were few. So few. Who cared where they put the linen closets in Hope House? He had cared very much out there in the light, just as he had cared about Sadie Baxter hanging up her car keys, and Buck Leeper coming to terms with his Creator, and Dooley Barlowe growing up and having a life that no one could take from him, no matter what.

He had cared that Lord's Chapel was running several thousand dollars behind budget, and that two of his favorite families had gone over to the Presbyterians for no reason he could understand. It was his job to care, but what he was beginning to understand, sitting here in this unspeakable darkness, was that God cared more.

Whether Tim Kavanagh cared wasn't the point, after all, and whether Tim Kavanagh was in control didn't matter in the least. God was fully in control—firmly and finally and awfully—and he knew it for the first time in his heart, instead of in his head.

He felt himself smiling, and wondered at the laughter welling up in him, like a spring seeping into a field where the plow had passed.

But he wouldn't wake her, not for anything, and he pushed the laughter back, and felt its warmth spreading through him like the glowing of a coal.

"Father?" he whispered.

Come in and tell me why....

"I love you," he heard himself saying. "I forgive you. It's all right."

Cynthia murmured in her sleep, and the surge of inexpressible tenderness that stirred in him was unlike anything he'd known before.

He sensed that everything was possible—yet he had no idea what that meant, nor what everything might be.

❋

Maybe he, too, had fallen asleep and was dreaming.

But he wasn't dreaming.

He heard it again—a kind of woofing or huffing. He sat, frozen, afraid he had imagined it.

Woof, woof!

"It's Barnabas!" he shouted. It was the mighty voice of a Wurlitzer, it was the voice of angels on high, it was his dog!

He heard himself yelling in odd harmony with Cynthia's ear-splitting scream, their voices raised in a single, joyful invective against the primordial dark.

The miner's lamp attached to his collar wildly illuminated the walls as Barnabas licked every exposed part of their bodies, pausing only to bark for the rescue team.

The faces of Larry Johnson and Joe Joe Guthrie finally bobbed toward them under hats with miner's lamps.

"Lord have mercy, are y'all OK?" yelled Joe Joe, tripping over the long rope leash they'd anchored to Barnabas.

"Fine! Wonderful!" shouted the rector.

"I ought to kick your butt," said Larry Johnson, meaning it.

❋

They stumbled out of the opening into the light, which issued from a ring of lanterns and the flash of J.C. Hogan's Nikon.

J.C. walked backward as they advanced from the cave, shooting at close range, and crashed into the underbrush.

Cynthia, who was covered with mud from head to toe, embraced various members of the exultant youth group and shouted, "Hallelujah!"

"What time is it?" asked the rector.

"Ten o'clock!" announced Bo Derbin, proud to be asked. "We

thought Indians were living in that cave and had scalped you or made you their slaves."

Mule Skinner appeared, carrying a lantern. "Lord help, look at that gash on your head! I hope you're up to walkin' th' two miles out of here. We got to get you to th' hospital."

"We're fine," he said. "No harm done!"

"We was goin' to radio for a helicopter in case you was in real *bad* shape," said a police officer, who appeared disappointed.

Father Tim felt positively humiliated by all this ruckus. Not only had he and Cynthia spoiled the camping trip, they'd brought out the police and the press, who, worse yet, had to hump it on foot across two miles of rough terrain.

"Cave!" said Larry Johnson. "That's all I had to hear. I gave you an hour and we started looking. We called and hollered, then went a little ways in and poked around, but couldn't see for squat, even with a lantern and flashlight. I walked out to the van, drove to the nearest phone, and called Rodney."

"I was down at th' station chewin' th' fat when Larry called," said Mule. "I told 'em how my daddy was lost in a cave in Kentucky, and they like to never found 'im 'til they sent in his Blue Tick hound. So Rodney collected th' boys and went to your house and got Barnabas."

"A stroke of genius."

Larry leaned close to the rector's ear. "I hate to tell you that Rodney took a wrong turn outside Farmer and every one of 'em were lost as the tribes of Israel for two hours."

"We followed Barnabas as hard as we could go," said Joe Joe. "The way he tracked you, y'all must've been runnin' around in there like chickens with their heads cut off."

"Tell me about it," said the rector.

"Actually," Cynthia informed J.C., "it was a very *interesting* experience. So sorry we alarmed everybody."

"Want my last package of peanut butter?" Lee Lookabill asked Cynthia.

"If you'll *knead* it first, I'll eat it," she said. "I never thought it would come to this."

Rodney Underwood looked at the rector sternly and hitched up his holster belt. "I don't know when I've had to fool with a man who was lost in a cave. I just radio'd th' county sheriff. He says this cave is totally unexplored."

"Not anymore it ain't," said Mule, grinning proudly.

✳

Emma Newland was making her pronouncement.

"Anybody who'd step *foot* in a cave *deserves* to get lost!"

"It was a very interesting experience," he said, quoting his wife.

"Interesting? With *bats* swarmin' around your head, and steppin' in water out th' *kazoo*?"

"We never saw a bat, actually."

"Never *saw* a bat? That's where bats *live*—in *caves*!"

"So sue me," he said.

✳

Merely walking out the door of the rectory was invigorating. It was as if he'd come back from the grave, given the dazzling, living energy of every green thing he saw.

He had escaped the tomb, and felt his spirit quicken in response. In a way, it was his own Eastertide.

"Lost in a cave?" said Bill Sprouse, who passed him on the way to the Grill. "That'll preach, Brother, that'll preach!"

✳

"For you," said Percy, "a dollar off th' special."

"Why a dollar off?" He was leery of Percy's specials.

"You been lost in a cave! You're a big gun!"

He grinned. "Big gun, is it? Well, then, bring on the special."

"Velma," Percy called to his wife, "th' father'll have th' special! Coffee's on th' house."

"What, ah, is the special?" he inquired.

"Grilled horned toad on a bed of fresh mustard greens," said Percy, looking solemn.

"Give me a side of salsa with that," replied the rector.

Percy doubled over with laughter, slapping his leg. Clearly, the week that Percy and Velma had spent in Hawaii last summer was still working wonders with the proprietor's sense of humor.

❋

"You got lost in a dern *cave*?" Dooley yelled into the phone.

"Totally!" Where Dooley Barlowe was concerned, only the bald truth would do. "Completely!"

"Totally, completely lost? Man!"

"Want to do it sometime?"

"What? Get lost in a cave? No way."

"You don't know what you're missing," he said.

"Did ol' Cynthia get scared?"

"Terrified."

Dooley cackled. "Did you get scared?"

"What do you think?"

"I think it scared th' poop outta you, is what I think."

"You hit the nail on the head, buddy."

Dooley Barlowe sounded as if he were rolling on the floor. Maybe, just maybe, hearing Dooley laugh was the payoff for that miserable experience.

❋

A dollar off a horned toad that turned out to be tuna salad, and a ripping good laugh out of Dooley Barlowe....

So far, so good, for a couple of hours spent stumbling around in the dark.

When he arrived home at five-thirty, he thought he had never smelled such a seductive aroma in his life, though something in his stomach was definitely off.

"Leg of lamb!" exclaimed Cynthia.

"Man!" Sometimes there was nothing else to do but quote Dooley Barlowe.

"And glazed carrots, and roasted potatoes with rosemary."

"The very gates of heaven."

"Dearest," she said, putting her arms around his neck, "there's something different about you...."

"What? Exhaustion, maybe, from only four hours of sleep."

She kissed his chin. "No. Something deeper. I don't know what it is."

"Something good, I fondly hope."

"Yes. Very good. I can't put my finger on it, exactly. Oh. I forgot—and a salad with oranges and scallions, and your favorite dressing."

"But why all this?"

"Because you were so brave when we were lost in that horrible cave."

The payoff was definitely improving. He brushed her hair back and kissed her forehead. "It wasn't so horrible."

"Timothy ..."

"OK," he said, "I was scared out of my wits."

She laughed. "I knew that!"

"You did not."

"Did so."

"Did not."

"Are y'uns havin' a fuss?" Uncle Billy peered through the screen door.

"Not yet," said the rector. "Come in and sit!"

"I cain't. I dragged m'self down here t' give you m' tithe, as Rose is on to me akeepin' it in th' newspapers. She's done gone through a big stack alookin' for it, don't you know. It's a scandal what a man with a little cash money has t' put up with, ain't it?"

"I don't have a clue, Uncle Billy. I never had much cash money."

"I hear you'n th' missus was lost in a cave. I got lost in a cave when I was a boy. Hit's somethin' you don't never forget. Them red Inyuns that roamed these mountains, they knowed caves like th' back of their hands, but th' white feller cain't hardly go a step without broad daylight in 'is face."

"That's a fact," he said.

"I hear your dog pulled you out, or y'uns might've been in there 'til Christmas."

Barnabas, who was lying under the kitchen table, thumped his tail on the floor.

"He's the man of the hour, all right," said the rector, stepping outside. "They say he led them straight to us, nearly a quarter of a mile in. We got to bed about three o'clock this morning."

"I hope y'uns didn't drink no water while you was in there."

"Why's that?"

"Oh, law, that cave water can send you high-steppin', don't you know. It don't hit you right off, might take a while, but let them cave germs git t' workin', and first thing you know ..." The old man shook his head, grinning.

"Uncle Billy, would you do us a favor?" Cynthia asked through the screen door.

"If they was anybody I'd do a favor, hit'd be you 'uns."

"Would you take the nice, fresh chocolate cake Esther brought today? We can't touch a bite. We'd just have to throw it out."

"Oh, law!" said Uncle Billy, stricken at the thought. "Me an' Rose'll be glad to take it off y'r hands if hit'll help y'uns out."

"Thanks be to God!" she said when Uncle Billy left with his

foil-wrapped parcel. "If he hadn't taken it, I would have eaten the whole thing! I would have absolutely stuffed it in my ears."

"Dodged a bullet," he said, feeling his stomach wrench.

She sat down suddenly in a kitchen chair.

"What is it? You're white as a bed sheet."

"I don't know. Oh, dear. Oh, no!" She bounded from the chair and sprinted down the hall to the guest bathroom, clutching her stomach.

His own stomach gave a loud, empathetic gurgle, signaling what he recognized as a dire emergency.

"Cave germs!" he shouted, racing upstairs.

✳

Dog Rescues Rector and Wife
Lost Fourteen Hours
In Hidden Cave

He peered at the latest edition of the *Muse.*

That Cynthia Kavanagh looked terrific, even when smeared with mud from head to toe, was no surprise.

As for himself, his face looked oddly like a turnip that had just been yanked from the ground. Worse yet, the photo of them staggering out of the cave was shot at such close range, he could see the whites of his own eyes. Not a pretty sight.

The photo of Barnabas, on the other hand, was snapped from such a great distance that it appeared to be a ground squirrel that had led the rescue team.

He fogged his glasses, wiped them on the lapel of his old burgundy bathrobe, and scanned the story.

He had *not* said they found the fossil remains of a dinosaur, much less discovered a *vase* in a vault.

And he certainly didn't care for J.C.'s insinuation that all they'd done was sit around eating candy, waiting to be rescued.

In any case, he made a mental note to pick up extra copies of the paper for Walter and Katherine, and one for Father Roland in Canada, all of whom were patently wrong to believe he led a rustic and uneventful life.

*

The mayor called at 5:00 a.m. and asked him to hotfoot it to the hospital, where Puny's labor was intense, and they were worried.

He had barely skidded into the deserted hallway when Nurse Herman found him and steered him toward the delivery room.

"I can't go in there," he said.

"Why not?" demanded Nurse Herman. "Everybody else does. It's the latest thing to watch the birth."

What could people be thinking, to stand around and watch babies being born, as if the whole affair were some daytime TV show? Didn't they have anything else to do, like mow their lawns or work for a living?

"Besides, th' mayor wants you to pray," said Nurse Herman.

He ran a finger around his collar, which suddenly seemed constricting. "I can do that standing in the hall!"

Esther Cunningham opened the door and poked her head into the hallway. "There you are!" she snapped, as if he had taken hours to arrive. "One just popped out, it's a girl, we're on a roll."

Nurse Herman shoved him into the room, where he saw Joe Joe sitting by Puny, her sweat-drenched red hair spread over the pillow. Joe Joe's mother, Marcie Guthrie, stood across the room covering her face with her hands, but observing the proceedings through her fingers. At the sink, a nurse cleaned up a red-haired infant, who was crying lustily.

"Bear down!" said Joe Joe.

"Pray!" said the mayor.

"Breathe!" said Dr. Wilson.

"Oh, *Lord!*" said Marcie Guthrie.

The mayor's husband, Ray, leaned unsteadily on a chair, wearing a look of mortified horror.

"Ray's not up to this," said the mayor, "but it's the latest thing to do, and he likes to keep current."

The rector thought the whole event was closely akin to a political barbecue.

"Here it comes!" shouted Esther.

"Hallelujah!" whooped Marcie.

"It's a girl!" announced the doctor.

"Catch him!" cried Nurse Herman, as the rector toppled toward the floor.

✳

"Sissy and Sassy?" he inquired.

"It's really Kaitlin and Kirsten," said Puny, smiling hugely. "But we decided to call 'em Sissy and Sassy." She was holding one infant on either side. The whole lot had mops of red hair like he'd never seen before in his life.

"Which is, ah, Sissy and which is … ?"

"This," said Puny, shrugging her right shoulder, "is Sissy. And this," she said, shrugging her left shoulder, "is Sassy. You'll get to know 'em apart when they come to work with me."

"Take your time on that," he said, meaning it. "No hurry. Why not take a month? Or take two—we can manage!"

Puny looked at him, wide-eyed. "We'd never pay our bills if I laid out for a month or two! You know that bathroom we added on, our *own* self? It cost four thousand dollars, and that's without a toilet! Lord only knows when we can git a toilet!"

"Aha."

"They say you fainted when Sassy popped out!"

"Went black," he said, grinning. If Nurse Herman hadn't snatched him up, he might have cracked his skull on the tile floor.

"Don't y'all worry about a thing," Puny assured him. "I'll be back in two weeks, good as new."

He gazed at the new mother and her little brood, feeling a glad delight for the young woman who had taken over his home and his heart, all to his very great relief.

"You're the best, Puny Guthrie."

"I'll bake you a cake of cornbread first thing," she said, smiling happily.

✳

He had never bought a toilet before, but after some discussion about a wooden, plastic, or soft seat, and the new, economical tank capacity, he decided on a standard model and, to save the delivery fee, had it put in his trunk in two boxes and drove it to the Guthries' little cottage, where, with no small difficulty, he wrestled the boxes out of the car and onto the porch, and assembled the thing on the spot with the aid of his auto repair kit.

He couldn't help but observe, as he drove away, that it had a certain panache sitting there.

✳

He sat up in bed and listened. Was it the wind? The shadows on the ceiling weren't moving.

In the hall, Barnabas growled.

"What is it?" Cynthia asked.

"I heard something."

She sat up with him.

Someone was knocking at the door. Barnabas raced down the stairs and stood barking in the foyer.

When he reached the foyer, he turned on the porch light, grabbed his dog by the collar, and opened the door.

As long as he lived, he would never forget what he saw.

It was a girl, he knew that from the long blond hair that fell over her shoulders, but she had been beaten so brutally that her face made little sense to him.

"Good God!" he said.

She fell toward him, and he saw the smear of blood in her hair.

"Lace Turner," she murmured.

It was the girl who had jumped from the tree and landed at Absalom's feet, the girl who had stolen the ferns and run.

TWELVE

Lace

Barnabas barked wildly as the girl leaned against Father Tim to steady herself. "I got t' lay down som'ers."

He gripped her arms and drew her into the hallway. "You're OK," he said, his heart thundering. "I've got you."

"Git that dog away from me."

Cynthia appeared on the stairs. "Who is it?"

"It's a girl. She's badly hurt. Put Barnabas in the garage."

"Dear God!"

"I'll take her to the study."

Her knees gave way, and he moved to pick her up. "Don't touch m' back!" she cried. "Git me laid down." The look of appeal on her face was crucifying.

"Put your arm over my shoulder," he said. "I'll help you walk."

"I cain't. It pulls m' back."

Together, he and Cynthia eased her along the hall and into the study. "Quit … jigglin' me," Lacey murmured through bruised lips.

As his wife hurriedly spread an old blanket over the sofa, he became aware of the strong scent of blood and body odor, and something unidentifiable that wrenched his stomach. He sensed that it was, somehow, the smell of violence itself.

"Lay me down easy."

"Right. Easy does it."

She cursed as they helped her down. "Not on m' back!" she said. "On m' side."

The blood on her arms had crusted, but fresh blood appeared to be coming from her head, staining her hair at the crown.

"I'll call Hoppy," he said. "She needs a doctor."

"Don't call no doctor!" yelled Lacey, trying to raise her head. "Don't call no doctor, I don't need no doctor—"

"You're badly hurt."

"I been hurt worser. I ain't killed."

"You could be hurt internally."

"I ain't, I know m'self. If you call a doctor, I'm leavin'. Wash me off, git some salve on m' back."

"Can you do that?" he asked his wife.

"Yes," she said, looking pale. "Get hot water and soap and clean rags—those old diapers I use to clean silver. And bring the peroxide—and the bandages."

"Done," he said, going from the room, shaken.

✳

They sat in the study with a single lamp burning against the dark.

Cynthia had bathed Lacey's wounds and patiently worked the fibers of her shirt from the raw flesh on her back. She had cried out only once when the peroxide was swabbed into the swelling lesions, and said nothing as Cynthia applied an antibiotic ointment and bandages.

He made a strong, dark tea with sugar and lemon, and Cynthia spooned it onto Lacey's tongue, avoiding her swollen lips, then helped her lie again on her side, covered with a light blanket. She was silent, except for occasional sharp intakes of breath through her teeth.

He looked at his wife, sitting on a footstool drawn close to the sofa, and saw the suffering in her own face. She was moved to tears or laughter with nearly anyone at all, being as open as a door to the feelings of others.

"You're safe here," she told Lacey. "I want you to know that."

The girl nodded.

"How did you come to us?"

"Ol' Preacher Greer. I met 'im in th' road here lately. He said if I was ever to git bad hurt, run to th' preacher in th' collar, he takes in young 'uns."

"Did you know," asked the rector, "that the preacher in the collar was the same person you saw in the ferns?"

"I tol' Preacher Greer I couldn't run t' you, you'd done caught me stealin'. He said go on, anyway, he'll he'p you."

"You were brave to come to a strange house in the night," said Cynthia.

"I was s' skeered of Pap, it didn't make no mind t' me where I hid at. Preacher Greer wouldn't tell me wrong, so I come. Always before, I run t' Widder Fox, but she went off to th' ol' people's home. You cain't tell nobody I come here, or Pap'll lick me worse'n this."

"Why did your pap lick you, Lacey?"

"I don't go by Lacey, I go by Lace."

"Lace, then," said Cynthia. "Why did your pap lick you?"

"'Cause he was drunk and you cain't say nothin' to 'im if he's drunk. I knowed better, I should've hid under th' house or som'ers, but he come in th' house s' quick, I couldn't do nothin'. I quit diggin' ferns and rhodos, is what it was, an' he seen m' sack was empty. Two or three times, I repented of stealin' an' quit, and ever' time, he licked me bad.

"Me'n Jess is got t' dig twenty-five fern and sixteen rhodo a week when th' weather's good, and I ain't dug my half n'r nowhere near. So he said he was goin' to knock m' teeth out to where I couldn't eat nothin', as I wadn't doin' my part t' earn nothin' t' eat, then he took off 'is belt and got me with th' buckle. He was goin' to beat m' head in, but I give 'im m' back or he'd of killed me."

"Your mother ... can't she do something?"

"M' mam's got a blood ailment and cain't git outta th' bed. She lays there and hollers f'r 'im t' quit, but he don't."

His heart weighed in him like a stone. "Are you hungry?" he asked.

"I ain't eat, but I ain't hungry, neither. M' head's asplittin'."

"The capsules I gave you should help," said Cynthia. "Lace— please let us take you to the doctor, we'll pay for it, and there's no need for your father to know—"

"I ain't goin' t' no doctor—no way, nohow," she said, and sucked in her breath.

"The guest room ..." said the rector. "We could put her in bed so she can sleep."

"I cain't sleep. I got t' git back by daylight."

"You mustn't go back. You're in no condition—"

"I got t' feed m' mam. She won't eat a bite f'r nobody but me. M' pap, he'll be sleepin', an' Jess won't do nothin'. My mam'll die 'ithout me, she said she would."

"I don't think you should get up and go anywhere," said Cynthia. "There must be someone who can take care of your mother while you—"

"They ain't nobody, an' I ain't stayin'!" Lace said vehemently. "Leave me be 'til I can git up an' go, an' I don't aim t' argue about it, neither. I hate town people. I hate th' guts of town people. You talk stupid." She cursed again, with the same feeling he had heard in Buck Leeper.

"We'll sit with you," Cynthia told her.

Like he had sat with Buck Leeper last year, through Buck's suffering. Unable to walk away, he had stuck with Buck's rage and lasted it out.

The clock ticked in the silent room as the hands moved slowly toward one in the morning.

Lord have mercy, he prayed silently, *Christ have mercy …*

✳

He dozed in the chair until five-thirty, when he heard Cynthia in the kitchen and went in and called Rodney Underwood at home.

Lace had slept fitfully, occasionally talking in her sleep or waking and asking for water. At a little past six, he helped her up, and she sat on the edge of the sofa.

He placed his hands on her head gently, over the place that had bled, and prayed for her. It was madness to let her leave, but her determination to go to her mother was final and complete; he felt the sheer, unswerving power of it.

Cynthia wiped the girl's face with a damp cloth, helped her swallow hot cocoa from a spoon, then knelt to put her shoes on.

"I've brought you some socks," Cynthia said.

"I don't want no socks. Pap'll be wantin' t' know where they come from."

"You'll need peroxide and ointment on your back every day for a while. Can you come and let me treat you?"

"They ain't no way."

"Will your father be up when you get home?"

"He'll lay asleep 'til up in th' day, but my mam, she'll be needin' me. She'll want 'er egg and coffee, she cain't go 'ithout it."

"Your school … is it over yet?"

"I don't go t' no school. I laid out s' long, they come lookin' f'r me, but Pap told 'em I'd went t' Tennessee t' live with 'is kin people."

He saw the pain in Cynthia's face as she tied the laces of the battered work shoes. "I've packed your breakfast. There's hard-boiled eggs and rolls and bacon and fruit and cheese. You must eat, Lace, and keep your strength."

"If I git a notion...."

They helped her up and led her through the kitchen, where he opened the screen door and held it. "What can we do?" he asked, hoarse with feeling.

"Nothin'. I thank you f'r washin' me an' all."

Cynthia touched the girl's hand. "Come back, Lace," she said.

"Anytime," he added.

They watched her go across the yard, walking as if bent with age. She passed through the hedge that gave way to Baxter Park, and vanished in the cool morning mist.

They stood silent, then turned back to the kitchen, where they poured coffee and sat at the table.

Cynthia put her head in her hands. "We lead a sheltered life, Timothy ... out of the fray."

"The fray," he said, "has come to us."

※

According to Rodney, he'd have to go to social services and file a statement that Lacey Turner said she was being battered. A law enforcement officer could go along to investigate, but that was up to social services.

When he finally found the right office in Wesley and told what he knew, the social worker said matter-of-factly, "It happens all the time."

"How long will it take you to investigate and get back to me?"

"I'll put the report in today. Depends. Five days, a week at the most."

A week. Someone could be killed in a week.

He felt useless, impotent—stupid, somehow, like Lace Turner had said.

※

Dooley would be home from school in a matter of days. He'd ride down with a boy and his family on their way to Holding, and be delivered to the rectory. A blessed relief, given the demands of Cynthia's new book and his own commitments, which included plans for a surprise celebration of Miss Sadie's ninetieth birthday, to be held in the parish hall Sunday after next.

There was no question in his mind that a blowout was in order.

Hadn't Sadie Baxter given five million dollars to Lord's Chapel, to build one of the finest nursing homes in the state? And hadn't her father, and then Miss Sadie herself, kept a roof on the church building throughout its long history?

He called the bishop, to ask whether he could attend, but Stuart Cullen had no fewer than four events on the Sunday in question, all of them miles from Mitford.

"Emma," he said, "call the entire parish and tell them they're invited."

Emma's lip curled. "Call th' whole bloomin' mailin' list?"

"The whole blooming list," he said, his excitement mounting.

"That's a hundred and twenty households, you know."

"Oh, I know." He was pleased with the number, especially as it had risen by seven percent in two years, even with the recent loss to the Presbyterian camp.

"I suppose you realize that nobody's ever home anymore, to *answer* the phone."

He couldn't argue that point. "So have cards done at QuikCopy. But you'll have to get them in the mail no later than tomorrow. Oh. And remember to say it's a surprise."

"It's certainly a surprise to me."

"When we get our computer," he said jauntily, "it'll knock the labels out in no time. Until then …"

She glared at him darkly. "I'll have to address every blasted one by hand."

"Every blasted one," he said, swiveling around in his chair and dialing Esther Bolick. This was an occasion for a three-tier orange marmalade cake, and no two ways about it.

✳

"Have you found out anything?" he asked the social worker. It had been only four days since he had filed the complaint, but it didn't hurt to ask.

"I can't say. I haven't seen anything on it."

"Have you investigated?"

"The person responsible for the investigation isn't in today. You'll be advised as soon as possible."

"I'll call back," he said.

✳

Cynthia agreed to buy the birthday present in Wesley when she went to get new towels and washcloths for the rectory. She thought it should be a cardigan sweater, a blend of wool and cotton, even silk.

"Spare no expense!" he said, feeling a warm largesse toward his all-time favorite parishioner.

Emma softened and bought a silver-plated letter opener, as Miss Sadie had lost hers and was using a kitchen knife with a serrated edge. "She goan cut her han' off jus' openin' th' 'lectric bill," Louella said. "An' th' 'lectric company already takin' a arm an' a leg."

He called Katherine in New Jersey, thinking she might like to drop a card to the lady who'd been kind to her on a long-ago visit to Mitford.

Katherine proceeded to give yet another of her sermons on why he and Cynthia should go to Ireland with them in August, and he responded with yet another sermon on why they could not, the chief reason being that Dooley Barlowe would still be home from school, and he wanted to spend every possible moment with the boy.

"Oh, well," said his cousin's wife, "I'll keep trying. In the meantime, I'll send Miss Sadie two of the pot holders I'm making for our church bazaar."

He didn't mention that the pot holders she once sent him had unraveled to the size of petits fours, and faded in the wash on his underwear.

The Sweet Stuff Bakery volunteered to make vegetable sandwiches, and the ECW promised to round up trays of lemon squares, brownies, and ham biscuits, not to mention a heap of Miss Sadie's favorite party food, which was peanut butter and jelly on triangles of white bread without crusts.

He jogged up Old Church Lane to the Hope House site to render an invitation to Buck Leeper, and marveled at the way construction was humming along. The windows, at last set in place, reflected the afternoon sun like so many squares of gold. Dazzling!

Buck would, indeed, come to the party, though the fact that it was being held in a church building did not appear to increase his eagerness.

Father Tim ordered ice cream, and plenty of it, vanilla *and* chocolate, and rummaged through drawers in the parish hall kitchen for birthday candles. He came up with fewer than twenty-one pink candles, and made a note to pick up more at the drugstore, along with a container of rouge called Wild Coral, which Miss Sadie once said she liked.

Esther Bolick would play the piano, Mayor Cunningham would deliver a speech, and Dooley Barlowe, he felt certain, would sing.

In advance of the occasion, Cynthia brushed his best dark suit and picked one of two silk squares for his jacket pocket. He shined his shoes and wrote, in longhand, a poem that he would read aloud. He rifled through his study library to find any references to "birthday" that might be funny, wise, thought-provoking, or all of the above.

He supposed he should let Louella in on it, and popped over to Lilac Road during Miss Sadie's nap time.

"You ain't!" said Louella. "You ain't gone an' done all that!"

"I certainly have," he said, suspicious of her frown.

"Miss Sadie don't want no big doin's for her birthday, she done tol' me that."

"What do you mean?"

"She say, 'Louella, don't you let nobody be singin' and jumpin' aroun'.'"

"But Miss Sadie likes singing and jumping around!"

"Not this time, she don't. She ain't feelin' herself. Ever since she fell off th' sofa and broke her wris' bone, she been grumpy as you ever seen." Louella shook her head. "I don' know. She ain't sick, she ain't ailin', she jus' ain't th' same Miss Sadie."

"Let me have a word with her." Sadie Baxter was not a grumpy person. She was sunshine itself. Maybe he should tell her about the party, how excited people were. That would fix everything, no problem.

"Come eat with us Wednesday, after Holy Euc'ris'," said Louella. "I'll have a pot of snap beans an' a cake of cornbread. It puts her in a good mood t' have comp'ny."

"Done!" he said, feeling encouraged.

✳

It was the last thing he needed in his life, the very last thing he needed on the whole of this earth. The prospect made a series of root canals seem nothing at all, a picnic.

"We'll be there tomorrow," said the computer technician.

✳

He went to the Grill for breakfast, as Cynthia had been up since four-thirty working on an illustration due in New York, pronto.

Sliding into the booth, he felt as if breakfast were his last supper.

"Business has fell off," said Percy, looking gloomy.

"Looks th' same to me," said Mule, eyeing the room. "An empty stool or two ..."

"I cain't afford a empty stool or two, especially with th' new help I've got on th' breakfast shift. Th' doc said, 'Percy, take a load off your feet,' so here I set, swillin' coffee like th' rest of th' loafers."

"You'll catch up," said J.C., unusually consoling.

"I cain't see how. Th' price of cookin' oil is up, th' price of eggs is up, even bread has went up. I need to expand my customer base."

"You've got us," said Mule. "We come in regular as clockwork. That ought to count for something."

"I cain't make a livin' off a preacher, a part-time realtor, and a jack-leg newspaper man. I got to advertise."

"I can't believe you used that dirty word," said J.C., chewing a combination mouthful of sausage, eggs, toast, and grits. "You've fought advertisin' like a chicken fights a hawk."

"I'm not talkin' ordinary, run of th' mill advertisin' like news-papers and such."

"Thanks a lot."

"I'm talkin' a banner to hang over my awnin'."

"A banner," said J.C., obviously bored with the conversation.

"Happy Endings uses banners, th' Collar Button puts up two banners a year at sale time ... an' remember how they lined up when Th' Local did a banner on fresh collards last October?"

"Who can keep up with such as that?" asked Velma, refilling their cups. "Lord, I hardly know where I was yesterday, much less who lined up for collards last October."

"You was here yesterday," Percy said helpfully. "From ten t' two. I needed you from eight t' two, but you was havin' your hair dyed."

"Put that on a banner," Velma snapped. "Most people think this is my natural color."

"What do you want the banner to say?" asked the rector.

"Dern if I know, I just this mornin' decided to do it."

"How much does a banner cost?" Mule asked.

"Two hundred dollars."

Mule blew on his coffee. "What it says better be good, then."

"Memorable," suggested the rector.

"Right," said Mule.

Percy looked at Father Tim. "What do you think it ought to say? You write sermons and put those snappy little notions on your wayside pulpit. And here sets th' editor of th' local paper, a scribbler and a half, to my mind. Seems like between th' two of you, you could come up with what to say."

"How many words?" asked J.C.

"No more'n ten. More'n ten, th' price goes up and readership goes down. That's th' rule for billboards same as banners, is what th' banner man says."

"Homeless Hobbes," said the rector. "He's your man. He was in advertising. Did cereal, automotive, and toothpaste."

"I don't have time to go stumblin' around th' Creek, gettin' my head shot off by one of them hillbillies. I got to get right on this thing."

"When it comes to advertising," said J.C., "there's always some big deadline deal. You waited this long, why can't you give a man a day or two to come up with the copy?"

"If I call it in today, th' paint dries Thursday, an' it's delivered Friday. That way, I get drive-by recognition all weekend, and when I open th' door on Monday mornin'—full house!" It was a rare occasion when Percy Mosely smiled.

J.C. sopped his toast around his plate and handed the plate to Velma as she walked by. "No need to wash that." He took out a handkerchief and mopped his face. "So why don't we come up with a line right now?"

"Right now?"

"Why not? I can't be laborin' over a dadblame banner like I got nothing else to do."

"I'll throw in a free breakfast, two mornin's," said Percy.

"Two mornings?"

"Three."

"With sausage?"

"Links or patties, your call."

"Deal," said J.C., taking a legal pad from his bulging briefcase and a pencil from his shirt pocket. "OK, what's the occasion? Free refills on coffee? Twenty percent off for senior citizens?"

"Just general."

"General? You can't write great advertising about general. You got to have particular. In fact, outstanding particular. The finest pies, the cheapest breakfasts, the biggest salad bar. Like that."

"I got one," said Mule. "*This is the best place to eat in town.*"

J.C. rolled his eyes. "This is the only place to eat in town."

"Scratch that," said Mule.

The rector smoothed his paper napkin and took out the pen he won in an American Legion raffle. "Since this is the only place, being better than somebody else won't hack it. Maybe you need to give something away."

"Balloons!" said Mule. "Bumper stickers! Mugs!" He looked around the table. "How about refrigerator magnets?"

Percy wagged his head vigorously. "I ain't givin' nothin' away. Look what I'm givin' away now—breakfast, two ninety-nine; cheeseburgers, a buck-fifty; BLTs, a buck-eighty when I ought t' be haulin' down two dollars ... nossir, I ain't givin' nothin' else away."

"Right," said Velma.

"Th' deal," Percy said, "is to pull in some new people, people that could be stoppin' by on their way to work in Wesley or Holding, like that. Or people that's packin' their lunch and could be eatin' right here just as cheap."

"OK," said Father Tim, "what about a line ... something like ... these aren't the words, just the gist of it ... something like, check us out and you'll come back again and again. I don't know. This is hard."

"That doesn't have any spin on it," said J.C., chewing the pencil.

"Spin?" said Percy. "What's that?"

"What time is it?" asked the rector, checking his watch. "Good Lord! I'm out of here."

"What's th' hurry?" said Mule. "The fun's just beginnin'."

That, thought the rector as he raced to the office, was not how he would describe things, at all.

✳

"There you go," said the technician, slapping a manual on his desk.

The rector picked it up and stared at it. It was heavier than his study edition of the Old Testament, something close to the weight of a truck tire.

He thumbed through to the back as the technician plugged in the keyboard. Eight hundred and twenty-nine pages! If this didn't turn out to be the worst experience of his life, he'd eat the index—a mere ten pages, including appendices.

Emma had scarcely moved since he arrived at the office. She sat at her desk, as frozen as a halibut, and deathly pale under two spots of rouge. He could not come up with one word of consolation.

"Before we go into your spreadsheet application," said the

technician, whose name was Dave, "let's take a look at your word processing toolbars."

"Aha."

"Would you like to hide your toolbars or display them?"

Honesty was the best policy. "I don't have a clue."

"OK, so let's get basic."

"Right."

"Let's start with your mouse, and practice pointing, clicking, and dragging."

Emma didn't move her head, but rolled her eyes around to watch the demonstration.

"OK, put your hand on your mouse like this...." Dave demonstrated. "Click it. Fun, right? You're off and running. Now, let's choose a menu option. Or would you rather use a keyboard shortcut?"

"What do you, ah, recommend?" he asked.

"Hey, I bet you'd like choosing a keyboard shortcut."

"I'm a shortcut kind of guy," he said.

Emma rolled her eyes, but still didn't move her head.

"OK, great. Position the insertion point in the text ... oops, hey, no problem. OK, click your mouse button. Right. Very good. And press this key. No, the other one. Lost that.

"OK. Here we are in Dialog Boxes. You'll really like Dialog Boxes. Hey, there are your Fonts! And look, there's Roman. Being Catholic, you'll probably go for that, ha ha, just kidding. I'll be darned. Never seen that before. Things change so fast in this business, you can't keep up. I was in chicken feed before I got into computers.

"Man, look at this, you'll love this, it's a zoom box ... right there on your standard toolbar. Just click the down arrow to select the percentage you want ... right ... hey, two hundred percent, you're a high roller. Terrific.

"Actually," said Dave, looking suddenly profound, "I should probably show you how to create a document ... or would you rather learn to save one?"

"With the, ah, little I know about it, it seems you can't save something you haven't created."

"Great line. A little religion there, right? OK. Creating a document. Click your New button on your standard toolbar. Hey. Very good. First thing you know, we'll be into typing, editing, opening, and saving."

Emma lunged from her chair and ran into the bathroom, slamming the door.

*

He went home early.

Parked outside his back stoop was a baby carriage. A double baby carriage, with a cheerful striped awning. Standing at the screen door, he heard a lively combination of sounds, including his dryer set on spin, his washing machine in the rinse cycle, his vacuum cleaner going full throttle, and something like rusty gate hinges moving back and forth.

Stepping inside, he discovered the gate hinges were squeals of joy and shrieks of delight. There on the kitchen floor in front of his stove were Sissy and Sassy, belted into small recliners that appeared to be rocking or jiggling.

Their attention was riveted on something hanging above them, which was attached to the light fixture. It was a gaggle of geese, and not only were they moving in a circle, but they were bobbing their heads and quacking.

"Well, well, well," he said, peering down at two happy faces.

"Father!" said Puny, coming down the hall at a trot. "We're glad as anything to see you! Th' girls are jus' dyin' to git t' know you! Looky here, Sassy, it's th' father, and Sissy, honey, you are soppin'! Father, wouldn't you like t' play with Sassy while I change Sissy? Then you can hold Sissy while I feed Sassy! Won't that be fun?"

✳

Cynthia breezed in the back door at six o'clock, carrying a pink rattle she had found in the yard. "Hello, darling! Aren't those twins adorable?"

She laid the rattle on the table and peered at him. "Oh, dear, you don't look so good."

"You never mince words, Mrs. Kavanagh."

"Well, but dearest, you don't. Are you all right?"

"Oh ..." He shrugged, speechless.

"And what's that on your shoulder? It looks like pigeon poop."

"Really?"

"And your hair. It's standing up funny on both sides."

"No kidding."

"Your eyes ..." she said, unrelenting, "they're sort of ... glazed over."

"I'll be darned."

"If you were a drinking man, I'd offer you a double scotch."

"If I were a drinking man," he said, "I'd take it."

THIRTEEN

Homecoming

He checked his calendar.

Following Holy Eucharist at eleven, he was having lunch with Miss Sadie and Louella, then racing home to put the new spread on Dooley's bed, which he'd buy in Wesley following a nine o'clock meeting at the Children's Hospital, during which he would try to wrestle money from a donor—a job he hated more than anything on earth.

Dooley was arriving at the rectory at two-thirty, and they'd promised to give his friend's parents a quick refreshment before they continued down the mountain to Holding.

Cheese and crackers ...

He was supposed to pick up cheese and crackers right after the meeting at the hospital—and don't forget livermush. Russell Jacks was primed for livermush, and no two ways about it. The rector determined to buy six pounds and freeze four, and let Dooley make a delivery to his grandfather tomorrow morning. A fine boy in clean clothes, talking like a scholar and bearing two pounds of livermush? It was enough to make a man's heart fairly burst with pride—his own as well as Russell's.

He could hardly wait to see Dooley Barlowe, and Cynthia was preoccupied with her own excitement. She had cleaned the boy's room to a fare-thee-well, hung new curtains, and bought a remote for his TV set.

After showing him her handiwork, they had passed the guest room and paused to look in.

"Next fall," she said, eyeing the bare wall at the foot of the bed, "the armoire."

"Next fall—the armoire," he repeated.

"Right there," she said, staring at the wall. "Perfect."

"Next fall," he said. "Perfect."

✳

Miss Sadie was wearing a blue dress with an ecru lace collar and one of her mother's hand-painted brooches. He didn't think he'd ever seen her looking finer. Her wrist appeared almost normal, and the car key was hanging on a hook in the kitchen, untouched in recent months, thanks be to God!

They sat down to green beans and cornbread, with glasses of cold milk all around, and held hands as he asked the blessing.

"Lord, we thank you for the richness of this life and our friendship, and for this hot, golden-crusted cornbread. Please bless the hands that prepared it, and make us ever mindful of the needs of others."

They had hardly said "Amen" when Miss Sadie shook out her paper napkin as if it were starched damask and peered at him.

"I hear," she said sternly, "that you're fixing up a surprise party for my birthday."

He glanced at Louella.

"Don' look at me, honey, I didn' say nothin'."

"Esther Cunningham slipped and told me without meaning to." Miss Sadie looked disgusted. "She went red as a turkey gobbler, and said she ought to slap her own face for doing that."

"Th' mayor done blabbed it," Louella said, in case he hadn't heard right.

"I thought you liked parties," he said. There it was again, the feeling that he was twelve years old.

"I do like parties."

"Well, then?"

"I don't want a party on an even year. It's bad luck, and everybody in creation knows it."

"I never heard that in my whole life," he said, and he hadn't. He yearned to light into his cornbread, but waited for Miss Sadie to pick up her fork.

"You should have had a party last year when I was eighty-nine," his hostess told him, as if he didn't possess enough sense to get in out of the rain. "Now it's too late."

"Too late?" he said, offended. "Miss Sadie, need I remind you that it's never too late?" He didn't have time to stand on ceremony. He buttered his cornbread and broke it and took a bite. Man alive! Crunchy on the outside, soft and steaming on the inside. Had he died on the way up Old Church Lane and gone to heaven?

Miss Sadie forked a bean and looked at it.

"You didn' say nothin' to th' Lord 'bout my beans," Louella reminded him.

"I didn't?"

"Jus' th' cornbread," she said darkly.

What was the matter with people around here, anyway? Fernbank had been a place where the sun shone, birds sang, and flowers bloomed in the dead of winter. And now look. Louella once told him that if Miss Sadie cried, she cried, and if Miss Sadie laughed, she laughed. She said her joints ached when Miss Sadie's did, and their necks got stiff at the same time. There you have it, he thought. Miss Sadie was the culprit, and he was going to fix the problem or bust.

"Miss Sadie, I think you owe it to everybody to let them give you a surprise birthday party."

"Who is everybody?"

"Why, the entire parish! One hundred and twenty families! People who know you and care about you."

That got her, he could tell. But he'd have to step on it if he wanted to build any kind of momentum. "Besides, Sunday after next, you won't even *be* ninety."

"I won't?"

"Certainly not. Your birthday falls on Saturday, so guess what?"

"What?"

"On Sunday, you'll already be in your ninety-first year." Smoke that over, he thought, pleased with himself.

"Thass right," said Louella, crumbling the cornbread and dumping it in her milk.

Two against one, he observed. He helped himself to another piece of cornbread and laid on the butter. If his wife knew he was doing this ...

"I'm too old to be jumping around at a birthday party," his hostess declared.

"Nonsense!" he said, with feeling. "Nonsense!"

He had never spoken to Sadie Baxter like that in his life. Lightning might strike at any moment. He was ready to duck.

"You've certainly gotten cheeky in your old age, Father!" She sat back in her chair and looked at him imperiously.

Louella tried to suppress a laugh, but failed, and clapped her hand over her mouth.

Miss Sadie glared at her and then at him. He was ready to duck, all right.

Then she began to laugh. She laughed and laughed some more. So did he. So did Louella. They roared, they rocked in their chairs, they slapped the table.

He hauled out his handkerchief, Miss Sadie used her napkin, and Louella fetched a paper towel from over the sink.

They wiped their eyes. They blew their noses.

"Two o'clock in the parish hall, Sunday the fourteenth!" he announced. "Be there or be square!"

*

A little depression, he mused, as he drove toward the rectory. That's what had gotten into Sadie Baxter. Too much sitting around. Not enough hurtling through the streets in her green 1958 Plymouth. And no rummaging through the attic at Fernbank, which had been one of her favorite pastimes.

He'd had a call or two from prospective chaplains for Hope House, and needed to respond to at least five letters of inquiry. As soon as the search process was seriously under way, he'd ask Miss Sadie to look over the applications with him. That might help her spirits. In the meantime …

He had received a letter this morning from social services. The letter, which he suspected of being a form letter, said they were continuing the investigation and would advise him further.

He glanced at the copy of the New Testament on the front seat of his car as he parked in the garage. How he wished he had given it to Lacey Turner. Could she read? He thought he might call the social worker again, in case they had learned something....

Barnabas leaped up as he came into the kitchen, barking to beat thunder. He didn't bother to haul forth a Scripture verse; he took the lavish licking on both ears and was darned glad to get it. Today was the day! Today, Dooley Barlowe was coming home.

"Where's your wife at?"

He turned and saw Lacey Turner on the other side of the screen door.

"Lace!" She was filthy. The sight of her pierced his heart. Blond hair spilled from under the old hat she'd left behind in the fern grove.

"Come in!" He held the door open as she stared at his dog.

"Not 'til you put that dog som'ers else."

"This dog," he said, holding Barnabas by the collar and propping the door open with his foot, "is harmless. Look." He stroked his dog's head to prove his point.

"I don't trust dogs."

"Barnabas would protect you, not hurt you."

"My back's itchin' s' bad I cain't hardly stand it. I cain't reach back there, an' Pauline ain't home an' my mama cain't do nothin'. Where's your wife at?"

"She's next door. I'll get her. Look, come in. Barnabas will lie down right there, don't worry." He instructed his dog to lie on the rug by his water bowl, which he did at once. "We'll get your bandages changed. Sounds like the itching means you're healing up."

"Pap tried t' git me agin las' night, but I dodged 'im an' hid under th' house. Some ol' car oil was under there." Frowning, she brushed at her shirtsleeve as if to remove the dark stain.

"Sit here," he said, pulling out a kitchen chair. "And look, how about a glass of milk and"—of course!—"a bologna sandwich?" This household was ready for Dooley Barlowe, all right. They'd bought a deluxe family pack of his favorite lunch meat only yesterday.

"Don' put nothin' on it, I like t' died from eatin' mayonnaise onc't."

The rector dialed the little yellow house as Barnabas lay with his head on his paws, blinking at the girl.

"Lace is here. Yes. She's going to eat a bite. Her back is itching, and she's asking for you. Right."

"She's on her way," he said. What a good thing to have a wife to call at a time like this. He put two slices of bologna between two slices of bread and added chips to the plate.

"I cain't eat no pickles," she said, watching him take the jar from the refrigerator. "They sour m' stomach."

He looked at her hands. Not a pretty sight. "Want to wash up?"

"I done washed."

He set the sandwich before her and turned to pour a glass of milk. When he turned again, the sandwich had vanished.

"I'll fix you another one," he said, oddly happy.

"No more bread, jis' meat." The hat sat so low on her head, he could barely see her hazel eyes.

He was putting slices of bologna on her plate when he heard the front door open, and voices in the hallway.

"Lovely!" said a woman. "So old and charming! My grandfather was a minister."

"He gets his house from the church," said a man's voice. But it wasn't a man's voice, it was ...

His heart pounded for joy. Dooley Barlowe was home!

He handed the plate to Lace. "I'll be back!" he said, and bounded down the hall with Barnabas, who made a beeline for the woman and backed her into a corner by the door.

"Take no thought for the morrow!" the rector quoted loudly from Matthew. "For the morrow will take thought for the things of itself! Sufficient unto the day ..."

Barnabas collapsed obediently, as Dooley Barlowe came toward him, grinning. It was a sight he wanted never to forget. "Dooley!" he said, hugging the boy in the school blazer.

"Hey," said Dooley.

"Hey, yourself!"

Dooley stooped to scratch Barnabas under a floppy ear. "How's this ol' dog?"

"Father? Vince Barnhardt. I'm afraid we're a bit early." A portly man extended a hand.

"And I'm Susan Barnhardt," announced the smartly dressed woman, grabbing his hand and shaking it.

"Sorry about my dog," he said, shaking back.

Another hand came his way. "Joseph, sir. How do you do?"

He felt enough energy pumping through the rectory to light up downtown Wesley.

"Hello!" said Cynthia, coming along the hall and embracing Dooley. "Why, you big lug, look how you've grown, I can't bear it. Squeeze down a couple of inches this minute!" She gave Dooley a resounding kiss on the cheek, which caused his face to turn red.

"Isn't it amazing how they grow in school?" asked Susan, who was now shaking Cynthia's hand.

"Amazing! Come into the dining room," said his wife. "I've set out lemonade and cookies, and cheese and crackers, and I'm just popping back to the kitchen a moment. Please excuse me."

Cynthia slid away, leaving him with what seemed a swarm of people, who were noting everything from his grandmother's silver service to the "unusual" color of the dining room walls to the size of his dog and the generous platter of walnut cookies.

He had entertained to a fare-thee-well as a bachelor, but now, let his wife leave it up to him for five minutes, and he was dashed if he could remember how to pull it off.

"How was your drive down?" he asked, pouring lemonade into glasses.

"Wonderful!" said Susan Barnhardt. "Dooley kept us entertained the whole way."

Dooley? Kept them entertained? A new thought.

"I want some milk," said Dooley, going off to the kitchen.

"I can't eat nuts," announced Joseph, peering at the cookies. "I have braces."

"I can eat nuts," said his father. After piling several cookies on a plate, he turned to the rector. "I've always wondered—what's it like to be a preacher?"

"Have a seat in the living room," said the rector, "and I'll try to answer that."

When everyone was seated with glasses and coasters and cookies and cheese and crackers and napkins, he sat on the piano bench and tried to address the question. How did he know what it was like to be a preacher? He never considered what it was like. He just did it, and that was that.

"Well," he said, wishing for his wife. "Let's see ..."

"It must be interesting," said Vince.

"Oh, it is."

"Busy?"

"Absolutely. Keeps me hopping."

"Has its stresses, I suppose."

"Definitely. Definitely. What's your calling, Vince?"

"Prosthetics," said Vince.

"Aha. And what's it like to be in prosthetics?" By George ...

Dooley walked in with a plate of cookies and a glass of milk. "Cynthia said she'll be here in a minute. Who's that in the kitchen?"

"That's Lacey Turner."

"Gross," said Dooley, with obvious distaste.

＊

"Don't go to your room yet," he told Dooley. He had left the new spread on the backseat of his car and wanted to put it on the bed before Dooley saw his renovated room.

"I already went," said Dooley. "I took Joseph up there while you all talked about artificial legs."

"Arms. I bought you a new bedspread. It looks like an Indian blanket."

"Neat. I like my remote. But you still get the same old three channels. At school, we get fifty-four."

"Fifty-four? Amazing."

"It's not amazing, it's cable. You could get cable."

He had once entertained the idea, but decided to send the twenty dollars a month to the Children's Hospital. What did he need with the native dances of Malaysia, anyway, much less all the sports he could watch, when he never watched sports?

"You'll be too busy to lie around this summer watching fifty-four channels. Tommy wants you to go to his grandmother's place in Arkansas for two weeks, there's the town festival where you said you'd like to have a cold-drink stand, and I know Hal and Marge want you to come and visit—"

"I'm going out there to stay," said Dooley.

"What's that?"

"I'm going to spend the summer at Meadowgate Farm, helping out Doc Owen."

He felt his throat tighten. Had he heard wrong? "What do you mean, spend the summer at Meadowgate? We never talked about that."

"I wrote Miz Owen and asked her and she wrote back and said if it was all right with you, I could do it."

He felt an odd chill. "But I never said ... we never talked about ..."

"I knew you wouldn't care."

"But I do care. And Cynthia cares. We've been looking forward to seeing you, to having you home." He felt a kind of anguish, as if he would burst into tears. Then he felt the anger.

Dooley looked at him and shrugged.

✳

Hot.

He got up and took off his pajamas, and padded to the bathroom.

All the windows were open, but no breeze was stirring.

He went to the closet and, as quietly as he could, took the fan off the shelf without turning on the light. He removed the clock from the night table, set the fan in its place, and plugged the cord into the socket by the bed.

"Timothy, what in heaven's name are you doing? You sound like the charge of the light brigade."

"Plugging in the fan."

"With a large crew of helpers, I take it."

"Sorry," he said. "It's hot."

"Like a sauna."

He aimed the fan at the bed, turned it on high, and climbed in beside her.

"Wonderful," she said. "Well done."

They lay there, looking at the shadow of leaves on the ceiling.

"What is it?" she asked, finding his hand and holding it.

"What do you mean?"

"What's on your mind? I always know, you know."

Marriage had many benefits. But a wife who could read your mind didn't seem, at the moment, to be one of them.

"Dooley," he said.

She waited.

"He wants to go to Meadowgate for the summer."

"No!"

"Yes. And determined to do it, too."

"But why? Why not just a visit?"

"He wants to work with Hal, said he wrote Marge and she said he could do it if we agreed."

"Do we agree?"

"No! No, blast it."

"I hate this," she whispered. "We thought he'd be glad to come home."

"The truth is," he said, bitterly, "only we were glad. It was a one-way street."

"Why hasn't Marge mentioned this to us?"

"I don't know." Marge Owen was his oldest friend in Mitford, the first friend he had made here, fifteen years ago. He and Hal and Marge had been as thick as thieves until Dooley came to the rectory and Rebecca Jane was born to Meadowgate. Then they had drifted apart, but never, he thought, in their affections. They knew very well how he cherished the boy, but they cherished him, too, had grown close to him....

"Let me talk to Marge," said Cynthia.

"No, leave it. He wants to go. That's the whole point, after all. Not whether they somehow instigated this or how we feel about losing him. The point is, he wants to go."

Devastated. That's how he felt. Empty, yet filled with heaviness.

❋

He occasionally thought about the cave, how frightened they had been, and about the peace he had felt toward the end. He had learned something in there, but he didn't know what. Perhaps he didn't know what because he hadn't allowed himself to think about it, to chew over it. Things had been so busy, after all, there was no time for reflection.

Feast or famine, he mused, walking from the office toward the church. As a bachelor, he had nothing but time in the evenings. This was a different life, all right, and he was glad of it. Having his wife sit on his lap and muss what was left of his hair, waking up to a kiss that sent him reeling, spending hours with someone whose company he relished, who made his conversation seem witty when clearly it wasn't ...

Once again, mice had been gnawing at the retable, that venerable shelf to the left of the altar. According to the junior warden, they may need to replace the side paneling, would he have a look?

Mice had always been attracted to that particular spot, as if the wood were infused with Vermont cheddar.

While he was there, Emma said, he should check whether the coffeepot was left on from the lay readers' meeting in the parish hall last night. According to her, lay readers loved to leave the pot on 'til the contents turned to mud. Lay readers were, in her opinion, at the bottom of the church ladder, having no candles to light, no wine to dispense, no cross to carry, no linen to wash and iron, no sacramental bread to bake, no flowers to arrange, no music to learn—all they had to do was stand up there and read from a *book*.

He regretted not having time to spend with Lacey. She had gone before he could get away from the Barnhardts. He wanted to learn how her prayer on the creek bank had affected her heart and her spirit, what it had meant to her. What had it meant to the other people who flowed down the bank into the water, to be baptized in the name of the Father, the Son, and the Holy Ghost? What had changed back there on the Creek, that place where even angels feared to tread?

He unlocked the door to the narthex and went in, feeling at once his gladness to be there.

He was seldom alone in the church anymore—the parish was growing, and more and more often, someone was puttering about or having a meeting, or the tourists were trying to get in and see the ancient Mortlake tapestry, which was insured to the hilt.

He bowed before the altar and sat down in the second pew on the gospel side, and kicked his shoes off.

This was home.

He didn't much care about the mice, who were not, at least for the moment, dining on the retable. He wanted merely to sit and let the peace soak in, and the fragrance of the chestnut walls, and the years of incense and dried hydrangeas and fresh flowers and beeswax and lemon oil.

He had loved the smell of his churches over the years, perhaps especially the little mission church by the sea. With the windows cranked open to the fresh salt breezes, and the incense wafting about on high holy days, it was enough to send a man to the moon. The Protestants didn't think much of incense, and the culture of the Sixties hadn't done anything for its reputation, either, but he was all for it.

When the Lord was laying out the plan for the Tent of Meeting to Moses, He was pretty clear about it. He asked that Aaron "burn sweet spices every morning" when he trimmed and filled the lamps, and to burn them again in the evening. Bottom line, there was to be "a perpetual incense before the Lord, throughout the generations."

Ah, well, it wasn't worth wrangling over, incense. In the end, it was just one more snare of church politics.

Why are church politics so bitter? someone recently asked. Because the stakes are so small, was the answer.

He chuckled.

Lord's Chapel had had its share of political squabbles, but thanks be to God, not in the last three or four years. No, things had gone smoothly enough, and he was grateful.

But why was he musing on politics, when the church was so sweetly hushed and somehow expectant? The light poured through the stained-glass depiction of the boy preaching in the temple, through purple and scarlet and gold, and the azure of the boy's robe as he stood before the elders. That was one smart, courageous kid, he thought. I'm glad I know him.

"Rest. Rest. Rest in God's love," Madame Guyon had written. "The only work you are required now to do is to give your most intense attention to His still, small voice within."

He sighed and moved forward in the worn pew, and fell to his knees on the cushion.

"Lord," he said aloud, "I'm not going to pray, I only want to listen. Why does Dooley turn away from us?

"And what was the lesson of the cave?"

✳

Cynthia wasn't interested in pulling punches.

"I don't want to make Dooley feel guilty, that's not the point. What I want is for him to know how I feel. That's fair. And besides, why didn't he let us know?"

His style was to give the issue to God and haul it back again, ad infinitum, 'til the cows came home, until the thing finally wore itself out in him. His wife, however, had her own style.

"Dooley," she said over dinner at the kitchen table, "we were looking forward to your homecoming."

Dooley nodded.

"We love you, and we've been excited about having you home for the summer."

Dooley stared at the wall.

"It makes us sad that you're choosing to go to the farm."

Dooley took a mouthful of lasagna.

"We wanted to spend time together, but we respect your choice and want you to have a good summer and learn a lot from Dr. Owen."

Dooley nodded.

"But that's only part of how I feel. Here's the other part." She made eye contact with Dooley and held it. "You have hurt my feelings and made me mad as heck. Sometimes, I think you act like a creep."

Dooley gulped.

So did the rector.

So be it.

✳

"Did you see it?" asked Percy.

"See what?"

"Th' banner."

"Aha! Got it up, did you?"

Percy looked grim. "Went up this mornin' at ten o'clock. Caused a stir."

"It's hard to see a banner when it's on an awning over your head. I'll step across the street and take a look."

"They left a letter out of th' dadgum thing."

"You don't mean it."

"But they knocked fifty bucks off th' price."

"The least they could do."

"I started to tell 'em to jus' shove th' whole business, but ..." Percy shrugged, despondent.

"Go ahead and make me a tuna melt. I've got some leeway in my diet today. Be right back."

He jaywalked toward the other side of the street, barely dodging Esther Bolick in her husband's pickup truck. Esther screeched to a halt and leaned out the window. "I hear th' mayor leaked the news to Miss Sadie."

"We're forging ahead."

"I'm not doing orange marmalade," said Esther. "I'm doing peanut butter. Three layers, with jelly in between. Apple or grape?"

"Grape!"

"For gosh sake, get out of the street before somebody nails you," she said, roaring off.

Safely on the other side, he turned and peered at the banner over Percy's awning.

Eat Here Once, And You'll Be Regular

He guffawed, slapping his leg.

But whoa. He couldn't stand here laughing. What if Percy looked out the window and saw him?

He turned his back to the Grill as if he were examining the brickwork in the post office, and hooted. The postmaster stuck his head out the door and pointed to the banner, grinning. "I've also known it to be otherwise," he reported.

He trotted across the street. "Percy," he said, soberly, "I'd give the banner company their fifty dollars back."

"What do you mean?"

"I mean that banner is going to be the talk of the town."

Percy brightened. "You think so?"

"That's what advertising is all about, isn't it?"

"Well ..." said Percy.

"Trust me on this," said the rector.

✳

Cynthia put her arm around his waist. "You want me to do it?"

"I'll do it," he said.

He went to the study and sat at his desk and dialed the Owens. Barnabas followed and lay down at his feet.

"Hello? Meadowgate here."

"Marge? Timothy."

"Timothy!"

"I won't keep you ..."

"That's OK, Rebecca is sleeping and Hal is at a Grange meeting. How are you?"

"Good. Dooley says he's coming out to you for the summer."

"Is he? I ... I didn't know, exactly. I said if you all agreed ..."

"It's what he wants to do. Just wanted you to know that I'll need him here until Miss Sadie's party on Sunday the fourteenth."

"Of course! Well ... yes. Miss Sadie's party. We're looking forward to it."

"He's singing, you see."

"I see."

Long pause.

"Well, Marge. Thanks for everything. When shall we have him out there?"

"Oh … anytime. Just anytime that suits. Perhaps you could … send him home with us after the party?"

"Good. All the best to Hal, then."

"Yes, and to Cynthia."

He hung up, feeling his stomach wrench. He had never before been uncomfortable with Marge Owen; she had, in fact, been the one who had made him most comfortable from the very beginning. How often had he put his feet under their table, in the peace of the old farmhouse, while the duties of a new and difficult parish kept him spinning?

Another thing. It was clear that Dooley Barlowe hadn't exercised the good sense or common courtesy even to tell them he was definitely coming.

He hated this. He hated it.

✳

"I'm excited, Father, I just wanted you to know it." It was Sadie Baxter, and the old zing was back in her voice.

"That's what I like to hear. We're excited, too. It's mighty hard to dig up a brass band these days, but we're trying."

"Don't you go to any trouble, now!"

"Trouble? Why, Miss Sadie, trouble is what it's all about! If nobody went to any trouble in this world, the church would never have a roof. Cornbread would never get baked. Boys would never go to school."

She laughed. "Cynthia says Dooley is coming to visit us today."

"Around two o'clock, I think. You'll be looking at a new boy."

"Not so new he won't be hungry. You tell him not to stand on ceremony. Louella is fixing lemonade and cinnamon stickies just like Mama used to make."

"I'm jealous."

"You're a case is what you are!"

"Worse has been said," he assured her.

*

He woke up with it on his mind, and went downstairs to his study, padding as quietly as he could through the bedroom.

Five o'clock.

He had been getting up at 5:00 a.m. for years. It had become his appointed hour, even if he'd gone to sleep wretchedly late.

He leaned against the mantel and stretched, breathing the prayer he learned from his grandmother: *Lord, make me a blessing to someone today.*

Good. So good to stretch, to come alive, he thought, pushing up on the balls of his feet.

He would make coffee, he would read the Morning Office and pray, he would sit quietly for twenty minutes; then he'd go to the hospital, a round he made every morning, with rare exceptions.

Visiting the sick continued to be good medicine, as far as he was concerned. If he was having a rough go of it, all he had to do was pop up the hill to the hospital and self-concern went out the window.

When he retired, he intended to keep at that very thing....

When he retired?

He let the tension go from his arms and stood holding the mantel.

When he *retired*. Where had that come from?

He went to the kitchen and ground the beans and brewed the coffee, feeling an odd blessing in this simple daily ritual. A ritual of well-being, of safekeeping, in the still and slumbering house.

He took the steaming cup and set it next to his wing chair, then turned on the lamp and picked up his worn prayer book.

This was the time to fill the tank for the day's ride. He could put in a quarter of a tank and, later, get stranded on the road, or he could pump in a full measure now and go the distance.

But something was pushing ahead of the Morning Office.

Why haven't you answered those questions? he asked silently.

He had received nothing in that hour at the church but a sense of calm. That in itself was an answer, but not the one he was looking for.

Forgiveness.

He felt the word slowly inscribe itself on his heart, and knew at once. This simple thing was the answer.

"Forgiveness," he said aloud. "Forgiveness is the lesson of the cave...."

He sat still, and waited.

"And what about Dooley, Lord? Why does Dooley pull away from us?"

Again, a kind of inscription.

Ditto.

He shook his head. Ditto? God didn't talk like that; God didn't say ditto. He laughed out loud. Ditto?

He felt his spirit lifting.

Ditto! Of course God talks like that, if He wants to.

He got up and walked to the window and looked out at the new dawn.

He would have to forgive Dooley Barlowe and Marge and Hal Owen, whether he liked it or not.

FOURTEEN

The One for the Job

Coot Hendrick passed the rear booth on his way to the men's room. "I bin eatin' here thirty years," he said, "an' I ain't regular yet."

"Percy'll give you a dish of prunes," said Mule. Mule looked at the rector and dropped his voice. "Did you see who came in behind you?"

"Who?"

"Officer Lynwood. She's sittin' at th' counter."

"Aha."

Mule whistled. "Man ..."

"Man what?"

"What makes J.C. think he can handle that? She's packin' a nine-millimeter."

The rector laughed.

"Yogurt and dry toast won't hack that, in my opinion."

"J.C.'s not interested in your opinion."

"No kidding. What's your boy doin' this summer?"

"He's going to Meadowgate to help Hal Owen."

"I thought you were planning some big surprise camping trip, just you and him."

"I was planning that, but I've recently had enough surprise camping, thank you."

"There's J.C. comin' in. Well, I'll be ... he nodded to her like he never saw her before in his life."

"That's standard."

"It is?"

"When you're in love, sometimes you act like you don't know the other person."

"Is that a fact? I never acted like that. Did you?"

"Over and over again," said the rector.

"Why?"

"Beats me."

"Whoa, he's sittin' down right next to her. But he's not even lookin' her way."

"That's a sure sign."

"Of what?"

"Of something serious."

A long silence ensued while Mule peered toward the counter.

"Seems like he'd at least step back here and speak to his friends. After all, we've been meetin' in this booth for fifteen years. Maybe he's just chewin' the fat with Percy, maybe he'll walk on back in a minute or two. Dadgum. Percy just handed him a cup of coffee and some silverware. I can't believe it—th' blame fool is goin' to eat at the counter."

"He's outta here," said the rector.

"What'll y'all have?" asked Velma.

"Who cares?" sighed Mule, looking despondent.

※

It took innumerable phone calls and the repeated qualifier that he was clergy. When he finally received a return call from the social services investigator, he felt as if he'd gotten through to the Pentagon.

"According to all we can learn, it's true that Lacey Turner doesn't live in the Creek community. One neighbor said West Virginia, another said Tennessee. No one came to the door at the Turner house. We left a note for the family to contact us, but we don't have much hope of that happening."

"The girl is living there. I know it for a fact."

"We've had a confidential source on the Creek for some years, but she's gone to a county nursing home. Until we can locate another source of reliable information, we're forced to deal with the information at hand."

"You've got to do something. I'm telling you, this is an urgent situation."

"We can go in with a law enforcement officer, but that puts a different cast on it. The Creek shuts up like a clam when they see a uniform.... They shot three deputies in there in the last twelve, thirteen years. I don't think that's the way to go."

"What is the way to go?" He regretted the coldness in his voice.

"We could use a court order. That gets us inside the house to check, and might at least produce the girl."

"What would you do with the girl if you found her?"

"If things are like you say, she'd be removed from the home. But first we'd do a medical exam, check for any evidence of abuse."

"Removed from the home to where?"

"We'd look for a suitable relative, and if that didn't work— foster care."

"What excuse would you use for the court order?" he asked.

"The truth. A complaint of child abuse."

"What if you can't find the girl?"

"We're required by law to try and substantiate your report. Ideally, we substantiate it by locating the abuse victim and doing a medical exam. If we can't find her, we can use your report as substantiation, along with another witness who's seen her bruises. In this case, that could be your wife."

"Then?"

"Then it's turned over to the district attorney's office. They'll do a complete and thorough search to locate Lacey."

He felt shaken.

"You need to know," said the investigator, "that she probably doesn't want to leave the home. It may be a violent situation, but it's a known situation. However, a minor doesn't have the right to refuse help, and we'd be required to take her out of there."

"The mother ... she's an invalid. If Lacey leaves ..."

"If she's a mentally competent adult, she has a right to choose between leaving or staying. The odds are, she won't leave."

He was silent.

"There's something you ought to know, Father. In cases like this, there are very few happy endings."

"What," he asked, "is the bottom line here?"

"You did what the law requires you to do—you reported it. Bottom line, we have to do what the law requires us to do, which is try and locate the girl. We'll pursue a few other avenues, and if those fail, we'll use your report as substantiation—and the DA's office steps in."

He hung up the phone, distraught. If they found Lacey, they would take her away from her mother, which would be devastating to both. If Lacey managed to hide, God knows what her father might do to retaliate for the investigation.

He felt a weight unlike anything he'd known in years.

Who was he to cause more breakage in lives already broken?

※

He turned left at Winnie Ivey's cottage and headed along the creek to visit his old friend.

Homeless Hobbes knew the Creek community like the back of his hand—didn't he live on the edge of it, and feed half the neighborhood every Wednesday night from his big soup pot?

As he approached the minuscule house on the bank of Little Mitford Creek, he saw Homeless sitting on the front step reading, and Barkless trying unsuccessfully to bark.

"I'm seein' things," said Homeless, dropping the book and rubbing his eyes. "It's a vision of John th' Baptist, or is it one of th' old prophets wanderin' th' wilderness? Where you been?"

"Married, my friend, married. The days fly by, and the first thing you know …"

"You've fell off to a total stranger. Come and get you some lemonade before you have a heat stroke."

He followed Homeless and Barkless into the house, which, even with its thin walls, seemed sweetly cool inside the oven of summer.

He saw that his friend, who often boasted of owning only one pair of britches, was clad in a fine pair of corduroy trousers with leather braces.

"Homeless, you're looking natty."

"Found these in th' Dumpster off Kildale Road, same as Miss Rose Watson used to plunder when she could hitch a ride that way. These come from a widder woman whose husband kicked. They say she didn't give a plugged nickel for th' fella, jus' loaded all he had in her yardman's pickup an' sent it out to Kildale. I was standin' there like I knowed he was comin.' There was a watch in th' pocket of these britches. I sold it to Avis Packard for sixty dollars and give th' rest of th' stuff away."

"Well done!"

"Have a seat right here," said his host, offering the only chair in the house. "That money paid for a crib mattress and blankets for Sis Thompson's granbaby. It was sleepin' on sacks." Homeless eyed his braces ruefully. "I don't know if I'll keep this getup or not. I might get stuck on m'self."

After thoroughly sniffing the rector's shoes and pants, Barkless leaped into the rector's lap and settled down contentedly.

"Ain't he a sight?" Homeless said. "That's th' most comfort a man could ever want, rolled up in nine pounds of brown an' white spots. How's ol' Barnabas? I hear he bailed you out of that cave."

"He did, and deserves a medal for it. My advice is, stay out of holes in the side of a hill."

"I ain't foolin' with nothin' I can't go in standin' up."

The rector rubbed the dog's ears. "I wanted to ask you about that night at camp meeting...."

"The night so many got saved? To my way of thinkin', it was somethin' only a few see in a lifetime."

"There was a young girl...."

"Lace Turner."

"Tell me everything you know about her."

"Hard life, that 'un. They live across th' creek and up th' hill, I'm kind of divided from that hardscrabble section, but I hear this 'n that. She's smart, and can read like a son of a gun. She's got a quick hand, too, with stealin'. Her daddy beats her bad, and her mama's an invalid. Last news was, Lace picked up and went to live somewhere else."

"She's still living at home. We want to help get her out of there if we can."

"You'll have to get her mama out before you'll get her out, is my guess. Her daddy's threatened to hurt her mama if Lace talks to anybody about what's goin' on."

"Tell me about her father."

"Name's Cate—he's bad business, people cut a wide circle around 'im. I've seen 'im a time or two, and that's enough for me. You don't mix a hair-trigger temper with rotgut alcohol."

"Job?"

"Off an' on, I take it. Worked on that new bridge over th' Shantee River, but that's been built a good while."

"I believe there's a brother."

"Jess. Eighteen, twenty years old. His elevator don't go all th' way to th' top, th' way I see it."

The rector pondered this as he stroked the dog's ears. "What did the camp meeting do to the Creek? Have any lives been changed?"

"Oh, they have. Sis Thompson's one of 'em. Sis had a mouth on 'er like you'd never want to hear. She didn't drink, but she was mean and carried a knife. Sis ain't th' same woman, I can vouch for that. Th' Lord's give her as tender a heart as you'll ever see."

"Anybody else?"

"Slap Jones. There's a changed man. Slap runs me to town to pick up what your grocery throws out, carries me around to th' Dumpsters, helps run soup to th' sick. I read th' Bible to 'im now and again, he's comin' along in th' Lord." Homeless paused and looked at the rector. "Slap did time for killin' his brother."

"You need somebody back here, a young Absalom Greer."

"Yessir, we do. Sometimes a changed life stays changed, sometimes it falls right back into meanness. Meanness is awful easy to fall back into, as I recollect."

"I don't know what to do, Homeless. Mitford clergy is uneasy about coming in here; it's out of our police jurisdiction, it's a whole other school district and a different social services department...."

"I'd go to preachin' myself, but th' Lord won't call me."

"He's already called you. You've got a ministry."

"Th' way I see it, soup ain't much of a ministry."

"That may be the first thing we ever disagreed on. In truth, I disagree strongly."

"Have some lemonade, then, and we'll square off about it," said Homeless, sounding his rasping laugh.

He opened the door of the ancient refrigerator and removed an ice tray. "You were askin' about changed lives. Another one comes to mind is Pauline Barlowe. Boys, there was as bad a case of alcohol as you'd ever want to see. An' I ought to know, as I was a five-star sot for thirty years."

"Pauline … ?"

"Barlowe. Right good-lookin' woman, got a young 'un, moved up there a while back with some low-down jackleg that uses th' butt end of a shotgun to keep 'er in line."

He felt sick to his stomach.

"She was one that jumped out an' prayed with Brother Greer. She's turned around since then, kind of an inspiration to some folks, I hear. Time will tell."

Homeless continued to talk, but the rector couldn't concentrate on what he was saying.

Pauline Barlowe was Dooley's missing mother.

※

There was still no breeze in the warm June night, except for the steady flow of air coming from their bedside fan.

"What are we going to do?" he asked, suffering.

"I don't feel we should do anything at all. She left Dooley in the care of his grandfather, and there, in a sense, he remains. Through you, through us, his grandfather is taking care of him. She hasn't come forward to change that. It's a precarious time in Dooley's life—look how he's growing, Timothy. Yes, he hurt us, but consider why—he wants to spend the summer learning more about what may be his life's work.

"Think of it! A boy who came to you in ragged overalls, with no knowledge that anyone could even *have* a life's work …"

He took her hand.

"She may not know he's here. And there's no reason for him to know she's there. No reason at all," she said with feeling. "Put this out of your mind. We'll pray that his mother is healing, as Dooley is healing. Leave it alone. Let God handle it."

"Thank you," he said. "I needed to hear that."

But what if Pauline Barlowe came for Dooley and demanded him back?

Even in the close, humid heat, he felt a sudden chill.

"Then there's Lace," he said. Cut from the same rough bolt of cloth as Dooley Barlowe.

Why had God sent her on Dooley's very heels? Maybe he hadn't gotten it right the first time and was being given another chance.

He turned on his side and Cynthia drew close, putting her arm around him.

"Mind your deacon, dearest, and go to sleep."

He tried to mind her, but couldn't.

✳

He was sitting at his desk when the door opened and a tall, slender young man walked into the office.

"Father Kavanagh? Scott Murphy."

He looked into the pleasant face of someone he might have known for years, but had never seen before in his life.

"Come in, Scott! Have a seat."

Scott Murphy adjusted his glasses. "I hear you're looking for a chaplain, sir, for Hope House. I'm here to say ... I believe I'm your man."

The rector stood and shook his hand, laughing. Scott Murphy had made that statement as if he believed it utterly.

"I like that," he said, sitting again. "Tell me why you think so." This was certainly not going to be the morning he'd expected.

"Well, Father, I'm willing to work hard, that's the first thing. I would give myself freely—not to the job, but to the patients. I've got the background, but more than that, I like being with the elderly. I care about them very much." The young man stopped and smiled.

"Anything else?"

Scott Murphy sat on the visitor's bench. "No, sir. That's it."

Disarmed. Caught off guard. It had a certain charm, after all. "Well, Scott, if that's true, I want to hear more. Who sent you?"

"I had a dream. It may be hard to believe, Father. All I can say is, you'll have to go with me on this."

"I'll go with you," he said, intrigued. "Will you have a cup of coffee?"

"No, sir. Coffee makes me jump."

"A sight I'd like to see sometime."

They laughed together easily.

"Father, when I was nine years old, a terrible thing happened to us, to our family." Scott took a deep breath and leaned against the wall behind the bench.

"My father's and mother's parents were good friends. They lived in the same little town, Redwing, Kansas, not far from where we lived. My two sets of grandparents shared their garden produce and took a lot of their meals together, and went to the same church.

"Every summer, I could hardly wait for school to let out. I'd get on a bus to Redwing, and there I'd stay for three months, going back and forth from Granma and Granpa Murphy's house to Granma and Granpa Lewis's farm.

"Being with them was a wonderful experience. There was love coming at me from all four directions, and all at the same time. It was as concentrated and direct as a laser beam."

Scott Murphy adjusted his glasses and grinned.

"They took me to the zoo, they gave me a pony, they built me a tree house, they let me work my own garden—they did every-thing anybody could ever do to make a kid feel great about life in general.

"But it wasn't stuff like the pony or the tree house that made the difference, sir. What made the difference was their love. It had a force to it, and it stayed with me all the time. Looking back, I'd say it made me feel ... invincible."

The rector nodded.

"One night, it was in the winter, all four of my grandparents piled into Granpa Murphy's new Chevrolet Caprice and drove to the next town to see a Disney movie. Granma Murphy loved Walt Disney. On the way home ..."

Scott lowered his eyes for a moment, then looked at Father Tim.

"On the way home, they were hit head-on by a truck."

The bookshelf clock ticked against the brief silence.

"Granma and Granpa Lewis were killed instantly, and so was Granpa Murphy. Granma Murphy was still alive when the ambu-lance reached the hospital, but she was in a deep coma."

Over the years, how many tales that went beyond bearing, even beyond repeating outside these walls, had been poured out in this one small room?

"I can't remember anything from then until I was about twelve or thirteen. There's a blank there, like I was hit on the head and didn't come to for a long time.

"You might say that accident left no survivors. Mom and Dad ... we couldn't seem to get over it, to go on." Scott shook his head. "You'd think that all the love I felt from my grandpar-ents would stay with me like some kind of armor plating. Instead, I felt it had been stripped away. Whatever they'd given me, I lost it."

"I understand."

"Can you understand that whatever faith I had in God was lost, too?"

"Yes. It can happen like that."

"We pretty much stayed away from the nursing home where Granma Murphy lived—if you could call it living. One reason we didn't go was because she never knew who we were.

"Something about that bothered me, the staying away because she didn't recognize us. But I was in school, and ever since the accident, school had been hard for me. There was a while when I didn't think I'd make it to my senior year. I had plenty on my mind, so not going to see her didn't trouble me too much. But something kept gnawing at me.

"One day, I was out on my bike, and I stopped by a picnic area and I looked at those tables sitting there with no one around, and I thought of all the picnics my grandparents had taken me on, and I was overwhelmed with … with grief, with something I had never allowed myself to feel. I thought I would die from the pain."

He let out a deep breath. "That was the best thing that could have happened to me, that I stopped and felt the pain.

"I knew right then that I had to go see Granma Murphy, really go see her, look at her, touch her, tell her I loved her. I can't tell you the urgency I felt.

"We had put her in a nursing home about twenty miles away. I hardly remember that bike ride—twenty miles and I hardly remember it, something else was pumping those pedals. It was like I was divinely guided, given wings."

Scott Murphy's face was beaming. "I slammed my bike down outside the door and ran down the hall and found Granma…."

Tears streamed down the young man's face, and he took off his glasses and wiped his eyes, but he was still smiling. "And I kissed her face and her hands and told her I loved her, and that I would always love her.

"I also told her I'd be back.

"I could see she didn't know me. And Father … it was OK that she didn't know me. A lot of people stop going to see someone they love because that person doesn't recognize them. Right then, I thought, who cares if she doesn't recognize me? One out of two people in this room knows their identity, and those odds are good enough for me."

"Yes!"

"I went back twice a week, it was like the old days, like the beginning of summer—I couldn't wait to go see Granma. I just believed that somewhere in there, behind the eyes that didn't appear to see, and the ears that didn't seem to hear, was a heart still full of love, a heart that still wanted to give and still wanted to receive.

"You can imagine that I've told this story a few times in my work, and once in a while, people ask how some teenage kid knew to think like that.

"I've got to tell you, I didn't know how to think like that. I was just a tall, gangly, mixed-up kid like a lot of other kids that age. Something else was at work in me.

"My parents started going, too. And somehow, we just began pouring love into my Granma, and talking to her as if she understood everything we said. My dad would tell her jokes, she always loved jokes, and we believed she could hear and was laughing somewhere inside. We just stopped doubting that she knew us and could hear us."

Scott paused and grinned.

"Go on!" said the rector.

"Today, my Granma is one of the activity leaders in her nursing home."

"Hallelujah!" he nearly shouted.

Scott looked at his watch. "Two-thirty. She's in crafts class right now. They're painting canister sets for their children and grandchildren."

The rector burst into laughter. Painting canister sets! How ordinary and insignificant that would seem to the world. He wanted to clap and shout.

"Some people," said Scott, "ask if I prayed while she was in that coma. Once in a while, I'd say something like, 'God, I'm really mad at you, but I still believe you're God and you can do anything you want to, and I want you to heal Granma. Period.'"

"What do you think happened?"

"I think he healed Granma, just like I asked him to. I think he did it with love, and he used us to help. He could have used anybody—a nurse, an old friend, maybe—but it was us, and I'm grateful.

"I came away from that time in my life with a special sense of a couple of verses in Second Corinthians:

"'For our light affliction, which is but for a moment, works for us a far more exceeding and eternal weight of glory; while we look not at the things which are seen, but at the things which are not seen: for the things which are seen are temporal; but the things which are not seen are eternal.'

"In my ministry as a chaplain, I try to look for the things which aren't seen."

"Well done."

Scott stood up and stretched. "Excuse me, sir, but I haven't been running in a while, and I can feel it."

"I've slacked off, too, in the last few days. How long are you going to be around?"

"I don't know. Maybe I should tell you the rest of the story...."

"Please."

Scott Murphy sat back down and leaned against the wall behind the bench.

"I think I got my calling to be a chaplain during the time we were visiting Granma. And so, when college came around, it just seemed the natural thing to do to go to Fuller, where a couple of uncles had gone. I got my M. Div. there, and did a C.P.E. year in a hospital working with geriatric patients.

"Then I was hired as chaplain at a large eldercare center in Boston. It's all in my résumé, sir, and I have several letters of recommendation."

"I look forward to seeing them."

"I've been at the center for three years, and I've worked hard and I've learned a lot, but somehow, it's time to move on. All I can say is, I've been feeling restless, and I haven't really known why.

"I've done a lot of praying about where I'm supposed to be, and two or three months ago, I had a dream. In the Old Testament, God does some pretty incredible stuff with dreams."

"You can say that again."

"In the dream, this black curtain came down in my mind, with a word on it. The letters were white, and they were big and they were printed. 'Mitford' was the word.

"Somehow, I felt this was the answer, but it sure didn't come with any instruction manual. I didn't have a clue what to do about dealing with this answer. So I went to the little neighborhood library down the street and cross-referenced that word 'til it was chopped liver. Geriatric centers, military schools, you name it. Nothing. Then, I was looking through an atlas, because I like maps a lot, and it hit me—maybe Mitford was a place."

"Good shot!"

"I found a lot of Milfords. They're everywhere. But there's only one Mitford in the whole country.

"I did some research on the Web, and learned you're building a five-million-dollar nursing home here."

Scott looked at the computer sitting on Emma's desk. "Are you on the Web?"

"You don't want to know," said the rector, grimacing.

Scott Murphy laughed. "So, I waited for a four-day break, and I got in my car and I drove down here.

"I won't ask if that sounds crazy, sir, because I know it does. I spent last night in Wesley, and I've been walking around your town all morning, and I've just been up to see Hope House. It's an outstanding facility, sir, the best I've ever seen. The space is filled with light ... everything about it lives up to its name.

"I like your town a lot. People have been very friendly to us all morning, especially to Luke and Lizzie."

"Luke and Lizzie?"

"My Jack Russells, sir. They're two years old. You might say they work with me."

"Aha."

"The elderly love dogs, and Luke and Lizzie love them. So, we're a team, sir." Scott smiled. "Hope House, your town, the people ... it all seems right to me, Father. It all seems very right. I just lay it out to you like it is, with no window dressing."

Scott Murphy stood up from the visitor's bench and put his hands behind his back like a schoolboy about to deliver a review of *War and Peace*.

"There's only one more thing I want to say, Father. And that is, I'd like very much to have this job."

The rector got up and walked over to Scott Murphy. He looked into the young man's urgent brown eyes and shook his hand.

"You're hired," he said.

✳

Good Lord! He had hired a man who should have been reviewed by the vestry, not to mention Hoppy Harper, and—last, but definitely, absolutely not least—Sadie Baxter.

If Sadie Baxter, who was footing the bill, didn't approve of Scott Murphy, Timothy Kavanagh was dead meat.

"Scott, I want you to visit Miss Sadie Baxter for a half hour or so, and please don't mention that I just hired you."

Scott laid his résumé folder on the rector's desk. "Yes, sir."

He dialed the number on Lilac Road.

"Miss Sadie, if it's convenient, I'm sending over a candidate for chaplain. I hope you'll give him a few minutes of your time."

"What do you think of him, Father?"

He was tempted to say he thought Scott Murphy uniquely suited to the job. But, no. Something held him back.

"Qualified. Good fellow," he said, trying to sound casual. "Call me when you can."

If this didn't work, he didn't even want to guess the outcome. Bottom line, he would be retired long before his time.

Two hours passed, then three, when the phone rang.

"Father?" said Miss Sadie. "I think Scott Murphy is the one for the job. Hire him!"

"Consider it done," he said.

FIFTEEN

And Many More

Foxgloves had to be staked earlier than usual, and the hosta, growing in lush groves throughout the village, produced rows of tight, urgent buds along erect stems.

Cream-colored bank roses bloomed along Old Church Lane, forming billowy clouds over the emerald grass. Pink and fuchsia climbers massed themselves on trellises, and in one yard, a vast stand of old shrub roses cast their rich, heady perfume on the air.

The scoop on June was captured by Winnie Ivey, who was never much on words:

"It's a dazzler!" she was quoted as saying in Hessie Mayhew's column.

He could scarcely appreciate the dazzle, given the fact that another computer session awaited him at the office.

He could, of course, fail to show up and let Emma take the heat. He could call in sick with the flu. He could fall in a ditch while jogging—heaven knows he had once done that very thing, and banged up his leg pretty badly.

He knew Stuart Cullen wasn't sitting over there at diocesan

headquarters pushing a mouse around. No indeed, Stuart could dish it out, but …

Dave was waiting in front of the church office.

"Hey, big guy! How's it going?"

"I'm over toolbars," replied the rector, unlocking the door. "What's the agenda for today?"

"Typing and Revising, Finding and Replacing," said Dave, obviously excited, "with a smidgen of Editing and Proofing."

If he were anything other than the responsible stick-in-the-mud that everyone knew him to be, he would get in his car and head for the county line.

✳

He had loaded a font, he had formatted a paragraph, he had bulleted a list, he had selected a font, he had embedded a graph, he had kerned a headline, he had set margins, and he was exhausted.

He went home early, and did something he hadn't done since he was a boy.

With a cool spring rain drumming on the roof, he got between the covers without removing his clothes, where he slept until Cynthia arrived, looking pale from hours of labor over a drawing board.

"Good idea," she said, crawling in beside him and falling sound asleep.

A fine pair they made, and newlywed into the bargain.

✳

They were getting dressed for Miss Sadie's party, and Dooley was presenting himself to them in blue jeans, a starched shirt, and his navy school blazer.

"Stunning!" said Cynthia. "Where's the camera?"

"Top shelf in the closet," said the rector.

"We'll get someone to shoot us at church," she said, taking it off the shelf and putting it in her handbag.

"Can I take my TV to the farm?" asked Dooley.

Were the boy's loafers newly shined, or was he imagining things? "Well, sure."

"Thanks," said Dooley, leaving the room.

"He told me he's helping Hal with a sick calf tonight," said Cynthia. "He is compassionate, Timothy."

"Compassion for animals does not make up for being indifferent to humans."

She was silent for a moment. "This is a pressing day for you, dearest—two services, adult Sunday School, a major party, and Evensong—I'm making dinner at my house tonight and giving us a retreat."

He smiled at his wife, who was putting on something the color of his favorite clematis. "Terrific. When I retire, I hope we'll have many retreats."

"When you … what?"

"When I … retire." He had said it; it had slipped forth without his knowing.

Cynthia's eyes shone. "Well, I'll be et for a tater!"

"We'll … talk about it sometime," he said, coloring.

"Good! I love to talk about the future."

"Cynthia, Cynthia," he said, putting on a fresh tab collar, "what don't you love?"

"Daytime TV, pickled onions, and cheap ballpoint pens."

He laughed easily. A retreat at the little yellow house. It might have been the south of France for the odd pleasure he took in thinking of it.

※

Sadie Baxter had been a member of Lord's Chapel for eighty years. Hardly anyone ever did anything, he mused, for eighty years. This was a blessing not to be taken lightly.

The children lined up and stationed themselves behind Ray

Cunningham, who stood at the open door of the parish hall with a video camera on his shoulder.

The rector gazed at the eager faces of thirteen children, ranging in ages from four and a half to twelve years, all with their own excitement over the event.

In today's world, how many children got to mix with the elderly? How did one ever "learn" what it meant to grow old?

In his time, all that had been in place, there were models for aging everywhere—up and down the street, talking on porches, working in the yard, sitting on benches—visible, out there.

"Here she comes!" shouted Ray.

Esther Bolick banged on a dishpan with a wooden spoon. "Quiet, get ready, here she comes!" Esther threw down the dishpan and took her place at the piano.

"I hope I don't break your camera!" said Miss Sadie, arriving with Louella and Ron Malcolm, and her best silver-tipped cane.

"Hit it!" shouted Esther.

> *Happy Birthday to you!*
> *Happy Birthday to you!*
> *Happy Birthday, Miss Sadie,*
> *Happy birthday to you!*
> *And many mo-oh-ore!*

"Happy Birthday, Miss Sadie!" chorused the children, holding up posters they had made for the occasion.

The entire room burst into hoots, cheers, and applause as he offered his arm and led the guest of honor to a chair in front of the fireplace.

"I'd better sit down before I fall down!" she warbled.

Laughter all around.

"Please come and pay your respects to our precious friend on the occasion of her ninetieth birthday," said the rector. "Help yourself to the refreshments, and save room for cake and ice cream after the mayor's speech. But first, let's pray!"

Much shuffling around and grabbing of loose toddlers.

"Our Father, we thank You profoundly for this day, that we might gather to celebrate ninety years of a life well-lived, of time well-spent in your service.

"We thank you for the roof on this house which was given by your child, Sadie Baxter, and for all the gifts she freely shares from what you graciously provide.

"We thank you for her good health, her strong spirits, her bright hope, and her laughter. We thank you for Louella, who brings the zestful seasoning of love into our lives. And we thank you, Lord, for the food you've bestowed on this celebration, and regard with thanksgiving how blessed we are in all things. Continue to go with Sadie, we pray, and keep her as the apple of your eye. We ask this in Jesus' name."

"Amen!" chorused the assembly, who either broke into a stampede to the food table or queued up to deliver felicitations to the honored guest.

He saw Buck Leeper, the job superintendent of Hope House, bow awkwardly in front of Miss Sadie and move quickly toward the door.

He was enthralled to see the children approach her one by one, each with a small, wrapped box—all of which contained, he was told on good authority, peanut butter candy.

Mostly, he loved the sight of Absalom Greer, who, to pay his earnest respects, and regardless of advanced arthritis, knelt by Miss Sadie's chair on one knee.

And many more! he thought, smiling. And many more, indeed.

❋

They walked home from church, Cynthia carrying a wrapped

parcel of the peanut butter and jelly birthday cake, which had been a dubious hit.

"Dooley," she said, "you sang so beautifully, the top of my head tingled."

The rector put his arm around the boy's shoulders. "And I got cold chills."

"Miz Bolick hammered down on that piano pretty good. You ought to get it tuned."

"We'll see to it," promised the rector. "Run in and finish getting your things together. Marge and Hal will be along in a few minutes."

"I want to take that cage Jack used to stay in, in case I find a rabbit or anything hurt."

"Take it."

Dooley dashed into the rectory ahead of them, and they paused on the stoop.

"How are you?" asked Cynthia.

"Struggling."

She put her hand on his arm. "Nobody knew it. The party was a huge success! Miss Sadie wept when Dooley sang, and everyone loved your poem."

"Ummm."

"Do you think we'd have celebrated Miss Sadie like that if she hadn't put the roof on and given the nursing home?"

"Definitely! Absolutely!"

"Good." She started inside as Dooley came along the hallway.

"That girl's here again," he said, looking coldly at them.

"Lacey ..."

"In the kitchen. Man, she stinks."

"Get your things," said the rector, and turned to his wife. "Would you see if he's rounded up what he needs? I'll look in on Lacey."

He found her slumped in a chair at the kitchen table, her hair pushed under the battered hat.

"Y'r door won't locked, so I come in."

He sat opposite her. "How are you?"

"M' pap's gone t' Tennessee t' work on th' bridge."

"Wonderful!" he said.

"He'll come home Fridays. They ain't nothin' t' eat in th' house, he done cleaned out what we had and took it."

"We'll handle that. How's your mother?"

"Bad off."

He heard the emptiness in her voice. "I'm sorry, Lacey."

She looked at him coolly. "I said t' call me Lace."

"Yes. Has your mother got her medicine?"

"Yeah."

"What about a hot bath? It'll be good for you, and good for your back, and we'll fix you something to eat."

"I don't need no bath."

Dooley and Cynthia came into the kitchen. "Lace! We're glad you're here! Dooley Barlowe, Lace Turner."

Dooley glared at the girl, and she glared back.

"Everything's at the front door," said Cynthia, unwrapping the cake. "I'm just going to cut some of this to send to the farm."

"I'd eat a piece of that if you was t' give it t' me," said Lace.

"I'm taking it with me," Dooley announced. "It's mine."

"Actually, it's ours," Cynthia said. "And she may have a piece."

Dooley gave the girl a withering look. "Where'd you come from?"

"None of y'r business."

The phone rang, and Dooley bolted for it. "Hello!" He listened intently. "Yes, ma'am. I liked doing it. I hope you have a real good birthday and … many more. Thank you for doing stuff for me. Yes, ma'am. I will. 'Bye."

"Miss Sadie?" queried Cynthia.

"She said she appreciated that I sang her favorite hymn. I hated to make her cry."

"Oh, but it was a good cry!" said Cynthia, giving Lace a piece of cake. Lace took it from the plate with both hands and devoured it.

Dooley glowered at her. "You ought to say thank you."

Lace licked her fingers and gave him an insolent look. "You ain't my boss."

"Step out front with me, son," said the rector, "and we'll visit 'til Marge and Hal get here."

They carried the bags to the front porch, where Dooley thumped down on the top step. "If she wasn't a girl, I'd knock her head off."

"What would that accomplish?" the rector asked.

"She'd know who she was talkin' to, that's what."

"Who would she be talking to?"

"I bet you're lettin' her move in here, lettin' her eat here and everything. She sure as heck better stay out of my room—and why's she tryin' to look like a guy, anyway? Gag. Puke."

He noticed that Dooley's prep school varnish was peeling off pretty fast. "Calm down," he said. "If you knew her circumstances ..."

Hal Owen pulled his red pickup to the curb, and Rebecca Jane leaned out the window. "Uncle Dools!"

Dooley grabbed a heavy bag in each hand, and the rector hoisted the duffle and the rabbit cage.

His heart beat dully. It seemed they had welcomed him home only yesterday, and now ...

Swallow it down, he thought, going to the curb. Swallow it down.

Hal got out and came around to help. "We'll just put your stuff in the back. Everything zipped up tight?"

"Yes, sir," said Dooley.

Marge opened the door and pulled Rebecca Jane onto her lap. "Climb in," she said.

"Marge ... " He didn't know what else to say.

"Timothy, I ... " She lifted her hands and let them fall.

Hal slapped the rector on the back. "We'll take care of him, and you and Cynthia come out anytime. We mean it."

"Anytime," said Marge, nearly whispering.

He reached in and patted Rebecca Jane, who displayed teeth like seed corn when she smiled. "Come with us!" she said.

The rector managed to smile back. "Not today."

Cynthia ran down the walk with the bag. "Wait! Esther's cake!"

Cynthia stuck her head in the truck cab and gave Rebecca Jane a kiss. "Take care of Uncle Dools for us."

"We will," said the little girl, nodding soberly.

She kissed Dooley. "Call us."

"OK."

"We love you, buddy," he said, suffering. He looked into the boy's eyes. Would the pain he saw there never go away?

✳

"Mam says if you wash an' go outside, y'r pores'll be open an' y'll git sick."

Cynthia passed her another piece of roast chicken. "This is June, though, Lace, and that's not likely to happen. Washing and going out in winter is probably what she meant. In any case, I want to look at your back."

Lace thought for a moment. "I thank y'uns, but I ain't goin' t' take no bath."

"Fine. How do you like the chicken?"

"I like chicken, it's m' favorite."

"Mine, too," said Cynthia.

"I'd like it better if it was fried."

There was a long silence as they ate their hastily prepared dinner.

"Lace ..." said Cynthia.

"Huh?"

"How do you feel about your father?"

"I hate 'im." More silence. "But I used t' like 'im."

"What did you like about him?"

"He was good t' me when I was a baby. They said I was s' little, I slep' in Pap's beard 'til I growed out of it. He used t' be nice t' me, bring me candy an' all, then liquor got 'im and he went down."

"Went down," said the rector.

"Yeah."

"Has he actually threatened to kill you?"

"Lots of times. An' he said if I tol' anybody anything, or let th' school people catch me, he'd hit Mam a lick she wouldn't forgit."

"I hear," he said, "that a woman named Pauline Barlowe lives at the Creek. Do you know her?"

"Yeah."

"What do you know about her?"

"She's nice, she's good. She he'ps me sometimes, but 'er man don't like her doin' it."

"What's nice about her?"

"She prayed that prayer I prayed, an' it made 'er different, she smiles an' all, an' does things f'r people."

"I heard she has a child."

"She's got Poobaw, he's ten."

"That prayer you prayed, Lace ... did it make you different?"

The girl shrugged. "Made me want t' quit stealin'. I know it ain't right, m' mam knows it ain't right."

"Anything else?"

She stared at them coldly. "Y'uns ask a lot of questions."

He didn't know why, but that struck him as funny, and he burst into laughter, liking the feeling. Cynthia laughed, too.

And then, so did Lace.

❋

She paused at the back door, clutching the parcel of food. "I'll be back, now an' agin."

"If I were to give you this," he said, holding a twenty-dollar bill, "what would you do with it?"

"I'd buy Mam some goobers, she loves goobers, an' I'd spend th' rest on somethin' t' eat, like ham an' all."

"Do you go to the store?"

"I don't go t' no stores n'r anywhere th' school people can catch me. I dress like a boy, an' know how t' duck around so people cain't see me. Like when I come here, I come th' back way—down th' creek and th'ough th' apple trees an' acrost th' park."

"Who goes to the store for you, then?"

"Pauline, most of th' time."

"She's honest?"

"Yeah. Honester'n anybody 'cept Mam."

He handed her the money. "Take it. And I'd also like you to take this. I know you have a place to hide it, if you need to." He pulled a small edition of the New Testament from his pocket and gave it to her.

She looked at it without comment and dropped it inside the bag of food.

"When you send to the store," said Cynthia, "please get a bar of soap and wash yourself." He thought his wife sounded as if she meant it.

"I might," said Lace. "If I take a notion."

As they watched her pass through the hedge, he remembered

that social services was looking for her. The very thought horri-
fied him one moment, and gave him relief the next.

✳

At Cynthia's house, a cool breeze blew through the open
kitchen window, and another from the living room met it in the
hallway. In the bedroom upstairs, he found she had turned the
covers back, and a vase of flowers sat on the small table she kept
before the fireplace.

Violet lay curled on the vanity seat, and a breeze puffed the
curtains out.

"Thank God!" he exclaimed, surveying the peace of it.

"Undress, dearest. I've got your robe hanging on the bathroom
door."

He turned and kissed her on the forehead. "I'm dashed if I
have a clue how I ever made it without you."

"Don't try and figure it out," she said gently. "Don't try and figure anything out. This is a retreat!"

✳

They were sprawled in bed, listening to the patter of a
summer rain. The crumbs of a shared piece of cake sat in a
plate on the nightstand, and glasses of lemonade perspired on
coasters.

"It's like going on holiday," he said, yawning hugely.

"What do you know about going on holiday, you big lug? You
never go on holiday unless forced by a direct command from the
bishop."

"True enough. But that's going to change."

"It is?" she said, looking hopeful.

"Absolutely."

"That's wonderful news, darling! Someone said that people
who can't find time for recreation are obliged sooner or later to
find time to be sick."

"I don't doubt it. Where do you want to go this summer? August is a good time for me to get away. How about you?"

"Perfect. The book will be out of my hands, and I'll be able to kick up my heels. What about ..." she threw her arms open wide, "northern Italy?"

"I was thinking of something more ... within driving distance."

"Of course. You didn't say you were going to get over your fear of flying, just your fear of having fun."

"Right."

"How about Mississippi? You could show me where you lived when you raised rabbits!"

"Mississippi in August? I don't think so."

"How about Massachusetts, then, and I'll show you where I lived when I learned to whistle."

"You may be on to something, Kavanagh. And while we're at it, I've been meaning to ask you another question."

"What's that?"

He cleared his throat. Could he actually talk about this? Yes. Yes, he could. In fact, he felt a small tremor of excitement. "Where would you like to live when we ... retire?"

The faint ticking of the clock merged with the sound of the rain.

"Goodness! I've steeled myself not to think about it, so now I don't have a clue," she said. "Somewhere warm in winter?"

"That's for sissies."

She peered at him. "So you like having your face blistered by the wind, and your feet go numb on the short walk between our house and The Local?"

"Crazy about it."

"So am I, actually."

He laughed. "So we're both keen on four distinct seasons...."

"Quite."

"Possibly somewhere near water?" he mused.

"Possibly."

"But nothing flat."

"No! Absolutely nothing flat."

They listened to the rain for a time, and felt the ravishing coolness of the breeze on their faces.

"Something rather small," she said happily.

"Right. Fine. But with a big yard."

"Small house, big yard. OK. I plant, you mow."

"No way. We plant, we mow."

They shook hands, grinning.

"Well," he said, "we have lots of time to think about it."

"Really?" she inquired. "How *much* time, do you imagine? Just asking, of course."

"Oh. Maybe a couple of years."

"Ummm. Yes. A couple of years sounds perfect to me."

"Good! Then it's settled."

"What's settled?"

"It's settled that we have a future," he said. "Don't you like having a future?"

"Like it?" she exclaimed. "I love it!"

Holding her close, he drifted into sleep as peacefully as a child.

The cave had been about forgiveness. And because of that, it had also been about freedom.

✳

He glanced at the clock when the phone rang. Three in the morning. "Hello?" he answered, dreading the news.

"Miss Sadie done fell ag'in," moaned Louella. "Come quick."

✳

He increased the speed of the windshield wipers.

Thank heaven they'd given the party, and not a moment too

soon. But if God's timing had been perfect for the party, he had to believe it had been perfect, as well, for allowing this hard thing. Like it or lump it, nothing happened to a child of God by accident, and Scripture inarguably proved that out.

"For all things work together for good …" he murmured, quoting from the book of Romans. "Use this for good," he prayed.

As he turned onto Lilac Road, he saw the attendants carrying the stretcher to the ambulance. He heard his heart beating as they closed the doors, and he followed them up the hill in the rain.

❋

How many times had he received grim news from Hoppy Harper?

"Bad break," said the doctor, shaking his head. "Very bad. We're taking her into surgery, but …" He paused and ran his fingers through disheveled hair. "I didn't want to tell you this."

"I didn't want to hear it."

Sadie Baxter would be among the first to need the nursing home she was building.

❋

During surgery, he sat in Hoppy's lamp-lit office with Louella and Cynthia and Olivia Harper.

"She say she spill a little drinkin' water goin' out of her bathroom to her bedroom, an' when she went to th' toilet in th' night, her foot hit that little patch of water and she went down."

Miss Sadie's friend and companion since childhood hugged herself as if she felt a chill. "This is a bad thing, honey, a bad thing. I can feel it in m' bones."

Olivia put her arm around Louella. "This strikes us all at the marrow," she said, trying to appear calm. Not long ago, Olivia had discovered Miss Sadie to be her great-aunt and only living relative. The bond had been, for both of them, one of the great joys of their lives.

They held hands and took turns praying as the clock ticked toward daylight.

✻

He swallowed hard before he went into Intensive Care, and could scarcely believe what he saw. It was Sadie Baxter with the light gone from her countenance; it was someone gray and suffering and very, very old.

He had to force down the cry that welled up in him, a cry that said, *This can't be, I can't accept this, this is wrong.*

✻

He stood at the study window and looked out to a drenching rain that made the rhododendron leaves glisten and dance. Beyond the hedge lay Baxter Park, a green pool of quiet and solitude in the summer dusk.

Cynthia came to him and put her arm around his waist. "What is it, my dearest?"

He clenched his jaw and spoke hoarsely. "It's Dooley. And Lace. And Sadie Baxter. And Sophia and Liza. And all the others."

"I'll go to the hospital tonight. You've had only three or four hours sleep."

"Thanks, but—"

"I'm your deacon, Timothy, you said so. Give me a chance to do my job."

He wanted to weep, he wanted to wail, he heard sounds forming somewhere in him that were unrecognizable, sounds of grieving he could never express.

"We'll go together," he said.

She went off to the kitchen. "I'll make us a cup of tea."

Sadie Baxter was tough, she was resilient, she was made of

strong stuff, and last but not least, her faith was up to the job. She could live to be a hundred. Still, he could not shake the dread he felt.

"And many more," he whispered urgently into the gathering dusk outside the window.

SIXTEEN

Loving Back

O"OK," said Puny, giving him a mischievous look, "which one is Sissy and which one is Sassy?"

"Now, Puny …"

"Oh, jis' try!"

He didn't have a clue, but figured the odds were pretty good. "This one is Sissy!"

"Wrong! That's Sassy!"

He was resting on the study sofa, under what he felt to be a veritable pile of fat, squirming babies, stuffed ducks, squashy monkeys, a rubber pig that squealed when he sat on it, and a stack of folded diapers.

"Blast," he said. "How do you tell?" As far as he could see, both had red hair, both had the same eye color, both were the same size, and they smelled exactly alike.

"See this?" said Puny, pointing to a fat cheek. "Sissy has a dimple on the left side, Sassy has a dimple on the right side."

Sissy, Sassy, left, right. He could hardly wait until they were walking and talking, at which time he would simply speak a name, and whoever came running, well, that's how he would know which was which.

"Would you like t' hold Sissy while I change Sassy? It won't take a minute. Or—*you* could change Sassy while *I* hold Sissy!"

She looked so excited and pleased about the prospect of either that he could hardly refuse. "The first thing you said," he mumbled.

"OK, here she is. Uh-oh. I need to change Sissy worse'n I need t' change Sassy!"

"If it's not one thing, it's two," he said, quoting a former bishop.

She hauled Sissy to his wing chair, plopped her in the seat, and did what she had to do. "Now!" she said, snapping the diaper in place. "Come and sit on your granpaw's lap!"

Granpaw! Granpaw? He'd better nip this thing in the bud while the nipping was good. "Ah ... Puny."

"Yes, sir?" She turned around with the baby in her arms, and he saw the prettiest sight this side of heaven—his one and only Puny, who had lit up the gloomy rectory with the glow of a thousand candles. Could he refuse her anything at all?

"Bring her on!" he said, holding out his arms, as Sissy landed him a swift kick.

❋

He had jogged, Puny had scooped up the babies and their ocean of paraphernalia and gone home, and Cynthia was arriving any minute. It was his night to cook dinner, and he was running behind.

Did he dare fix the boring and economical Parson's Meatloaf for a woman who had been his bride only a few months? He had spoiled her rotten with roasted this and glazed that, not to mention his barbecued ribs specialty, which she craved, plus a fairly deft output of everything from grilled quail and oyster stuffing to broiled mountain flounder with pecan sauce.

Was the honeymoon over? He bowled ahead with the meat-loaf, fervently hoping not.

He heard tapping at the back door and turned to see Olivia Harper peering through the screen. "Hello!" she said.

"Olivia! Hello, yourself! Come in!"

He held the screen door open and was dazzled, as was every-one, by the striking beauty of Sadie Baxter's great-niece. "This is a grand surprise. Cynthia's on her way any minute, and I've got kitchen duty tonight. Have you been up with Miss Sadie?"

"Yes," she said, sitting down at the table, "and she's in terrible pain, Father."

"I know."

"The bedpan is impossible with the kind of break she had, and getting up to use the potty chair is nearly more than she can bear. It hurts me so to see her suffer like this, and Hoppy says there's nothing we can do."

"I know. She's too small and too frail to medicate more heavily."

"I didn't want to come bringing doom and gloom," said Olivia.

He saw the grim concern that shaded her extraordinary violet eyes. "And you didn't," he assured her.

"I suppose I'm thinking of the future."

"Of sending her away to a rehab center," he said. "Then nurses around the clock when she comes home...."

"And possibly confined to bed for ... a long time."

"You know Cynthia and I will do whatever it takes. You're not in this alone. How is Louella today? I didn't see her when I went at three."

"Suffering, Father. This thing has aged them both at once."

"... the Lord do so to me, and more also," he quoted from the book of Ruth.

"... if ought but death part thee and me," she said, finishing the verse.

Cynthia and Lace came up the back steps and into the kitchen.

"Olivia!"

The two women embraced warmly. "Olivia, meet Lace Turner. Lace, this is Mrs. Olivia Daven ... oops, Harper."

Olivia extended her beautifully manicured hand to Lace, who looked at it for a fleeting moment, then awkwardly took it.

"I'm very pleased to meet you, Lace."

The girl dropped her head.

"Oh, Timothy," said Cynthia, "I'm so glad it's your night in the barrel. I thought it was mine, and I didn't have a clue what to fix. Maybe meatloaf, or something consoling."

"Meatloaf!" he said. "Just the ticket!" Great minds think alike.

"Lace came to see me," Cynthia said, "and I've been showing her my watercolors."

"She c'n draw!" Lace announced, sitting down and pushing her hat back on her head. "Looky here, she gave me these books." She hauled two *Violet* books from the belt of her workpants, and passed them to Olivia. He saw a sparkle in her eyes that he'd never seen before.

"I've seen them," said Olivia, "and they're grand! I can't draw a straight line, can you?"

"I can draw some." Lace rested her chin on her dirty hand and stared at Olivia. "You're real purty," she said.

"So are you, Lace."

"No, I ain't! You don't have t' tell me that 'cause I said it t' you."

"I didn't say it because you said it to me. I said it because it's true. You're a very pretty girl, with beautiful features and wonderful hazel eyes."

Lace blushed and pulled the hat down, nearly covering her eyes.

"I see you like hats," Olivia said. "I like hats, too."

"I can't wear a hat," said Cynthia, thumping into a chair at the table. "I look ridiculous."

The rector turned from dicing onions. "Don't be so modest. You look fetching in a baseball cap!"

Olivia laughed. "If you'd ever like to see my hats, Lace, I'd like to show them to you. I have hats that were made at the turn of the century, with glorious feathers and pins and veils. They came from someone in my family."

"This was m' pap's hat."

"Where do you go to school?"

"I don't go t' no school. I lay out."

"I see."

"M' pap won't let me go t' school. They'd land him in jail f'r whippin' me." She pulled up her shirtsleeve and showed Olivia the healing bruises, then suddenly yanked the sleeve down and stood up from the table.

"I got t' git home. Pap's comin' tonight." She collected the books and stuffed them under her belt.

"Wait, don't go just yet!" Cynthia went to the refrigerator, found cheese and tomatoes, and removed a loaf of bread from the freezer. She quickly put a jar of mayonnaise into a bag with a jar of pickles, cans of soup and baked beans, and two apples.

"There," she said, nearly out of breath. "Run home quickly, then, and hide it if you have to. You're in our prayers, all of you. Be safe, be careful—don't cross your father, and come back when you can."

Lace nodded and backed toward the door, clutching the bag. "Thank y'uns f'r th' stuff. I'll see y'uns now an' ag'in."

He stepped to the door and watched her walk toward Baxter Park. Today, he had seen the child in her, if only for a moment; he thought she nearly skipped through the hedge.

❋

He was getting ready to go to the hospital when the phone rang.

"Timothy?"

"Yes, Marge?"

"I … we need to talk. Is this a good time?"

"I was just stepping out the door to see Miss Sadie."

"Shall I call you tomorrow?"

"No. Let's talk now." He took the cordless into the study and sat in his wing chair.

"Timothy, there's a hard thing between us."

He didn't know what to say.

"Let me tell you how I feel. I feel … caught in the middle. You see, Dooley wrote and asked if he could come for the summer and, of course, I said he could, if that's what all of you wanted and agreed on. I thought he would talk to you about it, and you would talk to me. I'm so sorry it came as a surprise to you."

"We were both surprised, then."

"Yes. You know I treasure your friendship, and I love Dooley. Nothing can change that. Whatever I've done to hurt you, Timothy, please forgive me."

He thought he had forgiven her, but he hadn't. He felt the bile of it in him yet.

"I'm sorry, Marge. I'm sorry for being so …" What had he been? Possessive? Selfish?

"Then you forgive me?"

He heard the concern in her voice, and his heart softened. "Yes," he said eagerly. "Yes. There's nothing to forgive, nothing at all."

"I think I've had an insight about Dooley. When he helps Hal with a sick or wounded animal, I believe it's his way of loving his brothers and his little sister. Perhaps that's why he runs to the opportunity to help an animal, which makes it look like he's running from you and Cynthia."

"Yes," he said softly.

"I believe he hated to leave you the other day, that he was conflicted about it, but he sucked up and did it."

"Thank you, Marge, for talking this over. I'm ashamed of—"

"Don't be ashamed, old friend. Life is too short."

He chuckled. How good to have the weight off their hearts.

"Please come on Sunday afternoon and visit, you and Cynthia. Bring Barnabas, too. I'll give you chicken pie, your old favorite."

He felt a grin spreading across his face. "Consider it done. And thank you. Thank you."

"You know, Timothy, it's not having someone to love us that's so important—but having someone to love, don't you think?"

"Yes!" he said, knowing. "Oh, yes."

"I pray he'll be reunited with his family. Do you think that's possible?"

He was silent for a moment. "I don't know, Marge. With God, all things are possible. So, yes. The answer is yes."

✳

Miss Sadie was reported to have made a good turn, and was gathering strength. Before he reached the hospital on Wednesday morning to give her the Holy Eucharist, she sat up, according to the nurses, and sang the opening verse of "Love Divine, All Loves Excelling."

"It was a little squeaky," said Nurse Kennedy, "but she did it and we're thrilled!"

He sang it himself, barreling down the hill in his Buick to the noon service—shouted it, in fact, to whoever might be listening.

> *Love divine, all loves excelling,*
> *joy of heaven, to earth come down,*
> *fix in us Thy humble dwelling,*
> *all Thy faithful mercies crown.*

Jesus, Thou art all compassion,
pure, unbounded love Thou art;
visit us with Thy salvation,
enter every trembling heart.

✳

Sometimes, being elated drained him more than feeling despondent. His high at Miss Sadie's turnaround left him limp on Wednesday night.

His wife was propped up in bed, scribbling in a sketchbook, while he examined himself in the dresser mirror.

"You're tired, dearest?" she asked.

"A dash."

"More than a dash, I think. You know you can't shine if you don't fill your lamp."

"Where did you dig up that old platitude, Kavanagh?"

"Ummm. I can't remember."

He peered into the mirror, lamenting the new gray in what was left of his hair.

"Darling," she said, "I think your gray hair is wonderful. Very distinguished, in fact!"

He gave her a wicked sidelong glance. "Yes, and just because there's snow on the roof doesn't mean there's no fire in the furnace."

She went into gales of laughter. "Timothy! I can't believe you said such a thing."

"That may be only the first of the things you can't believe I said."

"Whatever do you mean?"

"I mean ... what do I mean? I mean, let's drive to Holding for dinner tomorrow evening, for starters. There's a new place, and it's foolishly expensive."

"I can't believe it!"

"You see? And another thing: Let's take in a movie. You can eat all my Milk Duds."

"Timothy! What is happening to you? If you don't watch out, you're going to be positively *fun*."

"I wouldn't go that far," he said, grinning.

"I'd love to do all of that! And now that Miss Sadie is feeling better, I can talk to you about something I've been thinking."

"And what's that?" he asked, coming to sit on the side of the bed.

"Having my will made last week reminded me … if I keel over before I get my roots touched up, don't let Fancy Skinner lay a hand on me, do you hear?"

He stared at her, blankly.

"You must send for a hairdresser in Charlotte, and I definitely want foil, not a cap. Understand?"

"I beg your pardon?"

"Foil! Not a cap! Oh, phoo, I'll write it down and put it in the envelope with the will. I did tell you where I put the will, didn't I?"

"I don't recall that you did." Good Lord, she sounded as if it were all coming down the pike tomorrow.

"In the top drawer of your desk in the study. Under the ledger."

"Right. So why are you concerned about your hair if you're going to be cremated?" Episcopalians were historically fond of ending up in an urn, which surely didn't require getting their roots touched up, much less by out-of-towners.

"I'm not going to be cremated! Just plopped in the old-fashioned casket that takes up all that room underground and is now politically incorrect from here to the Azores."

"Aha."

"I'll leave you a note about what I'm going to wear. I think it should be that plum-colored suit you like so much." She stopped and pondered. "Unless, of course, I keel over in the summer, which means that little piqué dress with the blue piping."

"Could we talk about something else?" he asked. When it came to discussing the future, he was far and away better at it than his wife, and he'd only recently begun.

✳

Sunday was all the perfection of June rolled into one fragile span of time, a golden day that no one would have end.

They feasted on Marge's chicken pie and raved over the flaky crust, and drank an entire pitcher of iced tea. Dooley rode Goosedown Owen around the barnyard, holding tightly to Rebecca Jane, who shared the saddle. Barnabas caroused with several of the Meadowgate dogs, and returned with a coat full of burrs, twigs, dead leaves, and other castoffs of nature.

The rector headed for the woods with his wife and her sketchbook, where they found a cushion of moss along the sunlit path.

"Dearest," she said, opening her box of colored pencils, "maybe we should buy a farm when you retire."

"That's a thought."

"I'd love to pick wildflowers and put them in Mason jars on a windowsill!" She peered at a grove of Indian pipes that had pushed through a layer of leaf mold, and sketched quickly. "And I'd love making deep-dish blackberry pies. Would you do the picking?"

"No way," he said.

"Why not?"

"The last time I picked blackberries, I was so covered with chigger bites, I was nearly unrecognizable."

"When was that?"

"Oh, when I was ten or eleven."

"And it put you off blackberry picking for life?"

"Absolutely."

"Maybe we'd better not buy a farm."

"Maybe not," he said laughing.

Dooley and Barnabas came crashing along the wooded path, followed by Bonemeal, one of Meadowgate's numerous canine residents.

"Hey!" said Dooley.

"Hey, yourself!" they replied in unison.

"I'm through watering the horses."

"Great. Come and sit while Cynthia draws."

Dooley thumped down on the moss as Barnabas sprawled on the Indian pipes.

"Get up, you big oaf!" cried Cynthia.

"Barnabas, old fellow, over here!" Barnabas lumbered over and lay next to his master, panting.

"Mashed pipes," said Cynthia. "Oh, well, Dooley, I'll draw you."

"Don't draw me," he said. "I ain't … I'm not … my hair's not combed and all."

"Perfect! It'll be a candid portrait."

Dooley covered his face with his hands.

"Uncover your funny face this minute!" said Cynthia, charcoal pencil at the ready.

Dooley kept his face covered, cackling with laughter.

"Nobody minds me," she sighed. "Timothy won't pick black-berries, Barnabas squashes my subject matter, and you hide your face. Rats, I'll just take a nap." She crashed back onto the moss.

"No, don't take a nap!" said Dooley. "You can draw me."

"Great!" she said springing up. "OK, hold still and look this way. Actually … look that way. Now, drop your chin. I love your freckles. Don't squint your eyes. Is that a cut on your forehead? What happened?" She sketched hurriedly. "Don't mash down your hair, it looks wonderful that way. Ummm, raise your chin a little. Just a tish. No, that's too much—"

"I hate this," said Dooley, as the rector shook with laughter.

"Why," asked Father Tim, "should you do all the drawing in the family, anyway? We'll draw you."

"No, no, a thousand times no, you will make my nose look like a squash."

"Tough," said Dooley.

"Yeah!" said the rector.

"Have a go, then," she said, finishing the drawing and giving Dooley her pencil and sketchbook.

"Look this way!" urged the rector.

"No, look that way!" said Dooley. "And get your hair out of your face!"

"Amazing!" said Father Tim, peering at the hastily completed sketch. "Your nose doesn't look like a squash at all. It looks like a gourd."

Dooley and the rector rolled with laughter, as Cynthia peered at them with stunning disdain.

"It certainly doesn't take much for you turkeys."

Dooley picked up the sketch she'd done of him and examined it carefully. "Man!" he said. "That's me, all right."

The rector looked into the boy's eager eyes. "You like it out here, buddy?"

"Yep."

"I'm glad you were such a big help with the calf."

"That calf is jumping around like new. Doc Owen said he couldn't have done it without me."

There were a few things that he, too, couldn't have done without Dooley Barlowe.

Smiling, he made a fist and scrubbed the top of Dooley's head. "We love you, big guy."

Dooley looked away, and said something. It was barely audible, but they heard it clearly. He said, "I love you back."

✳

"Where are Sissy and Sassy?" he asked, popping home for a meatloaf sandwich and a couple of books from his study shelves.

"Shhh," said Puny. "They're asleep in your study. You ought to see 'em, they've growed a foot!"

"I have to get a couple of books out of there," he said, keeping his voice low.

"I'll git 'em for you. You'd wake 'em up and oh, law, they didn't sleep five minutes straight last night. What d'you need?"

He scratched his head, trying to imagine the books on their particular shelves. "I need *Pilgrim's Progress*—I'm referring to it in a sermon—and a book called *In the Wake of Recovery*."

"Where're they at?" she whispered.

"Let's see. *Pilgrim's Progress* should be on the third or fourth shelf down, right-hand side, blue leather cover. The other one should be on the left-hand side, maybe the bottom shelf, I don't know what color the cover is."

"Third or fourth shelf, right side, blue cover, and left side, bottom shelf—what's th' name again?"

"*In the Wake of Recovery*."

"Shhh. OK, I'll be right back. Try not to rattle anything."

He opened the refrigerator door quietly, removed the meatloaf, and carefully pushed the door shut. He took the bread from the breadbox, and nearly jumped out of his skin when the round box lid crashed onto the floor, rolled under the table, and came to a window-rattling stop.

Crawling under the table after it, he decided to go next door to the little yellow house, where he could occasionally find crackers and cheese.

Puny returned to the kitchen, closing the door behind her. "Lord help!" she whispered. "What did you drop in here, your teeth? I cain't find nothin' with any pilgrims on th' cover. And this … is this what you were talkin' about on the bottom shelf?"

"It is, thank you. Well done! But I have to have *Pilgrim's Progress*, too."

"Does the cover have pilgrims with black hats and those funny shoe buckles and all?"

"No, there's no drawing or anything, just a plain blue cover and the title and the author's name, John Bunyan."

"That huge man that cut down trees? What do you need him for in a sermon? Or was that Davy Crockett?"

"Let me go in. I won't wake them up, I'll tiptoe."

"Men don't know how to tiptoe. You should hear Joe Joe tiptoeing—clunkety, clunk, slam, bam—"

"Puny ..."

"Oh, all right," she said, reluctant.

He took off his shoes and eased into the study like a burglar, dodging the floorboards that usually groaned when he passed. At the bookcase, he searched the right-hand shelves.... Where in blast was it, anyway?

He heard a squeal behind him and turned to look at the twins, who were bedded down in tandem on his sofa. One of them slept peacefully, while one gazed at him with wide, solemn eyes.

He made another frantic search of the shelf and fled the room, empty-handed.

Sliding into his loafers, he whispered to Puny, "One of the girls is awake, I saw her eyes—and trust me, I didn't do it!"

"Which one is awake?" inquired the concerned mother.

"Sassy!" he said, gambling. A great howl issued from the study.

He snatched the recovery book from the table and made a run for it.

※

"I thought you'd want to know," said Hoppy, calling early.

"I do."

"I was listening to her heartbeat this morning and something doesn't sound right. There's swelling in her ankles, looks like edema. My guess is early congestive heart failure."

"What can you do?"

"Medication. Some respond, some don't."

He was silent for a moment. "It's hard to get good news out of you, pal."

The doctor sighed. "Right. Let's just say I owe you one."

✳

When he arrived at the Grill for breakfast, he found Mule looking puzzled.

"So why do you think J.C. won't tell us about Adele Lynwood?"

"I think," said the rector, "that he doesn't want anybody to know he's getting overhauled. After what he's said about women to half the population in this town, he's probably trying to save face."

"I think he ought to come out with it and go on about his business. It looks like she's good for him, don't you think?"

"Considering he's dropped twenty-nine pounds, lowered his cholesterol, and carries a clean handkerchief, yes, I think so."

"Fancy Skinner's the best thing that ever happened to me," Mule said proudly.

"Is that right?"

"Yessir, I was rough as a cob when I met her. I'd never taken a drink in my life, but I was about to jump on some Beefeater gin my buddies had lifted off a transfer truck."

"No kidding."

"I was saved by the bell. Her daddy told me, he said, 'Mule, if I ever hear of you takin' a drink, I will personally whip your head to a very bad degree. My lips have never touched liquor,' he said, 'and lips that touch liquor will never touch Fancy's.' Buddy, he stood there in front of me, he was big as a house, her daddy, and I told him I wouldn't—and I didn't."

"Excellent."

"He bought us our first little home."

"Good fellow."

"Three rooms. Neat as a pin. I was sellin' Collier's encyclopedias."

"I didn't know that."

Velma set poached eggs and toast in front of the rector and gave the realtor a box of Wheaties and a bowl.

"Thank you," said Mule, responding to Velma's recent lament that customers seldom said thank you, much less left decent tips. "So is bein' married good for you?"

"Absolutely."

"You never look back?"

"Never. It's the best thing I ever did. Cynthia keeps me … real," he said, meaning it. He pushed the butter aside and took a bite of the dry whole wheat toast his wife insisted was good for him.

Mule stared into his empty bowl. "Velma didn't bring me any milk. No wonder nobody around here says thank you. How can you eat cereal without milk?"

"You can't," said the rector.

Mule looked up, brightening. "Well, I'll be dadgum! Here comes J.C., he's comin' back here straight as a shot. I declare! Speak of th' devil!"

J.C. threw his bulging briefcase under the table and slid in beside Mule, glowering.

Mule slapped him on the back. "Where you been, buddyroe?"

J.C. ignored the question and gave his order to Velma, who had followed him with her order pad. "I'll take two sausage patties, a double order of grits, two buttered biscuits, two eggs over well, and I wouldn't mind if you'd slip a piece of country ham in there."

J.C. removed a section of paper towel from his shirt pocket and mopped his face.

The rector and the realtor turned their heads and looked at each other, blinking.

✳

He pulled the chair close to her bed and sat down and took her hand. Oh, how small it was, and delicate and cool, with the blue veins shining through. He wanted the warmth of his own hand to radiate heat to hers, for his own vitality to flow out like a spring and emerge in her, so she could raise her head and sit up and tell him a story.

"Miss Sadie ..."

"Father."

They were quiet for a time.

"I need you," he said, but that was not at all what he meant to say. "I need you ... to tell me a story."

"Oh, Father. My stories are done."

That was what he had feared most. He could not bear to hear it.

"I don't want to believe that, so I ... I'll just go on believing there are stories yet to be told. Will you promise me one?" He would have to be positive in the face of this thing.

She smiled faintly. "You're a bother."

"I know it!" he said, encouraged. "I am!"

"Let me gather my strength," she said, and turned her head on the pillow to look at him. "And then, perhaps then ..."

"I'll appreciate it," he said, swallowing hard.

He kissed her hand and gently lowered her arm by her side. "There was the story of the 1916 flood you once mentioned."

"Ah. So long ago ..."

"And the story of the dentist who pulled the wrong tooth when you were a little girl. You never told me that from start to finish."

She closed her eyes and smiled. "I'm glad we hired Scott Murphy," she said.

"Yes, ma'am. That was a good thing."

"Go home, now, Father, and rest. If I'm going to tell you a story, I must have time to think which one."

He leaned down and kissed her cool cheek, not wanting to go.

At the door, he paused and looked back, thinking he would say something more, or wave, perhaps, but she had turned her head toward the window.

SEVENTEEN

Sing On!

When he dropped by to see Uncle Billy Watson, the old man welcomed him happily. "Preacher, come set in th' yard an' we'll watch th' traffic."

They walked across the grass, which had been recently mowed and watered by the town crew, and thumped down in chrome dinette chairs stationed by the sign that identified the Porter place as Mitford's Town Museum.

Uncle Billy spit in the bushes and drew his hand across his mouth. "Sadie Baxter ain't doin' too good, is she?"

"She sat up and sang a hymn the other day, but I don't know, Uncle Billy—she's weak."

"She's old!" said Uncle Billy. "That's what it is. Now you take Rose—Rose is startin' t' git s' old, she's losin' her hearin'. Yessir, cain't hardly understand a word I say and won't git aids."

The rector nodded.

"Like th' other day, Rose said t' me, 'Billy, I ain't got a dadblame thing t' do,' an' I said, 'Rose, you ought t' go in there an' start readin'.' Well, she like to had a fit. 'I ought t' go in there an' stop breathin'?' she said. 'You're tellin' me I ought t' go in there an' stop breathin'?' I said, 'Rose, I didn't say no such thing. I said you ought t' go in there an' start readin'.'"

He roared with laughter. "Uncle Billy, I'm sorry to laugh …"

"Oh, don't think nothin' of it, that's th' way I do—I keep laughin', don't you know."

"You're a good one."

"Nossir, I ain't. I lose heart, now'n ag'in."

They watched the traffic circle the monument. Coot Hendrick rattled by in his rusted pickup truck, waving, and they waved back. Ron Malcolm circled in his Cadillac and threw up a hand.

"Preacher, did you hear about th' deputy sheriff who caught a tourist drivin' too fast?"

"Don't believe I did."

"Well, sir, he pulled that tourist over and said, 'Where you from?' An' th' tourist said, 'Chicago.' 'Don't try pullin' that stuff on me,' said th' deputy. 'Your license plate says Illinoise.'"

The rector threw back his head and laughed.

"Did y' hear that 'un about th' feller whose driver's license said he had t' wear glasses when drivin'? Well, th' sheriff stopped 'im, don't you know, an' said, 'Buddy, you're agoin' t' jail for drivin' without glasses.' Th' feller said, 'But Sheriff, I have contacts.' An' th' sheriff said, 'I don't care who you know, you're agoin' t' jail.'"

"Bill Watson, you're good medicine!"

"One more an' I'll walk down th' street with you," said Uncle Billy. "Did y' hear about th' feller hit 'is first golf ball and made a hole in one? Well, sir, he th'owed 'is club down an' stomped off, said, 'Shoot, they ain't nothin' to this game. I quit.'"

He ought to be paying good money for this. "I've got to get down to my office," he said. "Come and walk with me."

Ray Cunningham roared around the monument in his RV and hammered down on the horn. They waved.

"Let me tell Rose I'm agoin' with th' preacher. She don't like me disappearin', don't you know." Uncle Billy creaked out of the chair, and they walked slowly across the yard and around to the side of the house.

"Rose!" called the old man, pounding on the screen door. "Rose, I'm agoin' off with th' preacher. I'll be back."

Miss Rose appeared in a chenille robe, argyle socks, and a shower cap. "You're going to see *Jack*?"

"Said I'll be back!"

"Be back by four o'clock, and I don't mean maybe!"

"See what I'm tellin' you?" said Uncle Billy as they made their way to the sidewalk. "Old age is settin' in t' ever'body! Rose cain't hear and I cain't half remember. What time did she say she wanted me back?"

✳

Winnie Ivey, bless her soul, was spending nights with Louella, who had seldom spent a night alone in her seventy-nine years.

He picked Winnie up when she closed the Sweet Stuff bakery at five-thirty, and, since her car was in the garage and her bunions didn't permit much walking, he drove her to her little house by the bridge, where she fed her cat before going to Louella's.

He sat in Winnie's porch swing and looked across Little Mitford Creek to the green woods. Somewhere in there, quite out of view from this peaceful place, was the community hardly anyone wanted to acknowledge.

Out of sight, out of mind....

When he arrived home at nearly six o'clock, Cynthia was drinking a cup of tea at the kitchen table, with Barnabas at her feet. He saw his wife's face and knew something was wrong.

"Timothy ..."

He pulled out a chair and sat down. "What is it?"

"They want me to sign a paper saying I've seen Lace's bruises, that I know she's been beaten. Then they'll get the district attorney's office involved, and they fully expect to find her and take her out of the home. This is too hard...."

"I know."

"It was one thing to want her out of there, but this is quite another. How can I be the one to sign the paper, to make a decision that will take her away from her mother? And yet, how can I not?"

"They'll give her mother the choice of staying or leaving."

"Yes, but they say she probably won't leave. I asked what might happen, and apparently people often choose the horror over help."

"We haven't seen Lace since her father came home. I wish we knew what's going on. I'd like to think that having work will help his drinking problem, but ..."

"But you don't think so."

"No, I don't think so. What did you tell them?"

"I said I'd let them know by Wednesday. If we do this thing and she's taken away, where will they send her?"

"They'll try to place her with a relative. Failing that, she'll be placed in foster care."

"What if ... that is ... should we consider being her foster care?"

"I have no idea how that works."

She was silent for a time before she spoke again. "I wish I could go to the Creek and see things for myself."

"What possible good would that do? What would that solve?"

"I don't know," she said vaguely. "I don't know."

✳

If there was anything a church had, it was lists, and in no time flat, according to Dave, they would have their lists formatted, bulleted, and numbered, not to mention sorted. Before Dave arrived, he hoisted the manual and read the following:

To change text appearing next to a number in the list, enter text in the Text Before box or the Text After box. To alter a number format or the bullet, select a number or bullet format under Number Format, Bullet Character, or Number or Bullet.

To change the indentation between sections of the list, enter a measurement in the Distance From Indent To Text box.

He noted that, to include hanging indents, he was to select the Hanging Indent box. He would not know a hanging indent if he met it in the street.

He looked with longing at his Royal manual, which sat mutely under its ancient black cover.

"There's only one problem with doin' lists today," Emma announced.

"More than one, to my mind."

"I can't find the folder with the lists in it. The ones we're supposed to key in this morning."

"It was right there on your desk two weeks ago, as I recall."

"Not anymore. I've searched high and low. Did you move it?"

"I never touch your desk." It might have been ringed with barbed wire for all the touching he ever did of her desk. "Which lists did it contain?"

"All the lists. Current membership, Sunday School roll with names, addresses, and phone numbers, lists of pledgers and non-pledgers, lists of people who've made special contributions and memorial gifts ... lists of people who worked on the roof since who-shot-Lizzie ... and oh, a list of all the costs to date on Hope House, and the projected expenses for next year's budget."

"Certainly those lists weren't the originals?" He didn't want to know the answer.

"Well, of course they were the *originals*; they were what I typed directly from all those messy notes you've been giving me since kingdom come. Plus, how was I going to make copies when the copier at the post office stays broken down half the time, and the one at the library's so little you can hardly get a postcard on it? Besides, we've been out of carbon paper practically since I went back to bein' a Baptist."

"We've got to find those lists."

"Fine," she said. "You look."

"Who else has been in here?"

"In the last two weeks? How am I supposed to remember? That chaplain you hired...." She looked at him as if Scott Murphy were the culprit, there was the answer right there.

"Emma ..."

"I know you're mad as a wet hen. But when things get so bad you can't leave a file folder on your own desk without somebody helping themselves, what do you expect?"

✳

"For God has not given us a spirit of fear, but of power, and of love, and of a sound mind," he read aloud from Paul's second letter to Timothy.

He remembered Katherine's passionate counsel on the phone last year before he proposed to Cynthia. He had been sorely afraid of letting go, and Katherine had reminded him in no uncertain terms where fear comes from. If, she reasoned, it doesn't come from God, there's only one other source to consider. "Teds," she said, "fear is of the Enemy." And she was right.

As a young seminarian, he had wanted to believe the letters were, in some supernatural way, written directly to him. There were oddly personal links throughout the letters, not the least of which was Paul's reference to Timothy's mother and grandmother as women of "unfeigned faith." No better description could have been rendered of his own mother and grandmother.

It was a long-standing tradition to read the letters on or near his birthday. Of course, there had been several years when he didn't have a clue that his birthday had come and gone, but this year was different. Now, there was more to celebrate about June 28, only days away, than his nativity in Holly Springs, Mississippi. Now it was also the date on which he'd proposed to his next-door neighbor.

He adjusted his glasses and read toward a favorite passage, a passage that, every year, seemed to stand apart for him.

"Continue in the things which you have learned and been assured of, knowing from whom you have learned them, and that from childhood you have known the Holy Scriptures, which are able to make you wise for salvation through faith which is in Christ Jesus."

He read on, toward the end of the second letter, where the chief apostle made a request. "Bring the cloak that I left with Carpus at Troas ... when you come ..." Because Paul was then almost certainly ill and dying, those few lines never failed to move him.

"Do thy diligence to come before winter," the letter said in closing. In other words, Hurry! Don't let me down. Soon, it will be bitterly cold.

In the end, would he be able to say with Paul, *I have fought a good fight! I have finished the course! I have kept the faith!*

Time, which tells everything, would tell that, also.

✷

He was running late and no help for it.

Opening the office door, he was about to say good morning to his secretary when something brown dashed from nowhere and attached itself to his right ankle, growling.

"What in the dickens?"

Emma lunged from her desk. "Snickers! Come here this minute!"

"Good heavens," he said, trying to shake his ankle free. The teeth weren't actually puncturing the skin, but if he made a wrong move ...

"Don't mind him," said Emma.

Don't *mind* him? This dog was determined to attach itself to his leg permanently.

"Don't pay any attention and he'll stop doing it."

"Oh." He walked to his desk, dragging the dog with him, as if it didn't exist.

"That's Snickers," said Emma. "Since you've pretty much quit bringing Barnabas to work, I thought I'd bring Snickers once in a while."

Was there *any* balm in Gilead?

"I suppose I could just leave my ankle in his mouth until he falls asleep," said the rector, taking the cover off his Royal manual.

Emma peered at him over her glasses. "You don't like my dog?"

"Well …"

"He certainly likes you," she said, offended.

✳

He had wired Roberto in Florence, asking if his grandfather might write a letter to Miss Sadie.

It would be good medicine to have word from her childhood friend, Leonardo. As a young boy, Leonardo had lived at Fernbank with his artist father for three years, transforming the ballroom ceiling into a heavenly dome alive with a host of angels.

When the letter arrived at the church office, carefully translated into English, he took it to the hospital at once.

"May I read it to you?" he asked, sitting by her bed.

She nodded, and he noticed how transparent her skin seemed. He had never noticed that before.

My dearest Sadie,

    Time continues to be money, my cherished friend, but I no longer care about such things.

What do I care about, then, and what moves me, still? Hearing Roberto sing your praises, and tell of the journey he made last June into the bosom of your family and friends, and of the grand occasion held in your ballroom, that same lovely room in which my father and I labored so happily.

I delight to listen again and again to Roberto's description of the ceiling, which had grown faded in memory, but which he has made vividly fresh and beautiful to me once more.

I care, Sadie, that I have lived my life doing what I loved most passionately—painting. That is all I ever wanted to do, I never once thought of being a banker, or pondered the lure of exporting, I was able to do what I loved! I consider this a most extraordinary miracle in a world which conspires to rob us of our dreams, and even of our passion.

Your priest tells us that you have fallen, but that your spirits are strong and you are singing in your bed! That is the Sadie Baxter who met us at the door so many years ago and said, Tempo e denaro! Time is money! Did you know that my father often pressed me to quicken my brushstrokes, in remembrance of what you said to us in greeting? He thought your father had asked you to say it, being too much a gentleman to press us himself.

I, also, lie in bed these days, and am not often up. My old enemy, arthritis, afflicts me savagely. Yet I, too, sing in my bed, Sadie, the old music from La Traviata. I have no voice left, it is my spirit which sings.

My dear friend, across half the world, I challenge you:

Sing on! Sing on!

You live forever in my soul.

Yours faithfully,

Leonardo Francesca

Miss Sadie nodded, which told him she had heard and was pleased.

"Where is Louella?" she asked, looking out the window.

"I'm going to get her at nine o'clock and bring her to see you."

"Oh, Father," she said slowly, "you don't have time to be ferrying people around."

"It's my job to ferry people around, if it has anything to do with you."

She turned her gaze to him. "I wasn't going to tell you this, Father, for it might give you the big head ..."

"Tell me!" he said, urgent. "Whatever it is, I promise I won't get the big head."

"We've had seven priests in my eighty years at Lord's Chapel, and you ... you are the one who has loved us best."

He swallowed hard. Whatever he did, he must seize the moment. "And the thanks I get from you is no more stories?"

She closed her eyes and smiled. "When you come again," she said. "But I hope you won't expect too much, Father. I think I've spoiled you with stories of angels and painted ceilings, and broken hearts that never mended."

"Miss Sadie, you can tell me anything. You can read me the phone book, for all I care! Just keep ..."

She looked at him.

"Just keep being Miss Sadie."

She closed her eyes again and he bent down and kissed her forehead. "Would you like me to bring you a bag of donut holes?" Please say yes, he thought.

"Oh, no. No."

He tried to sing "Love Divine, All Loves Excelling" as he drove down the hill, but he could not.

✳

"Happy birthday!" crowed his wife, kissing his face.

"What in the world?"

"Wake up, sleepyhead, it's your birthday! You're now a full seven years older than me, and I'm thrilled!"

"Being seven years older than you will last less than a month, so enjoy it while you can."

"Oh, I will, I will! Now sit up, I've brought your coffee."

"I've never had coffee in bed in my life, except for a cup Dooley brewed when I had the flu. What time is it, anyway? Good Lord, Kavanagh, it's not even daylight."

"I had to do it now because if I didn't, you'd be careening down Main Street in that funny jogging suit, or in your study doing the Morning Office."

"What is this?" he asked suspiciously, taking the tray on his lap and looking at something discreetly covered with a napkin.

"First, drink your coffee. Then I have a little present for you."

"A present? At five o'clock in the morning? This is earlier than I ever got up for Santa Claus when I was a kid."

"Isn't it fun?" she asked, sitting cross-legged on the bed.

"For you, maybe. I have my hospital visits, two meetings before noon, Winnie Ivey to fetch back to the bakery, and a sermon to finish so I can squire you out to dinner Saturday evening. Not to mention another round with the computer technician."

"Oh, dear. Dave?"

"Dave."

"Ummm. Drink your coffee, dearest."

"By the way," he said, "happy anniversary of ... well, you know."

"Say it, you big lug."

"Of the night I hauled myself down on one knee and recklessly abandoned my freedom, my liberty—"

"Your boring existence as a dry old crust ..."

"Exactly."

He had taken his first sip of coffee from his favorite mug when the phone rang. No, he thought. Please, not that....

It was Nurse Kennedy. Someone had been critically burned. Would he come and pray at the hospital, or did he want to do it at home?

"Pray," he told Cynthia as he hurriedly dressed. "A burn victim."

All he could think as he drove up the hill was, Why, God?

✳

"They don't know who it is, Father. It's somebody from the Creek, that's all I can tell you. Dr. Harper's having a trauma surgeon fly in who knows more about what to do. He and Dr. Wilson are both working in there. He says to pray like you've never prayed before."

"It's bad?"

"It's very bad."

Bill Sprouse had talked about families who got burned out at the Creek, but that was in winter, when kerosene stoves and open fireplaces posed a threat.

He didn't dare think....

He ran after the retreating nurse, his heart pounding. "Kennedy! Is it a girl?"

"I don't think so, Father. Is it important to know?"

"Yes!" he said. "Very!"

"I'll find out as soon as I can." She walked away quickly, the soles of her shoes making loud squishing noises along the empty hallway.

✳

Kennedy knocked lightly and opened Hoppy's office door. "One of the nurses says it's not a girl. It's an adult female."

"Do you know who it is, then?"

"No, sir. Nurse Gilbert says the patient can't talk, and whoever brought the patient didn't stay."

"No idea who she is?"

"They said she's wearing a bracelet with the initials LM. I think Dr. Harper wants you with her when she goes to isolation, that's what I heard—but he hasn't come and said anything to me."

"Whatever," he said, meaning it.

✳

There were two choices, Hoppy once told him. A doctor could believe the patient was going to live, or that the patient was going to die. He had referred to something a patient told him about her former physician. She said he hadn't believed she was going to live. In fact, she went on to say she felt like the doctor's attitude was killing her.

Nurse Kennedy rapped on the door and peered in.

"Father, Dr. Harper wants you in isolation in ten minutes. He asked me to give you a rundown.

"It's a forty percent burn, primarily on the left side of the body and mostly third-degree. No eye injury, but a lot of grafting will be necessary. They've put the patient on a respirator, to keep the airway open. It was a flash burn with kerosene, there was some inhalation injury, and swelling was occluding the airway. She can't talk, even without the endotracheal tube, and probably won't be able to for several days."

"Grafting ..." he said, remembering a seminary friend who was in a car accident.

"Yes, sir. They've just washed off the debris and given her another shot of morphine for the pain, but there's a lot of pain that can't be controlled. The trauma surgeon said to talk to her, it will calm her. We hope you don't mind doing it. You're so good at it."

"Of course I don't mind. Anything else I should know?"

"Dr. Harper will tell you anything else. They've admitted her as LM, for the time being. Want some coffee?"

If he had passed out when Sassy Guthrie came into the world, what might he do in the face of this hellish thing?

✳

Isolation.

As he opened the door to the gray room, he felt he was stepping into a place removed, out of time. And the smell. There was always the alien smell of fluids that didn't belong to the human frame, but could, nonetheless, sustain it.

The suffering beneath the mound of wet dressing was palpable. He felt the impact of it like a blow.

He walked to the bed and looked hard at what he could see of the patient. Only a small portion of the right side of her face was visible, distorted by the large tube that entered her mouth. The smell of saline, which permeated the dressings, came to him like a sour wind from the sea. Dear God. Could he speak?

The patient opened her eye and gazed into his, and he suddenly felt the power to do this thing surge through him.

"You're not alone. I'm with you."

Tears coursed from her eye onto the pillow, and he took a tissue from the box by the bed. He started to wipe her tears, but instinctively drew back, afraid of inflicting pain with his touch.

"I've asked the Holy Spirit to be with us, also."

He had seen eyes that beseeched him from the very soul, but he hadn't seen anything like this in his life as a priest.

He had no idea where the thought came from—it seemed to come from a place in him as deep as the patient's desperation. "I'm asking God to give me some of your pain," he said, hoarse with feeling. "I'll share this thing with you."

She looked at him again and closed her eye.

He brought the chair from the corner of the gray room and placed it next to her bed, and sat down.

Lord, give me power and grace to do what I just said I'd do. Whatever it takes.

✳

He called the little yellow house and told Cynthia what he knew.

"The decision has been made, then," she said.

"What do you mean?"

"The burn victim from the Creek—I was praying for a sign, something certain, and this is it. Lace must be taken out of that hell."

"Yes," he said.

"I can't imagine what's going on, why we haven't seen her. I'll call social services and find out if they've learned anything. Then I'll go and sign the papers."

"Let me know. I'll be home … sometime. Probably before dinner. I have the distinct sense I'm to stick here."

"I'll bring Louella to see Miss Sadie at eleven, and I'll fetch Winnie this evening. Against everything that strives to make it otherwise, I shall say it anyway—happy birthday, dearest love."

"You're precious to me, Kavanagh."

His wife gulped and hung up.

✳

He had missed Dave, the computer technician, but Emma had not. She'd been there, alone, for a two-hour session he presumed would put her over the edge.

The least he could do was call. "How was it?" he asked cautiously.

"It was terrific! It was fabulous!"

"It was?" Had his hearing failed utterly?

"Dave brought lunch, it was cheeseburgers all the way and fries with milkshakes. We ate ours and split yours."

"Glad to be of service." He dreaded the rest of the conversation.

"Finally, I don't know how it happened, but I just got … I don't know, it started coming together. You won't believe this …"

"Try me."

"I did the first page of the newsletter."

"No!"

"All the margins, a bulleted list, your message of the month, and the masthead."

"Fantastic!"

"Not to mention a border. And not just a bunch of those dumb rule lines, either."

"Really?"

"Greek keys," she said with feeling. "Dave brought me a free solitaire program, and you get *Learning the Books of the Bible.*"

"I'll be darned."

"You won't have to hire some young thing with her skirt up to here, after all," she crowed.

"Aha."

"But you will have to give me a raise."

"Well ..."

"And I don't mean maybe!"

He viewed this turn of events as the best birthday present, bar none, since Cynthia Coppersmith accepted his marriage proposal. If Emma Newland would take on the infernal nuisance of the whole thing, including hanging indents, he wouldn't oppose her raise for all the tea in China.

"By the way," said Emma, "I found the file folder with the lists in it."

"Where?"

"Under the seat cushion of Harold's recliner next to the TV in our sunroom."

He didn't inquire, because he didn't want to know.

✳

Hoppy creaked back in his desk chair, exhausted.

"What's the worst that can happen?" he asked, exhausted himself.

"Infection. Pneumonia. Setbacks. If we don't have one or all of these, it will be a minor miracle."

"Tell me everything."

"The burns are of mixed depths—some partial, but mostly full-thickness burns. I don't think there'll be any grafting to fat, but I won't know until Cornell Wyatt gets here. He'll fly in tomorrow with his burn nurse, and we expect to harvest the donor sites the following day."

"What areas will need new skin?"

"The left side of her face—we'll probably harvest the graft from behind the ear and neck on the right side. Her neck, shoulder, arm, upper body, and portion of the upper hip will also be recipient sites. It looks like an explosion, maybe the kerosene ignited in front of her and exploded as she turned away."

"I have a special feeling for this patient."

"Why?"

"I don't have a clue," he said. "Maybe it's the praying. I think when we pray for others, even total strangers, it bonds us in ways we can't understand."

"We're pulling this thing together by the seat of our pants. I've never had serious burn experience. Cornell owes me a big one, and this is a big one. By the way, LM lost her left ear."

"Blast."

"We'll be changing her dressings twice a day until the grafts are done, and no amount of morphine can kill the pain that comes with that. I'd like you to be with her after the dressing changes, whenever you can, around nine in the morning and eight at night. I know you're busy, this is not your job …"

"Actually, it is my job."

"LM," said Hoppy, abstractedly looking at the wall. "Cornell said if we could call her by her first name, it would help."

"What's the best that can happen?"

"With no pneumonia, no infection, no setbacks, she'll be here two, maybe three weeks, then to Winston-Salem for some very aggressive physical therapy. Best scenario, a long recovery and pronounced scarring."

"How is the grafting done?"

"You don't want to know."

"I do want to know."

"Picture a machine like an electric cheese slicer. You adjust the calibration to the desired thickness and width of the graft you need to harvest. I've heard burn patients say the sound of it gave them nightmares for years.

"In any case, it generally gives you a nice sheet of skin from the buttocks, which can be used for trunk and arm injuries. Bottom line, grafting is a big slice of hell for everybody—doctors, staff, and patient alike."

"I wouldn't have your job, pal."

"I wouldn't have yours."

"So, it's a wash," said the rector, managing a smile. "I'm going in to talk with LM a few minutes, then I'll step down the hall to Miss Sadie. How is she?"

Hoppy ran his fingers through his graying hair. He started to speak, then changed his mind.

✳

If Hoppy was short on burn experience, so was he. They were all flying by the seat of their pants.

He stood by her bed and held the rail, and watched the random flickering of the lid over her closed eye. Sleeping, perhaps, or lost in the mist produced by morphine. The air in the tube that formed her breath sounded harsh against the constant hiss and gurgle of the IV drips.

He prayed aloud, but kept his voice quiet. "Our Father, thank You for being with us, for we can't bear this alone. Cool and soothe, heal and restore, love and protect. Comfort and unite those who're concerned for her, and keep them in Your care.

We're asking for your best here, Lord, we're expecting it. In Jesus' name."

She opened her eye after a moment and he looked into the deep well of it, feeling a strangely familiar connection.

"Hey, there," he said, smiling foolishly.

EIGHTEEN

Every Trembling Heart

Sadie Eleanor Baxter died peacefully in her sleep on June 30, in the early hours of the morning.

When the rector of Lord's Chapel received the phone call, he went at once to the hospital room, where he took Miss Sadie's cold hand and knelt and prayed by her bedside.

He then drove to the church, climbed the stairs to the attic, and tolled the death bell twenty times. The mournful notes pealed out on the light summer air, waking the villagers to confusion, alarm, or a certain knowing.

"It's old Sadie Baxter," said Coot Hendrick's mother, sitting up in bed in a stocking cap. Coot, who was feeding a boxful of biddies he had bought to raise for fryers, called from the kitchen, "Lay back down, Mama!"

Mule Skinner turned over and listened, but didn't wake Fancy, who could have slept through the bombing of London. "There went Miss Baxter," he whispered to the darkened room.

J.C. Hogan heard the bells in his sleep and worked them into a dream of someone hammering spikes on a railroad being laid to

Tulsa, Oklahoma. *Bong, bong, bong, John Henry was a steel dri-vin' man ...*

Cynthia Kavanagh got up and prayed for her husband, whose pain she felt as if it were her own, and went to the kitchen and made coffee, and sat at the table in her robe, waiting until a reasonable hour to call Meadowgate Farm and all the others who'd want to know.

Winnie Ivey, awake since four-thirty, stopped in the middle of the kitchen on Lilac Road, where a dim light burned in the hood of the stove, and prayed, thanking God for the life of one who had cared about people and stood for something, and who, as far as she was concerned, would never be forgotten.

Louella Baxter Marshall had not been asleep when she heard the bells toll; she had been praying on and off throughout the night, and weeping and talking aloud to Miss Sadie and the Lord. When the tolling came, she sat up, and, without meaning to, exactly, exclaimed, "Thank you, Jesus! Thank you for takin' her home!"

Lew Boyd heard the bells and woke up and looked at his watch, which he never took off except in the shower, and saw the long line of automobiles snaking up to his gas pumps and buying his candy and cigarettes and canned drinks. Sadie Baxter's funeral would draw a crowd, he could count on it. He sighed and went back to sleep until his watch beeped.

Jena Ivey, who was up and entering figures in her ledger for Mitford Blossoms, shivered. She would have to hire on help to do the wreaths and sprays for this one. This would be bigger than old Parrish Guthrie's had ever hoped to be, the old so-and-so, and so what if Miss Sadie had never bought so much as a gloxinia from Mitford Blossoms, Sadie Baxter had been a lady and she had loved this town and done more for it than anybody else ever would, God rest her soul in peace.

Esther Bolick punched Gene and woke him up.

"Sadie Baxter's gone," she said.

"How d'you know?"

"The bells are tolling."

"Maybe it's th' president or somebody like that," said Gene, who remembered the hoopla over Roosevelt's passing.

"I don't think so," said his wife. "I saw the president on TV yesterday and he looked fit as a fiddle."

Percy Mosely was leaving his house at the edge of town when he heard the first tolling. He removed his hat and placed it over his heart and was surprised to feel a tear coursing down his cheek for someone he'd hardly ever exchanged five words with in his life, but whose presence above the town, at the crest of the steep fern bank, had been a consolation for as long as he could remember.

✳

After tolling the bell, the rector went to Lilac Road and sat with Louella and prayed the ancient prayer of commendation: "Acknowledge, we humbly beseech you, a sheep of your own fold, a lamb of your own flock.... Receive her into the arms of your mercy, into the blessed rest of everlasting peace, and into the glorious company of the saints...."

Then he did what others after him would do with Sadie Baxter's lifelong friend. He sat and wept with her, sobbing like a child.

✳

He dialed the number and listened to the odd, buzzing ring of a rural telephone.

"Brother Greer ..." he said.

"Is it Sadie?" asked the old man.

"It is."

"I'll come, then," said Absalom.

✳

He had done this for thirty-eight years—arranging the funeral, delivering the service, consoling the family. But now he was the family, and there was no consolation anywhere. It was as if a part of his own life had been suddenly lost, and there was no getting it back again.

✳

He signed the papers that allowed her body to be taken to Holding and cremated, and was wondering what to do about a marker and urn when the phone rang.

"Father Kavanagh? Lewis Cromwell of Cromwell, Cromwell and Lessing, in Wesley. We've been the Baxter family law firm since the turn of the century."

"Of course. Miss Sadie often spoke of you and your father and grandfather."

"I've just learned of her passing; Louella called this morning. I wanted you to know there's a letter here, and it was Miss Baxter's express wish that you have it immediately following her death."

"How shall I get it?"

"We'll send it over to you. I have a young assistant who must come that way to pick up produce at your local grocery store. You know how fond we Wesleyans are of your fine grocer."

"Avis Packard is almost as famous as his advertising professes."

"I know you were important to Miss Baxter, and we'd like to express our condolences to you, sir."

"Thank you."

"It's the end of an era," said Lewis Cromwell.

✳

It was delivered to the office as he was leaving for home.

He hardly knew what to do with it. Perhaps he should sit with it awhile before he opened it. She had inscribed his name on the front of the fat envelope in her spidery scrawl, and sealed it with Scotch tape that looked nearly fresh.

When he arrived home, he thumped down at the kitchen table, holding it in his hand.

"Take it to your study," said Cynthia, "and I'll bring you a pot of tea."

He didn't want tea. He didn't want to go to his study. He felt desperately worn and addled, as if he had overused his mind for something he couldn't even call to memory.

He wanted to lie down, that's what he wanted. But somehow, that was no way to read a letter, especially a letter from the departed. That seemed to warrant sitting up in a straight-back chair.

"Blast," he said to nothing and no one in particular.

"Then take it over to my house," she said, reading his mind. "Sit on my love seat in the studio. That's what I do when I need consolation."

He didn't want to go over to her small, empty house and sit on that small love seat in that small room.

"Why don't I just sit here and read it?" he asked, looking forlorn.

"Wonderful! Do you mind if I make dinner while you sit there?"

Mind? He couldn't think of anything he'd like better. He suddenly felt protected by his wife's close presence, the familiarity of the cooking ritual, the ordinariness of it all.

Brightening, he opened the letter with a table knife.

The date was September seventh of the previous year.

Dear Father,

We have just come home from your lovely wedding ceremony, and I don't know when our hearts have felt so refreshed. The joy of it makes my pen fairly fly over the page.

To see you taking a bride, even after so many years, seemed like the most natural thing in the world. Certainly no one can ever say that you married in haste to repent at leisure!

Long years ago when I loved Willard so dearly and hoped against hope that we might marry, I wrote down something Martin Luther said. He said, there is no more lovely, friendly and charming relationship, communion, or company than a good marriage.

May God bless you and Cynthia to enjoy a good marriage, and a long and happy life together.

As you know, I have given a lot of money to human institutions, and I would like to give something to a human individual for a change.

I have prayed about this and so has Louella and God has given us the go ahead.

I am leaving Mama's money to Dooley.

We think he has what it takes to be somebody. You know that Papa was never educated, and look what he became with no help at all. And Willard—look what he made of himself without any help from another soul.

Father, having no help can be a good thing. But having help can be even better—if the character is strong. I believe you are helping Dooley develop the kind of character that will go far in this world, and so the money is his when he reaches the age of twenty-one.

(I am old fashioned and believe that eighteen is far too young to receive an inheritance.)

I have put one and a quarter million dollars where it will grow, and have made provisions to complete his preparatory education. When he is eighteen, the income from the trust will help send him through college.

I am depending on you never to mention this to him until he is old enough to bear it with dignity. I am also depending on you to stick with him, Father, through thick and thin, just as you've done all along.

When you receive this letter, there are two things you will need to know at once. First, the urn for my ashes is in the attic at Fernbank. When you go up the stairs, turn to the right and go all the way to the back. I have left it there on a little table, it is from czarist Russia, which Papa once visited. Don't scatter me among any rose bushes, Father, I know how you think. Just stick the urn in the ground as far away from Parrish Guthrie as you can, cover it with enough dirt to support a tuft of moss, and add my little marker.

The other thing you need to know at once is that my marker is with Mr. Charles Hartley of Hartley's Monument Company in Holding. It is paid for. You might say it is on hold in Holding, ha ha. I think it is foolish nonsense to choose one's own epitaph, it makes one either overly modest or overly boastful. I leave this task to you, and trust you not to have anything fancy or high-toned engraved thereon, for I am now and always will be just plain Sadie.

I am going to lay down my pen and rest, but will take it up again this evening. It is so good to write this letter, which has been composing in my head for years! It was your wedding today which made me understand that one must get on with one's life, and that always includes the solemn consideration of one's death.

He looked up to see his wife rubbing a chicken with olive oil, and humming quietly to herself. An extraordinary sight, somehow, in view of this even more extraordinary letter.

He noted the renewed strength of Miss Sadie's handwriting as the letter resumed.

We are going to watch TV this evening and pop some corn, so I will make it snappy.

As for Fernbank, I ask you to go through the attic with Olivia and Cynthia and take whatever you like. Take anything that suits you from the house, also. I can't imagine what it might be, but I would like you to select something for Mr. Buck Leeper, who is doing such a lovely job with Hope House. Perhaps something of Papa's would be in order.

Whatever is left, please give it to the needy, or to your Children's Hospital. Do not offer anything for view at a yard sale or let people pick over the remains. I know you will understand.

I leave Fernbank to supply any future requirements of Hope House. Do with my homeplace what you will, but please treat it kindly. If I should pass before Louella, she has a home for life at Hope House, and provision to cover any special needs. I know you will do all in your power to look after her, she is my sister and beloved friend.

It would be grand if I could live to be a hundred, and go Home with a smile on my face. I believe I will! But if not, I have put all the buttons on my affairs, and feel a light spirit for whatever God has in store for me.

May our Lord continue to bless you, Father, you mean the world to

yours truly,

Sadie Eleanor Baxter

He looked up and met Cynthia's concerned gaze.

"What is it, dearest?"

"You mustn't speak this to another soul," he said.

"I won't. I promise."

"Sit down," he said. She sat.

"Dooley Barlowe," he told her, "is a millionaire."

＊

"No one ever thinks the preacher might be sad at a funeral," said Absalom Greer, who had come to the rector's office.

"You're right about that."

"They don't know we suffer, too."

The two men grew silent for a moment, drinking their coffee.

"How did you get here?" asked the rector.

"Th' man that keeps my orchard, he brought me in his truck. He'll bring me back for the memorial service."

"After the service, we'll take the urn to the churchyard. There'll be just a few of us for that. Will you come?"

"Oh, I will," said the old man. "I once told Sadie Baxter I'd love her to her grave, and I'm a man of my word." His blue eyes twinkled. "Lottie told me this morning, she said, 'Absalom, I forgive Sadie.' It was all I could do to keep from saying, 'This is a fine time to do it, after she's dead and gone.' If I was the Lord, I'd say that dog won't hunt."

"Thank heaven you're not the Lord," said the rector.

They laughed easily.

"I wonder who she left her money to," wondered Absalom. "The church, I'd say."

"That's a good guess."

"Sadie's life will preach up a storm. You'll have a fine subject and a big crowd. What do you want me to do?"

"I'd like you to sit with Louella and Olivia and Hoppy, as family."

"I will, and glad to."

"You sent Lacey Turner to see me," said the rector.

"I knew you'd help her, if you could."

"I want you to know we care about her. I reported the abuse, and the DA's office is looking for her. They'll put her in foster care if they can't locate a relative."

The old preacher nodded. "It's a hard case, Brother, a hard case. God help you to do what you can."

✳

Louella would sing a hymn in her throaty mezzo soprano, which was as consoling as raisins in warm bread. No, she wouldn't break down, she was wanting to do it! Hadn't she sung with Miss Sadie since they were both little children?

The choir director, who was known for inventiveness, suggested Dooley sing with Louella, but no one thought he would. The rector called the boy, anyway.

"What're we singing?" Dooley asked, already persuaded.

"'Love Divine, All Loves Excelling.'"

"No problem. What instruments?"

"Organ and trumpets."

"I can't sing over trumpets," said Dooley.

"You don't have to sing when the trumpets are playing."

"When is rehearsal?"

"Tomorrow at three o'clock. I'll see you at Meadowgate around two."

"I'm sorry she died," he said. "It seemed like she'd live a long time."

That, he thought, is the way it always seems with someone we love.

✳

He raced to the hospital to see LM. Who had sat with her after the last dressing change? How was the morphine doing? Any signs of infection? A few hours away from a desperate situation could seem interminable; he felt out of the loop.

"So far, so good," said Nurse Gilbert. "They start grafting in the morning. Dr. Wyatt got in last night with his nurse."

He let himself into the room and stood by her bed.

"Hey, there," he said, softly.

It appeared she had not moved since he first saw her. Still the great, swollen mass of wet dressings and the odor that stung the nostrils. Still the eye looking desperately into his, and the air pumping mechanically from the respirator into the green tube.

He didn't know why, but as he looked down at her, something in him connected with a new reality. It suddenly became real to him that Sadie Baxter was where the gospel had promised a redeemed soul would be—in Paradise. If he believed that so fully and completely, why was he grieving? Because it had taken time for such supernal knowledge to make its way from his heart to his head. Or was it from his head to his heart?

He realized that he was smiling uncontrollably, as he had smiled in those first months of his marriage. Tears sprang to his eyes, tears of joy, and he felt he should turn away from the woman lying there who felt no joy, whose tears were born of an agony he couldn't possibly know. But he couldn't turn away. He felt riveted there, beaming, as if his face were not his own.

He reached out to touch her right hand, the one that was completely and wholly well, and saw that he took it, and held it, and wept and did not turn away.

✳

"Father! It's Scott Murphy!"

"I needed to hear your voice, my friend."

"I'm excited about coming to Hope House, sir. September is only two months away, and I've already given my notice. How are things in Mitford?"

"Sadie Baxter has died. The memorial service is tomorrow." That was precisely how things were in Mitford—that one event had, for him, obscured all others.

"Miss Baxter? She died? She was ... so alive when I saw her!"

"She fell, and couldn't recover from the shock of what came with it. I want you to know how heartily she approved of you."

"I'll do my best to honor that, sir."

There was a comfortable silence.

"I'd like you to know what I've been thinking, Father, if it's not too premature to talk about it."

"Never too soon."

"I was wondering ... I've seen how positively the elderly respond to animals—rabbits, dogs, kittens, I've even worked with ponies. I was just wondering, sir, if there might be anything left in the Hope House budget to build a small ... kennel."

"A *kennel*?"

"Too rash?" asked Scott, concerned.

"You must admit it's not the ordinary line of thinking."

"But that's just it, Father. Ordinary lines of thinking don't extend far enough when reaching into the lives of people who're often losing touch."

"Keep talking."

"Only a small kennel, so the animals could visit on a regular basis. It's awkward to round up people who'll bring their dogs and cats in. As I recall, that area behind the parking garage might work for a kennel and a run. But it's just a thought, sir, only a thought. Actually, we have the greatest resource of all, right down the street from Hope House."

"We do?"

"At Lord's Chapel. The children, sir."

"Aha."

"I don't have to tell you what a positive influence children and old people can have on each other."

Where had his own enthusiasm gone? Had it flown with his youth?

"I'm also thinking of a garden. There's a plot behind the dining hall that would be perfect for the residents because it's easy to get to. A little digging in the dirt can be good for the soul."

"Absolutely!"

"Anyway, Father, I just wanted you to know that I'm very excited about my future in Mitford, and I thank you—and Miss Baxter—for asking me to come."

"It will be a fine thing, Scott, I know it in my bones."

"Speaking of bones, Luke and Lizzie send their regards."

He laughed when he hung up. Scott Murphy's new blood would be good, indeed, for this old rector, not to mention the forty residents of Hope House who, whether they liked it or not, would be forced to enjoy their last years.

✳

On his way down Main Street from Lew Boyd's, he saw the Independence Day parade forming behind the police station.

The Mitford School Chorus was at the front, as always, carrying the banner inscribed with the mayor's longtime political platform. *Mitford Takes Care of Its Own.*

Next came Coot Hendrick's truck, loaded with hay, and kids waving American flags.

The truck was followed by Fancy Skinner's pink Cadillac, with Mule's real estate sign on the hood and a Hair House sign on the rear. He saw Fancy, dressed in a pink sweater and Capri pants, polishing the hood ornament with a rag.

Still jockeying for position, it appeared, was a woman in a cowboy hat, leading two llamas. He heard the Presbyterian brass band strike up somewhere, and caught a glimpse of a drum majorette who, he presumed, was borrowed from Wesley.

As he drove down Main Street, already lined with spectators, he saw cars turning into the Lord's Chapel parking lot.

To other eyes, perhaps, the north end of Main was getting ready to celebrate while the south end was in mourning.

But he didn't see it that way. Not at all.

✳

While the trumpets sounded the good news of Sadie Baxter's presence in a glorious heaven, the electric cheese slicer would sound LM's entry into a living hell.

"Pray for LM," he said to Marge and Olivia before the memorial service.

Ron Malcolm overhead the request. "I'll pray, too," he said.

A priest was thankful for people who didn't need all the details, but took the smallest request to heart, and acted.

✳

"The people have gathered, the trumpets have sounded!" he exclaimed. "Sadie Eleanor Baxter is at home and at peace, and I charge us all to be filled with the joy of this simple, yet wondrous fact."

How often had people heard that, for a Christian, death is but the ultimate triumph, a thing to celebrate? The hope was that it cease being a fact merely believed with the head, and become a fact to know with the heart, as he now knew it.

He looked out to the congregation who packed the nave to bursting, and saw that they knew it too. They had caught the spark. A kind of warming fire ran through the place, kindled with excitement and wonder.

When Louella sang, her voice was steady as a rock, mingling sweetly, yet powerfully, with the boy's. Their music flooded the church with a high consolation.

Jesus, Thou art all compassion
Pure, unbounded love Thou art
Visit us with Thy salvation
Enter every trembling heart ...

Into the silence that followed the music, and true to his Baptist roots, Absalom Greer raised a heartfelt "Amen!"

The rector looked to the pew where Sadie Baxter had sat for the fifteen years he had been in this pulpit, and saw Olivia and Hoppy, Louella and Absalom holding hands. Those left behind....

"We don't know," he said, in closing, "who among us will be the next to go, whether the oldest or the youngest. We pray that he or she will be gently embraced by death, have a peaceful end, and a glorious resurrection in Christ.

"But for now, let us go in peace—to love and serve the Lord."

"Thanks be to God!" said the congregation, meaning it.

The trumpets blew mightily, and the people moved to the church lawn, where Esther Bolick's three-tiered cake sat on a fancy table, where the ECW had stationed jars of icy lemonade, and where, as any passerby could see, a grand celebration was under way.

✳

"There," he said, placing the small, engraved stone over the fresh earth. *Sadie Eleanor Baxter*, it read. *Beloved.*

✳

She didn't open her eyes at all. He had no way of knowing whether she realized he had come, or even cared.

He pulled the chair close to her bed and sat down. Today, they had taken sheets of skin from the back of her neck, her buttocks, and abdomen, and done all the grafting in one long ordeal, which he saw reflected in the face of every nurse he encountered in the hallway.

All of it was beyond words, but he did the best he could.

"Hey, there," he said.

✳

"Timothy!" It was Marge Owen.

"I thought you'd like to know that Dooley delivered twin calves this evening! Hal had gone to a Grange meeting, and Mr. Shuford called and said his prize heifer was having a bad time. I drove Dooley to his farm and ... he did it!"

He gulped.

"Maybe it wasn't strictly ethical, but ..."

"Someone had to do it!" he said, heady with pride. "Put him on if he's around."

He heard Marge calling, "Dooley! Dooley?"

Dooley.

"Hey," Dooley said in his grown-up voice.

"Hey, yourself. Tell me everything. Twins, was it?" Sissy and Sassy had started a trend.

"It was Mr. Shuford's best heifer, and Miz Shuford was out in the barn having a fit. She said that heifer was her best friend. I never heard of such a thing, but I knew I better get it right."

He laughed.

"The heifer was in dystocia. If somebody hadn't been there,

she could have died. I saw these feet sticking out, one front hoof and one back hoof, and when I reached in there, I could tell there was two calves. I like to died. I figured I had to match up the hooves before I started pulling or I could have strangled one of the calves or something.

"So I run my arm in there and found the front hoof that went with the back hoof that was sticking out, and started pulling, and pretty soon, we had two calves lying in the straw."

Dooley took a deep breath. "I can't exactly remember everything."

"What did Mrs. Shuford say?"

"She gave me a big hug and all, and Mr. Shuford, he gave me a twenty-dollar bill and said it was mine to keep."

"Phew! What a story. I'm proud as heck."

"Yeah," said Dooley. The rector could almost hear the grin spreading over the boy's face.

"I'd like you to tell Cynthia, but she's taking a bath. Can she call you in the morning?"

"She better call before seven. I'm going with Doc Owen to Asheville, to a vet meeting or something."

"Big doings, pal. Well, listen—we love you."

"I love you back!" said Dooley.

He literally jumped around the room, shouting.

"Yee hah!" he yelled. "Yee hah!"

※

There was no need to hurry back to Fernbank to go through her possessions. That could wait until things slowed down, when it would be a pleasure and not a burden.

He had checked the house carefully when he went for the urn. The roof was still leaking, but not enough to pose a problem as long as he left the pots where they were.

Winnie Ivey had agreed to spend her nights with Louella until

Hope House opened in the fall. Winnie appreciated the extra money, but better than that, she and Louella liked each other's company.

All he had to do was go to the law office in Wesley and sign a few papers, which he'd take care of next week.

He mused that he might drive Cynthia to Meadowgate on Sunday, and they'd all troop over to the Shufords and see the twins. It made him grin, just thinking about it.

Cynthia offered to sit with LM in the evening; in fact, she insisted on it.

"Can you handle it?" he asked. "It's not ... easy, exactly."

"Of course I can handle it. I'm your deacon."

She brought his supper on a tray, and did everything but feed him with a spoon. "Now, rest," she told him, stern as any school principal, "and I don't mean maybe."

Which was worse? Emma Newland or his own wife?

"Yes, ma'am," he said, lying on the sofa and stuffing a pillow under his head. Barnabas leaped up and crashed on top of him, sighing. What more could he ask of life, after all?

He had just fallen asleep when the phone rang.

"Timothy? She wants you."

"Who?" he said, feeling groggy.

"LM. They say she's looking around the room for you, and seems agitated. I wasn't going to disturb you, no matter what, but ... even I feel this desperation in her. They're taking the breathing tube out in a little while. Can you come?"

"I'll be right up."

The questions he'd been storing were endless.

Who are you? Why hasn't your family been here? How did this happen? What does LM stand for? He had thought Lillian, perhaps, for no sensible reason. How old are you? What do you do? What can I do?

When he arrived at the hospital, Cynthia went home to work on her book, which was due at the publisher in only four weeks.

"Stop at my house as soon as you get home," she said, looking anguished. "I want to know."

In the hallway, he met Hoppy, who grinned at him with relief. "You can come in while we take out the breathing tube. We're so used to you, it's like you work here."

He waited until the thing was finished, the tube out, and went and stood by the bed. "You probably can't say much for a day or two," Hoppy told his patient. "This thing was inserted between your vocal cords, which means your throat will be sore, and talking won't feel so good. Go easy."

He knew Hoppy was also curious to know more about his patient, but respectfully let the rector have the first round while he took a much-needed break down the hall.

The doctor and the nurse closed the door as they left.

She was swathed in fresh dressings over the grafts. "You're looking good," he said.

She whispered something that was barely audible, and he leaned down to hear it again. "My ... kids."

"Tell me what I can do."

She only looked at him and shook her head slowly.

What was her name? Was it Lillian? He didn't think he could wait any longer. "What is your name?"

She struggled to swallow.

"What does LM stand for?"

She shook her head. No. "That's ... th' name of ..." the tears began, "th' man who ..."

"Who did this to you?" he said, suddenly knowing.

She nodded her head. Yes.

"Can you tell me your name?" She would like to hear her own name spoken; according to Wyatt, it would be a consolation.

The tears came freely, now, and she worked to open her mouth and speak. "Pauline," she whispered.

"Barlowe," he said, his heart pounding.

She looked at him for what seemed a long time, then nodded her head.

Yes.

NINETEEN

Starting Over

P"Poobaw," she whispered.

"Your son." Dooley's little brother, now ten years old.

"Where …?" She swallowed and grimaced. "How is he?"

He knew at once that he would lie. "Fine. Don't worry." What if it was, in fact, a lie? Could LM have done something as sinister to the boy? He would face that later.

"Who … has him?"

"He's in good hands."

The tears continued. "So much … to tell you," she managed to say.

"I want to hear."

"Th' pain …"

"Yes." They had given her a shot only minutes before.

"I want you to know …" Her eye closed, and she began to breathe quietly.

"Yes?" he said.

"That I can bear it."

"'I can do all things through Christ …,'" he said, quoting the first part of Olivia's favorite verse from Philippians. He could scarcely hear her response.

"'… who strengthens me,'" she whispered.

❋

"What're you havin'?" asked Velma, as J.C. slid into the booth.

"Wheaties and skim milk."

Velma raised her eyebrows. "No coffee?"

"I'm off coffee."

Mule sighed. "Here we go again," he said, as Velma moved to the next booth.

"What's that supposed to mean?" glowered the editor.

"I mean, why don't you marry th' woman and get it over with?"

"What woman?"

"Adele Lynwood! Who else would I be talkin' about?"

The rector blew on his steaming coffee, ready to duck. It was clear that Mule Skinner was tired of intrigue and cover-up. He wanted to see cards on the table.

J.C. sat back in the booth, looking exhausted, and wiped his face with a handkerchief. "Dadblame it," he said.

"Dadblame what?" queried Mule, pressing on.

"I guess you know about Adele."

"Any ninny can see you're sweet on her. What we don't know is—what in th' dickens is goin' on?"

"Dern if I can figure it out," said J.C. "One minute it's on, the next minute it's off."

"One minute it's Wheaties, the next minute it's grits," said the rector.

"Right," said Mule.

The rector swigged his coffee. "Sounds pretty typical to me."

J.C. leaned forward. "It does?"

"Sure. One day you know, one day you don't. Pretty soon, if it's right, you *really* know."

"Oh."

"But how do you know if you really know?" asked J.C.

The rector looked slightly dazed. "I don't know," he said, meaning it.

Mule sighed. "We're kind of rusty at this."

"How come she wants me to get off coffee and axe the fat and lower my cholesterol if she wouldn't go out with me last night? I mean, what's th' deal?"

"Maybe she had to work," said Mule, wanting to help.

"No way. She was home cleanin' her gun."

"How do you know?"

"Because I called her up and that's what she said she was doing."

"Where had you offered to take her?" asked the rector.

"To Brendle's, they were having a sale on Tri-X film."

"No wonder she stayed home to clean a gun," said Mule.

"Have you sent her flowers?" asked Father Tim. "That's a good thing to do."

"Flowers? To a woman who carries a nine-millimeter?"

"Whoa, buddy," said Mule. "You're soundin' mighty macho there. It's th' woman's *job* to carry a gun."

"Women like flowers," said the rector. "It's that simple. Maybe she's trying to look after your best interests, and you're not looking after hers."

J.C. scratched his head. "I don't think that's it. I sent my first wife flowers once, and look what happened."

"Once won't cut it," said the rector.

"Right," said Mule.

"Do you care about her?" asked Father Tim.

J.C. turned red. "Yeah. I care about her. We go out. We do stuff."

"What stuff?"

"Oh, this and that. She cooks at her place pretty often, I took pork chops once."

Mule looked at the rector.

"Sounds like there's a whole lot of *once* in the way you operate," said Father Tim. "Once you sent flowers, once you took pork chops."

"Yeah," said Mule.

"There's the problem," said the rector.

"So? So I'm supposed to go crawling on my belly like a snake to get this woman interested in me again?"

"Sending flowers is not crawling on your belly."

"And why take pork chops," asked Mule, "if she's tryin' to get you off fat and cholesterol? You ought to take ... let's see ..."

"Tofu," said the rector.

"Man!" said J.C., mopping his face. "If I listen to you turkeys, I'll be in up to my neck."

Mule leaned back for Velma to set his plate down. "You're in so deep now, you need a bloomin' shovel. And why not listen to us? We've got credentials."

"Right," said the rector. "We're married."

"By th' dern grace of God, if you ask me," said J.C.

"Right again," agreed Father Tim.

"OK, I'll listen," sighed the editor. "But just this once."

✳

He could hardly wait to leave the office and get to the hospital, where, according to Nurse Kennedy, Pauline Barlowe had been up to the bathroom and was drinking juice.

We're still praying, Kennedy had said, pneumonia is a possibility, infection is a likelihood—we're not out of the woods by a long shot.

He was finishing his sermon notes, which Emma, God love her, had offered to key into the computer, when he heard a knock on the door.

"Father?"

Olivia Harper stuck her head in the office and smiled. "Is this a good time?"

He got up and went to greet her. "It's always a good time for you."

"I just wanted to talk to you about something at Aunt Sadie's."

"Sit in Emma's chair. Want some bubble gum?"

She took a piece. "What in the world are you doing with bubble gum?"

"Amy Larkin keeps me supplied."

She laughed. "Who doesn't love you?"

"Don't tell me that. I'll get the big head."

"You know we were thrilled with Aunt Sadie's memorial service. Thank you for talking about who she was and what she stood for."

"It's important to do that in a small community, important to talk about the loved one. It departs a bit from the traditional Anglican burial service, but ..."

"But this is the *South!*" she said, laughing.

He grinned. "What's up?"

"There's a mahogany chest of drawers at Fernbank, which Louella says I should have. I just wanted to check with you before I go rifling through."

"My dear, you don't have to check with me. Take whatever you want, and after Louella's gone through, Cynthia and I will go through. Miss Sadie would have wanted it that way, she just assumed we'd know that. After all, you're blood kin."

"I had my great-aunt for such a short time."

"That you had her at all was supernatural."

"You're so right," she said, as the phone rang.

"Lord's Chapel, Father Kavanagh speaking."

"Father Kavanagh, Doug Wyeth at social services in Wesley. We thought you'd like to know the DA's office was successful."

"They were?"

"We have Lacey."

He felt caught off guard.

"We're looking for a foster home, but so far nothing has worked out. We've established there are no other relatives, at least none that we can locate."

"What will you do, then?" he asked.

"If we can't work out the foster care, she'll have to go down the mountain to an emergency shelter."

That didn't sound good.

"I know your interest in this case, Father. Would you be open to taking her on a temporary basis? You're not licensed for foster care, but we could get you authorized temporarily."

"Let me ... think about it," he said. "I'd have to ... Let me call you back in, what, half an hour?"

"Fine. You have my number."

"How is Lace?"

"Angry," said Doug Wyeth.

He put the phone down and shook his head.

"Lace?" asked Olivia.

"The district attorney's office. They found her—she's with social services. They're trying to get her in foster care, but haven't been successful yet."

Olivia sat forward in the chair. "Let us take her, Father."

"Good Lord, Olivia! You can't know what you're saying."

"But I do. Hoppy and I, we've talked about taking someone in. We thought it would be Louella until Hope House opens, but it worked out so beautifully for Winnie to keep Louella company. I liked Lace. We can do it."

"But surely it would be too much...." The idea seemed wildly improbable.

"Father, God spared my life! Against impossible odds, he gave me a new heart. I believe to this day it was yours and Hoppy's prayers that opened the gates of heaven and worked miracles with my transplant. All that for what?" she asked, her violet eyes dark with feeling.

"To be the happy wife of a wonderful man? I need to give something back. I may not do it well, but I shall give it everything I've got. Let us take Lace."

Why shouldn't he grant this request to the woman whose lifetime verse was one he'd just quoted to Pauline Barlowe?

"Besides," she said, pressing on, "look what you've done with Dooley."

Surely, as clergy, his word could help get the Harpers authorized.

"Call them back," she urged, meaning it.

✳

She was hoarse, still, and could only whisper. "When you looked at me ..." she said, trying to swallow.

He waited.

"... and cried, I felt some of the pain leave me."

"Really?" He was croaking like a frog. Who could tell which one of them had had a tube shoved down their trachea? "I'm glad."

"I think I always know when you come, no matter how much morphine."

"Yes. Good."

"Why?" she asked.

"Why what?"

"Why do you care?"

"Because ..." What could he say, after all? Because I love your son with all my heart? Because any mother of his is a friend of mine? Because you were suffering and that was enough for me? Who knows why? The truth was, he had come because they called him, and then he started caring and couldn't stop.

"I've done ... terrible things."

"Haven't we all?" he asked with feeling.

Her tears came freely. "Terrible," she said again.

He stood with her and waited.

"My children. I gave 'em away."

He nodded, understanding that the tears would swell her eyes and cause more pain and discomfort. Pain, and endless pain, he thought.

"What ... is your name?" she asked.

"Timothy Kavanagh. Father Kavanagh."

"You're the one who has Dooley."

"Yes."

"I knew you had him. They said ..."

"What did they say?" he asked gently.

"They said you sent him ... to school."

"A friend sent him. It's helping. He's healing."

"Healing." She closed her eye, and the tears continued to flow. She was silent for a long time. "I wanted to see him.... I sat in front of your house twice, hoping to see him. But I heard you were good to him, and so ... I let him be."

He nodded.

"A while back, I said a prayer ... with old Preacher Greer ..."

He waited.

"When I done that, I seen what a mess I'd made of my life ... an' th' pain was ... so big, so terrible."

She swallowed and looked at him. "But for the first time ..."

"Yes?"

"I had the strength to bear it."

"It often happens that way."

"Th' reason I used to drink whiskey and anything I could lay my hands on was because … I couldn't bear it."

He nodded.

"I lost my ear," she whispered.

"Yes. I'm sorry." He realized he'd been whispering, too.

"I've asked God to help me forgive Lester Marshall. I knowed it was wrong to go on livin' with him, but …" She moved her right hand toward the rector. "Pray for me," she implored, "to get my children back."

He stood there, frozen, and saw her hand move toward his as if in slow motion.

Pray for her to take Dooley? Ask God to let the unthinkable happen?

The recent events of his life had forced more than one truth to the surface, and now another came.

Dooley did not belong to Pauline Barlowe. Nor did he belong to him. Dooley belonged to God. Period. Dooley was not his to give back.

✳

"I been drivin' Harley Welch's ol' truck since I was twelve. I can haul butt."

Lacey sat on a high stool in the small office, swinging her leg and chewing gum. She was wearing the hat, and her clothes were caked with engine oil and mud.

"So when I heard Pauline hollerin', I run down there and th' son of a—" She stopped and looked at the rector. "Th' son of a gun was tryin' to burn 'er up. He run out of th' house, and I th'owed a blanket around 'er and hauled 'er out to th' porch. I went an' got Harley's truck and we put 'er in it, and I took 'er to th' hospital. I left th' hospital before they knowed anything, 'cause I heard police was lookin' for me."

"Where's Poobaw?" asked the rector.

"I ain't tellin' that."

"No harm will come to him or you, Lace."

"I still ain't tellin'."

"His mother would like to know. Is he safe?"

She shrugged. "I don't know, how do I know? I was th' one lookin' out for 'im. Now y'll done ruint that."

"We're going to be placing you in foster care," said Doug Wyeth. "We'll just need—"

She jumped off the stool. "You ain't doin' any such thing!" she shouted. "I thought you brung me in here 'cause of drivin' without a license."

Cursing, she made a run for the door. It took two social workers to stop her and hold her.

If Olivia Harper could handle this, he thought, she could become a canonized saint.

✳

They lay in bed, looking at the ceiling. Rain had pounded the village all day, and shadows cast by the tossing leaves danced above them.

"It's not a question of if, but when," he said.

"I feel we should let him see her right away. He can handle it. Surely she can't take him out of school or even away from Meadowgate, because she has no place to live. Also, she's facing months of physical therapy."

"I'll call him. What time is it?"

"Eight-thirty. Good heavens, don't ever tell anybody we're in bed this early. We'd be the laughingstock."

"If you only knew how many people are sawing wood in this town, even as we speak."

"I've become a rustic," she sighed.

"And no help for it."

Why think about it and ponder it and try to make up the right thing to say? He'd just say it simply, and go on, believing the best.

He was reaching for the phone when it rang.

"Hey," said Dooley.

"Hey, yourself, buddy."

"Miz Shuford asked me to name them calves."

"That's terrific. And what did you name them?"

"Jessie and Kenny."

"Ah. Good. That's good." The names of his little sister and younger brother.

"I was going to name them Lillie and Willie."

"I like Jessie and Kenny."

"How's ol' Cynthia?"

"Couldn't be better. Want to say hello?"

"Yeah."

"Dooley, you big lug. How are you?"

"I named the calves Jessie and Kenny."

"Dr. Dooley Barlowe, full-service vet. I heal, I deliver, I name. You're great!"

"You coming out Sunday?"

"Yes, we want to see Jessie and Kenny."

"Good. They're real healthy. You'll like 'em."

"I like you!"

"I like you back."

She reached across him and hung up the phone.

"I couldn't do it," she said.

"I couldn't, either."

"We're letting him have two more days of innocent boyhood," she said. "We can tell him on Sunday."

"Right. I'll tell Pauline he's coming to see her."

They were silent for a long time, holding hands.

"Are you ever sorry you married a parson?"

"Why should I be?"

"I can't leave my work at the office."

"Of course you can't. Your job isn't nine to five, it's noon to noon. I knew that, dearest. Besides, I love your work, too. Remember, I'm your deacon."

He rolled over and kissed her and felt the softness of her body against his. "Such a deal," he murmured. "Every clergyman in the nation would be wildly jealous."

✳

It was ponytail time again, if he didn't act soon.

Hadn't he just had his hair cut? What a blasted aggravation that, while no hair ever grew on top, the rest of his head appeared to be fertilized with Miracle-Gro.

Another aggravation was whether to slip around behind Joe Ivey's back and see Fancy, or be loyal, as was his bent, and force himself up the stairs to Joe's chair, where, according to Fancy, those chipmunk puffs over his ears were made to prosper and flourish.

Dadgum it, it seemed a man should at least be able to get a haircut without a hassle.

"Six hundred and thirty-two," said Emma, keying in the previous week's collections. "No, six hundred and seventy-five. You need a haircut."

"Where should I get it?" he asked, thrilled to pass on the responsibility of a decision.

"Go to Fancy. Joe makes you look like a chipmunk," she said without looking away from the computer screen.

He was liking Emma Newland better every day.

"Has your raise come through yet?" he asked.

"Not unless Harold's goat ate it out of th' mailbox."

"I'll take care of it," he said, glad to be of service.

✳

"We're bringing Dooley to see you," he said. "Either Sunday evening or Monday."

"I don't deserve it."

"God's grace isn't about deserving," he said, taking her hand.

She smiled. It was the first time he had seen her smile.

"May I … call you Father?"

"Please. And would you like to see your own father? He's well and well cared for. It will give him joy."

She nodded yes.

"I've been … thinking, Father."

"Tell me."

"You should keep Dooley 'til he's out of school. School is a good thing—my mother tried to tell me that. Then he can do whatever God wants him to do. I won't try … to take him back."

"Good," he said. "That's best."

"But my other kids …"

"Where are they?"

"After I prayed that prayer, I tried to find them."

He was used to her tears. They were a kind of language that needed expression.

"Kenny, I gave him to …"

He sat in the chair by her bed and waited.

"To …"

"It's all right."

"… somebody for a gallon of whiskey an' … a hundred dollars."

He really didn't know if he could deal with this. He was only human, after all. Being clergy didn't equip him with some shield and suit of armor. No, this was too blasted much. He needed reinforcement. He didn't even want to hear any more.

"It hurts me to hear it," he said. Why beat around the bush?

She looked at him, imploring.

"Can we find Kenny?" he asked.

"He was in Oregon th' last time I knowed."

There was a long silence, which he didn't try to break.

"Poobaw," she said. "We call him that because he liked to tote around a pool ball I brought home, an' that's what he called it. He's ten, he's such a good boy, Father, always happy...."

"And Jessie?"

"She's four. So ... little. So ... pretty." She sobbed brokenly, and he wanted to turn away, to run out the door and not come back.

"Father ... I want so much ... to start over. Do you think God ... will let me start over?"

"That," he said, meaning it, "is what God is all about."

Nurse Gilbert's uniform rustled crisply as she walked in with a needle. "This will help," she said, going to Pauline.

If only it could, he thought.

❋

"Lord help! Look at this! Are you practicin' to be John the Baptist in a church play? Remember what happened to him, honey, his hair was so bad-lookin', they cut his head off.

"How's your wife, I saw her the other day, she was at the food bank givin' a ton of stuff, all I took was sweet potatoes and cream of mushroom soup, do you think that's OK? Do you know what all you can *do* with cream of mushroom soup? It's more versatile than Cheez Whiz, you can pour it over chicken and bake it covered, and Lord, it is the best thing you ever put in your mouth, Mule loves it, do you ever use it? Well, you should, you can also pour it over a roast, but you have to wrap that thing like a mummy for it to work, at least two sheets of foil, and let it go on three fifty for two hours.

"Speakin' of foil, I'm learning to highlight with foil, I used to use a cap, but that is outdated, nobody does that anymore who's up to the minute. Do you know what it costs to be up to the minute in this business? I went to a convention in Charlotte, you wouldn't believe the hotel rooms down there, they cost an arm and a leg and you open your curtains and all you see is a brick wall.

"Speakin' of walls, I hear Cynthia knocked holes in your kitchen, I said, 'Mule, what is that *about*?' Is that the latest thing, to knock holes in your wall? He said, 'Fancy, if you knock holes in our walls, I will personally knock your head off,' ha, ha. I'm sure she had a reason, she's so smart, we all like her, I think you did really great to get her.

"Oops, there I go, pokin' you with these nails, they're acrylic, mine won't grow because I never drank milk as a kid, don't you think it's awful the things you do when you're young and have to pay for down the road? Like layin' in th' sun. Look at these wrinkles around my mouth, see that? Sun! Too much sun. But I say, why quit now, if it's goin' to kill me, I've already had enough to keel me over two or three times.

"Speakin' of keelin' over, I hated to hear about ol' Miss Baxter, was she a friend of yours, I hope she left you some of that money she's been hoardin' back all these years. Whoa, baby, wouldn't it be a deal for a preacher to have big bucks? What would you do, probably go to the Caribbean on a cruise, I have always wanted to go on a cruise, Mule says next year. Have you ever been on a cruise? Do you think you would throw up? I might throw up. I hear that is the worst sick anybody can get, but the food, they say you eat twelve or fourteen times a day, which is enough right there to make you throw up.

"Sit still! I declare, men squirm like babies in this chair, I don't understand it. Did you know Buck Leeper had th' guts to come back and set down where you're settin' and was nice as anything you'd ever want to see? Remember I nearly scratched his eyes out th' last time because he sassed me so bad?

"Do you know who else comes in here? Adele Lynwood. Have you heard she goes out with J.C. Hogan? Can you believe it? Who would go out with J.C. Hogan? She's really nice. You ought to talk to her sometime, she has a son who's a cop in Deerfield—is that Connecticut or Massachusetts? And two of the cutest little granbabies you'll ever lay eyes on. Seriously, what do you think she sees in him? It is *beyond* me.

"Lord! Look at this stuff, I need a hay baler and a combine to clean up after you.

"But let me tell you, honey, it is lookin' *good*, your wife will eat you with a spoon! And I *am* talkin' a *spoon*!

"See there? What do you think? That'll be six dollars, you're clergy."

※

"Any infection?" he asked Hoppy.

"Nothing. No setback, no pneumonia, no infection."

"An answer to prayer?"

"I don't know. There's no way to know. But I have my opinion, and it's yes."

"So is this a miracle?"

Hoppy ran his fingers through his unruly hair. "Definitely un-typical. Definitely a minor miracle."

The rector grinned. "So why split hairs?" he asked.

※

He called Olivia. "How's it going?"

She laughed.

"Thank God you're laughing."

"One must, Father, don't you think?"

"Yes, and I need desperately to remember that. Tell me everything. How is she?"

"Very solemn. Did you know her mother has agreed to come out? They'll be putting her in a women's shelter in Wesley on Tuesday."

"Excellent! I'm relieved to hear that."

"I only hope this removes the impulse for Lace to run away. She's quite a character, I must say, but more than that, she has character."

"Yes. I think so, as well."

"She likes Hoppy enormously! Oh, and I've cleaned her up and she looks wonderful in a dress, but I don't think she likes it. Actually, I know she doesn't like it, so we've washed and ironed all her old clothes and will keep them in her closet."

"Sounds like you've got a handle on it."

"I don't know, Father, I think we mustn't try and remove all her identity at once. The way she dresses seems rude and unworthy to us, perhaps, but it's who she is, and we must let her grow up into a new creature without much forcing."

"I like your style."

"That hat, though ..."

He laughed. "A test, Olivia, a test."

"Mercy ..."

"I'll be up to look in on you. Does she think I had anything to do with what happened?"

"She's generally distrustful of us all. I'm only hoping she doesn't run away. But I don't think there's anywhere to run, now that her mother is leaving the Creek."

"I hope you're right. Has she mentioned Poobaw?"

"She said he was living under the house with her. They slept on a pile of blankets under the house, right under her mother's bed. She said she could remove the floorboards and go in and out of the house without being seen. She knew they were looking for her, and thought they'd be looking for the boy, too. She was protecting him. She said it was the only child Pauline had left."

"Where is he now?"

"She left him under the house when she went out to get food, and that's when she was picked up."

Please, God, give us a break here.

He wanted to move to Nova Scotia, one of the few places left that had home milk delivery, and be a milkman. It was not a high ambition, but the thought had always consoled him in times like these.

＊

"I like your hair," said Puny, who was peeling potatoes at the sink.

"I like yours."

She laughed.

"Where are Luke and Lizzie today?"

"*Who?*" She turned around and stared at him, blankly.

"Uh-oh." Luke and Lizzie, Sissy and Sassy, Jessie and Kenny ... how he'd ever keep them all sorted out was a blasted mystery.

＊

He went to the phone to call Miss Sadie and tell her that Dooley's mother was improving. He had his hand on the receiver when he stopped and shook his head, realizing all over again that Miss Sadie was not there.

＊

"Father," said Nurse Kennedy, "someone was here to see you about Miss Barlowe, but he didn't stay."

"Who was it?"

"Mr. Leeper—he's the supervisor at Hope House. He said he heard Dooley's mother was in here and he was sorry."

He was dumbfounded. Buck Leeper?

"He left this for Miss Barlowe."

Nurse Kennedy handed him a rose in a vase.

The man who had smashed furniture against his walls had left a rose in a vase?

He shook his head with a kind of wonder.

"There's something I've been wanting to ask you, Father," said Nurse Kennedy, walking with him along the hall.

"Shoot."

"Why is it God so often breaks our hearts?"

"Well. Sometimes He does it to increase our faith. That's the way He stretches us. But there's another reason, I think, why our hearts get broken."

She looked at him.

"Usually," he said, "what breaks is what's brittle."

She nodded thoughtfully. "So we have to be careful of getting hard-hearted?"

"Bingo," he said, putting his arm around her shoulders as they walked to the end of the hall.

TWENTY

Send Me

I"It's our retreat for the month," Cynthia announced, "and you have to come."

"No problem," he said, happy to mind his wife.

At twilight, they trooped through the backyard and out to Baxter Park, carrying a blanket.

She brought a little sackful of things and began setting them out. There were small candles in holders, which she lit with a match, then placed in the grass like so many fireflies caught in jars.

Two ripe peaches. A bottle of champagne. Crystal stemware. Two damask napkins.

"There!" she said, pleased with herself.

He fell back on the blanket, quietly intoxicated with an idea he couldn't have come up with in a hundred years. Tree frogs called, crickets whirred, a night bird swooped from the hedge and rushed over them.

"Ahhhh," said his wife, letting out her breath.

"What did you do today?" he asked, feeling a sudden tenderness for his wife's good instincts.

"The usual, of course. And I sat with Miss Pattie for an hour and a half."

He loved the familiarity of the question everyone asked of Evie Adams's elderly mother. "What's Miss Pattie done now?"

"Nothing much, actually. We were sitting on the sofa playing Who's Got the Button, that's her favorite, when she went sound asleep. She just sort of fell over on my shoulder and snored for ages."

"And what did you do?"

"I didn't want to move and wake her up, of course, so I just sat there and prayed for Pauline and Evie and Miss Pattie, then I made out our grocery list in my head, and figured out how to mix two blues together with a dash of green, for some feathers I'm painting."

He smiled. "Good work, Deacon. How's your book?"

"Wonderful! Just two more pages to go. Do you know I absolutely love painting birds?"

"What don't you love?"

"Three things. Stress, stress, and stress."

"We've certainly had all three lately. And all for good reason, of course, but ..."

"We shouldn't even have to *talk* about stress, much less *have* it. After all, we live in Mitford!"

"Right. A quaint little town where people value each other and nothing bad ever happens to anybody."

"Poop!" she said, with feeling.

"Where are we going to live when we retire?" he asked, seeing a star appear. "And where are we going in August, which is only next month? To the coast?"

"I can't swim!" she said.

"I can't tolerate sun," he confessed.

"I hate sand!"

"So that's out," he declared. "Let's open the champagne." They hadn't had champagne since …

"We haven't had champagne since our wedding," she said, handing him the bottle. "And please be careful. My nephew, David, drew out the cork one evening and looked in to see why it hadn't all come out."

"Uh-oh."

"That's when it came out! He wore the eyepatch for two months."

He drew out the cork and they heard it pop across the grass and into the rhododendron.

"Bingo!" exclaimed his wife.

They raised their glasses. "How did I ever find you?" he asked.

"You were poking around in the hedge, and there I was!"

"In your curlers," he said, grinning.

"To curlers!" she crowed. "Let's figure out August later, and dream of the other, now. We can paint retirement with a much bigger brush!"

"How about if I supply in Canada?" he asked, lying back and holding the glass on his chest.

"We could live in the wilds!"

"Wherever I'm called."

"I could do that," she said.

"Or England. We could live in England. We know the language. Roughly speaking, of course."

"I could do almost anything, dearest. And just think—I can work anywhere, as long as I have paints and a brush. By the way, I hear there's a little church at the coast with an apartment in the rear, and clergy from different denominations supply it every week or so. Of course we'd hate the sand, but we'd love the seafood. That might be fun."

"Maybe …" he said, smiling.

The champagne was going straight to his head. He saw himself wearing shoes with treads that might have been spliced from tractor tires. He would be a veritable globe-trotter; he would go here, he would go there …

"Timothy, dear?" She nudged him in the side. "Are you dropping off?"

He sat upright at once. "Who, me? Dropping off? Of course not!"

Good Lord! Where would he get the energy to go farther than his own backyard?

✳

Dooley came from his mother's hospital room, looking drawn and silent.

They drove slowly down Old Church Lane in a downpour, the windshield wipers turned on high.

"Your mother is going to be all right."

"She ain't got but one ear."

It was the old Dooley talking, the boy who still lived under the emblem on his prep school blazer.

"Do you want to stay with us awhile, and go see her every day?"

Dooley was quiet. Then he said, "I want t' go back to th' farm. I've got stuff t' do."

Two steps forward, one step back.

On Main Street, they passed Olivia Harper in the blue Volvo, who blew the horn and waved. He saw Lace sitting beside her, unsmiling, the old hat jammed on her head.

One for you and one for me, he thought, waving back.

✳

The Hope House project was booming along, even with the heavy rains. Buck Leeper was driving his crew to finish on time, and unbelievable as it seemed in today's world, he was still committed to bringing it in on budget.

"He'll kill himself one day," said Ron Malcolm. "He'll just fall over in an excavation and they'll throw the dirt over him. Or, he's going to blow like a volcano." Ron shook his head. "It's not worth it."

"Amen."

"How's the computer? And don't bite my head off for asking."

"My friend, I am a happy man. By some miracle I'll never understand, Emma likes the blasted thing, and has taken to it like a bee to clover. Go figure!"

Ron laughed. "Hope House is going to be a dazzler."

"Indeed. Have you found an administrator? I missed the last meeting."

"It looks like Hoppy has one," said Ron. "We'll be in the interview process in the next week or two. I hear she's tough."

"You'd have to be tough to run a forty-bed nursing home and make it go like clockwork."

"What do you know about tough?" Ron asked fondly.

"What do I know about tough? Plenty. More than I'd like to know."

"You've been looking all in, if you ask me. Are you taking care of your Big D?"

"Pretty well. I'm off my running schedule, but Scott Murphy will be here in September, we're going to try and run together. That'll get me going again."

Ron looked concerned. "I wouldn't wait for Scott Murphy to get you going."

※

"So?" said Mule, as a rain-soaked J.C. slammed into the booth.

"So what?" snapped J.C.

"Oh, no. Don't tell me …"

"I don't have any intention of telling you. It's none of your dadgum business."

"After all we did to help you, it's none of our business?" asked the rector.

"You didn't send the flowers," said Mule, looking depressed.

"I sent the bloomin' flowers."

"You forgot the reservation at the restaurant and they wouldn't seat you and you had to go to Hardee's," surmised the rector.

"I not only remembered the reservation, I shelled out sixty bucks for something on a lettuce leaf the size of snail droppings."

"Oh, law!" said Mule. "We told you not to go to that French place."

"Maybe it *was* snail droppings," said the rector, trying not to laugh.

"So, did you propose?"

"Propose? We never talked about me proposing."

"We didn't think we had to talk about it, we thought you got the drift. Did you at least tell her you love her?" asked Mule.

"Sort of."

The rector looked at the editor over his glasses. "What do you mean, sort of?"

"I said … well, you know."

"No, we don't know. And if we don't know, chances are she doesn't know, either. Have you ever thought of that? Read my lips," said the rector. "You have to say it outright, I l-o-v-e y-o-u. Get it?"

"I said something kind of like that."

"What was it?" asked Mule.

"I told her I really like the way she keeps her squad car clean."

Mule slapped himself on the forehead. "No way, no way, no way! You're hopeless." He turned to the rector. "We're wasting our time."

"Go back and try again," said Father Tim. "Send the flowers. Take her to dinner. Tell her you love her."

"Then give her a ring," said Mule. "Don't you know *anything* about th' birds and bees?"

"I might tell her I love her, but I'm not doin' flowers and snail stuff again."

The rector peered at J.C. "There's that one-time deal rearing its ugly head. Flowers one time, a fancy dinner one time. You're getting off the train before you get to the station, buddyroe."

"Whatever that's supposed to mean."

"Go back and start over," said Mule, looking grouchy.

J.C. gave a shuddering sigh and wiped his face with a Scot towel.

"See? Look at that! A paper towel. You're in such sorry shape, I can't believe it. If you're ever going to get a woman to look after you, the time is now, before you're too far gone."

"Right!" said the rector.

J.C. shambled out of the booth, dragging his bulging briefcase.

"Call her up!" said Mule.

"Right now!" instructed the rector.

"Lord have mercy," groaned J.C., heading for the door.

Mule blew on his coffee. "You don't think we were too hard on him, do you?"

✳

"Stuart? Tim Kavanagh."

"I'll be hanged, I was just thinking about you," said his bishop and seminary friend.

"What were you thinking?" asked the rector. "Do I want to know?"

"I was thinking that I hadn't heard from you in far too long. I'm curious about something."

"You're always curious about something. Nosy was what we called it when I was coming up."

"I admit, I'm nosy. Anyway, I want to know how you like being married."

"I like it greatly, as a matter of fact."

"Excellent! Not too much for you, then?"

"What do you mean, too much for me?"

"Cynthia's a live wire."

"So am I," he said.

"You? A live wire? Since when?"

"Since I decided to retire, which is why I'm calling."

"What?"

"What, indeed, my friend. I would have written you, but I can't find the time." He hoped that didn't sound cocky, but why worry about it when there were larger issues to occupy his mind?

"Keep talking."

"I've decided to retire in two years, and thought I'd go ahead and let you know now. I'll be sixty-five then, that's my cutoff date. I'm thinking that I definitely want to remain active, which means I'd like to supply. You can give us something in this diocese, of course, but not necessarily. I'm ready for some adventure in my life."

"Excuse me, is this Father *Timothy* Kavanagh?"

"One and the same."

"Being married has clearly loosened you up, Timothy! There's a new … tone in your voice."

"That's determination you hear, Stuart, determination. I'm determined to have a new life, which is not to say I don't like the one I've got. Actually, I like it vastly."

"I knew Cynthia would be good for you!"

"Cynthia is good for me, you're perfectly right. But she can't take all the credit."

"Really? How's that?"

"I foolishly—or wisely, as the case may be—dropped through a hole in the ground like the White Rabbit, and was lost in a cave. It gave me something to think about."

"You old stick-in-the-mud!" Stuart said fondly.

"I'm convinced that every stick-in-the-mud should get stuck in a hole in the ground."

Stuart laughed. "What did you learn down there?"

"For one thing, I learned something about my father and about my feelings. I've been chewing over it for weeks, and it strikes me that one reason I went into the priesthood was to minister to my father. I wanted his soul to be saved, but as far as I know, that never happened. I believed that if I kept going and never stopped, I could reach people like my father, and make up, somehow, for failing to reach him for Christ. I still feel the urgency to reach people, but bottom line, I don't feel the bondage anymore. I feel … the liberty."

Stuart was quiet. "Maybe I need to fall in a hole."

"Maybe," he said, boldly.

His bishop sighed. "There are a few old wounds I've kept licking over the years, but conveniently, I've kept too busy to deal with them."

"Fall in a hole and the only busy you'll be is trying to haul your tail out of there."

They laughed.

"I don't know when I've liked a phone call better," said Stuart. "So. You want to supply, and I can trade you around like a fancy baseball player to other bishops?"

"Something in the Caribbean, maybe."

"You dog."

"Seriously, Canada would be of interest to us, or England. Ireland, possibly. Virginia? Vermont? I don't know. I have the providence of a wife who finds all of life an adventure. And I think there's definitely something in me that needs airing out, so there you have it. Should I put it in writing to make it official?"

"Consider it official. Write me when you get around to it, just for the records. In the fullness of time, we'll get the search process started at Lord's Chapel. It can take up to a year and a half to put a new priest in place, given the tough parameters we're now using."

"Keep it quiet until we have to make it public. My parish is—"

"Your parish is devoted to you! I hope I'm in farthest Africa when the word gets out that I've allowed you to go."

"You're kind."

"I'm your friend."

"How many years?" asked the rector. "Thirty-six, thirty-seven?"

"Thirty-nine."

"Sorry I asked. How's Martha?"

"Trying to get me to slow down...."

"And having no success," he said.

"I see slowing down as a kind of death."

"You think slowing down to take your two adopted grandkids to the zoo or out to lunch is death? My friend, that is life."

"Don't preach me a sermon, Timothy."

"You've certainly been known to preach me one, Bishop."

"Go fly a kite," said Stuart, chuckling.

"Go step in a hole," said the rector, meaning it.

❋

Uncle Billy's arthur was so bad after the rain that he asked Father Tim to come fetch his tithe.

The rector arrived just before lunch, and went around to the back stoop. He should have sent his beautiful deacon, he thought, but the moment the old man opened the door, he was glad he'd come. If there was ever a face to give a preacher a lift, it was Bill Watson's.

"Come in an' take a load off y'r feet, hit's hot as blazes and Rose made us a pitcher of tea."

What the heck? He'd resisted Rose Watson's suspect refreshments for years on end, but maybe he'd loosen up, for once, and do the thing.

"Rose! Hit's th' preacher come t' have a glass of tea."

"Pour it yourself," she snapped, glaring at them from the hallway.

"Oh, law," said the old man, embarrassed, "hit's th' heat, she don't like it."

Miss Rose came and stood in the doorway and watched her husband pour tea for their guest. She was wearing a calf-length chenille bathrobe, the sling-back pumps Uncle Billy had ordered last year from an almanac, and the hat from Esther Cunningham's Waves uniform.

Uncle Billy passed him the glass of tea with a trembling hand. "That was some rain, won't it, Preacher?"

"Either that or a colossal dew!"

"Possum stew?" demanded Miss Rose. "What're you saying about possum stew?"

Where was his deacon?

"I'd never eat a bite of anything made with possum," said the old woman, "and I wouldn't think you would, either, being a preacher!"

"Yes, ma'am," he said, cowering in the corner.

He dearly loved his parishioners, but collections had never been his long suit.

✷

"Father? Scott Murphy! I hope I'm not making a pest of myself."

He instantly felt the grin spreading across his face. "Quite the reverse! How are you?"

"Great, sir. I'm back to running. How about you?"

"Off my schedule and no help for it."

"Go out there and do it, sir, and get in shape for September. I'm not going to hang back for you."

He laughed with delight. Here was someone who'd give him a run for his money, all right. "Consider it done. What's up?"

"I just called your friend, Mr. Skinner, about places for rent, and he said a Miss Winnie Ivey's cottage might be coming up."

"That's right." Olivia had invited Winnie to stay on in her home on Lilac Road, and graciously included Winnie's two elderly cats in the bargain. "I know that cottage well. It sits on a creek. Has a porch, a nice view, and it's private. Winnie runs the bakery here."

"Yes, I stopped in there and had a Napoleon."

"She's kept her little place as clean as a pin. And it's only a short run to Hope House, up the hill and past the orchards."

"Sounds too good to be true. I'll call Mr. Skinner back and tell him I'll take it. What's going on in your parish, Father?"

"I've had a boy with me for a couple of years, and his mother's just been terribly burned, but we're sorting that out. And there's a girl, thirteen ... we've just had her removed from a very bitter and violent situation in a blighted community we call the Creek."

"Poverty? Inbreeding? Drugs?"

"All that. It's said to be dangerous in there for law enforcement and clergy, and the upshot is—nobody does much about it, including myself, I'm ashamed to admit."

There was a thoughtful pause.

"I'll go in there, Father. When I come to Mitford, send me."

Send me. The words spoken by the prophet Isaiah, when God had a rotten job to get done.

"I don't know, Scott, maybe you need to ... look into it first."

"Well, sir, I believe the only way to look into something is to go in and look."

That wasn't an impertinence. What it was, was the truth.

"Remember how I said I felt invincible because of my grandparents' love?"

"I remember."

"Because I know so surely that God loves me, I feel that invin-
cibility all over again," said Scott. "When I come, let's talk about
it. I'll go in there and see what I can do. There has to be a way."

Scott was right, of course. There has to be a way. The rector
felt suddenly encouraged about something that had discouraged
him for months.

Was Scott Murphy's bravado just a lot of smoke and youthful
optimism? Time, which tells everything, would also tell this, he
reasoned.

✳

What could be done about Poobaw? Father Tim hadn't said a
word to Dooley about his little brother, and apparently Pauline
hadn't, either.

He went up to the Harpers' rambling mountain lodge and
found Olivia cutting out a dress for Lace on the dining-room table.

She looked peaked, to say the least.

"I'm not exactly wringing my hands yet, but I don't do very
well at … reaching her."

"That's to be expected," he said, grinning. "What you're talking about takes two or three hundred years to accomplish."

"Oh," said Olivia, laughing. "I thought I was supposed to do it
in two or three days."

"It's hard to reach someone who's been betrayed by everyone
she's ever known, including her mother."

"What do you mean?"

"I mean her mother's inability to look after herself and her
daughter has cost Lace great heartache. I know her mother is an
invalid, but even that has something of betrayal in it, since Lace
has had to be the mother."

Olivia sighed. "It's not that we haven't made any progress at all. So far, she's taken two baths and even let me scrub her hands and nails. Oh, and she allowed me to brush the tangles out of her hair, which is a miracle. I don't think anyone had ever done that for her."

"What does she like about living here, so far?"

"My makeup. Hoppy. Breakfast, lunch, and dinner. My hats."

"Terrific. You know you can be a lifelong blessing to her."

"If I hold up," said Olivia, who gave him a dazzling smile.

"If you can't hold up, nobody can. I need to talk with Lace. May I?"

Olivia brought Lace into the living room, and he found that he hardly recognized her in a skirt and blouse, with her hair tied back. He was, in fact, shocked at her surprising beauty.

"You look wonderful. Absolutely wonderful!" he said.

Lace glanced at him, then looked at the wall.

"I have a report on your mother. You can visit her tomorrow. She's doing very well and seems to feel stronger." Just in case she didn't get it, he drew the bottom line. "This is good news."

"Yeah," said Lace.

"I need to know everything you can tell me about Poobaw, and I need you to tell me now." He spoke gently, but he meant it and she knew it. "Let's sit down."

She sat in a chair, looking suddenly awkward in her new clothes. Odd, but he'd gotten used to the rags she'd worn.

"Pauline Barlowe is going to improve, but soon she'll go away for a long stay to a place where she'll learn to use her arm again and care for herself. She's just seen her oldest son, Dooley—you met him."

"He's a creep. I hate redheads."

"Some of my best friends are redheads, so I'll thank you to be kind. What she needs now is to see Poobaw, to know he's safe and taken care of." He let that sink in. "So tell me. Where is he? How can we find him?"

She looked at him.

"Listen to me, Lace. You don't trust me, and I don't blame you because you don't know me. But you've got to believe that no harm will come to Poobaw. We need to locate him and take him out of that place, and find someone for him to live with until Pauline is well and can take care of him herself."

She shrugged. "I told 'im t' go t' Harley's trailer if I didn't come back from gittin' us somethin' t' eat."

"Who is Harley?"

"Harley's crazy, but he's all right. He wouldn't tell nobody that Poobaw was there, an' if they come lookin' for Poobaw, I told Harley t' shoot their brains out, it's th' only kid Pauline had left. I didn't know about Dewey, or whatever 'is name is."

"Where does Harley live?"

"Down there where people dump stuff off th' side of th' hill. He's got a blue trailer and three dogs that'll eat your butt up, so you better step easy if you mess around there."

He was going to need Scott Murphy before September … way before September.

✳

Why did she have to tell Harley to shoot somebody's brains out if they came looking for Poobaw?

Every time he raised the courage to go get the boy himself, he thought about Harley and sank back. Blast, he hated cowardice. He had nearly lost Cynthia through a type of cowardice, and here he was a grown man in a free country, perspiring—no, sweating like a field hand—at the thought of stepping up to a door and knocking on it.

Rodney Underwood would be of no use—it wasn't his county.

And social services, by their own admission, could take days to get the wheels turning.

Right. But better them than him staring down the barrel of what had, in his mind, become crazy Harley Welch's twelve-gauge shotgun.

✳

The urge to do something would not let him alone; it was now on his heart constantly. This morning, Pauline had searched his face as she asked again, "Poobaw? Is he all right?"

Worse still, he recalled the anguish on Dooley's face, the kind of anguish he'd believed time would erase, and remembered how he and Dooley, long ago, had held hands and prayed for his sister and brothers, with a special sense of concern for Poobaw.

Why couldn't they call Harley and ask him to drive the boy to the hospital in his truck, for Pete's sake? He and Cynthia would take it from there.

He rang Olivia and asked to speak with Lace.

"Harley ain't got a phone. He ain't even got a toilet."

Was there any way she could get a message to Harley?

"Th' only way is to go up there."

"Up there?"

"Acrost th' creek and up th' bank. Hit's steep but I been up it a million times, don't anybody use that trail but me an' Granny Sykes."

"What about the dogs?"

"They know me pretty good, but anybody else goin' in there better tote a sack of meat."

When he hung up, he realized he was perspiring again. He thought he had hidden the idea from his conscious mind, but he had not.

He suddenly knew very clearly that he was going in there to get Poobaw.

✳

"We can't leave that boy in these circumstances," he told Olivia. "I know it's a crazy idea and there could be tremendous risk, but I feel we must do it. Would you agree?"

She didn't hesitate. "Yes," she said, her violet eyes dark with concern.

✳

"How many you feedin'?" asked Avis Packard at the meat counter of The Local.

"Three," he said. "But they're plenty hungry."

"Three pounds ought to do it, then."

"Better make it six pounds," he said, wiping his forehead with a handkerchief. "And it doesn't have to be your best."

Avis winked. "Must be entertainin' your vestry."

He laughed. "I'm not entertaining at all. This is …" Should he tell? Why not? It wouldn't reveal anything. "This is for dogs," he said.

"Six pounds of beef for three dogs. Must be some dogs."

"Oh, they are, they are."

The large, wrapped parcel seemed so conspicuous as he hit the sidewalk, he wanted to shove it under his coat.

✳

Be back soon, he wrote. Should he say, "Don't worry?" Of course not. That would make her worry. *Important meeting.* Wasn't that the truth? *Love, Timothy.*

✳

He kept the beam of the flashlight low to the ground.

"You better catch on right here if you don't want to bust your butt." Lace had gone up the muddy bank ahead of him, as nimbly as a squirrel.

"Slow down!" he whispered. The shoe treads he had envisioned the other night would sure come in handy.…

"You don't want t' lose y'r step along here or you'll end up some'ers around Leesville."

His heart was pounding—thundering, in fact. If somebody named Granny could negotiate this bank, so could he. However, somebody named Granny was not likely to have six pounds of red meat swinging in a sack lashed to her back.

"Git m' hat!" said Lace, keeping her voice low. "That bush knocked it off."

"Keep going," he said. "I've got it."

He jammed it on his head and hauled himself up by grabbing onto the exposed root of a tree.

What was he doing out here in the dark of the night, scrambling up a bank like some chicken-poaching thief? He had put Lace Turner and himself at senseless risk, and in a foolish and impetuous way, to boot. What if her father saw her? What if Lester Marshall was hanging around Harley's trailer? Not a living soul would be likely to forgive the local rector if anything happened.

However, if God's love had made Scott Murphy invincible, why wouldn't it do the same for him and for her? When it came to loving his children, God didn't pick favorites.

"We're gittin' there," she said. "You OK?"

"I'm hangin' in." He was so out of breath, he might have run a 10k. If he could only rest a minute …

"Don't be settin' down," she hissed. "I can see ol' Harley's TV shinin' th'ough th' winder."

The stench of garbage and mold had assaulted his nostrils all the way up the bank. In the moonlight, lining the trail to their left, he saw the pale, abandoned hulks of refrigerators and stoves, half-exposed in mounds of rain-soaked debris. That day in Omer's plane, he had looked down on this very place, never dreaming—

He heard skittering noises in the dump, and shivered.

They reached the top of the bank, where the ground leveled

off. "Set!" she whispered. "Git that sack out an' give it t' me."

He did, noting that his hands shook.

"They ain't nothin' t' be skeered of," she said. "I done this a million times. When we git beyond here, th' dogs'll start up. I'll th'ow down th' meat and you hit Harley's winder with these little rocks. Here." She handed him two pieces of gravel she had picked up from the creek. "That's m' signal f'r 'im t' let me in."

"What if he's sleeping?"

"He don't sleep 'til 'way up in th' night."

"What if he can't hear it hit the window?"

"He'll hear th' dogs start up an' listen f'r th' rocks."

He hoped her plan worked as well as she seemed to think it would. Six pounds of meat wouldn't last six minutes. If Barnabas Kavanagh was any indication, three seconds, maximum, was what they could count on.

"What about the dogs when we leave?" he whispered urgently. The sack of meat might work up front, but what strategy would they use to protect the rear?

"He'll call 'em off," she said. "You ready?"

"Ready." An outright lie.

✳

"Lord, if it ain't Lace," said Harley Welch, grinning. They were in the trailer with the door slammed behind them and three dogs pounding on it like jackhammers. He was breathing hard.

"You won't have t' feed them dogs f'r a couple of days," said Lace.

Harley shook his hand, still grinning. If there was a tooth in Harley's head, the rector didn't see it. He instantly liked this whiskered man whose eyes revealed genuine kindness.

"You 'uns come in. Th' boy's sleepin' an' I'm jis' havin' me a little snack." Harley held up a spoon.

The rector saw a cracked green vinyl sofa with an open food can sitting on one of the cushions. A lamp with a bare light bulb illuminated the corner of the room, and newspapers were taped over the windows.

"You 'uns want a bite?"

"I done eat," said Lace.

"Me, too," said the rector.

"I like y'r hat." Harley pointed to his head. "Ol' Lace has a hat jis' like it, 'cept I think your'n's in worser shape."

Lace sat on the arm of the sofa. "We come t' git Poobaw. Pauline's still half burned up in th' hospital."

"Yeah," said Harley, "an' th' law's done got 'er man."

There was some good news in this world, the rector thought.

"Better wake 'im up and git 'im started," she said. "Are they any of 'is clothes over here?"

"Ain't but what he had on," said Harley, still grinning. He picked up the can and rattled the spoon around in it. "Boys, if them beans didn't walk right out of there." He looked at the rector and said mischievously, "Ol' dump rat got 'em."

"Oh, hush, Harley, they ain't any rats in here. Rats stay as far away from you as they can git."

He cackled. "Ain't she a bird? I knowed 'er since she was knee high to a duck. Lace, your pap's done left, he raked ever'thing out and hauled it off."

Father Tim saw her face, and thought he could not bear to see another hurting soul in this world.

"Took y'r brother with 'im." Harley laughed. "Good riddance t' bad rubbish."

"There's ol' Poobaw," she said. The boy came into the room, rubbing his eyes.

"Hey," he murmured sleepily, smiling up at her.

Hey, yourself, he almost said, feeling his heart swell with a nameless joy.

✳

They were down the bank. They were across the creek. They were walking over the little bridge.

There was Winnie Ivey's small cottage, with the glow of a lamp in the window. And above them sailed a great orb of moon that washed the whole scene with a silvery light.

He felt the boy's hand in his and saw Lace walking ahead of them, her shoulders squared under the old coat she'd worn again for tonight.

He felt touched by something that, in all his years as a priest, he had never known and, for the moment, didn't even wish to understand or define.

✳

"Cynthia," he said, coming through the back door, "there's someone I'd like you to meet...."

The boy walked in, blinking in the bright light of the kitchen.

"Poobaw Barlowe!" the rector said.

If he thought he was thrilled, it was nothing compared to what he saw expressed in the face of his jubilant wife.

✳

"Pauline, there's someone here to see you."

He backed out the door as Poobaw went in.

"Mama?" said the boy, and ran to her bed.

He was closing the door as he saw Poobaw lift his hand and tenderly pat the right side of his mother's beaming face.

✳

"Dooley," he shouted, hailing him between the Meadowgate farmhouse and the barn, "there's someone here to see you. They're waiting on the porch!"

TWENTY-ONE

These High, Green Hills

Fields of broom sedge turned overnight into lakes of gold, and the scented vines of Lady's Mantle crept into hedges everywhere, as the sun moved and the light changed, and the brisk, clean days grew shorter.

"You always say this is the best fall we've ever had," Dora Pugh scolded a customer at the hardware. "How can every year be the best?"

Avis Packard put up a banner, Percy Mosely at last took his down, and the Collar Button was having its annual fall sale. The latter encouraged the rector to make a few purchases for Dooley Barlowe, now back at school, which included three pairs of khakis, four pairs of socks, and a couple of handkerchiefs that Dooley would never use for their intended purpose.

Pauline Barlowe was two hours away in a burn therapy center, Lace Turner was enrolled in seventh grade at Mitford School, and Poobaw—living with his grandfather, Russell Jacks, at the home of practical nurse Betty Craig—was enrolled in fourth grade.

Louella was pushing along with Winnie Ivey, Scott Murphy

had moved into the cottage on the creek with Luke, Lizzie, a bed, three chairs, and a wok, and J.C. Hogan had, only days ago, announced his news.

"I thought for a while there," said Mule, "that we'd have to do it for you—like that feller with th' big nose."

"Do what for me, and what big nose?" asked J.C.

"You know ..." Mule looked to the rector for help.

"Cyrano de Bergerac. He proposed to Roxane as proxy for Christian de Neuvillette."

"Never heard of him. Anyway, I pulled it it off myself, thank you."

"How'd you feel about proposing?" Mule asked.

"I threw up right after."

"I bet that was attractive. How'd you do it?"

"Just bent over the toilet and up it came."

"That," said Mule, "is not what I was askin'. How did you propose? I hope you didn't do one of those dumb tricks like put th' ring in a piece of cake."

J.C. looked surprised. "How'd you know? I was over at her place and she'd baked a cake for my birthday and while she was in the kitchen, I mashed the ring down in her piece—in the icing part."

"What if she'd bitten into it?" asked the rector.

"What if she'd swallowed it?" asked the realtor.

J.C. mopped his face with a handkerchief. "Bein' a working woman, she eats fast, and before you know it, she was bearin' down on that ring pretty hard, so I looked over and said, 'What in the dickens is that in your cake?' and she said, 'Well, I never, it's a ring.'"

"Then what did you say?" asked Mule.

"Y'all are worse'n a bunch of old women."

"It's true," admitted the rector.

"I said, 'Want to do it?' and she said, 'OK.'"

Mule rolled his eyes. "*Want to do it?* You said *that?*"

"If it was good enough for Officer Adele Lynwood," snapped J.C., "it ought to be good enough for you, buddyroe."

Mule peered across the table. "Did you get down on your knees or anything?"

"Are you kidding me?"

"So you proposed on your birthday!" exclaimed the rector.

"Right."

"That's what I did, you know."

Mule cackled: "You don't mean it. I didn't know that. I declare."

"It's a dadblame epidemic," said the editor, grinning.

Velma skidded up to the booth and glared at J.C. "OK, what'll you have, and don't take all day."

The rector and the realtor looked expectantly at J.C. "Low-fat yogurt and grapefruit juice ..."

"Here we go again," sighed Mule.

"With a side of sausage and grits," said the editor.

✳

"When it boots," Emma told him, "I have the configuration file install all the device drivers I'll need all day."

"Great!" he said, oiling the roller on his Royal manual.

"Can you believe the object linking and embedding capabilities allow me to make all my applications interactive?"

"I'll be darned," he said.

"Not only that, I can append to th' database, paste from th' clipboard, or drag and drop anywhere ..."

"No kidding!"

"... within seconds," she said, looking triumphant.

On what Emma called their now bimonthly "Tech Day," she hauled in everything from roast beef and green beans to macaroni and cheese, which she fed Dave in huge quantities. Over lunch at the rector's desk, which resembled a neighborhood cafeteria, they blithely spoke a language as foreign to him as Croatian.

On Tech Day, one thing was for certain: He was out of there.

Whenever he met Bill Sprouse, who always wanted to know how it was going, he answered from an assortment of enthusiastic responses, including "Terrific!" "Couldn't be better!" and his increasing favorite, "No problem!" With Emma Newland having taken to advanced technology like a duck to water, wasn't every word of that the everlasting truth?

Never say you can't teach an old dog new tricks, he thought, hoofing it to the Grill before Dave roared in at eleven-thirty.

He had dropped the Fernbank key in his pocket when he dressed to go running, and was standing in the middle of Miss Sadie's attic, trying to find the right thing. In a way, it was like shopping, without the blasted aggravation of a mall.

Hat boxes, trunks, rocking chairs, a rolltop desk. Old newspapers, neatly piled and the stacks numbered. Dozens of umbrellas, both Chinese paper and crumbling silk, lamp bases, a magnificent chair with wheels, piles of folded draperies covered with sheets, a child's rocker, a child's table and chairs, headboards, footboards, rusting bedsprings.

It was overwhelming, and only a little light fell in through the window.

There. A large trunk with the initials JB. Josiah Baxter.

A cracked leather chair, a floor lamp with a hand-painted parchment shade. Books, books, and more books. A series of boxes stacked on a Jacobean table.

He looked at the boxes, one by one, until he came to the traveling case fitted with a comb and brushes, a shoehorn, talcum powder, and empty, cut-crystal bottles for cologne.

He picked it up and brushed away the dust with his handkerchief. *JB*, read the dim monogram on the leather.

"Something of Papa's," Miss Sadie had said.

It was a little fancy for a man like Buck Leeper, but it would certainly do.

＊

"Retreat time!" she announced as he came in the back door, ready to do another few hours' work at home.

"Didn't we just have one?" he asked, scratching his head.

"Timothy, that was July! This is October."

"Oh," he said.

"I'm just packing up this hamper and we'll be off. The sunset should be glorious tonight; there was a red sky this morning!"

"Doesn't red sky in morning mean sailor take warning?"

"Whatever," she said happily, stuffing in a wedge of cheese.

Barnabas trudged with them up the hill, where, panting furiously, they all arrived at the stone wall.

"Don't really look at the view just yet, dearest. Let's save it until we finish setting up our picnic, shall we?"

He spread the old fringed cloth, which had belonged to a bishop's wife in the late Forties, over the wall, and Cynthia began unpacking what she'd just packed.

Why was he up here on the hill, lolling about like some gigolo, when he had a nursing home to officially open one week hence, and a thousand details to be ironed out, only two of which had kept him up until one o'clock in the morning? But no, let his wife finish a book and she went instantly into the lolling mode. Perhaps it was this very lolling mode of the last two months that had given her countenance the beatific look he'd lately noticed.

"The domestic retreat," she said, setting out a plate of crackers, "is an idea which could literally save the institution of marriage. Do you know that studies say husbands and wives speak to each other a total of only seventeen minutes a week?"

"We're so far over that quota, we've landed in another study."

"I'll say. Roasted garlic. Ripe pears. Toasted pecans. Saga bleu."

She pulled out napkins and two glasses and poured a round of raspberry tea.

"There!" she said. "Now we can look!"

The Land of Counterpane stretched beneath their feet, a wide panorama of rich Flemish colors under a perfectly blue and cloudless sky.

Church steeples poked up from groves of trees.

Plowed farmland appeared like velveteen scraps on a quilt, feather-stitched with hedgerows.

There, puffs of chimney smoke billowed heavenward, and over there, light gleamed on a pond that regularly supplied fresh trout to Avis Packard's Local.

"Look, dearest! Look at our high, green hills."

He gazed across the little valley and up, up to the green hills, where groves of blazing hardwoods topped the ridges, and fences laced the broad, uneven meadows.

"Aren't they beautiful in this light?"

"They are!" he said, meaning it.

"Where's the train?"

He peered at his watch. "Ten minutes!" The little train would come winding through the valley, over the trestle that spanned the gorge, and just as it broke through the trees by the red barn and the silo, they would see it. If Providence were with them, they would also hear the long, mournful blast of its horn.

Away to the east, he thought he saw a speck of some kind, a bird perhaps. But birds didn't gleam. Aha! It was a little plane. It was a little yellow plane. By jing, it was Omer Cunningham.

Dipping, rolling, gliding, soaring. Omer! He stood up on the wall and waved.

"What in the world …?" asked his wife.

"That's Omer," he said, gleeful.

"Who is Omer?"

He waved some more and thought he could see Omer waving back as the little plane dipped its right wing and roared into the blue.

"Omer. I declare." He felt a silly grin stretching all the way across his face.

"You know absolutely everybody," she said, impressed.

He sat back down and gazed around and gulped his tea. "Ah, well, we won't be doing this forever," he said.

"I know!" She raised her glass to his. "We'll be living in some far-off land filled with adventure!"

"Right."

She sighed.

"Why are you sighing?"

"Was I sighing? I didn't know I was sighing."

"Sighing often goes unnoticed by the sigher," he said.

"Ummm. What did we agree we wanted in the place where we'll retire?" she asked.

"Oh, as I recall, four distinct seasons …"

"Absolutely!" she said.

"A small house and a big yard."

"Oh, yes. Now I remember. We plant, we mow."

"You got it. And nothing flat, we said."

"Flat is so …" She paused, looking for words.

"*Flat,*" he remarked.

"Right!" she agreed.

"Didn't we say something about liking winters that freeze our glasses to our noses?"

"Definitely."

"Listen!" He cupped his hands to his ears. "Here it comes!"

A freight train broke into view at the red barn, blowing its horn as it rushed past a field, disappeared into the trees, and appeared again along a row of tiny houses.

She applauded, and turned to him, laughing. No, indeed, it didn't take much for his wife....

They tried the roasted garlic and spread the Saga bleu on crackers and munched the pecans and emptied the tea container and watched the sky blush with pink, then fuchsia.

"You're sighing again," he announced.

"I can't think why."

"You can't fool me. If anybody can think why they do something, it's you, Kavanagh."

"OK. I think I'll miss Mitford."

"Aha. So will I."

A bird called. Barnabas rolled over at his master's feet and yawned, and the rector leaned down to scratch the pink belly that was offered.

"So ..." she said, pausing thoughtfully.

"So?"

"It occurs to me that we've found a place that meets all our strict requirements."

"Hmmm. Small house, big yard," he mused.

"Winters that freeze our glasses to our noses ..."

"Nothing flat, lots of hills ..."

"No sand," she said.

They turned to each other and smiled. Then they laughed.

Neither said anything more as they packed up the hamper and folded up the cloth and went down the hill with their dog at their heels.

＊

Next year, they agreed, they'd be adding a large room to the back of the little yellow house. With lots of windows, said the rector. With gleaming hardwood floors, said his wife.

"'There are two things to aim at in life,'" he quoted from Logan Pearsall Smith. "'First, to get what you want, and after that, to enjoy it.'"

"There's the rub!" she said.

Using a Magic Marker, she inscribed the wisdom on the wall above her drawing board, relishing the freedom to do it, loving the notion of making the little yellow house larger, and living there forever.

There was so much to do and so much to think about, they had trouble sleeping at night. He'd even talked the vestry into building the kennel and dog run, and two men from Farmer had been working around the clock to complete the job.

The ECW was out in force, canvassing every garden and meadow for autumn flowers, dried herbs, pumpkins, and gourds to decorate the public rooms at Hope House. Cynthia volunteered to round up vases, buckets, and mounds of oasis from the florist, not to mention bake six dozen lemon squares for the reception.

J.C. Hogan's wedding was coming straight up, in the middle of the week after the grand opening, and the rector would not only officiate, but had offered to bake a ham.

Immediately following the police-station wedding at which Mule Skinner would be best man, they would troop to the Skinner household, where Fancy was giving a reception on the premises of Hair House, owing to the fact that their living quarters were being repainted.

For this affair, Cynthia had been asked to contribute four dozen vegetable sandwiches, four dozen lemon squares, and as many barbecued chicken drumettes as she could manage.

"I will not make drumettes, barbecued or otherwise," she told her husband. "There are two cardinal rules from which I will not depart—I will not cook with Cheez Whiz and I will not do drumettes. I will substitute meat balls in sauce."

Scott Murphy was collecting animals, large and small, having them vetted by Hal Owen, and installing them in the brand-new Hope House kennels, which were complete except for fencing in the runs.

The Presbyterian brass band was busy rehearsing three nights a week and could be heard through half the village. The Lord's Chapel Youth Choir was holding rehearsals in Jena Ivey's florist shop because the Sunday School rooms were overtaken by the ECW, who had twenty-seven major floral arrangements to pull together.

"Raffia!" cried the frantic Hope House chairperson for opening day events. "We need raffia!"

"What's raffia?" several volunteers wanted to know.

"Don't use raffia," said Jena Ivey. "The last I got had bugs in it."

Someone said Buck Leeper had bought a suit at the Collar Button that wasn't even on sale, and J.C. Hogan was seen leaving the Collar Button with a box the size of a small garage. He was reported to have been with Officer Lynwood, who was out of uniform and looking good in a pants suit.

Percy Mosely was running a special on a vegetable plate: collards, black-eyed peas, candied yams, cornbread, and banana pudding for two-fifty, during the week of the Hope House grand opening, only. After that, three bucks.

Happy Endings Bookstore was giving twenty percent off every title starting with H. "Does that include th' Holy Bible?" asked Uncle Billy Watson, who, when assured that it did, shelled out fourteen dollars on the spot, plus three-fifty for a magnifying glass.

Hardly anyone in the village was untouched by the excitement of the great glass and brick building at the crest of the hill, which stood where the town's first Episcopal church had burned to the ground in a tragic fire. Only one living person knew the full truth about that fire, thought the rector, and he was the one.

Sadie Baxter's attempt to right a wrong was a better thing than he could now imagine. Good things would come of Hope House; he could feel it in his bones.

✳

"I'm here," said Scott Murphy, "because God brought me here. And so are you."

Clearly, the chaplain's message was directed at the forty new residents of Hope House, most of whom were present, and all of whom were in unfamiliar circumstances.

"Because God has brought us here, we're going to honor him by having fun, and enjoying this wonderful and remarkable place.

"You need to know that I do not now, nor will I ever, consider this a nursing home, though some of you will need nursing. Good nursing care is vital, but it isn't everything."

The mayor looked at the rector and nodded.

Ron Malcolm sat back and relaxed.

A muscle jumped in Buck Leeper's jaw.

"We're going to sing here," said Scott Murphy, stepping from behind the pulpit and walking into the aisle. "We're going to dance here. We're going to pray here. We're going to laugh here, and love here. And we're going to do all that by sustaining the powerful, eternal, and life-giving spirit of hope through Jesus, the Christ.

"As your chaplain, I will not be working alone. That's because I come to you not as an individual, but as part of a team.

"Luke!"

A Jack Russell terrier trotted out from the behind the pulpit, wagged its tail, and sat down.

The audience laughed with surprise.

"Lizzie!"

Another Jack Russell, nearly identical, shyly poked its head around the side of the pulpit, then walked out and sat down next to Luke.

The audience applauded wildly, glad for laughter after the formality of a ribbon-cutting in a whipping October wind, a lengthy dedication with choral music, and a bombastic mayoral speech.

"You hit a home run with the chaplain," whispered the mayor to the rector.

"I wasn't the one who hit it," whispered the rector to the mayor.

✳

After the grand reception, held around the splashing fountain in the atrium, forty residents, many in wheelchairs, took occupancy of their new quarters.

Louella Baxter Marshall was escorted to Room Number One by Olivia and Hoppy Harper, Lacey Turner, Cynthia and Timothy Kavanagh, and Dooley Barlowe. Miss Pattie was led to Room Thirty-four by Evie Adams, who was weeping with gratitude and relief.

Up and down the corridors, families helped loved ones settle in, meeting nurses, talking with doctors, and admiring the lavish display of flowers that filled rooms and nursing stations.

"I'm movin' in here as soon as Gene kicks," said Esther Bolick.

"But you're not sick!" said Fancy Skinner.

"No, but I'm workin' on it," declared Esther, looking around at the rose-colored carpet, Palladian windows, and crystal chandeliers.

"Buck," said the rector, shaking the superintendent's rough hand, "this is as fine a job as I've ever seen done. Personally, I can't thank you enough, nor can Lord's Chapel."

Buck nodded, and the rector was suddenly moved by the reality of thousands of hours of labor, and a promise that, at great personal sacrifice, had been kept. He threw his arms around the man and hugged him. "May God bless you for this, Buck."

"No problem," said Buck Leeper, turning to walk away.

"Wait! When are you leaving?"

"I'll be pulling out tomorrow." The nerve twitched in his jaw.

He didn't want to see Buck Leeper go. No, he didn't want that at all.

"The church attic—all that space Miss Sadie's father wanted to turn into Sunday School rooms—is that job big enough for you? Could we get you back for that?"

Buck shrugged. "Maybe."

"Could you—would you come over for supper tonight? We'd love to have you."

"I've got a lot to pull together," said Buck Leeper, looking awkward.

The rector tried to smile. "Maybe another time."

He felt deflated as he and Cynthia drove home with Dooley. He was glad they'd had the plaque made, honoring Buck.

"What is it?" she asked, always knowing his heart.

He couldn't find the words, exactly. Tomorrow he'd start looking into the attic project, and how they might initiate fund-raising; he would call Buck's boss, whom he'd met at the country club, and put in a special request for his star superintendent.

Something told him very clearly that Buck Leeper was not finished in Mitford.

Not by a long shot.

✳

"Well, buddy."

Fall break was over and they had delivered Dooley back to school, taking Poobaw along for the ride.

"You know we love you," said the rector, giving the boy a hug. With the obvious exception of Miss Sadie, he couldn't remember ever hugging a millionaire before.

Cynthia kissed him on the cheek. "Yes, you big lug, we love you."

"I love you back," Dooley said, meeting their gaze.

Dooley squatted on one knee and put his hands on Poobaw's shoulders. "Stay cool, Poo."

"I will," said Poobaw, nodding and smiling. "I'll see y'uns later."

"Don't say y'uns," his brother admonished.

"What should I say?"

"Get them to tell you what to say." Dooley stood up and smiled, then turned around and was gone along the hallway.

✳

"Today's the day!" announced his wife, looking infernally pleased with herself.

"Today," he murmured, trying to accept the inevitable.

"It will be over in no time!" she said, beaming.

"Over in no time. Of course."

"So, let's roll up our sleeves and begin!"

He began rolling. "'He has half the deed done who has made a beginning.'"

"Plato!" crowed his wife.

"Horace!" he snapped.

Cynthia brushed her hair from her eyes and peered at him with cool disdain. "My escort to the junior prom, as I recall. I didn't realize you'd met."

✳

They emptied everything onto the floor in a pile that, he surmised, was altogether large enough to fill an eighteen-wheeler.

After removing the drawers and roping the doors shut, they

muscled the thing down the stairs and through the hallway, out to the stoop and down the steps, then across the side yard and through the hedge, where they set it on the flagstones.

He mopped his face.

She panted and moaned.

He squatted on his heels and looked at the ground.

She leaned against a tree and stared at the sky.

A bird called. An airplane roared over.

"Ready?" she inquired.

"Ready," he replied.

"Didn't I tell you we could do it?"

"You did."

"OK," she shouted, "one, two, three, lift!"

Off they bolted like two pack mules, across the side yard of the rectory, up the steps, and over the threshold, where the door was propped open with a broom handle.

Safely inside, they set their cargo down and fell exhausted into chairs at the table.

"Lemonade?" she asked after a labored pause.

"And step on it," he said, mopping again.

He looked at the alien thing sitting in his kitchen. A three-bedroom condo, at the very least. A shipping crate for a Canadian moose …

"There!" she said, handing him the lemonade and gulping hers.

If this wasn't the last blasted piece of decorating business on his wife's agenda, he was going to build a brick wall across the path through the hedge and be done with it.

"You might have waited for Puny to give us a hand," he said.

"I can't ask a new mother to be hauling heavy furniture."

"Heavy? Did I hear you say heavy? You've insisted for a year that this thing is light as a feather!"

"Oh, poop," she said darkly, "you know what I mean."

He downed his lemonade and stood up to take his medicine like a man. "Ready?"

"Ready," she said, eyeing him. "And don't scratch the hall floors. They've just been waxed."

Waxed, was it? He could see them taking one wrong step, skating up the hall, bursting through the front door, and landing in the street with the blooming thing on top of them. Bachelors didn't rearrange the decor, no, indeed. In fifteen years, he had scarcely moved a side chair from one place to another.

He sighed deeply.

"You're sighing," she said.

"A penetrating observation."

"One, two, three, lift!"

Away they went, lumbering down the hall. He tried to grip the slick floor with his toes, but they were imprisoned in his loafers.

✳

"There!" she said happily, stepping back from the guest room wall to take a look. "What do you think, darling?"

"It's wonderful!" he said, meaning it. "It belongs there. You were right all along, Kavanagh."

"We'll have so much more room for towels and linens …"

"Exactly!" he said, mopping his face. "Absolutely." What was that zapping pain that raced up his right leg? Or was it coming from his lower back?

"… and wonderful storage for sheets and pillowcases!"

"Well done," he said, ready to crash on the study sofa, next to the electric fan.

"However …" She stood still farther from the wall and peered over her glasses. She folded her arms across her chest and frowned.

"However, what?"

"When you consider the way the windows are situated in this room, it looks out of proportion to the wall. Rats! Do you see what I mean?"

He recognized the faraway look she often got when thinking up a book. "Not at all," he said. "I don't see that at all, it's wonderful right where it is, we should have done this ages ago." He regretted sounding desperate.

"In fact, Timothy, do you know where it would really look grand? In our bedroom! On the wall to the right as you go in the door, just where your family chest is. We could move the chest in here—it would look terrific. All *that* old, dark wood with all *this* old, dark wood. I think that's the answer."

He backed from the room, looking pale.

"But not today, dearest!" she said, coming after him and planting a kiss on his cheek. "More like … in the spring."

"Of course!" he said, feeling brighter. "In the spring!"

They walked across the hall and into their bedroom. "Right there!" she said, pointing at the wall behind the family chest. "Perfect!"

He took a deep breath.

"In the spring," he said, smiling at his determined wife. "Perfect!"

Readers' Guide

*For Personal Reflection
or Group Discussion*

Readers' Guide

1. What would you say to the idea that a Jan Karon novel is a kind of scrapbook? How many writers can you name whose work you first encountered in a Karon novel?

2. What do you make of the technique of skipping over the marriage and letting the details seep out over the course of this third book in the series?

3. In chapter 3, Karon slips in a tongue-in-cheek description of the minister every church wants: "The perfect pastor preaches exactly ten minutes. He condemns sin, but never hurts anybody's feelings. He works from eight in the morning until midnight and is also the church janitor. He is twenty-nine years old and has forty years experience. He makes fifteen house calls a day and is always in the office." Is there any truth here?

4. One of the themes of Karon's books, especially this one, seems to be that, in all of our longing for spectacular visions of God, we miss God "in the commonplace," as she puts it in chapter 6. How would you formulate the problem, and what can we do to avoid the trap?

5. In chapter 7, we hear that a bishop has predicted that Father Tim will be "the sort of priest God can use around his house." What does that mean?

6. Karon adds substantially to our understanding of Father Tim in this novel. We delve into a psychological dimension, heretofore unsuspected, when Father Tim speaks of his perfectionism as his "unwritten liturgy," in chapter 10. What do you make of these new revelations about the rector and his father? How do they affect your sense of the development of this story through the three novels? What is the lesson of the cave? Although this novel has fewer plotlines than the first two,

it features a really searching, psychological, and spiritual study of Father Tim. Could this novel be considered Father Tim's conversion story?

7. Have you noticed the absence of television, movies, video games, and the other trappings of popular culture in Karon's novels? Does this make the novels unrealistic somehow?

8. You certainly laugh along with Father Tim at Percy's advertisement in chapter 13: "Eat Here Once, And You'll Be Regular." How does Karon avoid the trap of hillbilly humor, the too-easy recourse to popular stereotypes and making fun of the small-town folks?

9. In what ways is *These High, Green Hills* a book about aging?

10. When Father Tim talks in chapter 15 about "God's timing," he is playing close to the big fire that believers call providence. How would you summarize the rector's take on this ancient Christian doctrine? Can you go along with him? Do you, like Father Tim, pray for signs?

11. So much of this story has to do with unitings and reunitings, and the idea seems to turn on the premise that having someone to love is as important as being loved. How has such an idea played out in your life?

12. Talk about Pauline. More than anything else, she wants "to start over," as she says in chapter 19. Do you still believe that starting over is really an option?

13. Karon says that writing of Miss Sadie's death in this novel "broke her heart." How did you respond?

14. When Cynthia and Father Tim talk in chapter 20 about stress and trouble in Mitford, the rector refers to Mitford as the "quaint little town where people value each other and nothing bad ever happens to anybody." The line seems a trifle sardonic, and Cynthia's response—"Poop!"—confirms that impression. Do you think Karon is here addressing those critics who see her books as escapist pulp?

15. What role does Romans 8:28 play in the Mitford series?

The Word at Work Around the World

A vital part of Cook Communications Ministries is our international outreach, Cook Communications Ministries International (CCMI). Your purchase of this book, and of other books and Christian-growth products from Cook, enables CCMI to provide Bibles and Christian literature to people in more than 150 languages in 65 countries.

Cook Communications Ministries is a not-for-profit, self-supporting organization. Revenues from sales of our books, Bible curricula, and other church and home products not only fund our U.S. ministry, but also fund our CCMI ministry around the world. One hundred percent of donations to CCMI go to our international literature programs.

CCMI reaches out internationally in three ways:

- Our premier International Christian Publishing Institute (ICPI) trains leaders from nationally led publishing houses around the world.

- We provide literature for pastors, evangelists, and Christian workers in their national language.

- We reach people at risk—refugees, AIDS victims, street children, and famine victims—with God's Word.

Word Power, God's Power

Faith Kidz, RiverOak, Honor, Life Journey, Victor, NexGen — every time you purchase a book produced by Cook Communications Ministries, you not only meet a vital personal need in your life or in the life of someone you love, but you're also a part of ministering to José in Colombia, Humberto in Chile, Gousa in India, or Lidiane in Brazil. You help make it possible for a pastor in China, a child in Peru, or a mother in West Africa to enjoy a life-changing book. And because you helped, children and adults around the world are learning God's Word and walking in his ways.

Thank you for your partnership in helping to disciple the world. May God bless you with the power of his Word in your life.

For more information about our international ministries, visit www.ccmi.org.

Additional copies of *THESE HIGH, GREEN HILLS*
and other RiverOak titles are available
wherever good books are sold.

If you have enjoyed this book,
or if it has had an impact on your life,
we would like to hear from you.

Please contact us at:

RIVEROAK BOOKS
Cook Communications Ministries, Dept. 201
4050 Lee Vance View
Colorado Springs, CO 80918

Or visit our Web site:
www.cookministries.com

RIVEROAK®
Good News in Fiction